Resounding praise for
PETER ROBINSON

"The novels of Peter Robinson are chilling, evocative,
deeply nuanced works of art."
Dennis Lehane

"Fans of P.D. James and Ruth Rendell who crave more
contemporary themes than either master has provided
of late should look no further."
Washington Post Book World

"Robinson is a skillful writer . . . Returning to the world
of Alan Banks is always a pleasure."
Houston Chronicle

"Able plotter and smooth stylist that he is, Robinson is
above all a gifted creator of fully fleshed and vividly
presented characters . . . He creates a suspense novel with
many of the dynamic qualities of more literary fiction."
Seattle Post-Intelligencer

"His characters are so believable you'll find
yourself wondering what they're doing after
Robinson stops writing."
San Jose Mercury News

"Robinson's skill . . . has been burnished to a high gloss."
Chicago Tribune

Also by Peter Robinson

Gallows View
A Dedicated Man
A Necessary End
The Hanging Valley
Past Reason Hated
Wednesday's Child
Final Account
Innocent Graves
Blood at the Root
In a Dry Season
Cold Is the Grave
Aftermath
Close to Home

Available in hardcover

Playing with Fire

PETER ROBINSON

INNOCENT GRAVES

A NOVEL OF SUSPENSE

AVON BOOKS

An Imprint of HarperCollinsPublishers

AVON BOOKS
An Imprint of HarperCollins*Publishers*
10 East 53rd Street
New York, New York 10022-5299

Copyright © 1996 by Peter Robinson
ISBN: 0-380-82043-9
www.avonbooks.com

First Avon Books paperback printing: April 2004

Avon Trademark Reg. U.S. Pat. Off. and in Other Countries, Marca Registrada, Hecho en U.S.A.
HarperCollins® is a trademark of HarperCollins Publishers Inc.

Printed in the U.S.A.

10 9 8 7 6 5 4 3 2 1

For Sheila

INNOCENT
GRAVES

Chapter 1

I

*T*he night it all began, a thick fog rolled down the dale and enfolded the town of Eastvale in its shroud. Fog in the market square, creeping in the cracks between the cobbles; fog muffling the sound of laughter from the Queen's Arms and muting the light through its red and amber panes; fog rubbing and licking against cool glass in curtained windows and insinuating its way through tiny gaps under doors.

And the fog seemed at its thickest in the graveyard of St. Mary's Church, where a beautiful woman with long auburn hair wandered barefoot and drunk, a wineglass full of Pinot Noir held precariously in her hand.

She weaved her way between the squat, gnarled yews and lichen-stained stones. Sometimes she thought she saw ghosts, gray, translucent shapes flitting among the tombs ahead, but they didn't frighten her.

And she came to the Inchcliffe Mausoleum.

It loomed ahead out of the fog, massive and magnificent: classical lines formed in marble, steps overgrown with weeds leading down to the heavy oak door.

But it was the angel she had come to see. She liked the angel. Its eyes were fixed on heaven, as if nothing earthly mattered, and its hands were clasped together in prayer.

Though it was solid marble, she often fancied it was so insubstantial she could pass her hand right through it.

She swayed slightly, raised her glass to the angel and drained half the wine at one gulp. She could feel the cold, damp earth and grass under her feet.

"Hello, Gabriel," she said, voice a little slurred. "I'm sorry but I've sinned again." She hiccupped and put her hand to her mouth. " 'Scuse me, but I just can't seem to—"

Then she saw something, a black-and-white shape, sticking out from behind the mausoleum. Curious, she squinted and stumbled towards it. Only when she was about a yard away did she realize it was a black shoe and a white sock. With a foot still in it.

She tottered back, hand to her mouth, then circled around the back of the tomb. All she could make out were the pale legs, the fair hair, the open satchel and the maroon uniform of St. Mary's School for Girls.

She screamed and dropped her glass. It shattered on a stone.

Then Rebecca Charters, wife of the vicar of St. Mary's, fell to her knees on the broken glass and started to vomit.

II

The fog tasted of ashes, thought Detective Chief Inspector Alan Banks, as he pulled up his raincoat collar and hurried down the tarmac path towards the faint, gauzy light. Or perhaps he was being fanciful. Even though he hadn't seen the body yet, he felt that familiar clenching in his stomach that murder always brought.

When he reached the scene, just off a narrow gravel path past the shrubbery, he saw the blurred silhouette of Dr. Glendenning through the canvas screen, bent over a vague shape lying on the ground, like a dumb-show in a Jacobean drama.

Fog had played havoc with the usual order of arrival. Banks himself had been at a senior officers' meeting in

Northallerton when he got the call, and he was consequently almost the last person to arrive. Peter Darby, crime-scene photographer, was there already, and so was Detective Inspector Barry Stott, who, for reasons clear to anyone who saw him, was more commonly known as "Jug-ears." Stott, who had recently been transferred from Salford upon his promotion from detective sergeant, was a temporary replacement for DS Philip Richmond, who had gone to Scotland Yard to join a special computer unit.

Banks took a deep breath and walked behind the screen. Dr. Glendenning looked up, cigarette dangling from his mouth, its smoke indistinguishable from the fog that surrounded them.

"Ah, Banks . . ." he said in his lilting Edinburgh accent, then he shook his head slowly.

Banks looked down at the body. In all his years in Eastvale, he hadn't had to deal with a crime like this. He had seen worse in London, of course, which was part of the reason he had left the Met and transferred up north. But you clearly couldn't hide from it any more now. Not anywhere. George Orwell was right about the decline of the English murder, and this was exactly the kind of thing it had declined into.

The girl, about fifteen or sixteen by the look of her, lay on her back in the long grass behind a huge Victorian sepulchre, upon which stood a marble statue of an angel. The angel had its back turned to her, and through the fog Banks could make out the chipped feathers of its wings.

Her eyes stared into the fog, her long blonde hair lay fanned out around her head like a halo, and her face had a reddish-purple hue. There was a little cut by her left eye and some discoloration around her neck. A trickle of blood the shape of a large teardrop ran out of her left nostril.

Her maroon school blazer lay bunched up on the ground beside her, and her white blouse had been ripped open at the front; her bra had then been removed—roughly, by the looks of it.

Banks felt the urge to cover her. In his job, he had already seen far more than a man should, and it was little things like this that sometimes affected him more than the blood and guts. The girl looked so vulnerable, so callously violated. He could imagine her shame at being exposed this way, how she would blush and hurry to cover herself if she were alive. But she was beyond shame now.

Below her waist, someone had pulled her skirt up to reveal her thighs and pubic region. Her long legs lay open at a forty-five-degree angle. Her white socks were down around her ankles. She wore shiny black shoes with buckles fastened at the sides.

Lying beside her was an open satchel. The strap had come free of the metal ring at one end. Using his pen, Banks pushed back the flap and read the neatly inked address:

Miss Deborah Catherine Harrison
28 Hawthorn Close
Eastvale
North Yorkshire
England
United Kingdom of Great Britain and Northern
    Ireland
European Community
Earth
Solar System
Milky Way
The Universe.

He smiled sadly to himself. It was a typical teenager's sense of playfulness, exactly the same thing he had done at school.

Hawthorn Close meant money, as did St. Mary's in general. It was an area of large, mostly detached houses, each with an acre or two of garden, long drives and croquet lawns shaded by copper beeches. To live there, you had to make enough money to employ a gardener, at the very least. St. Mary's School required money, too—about £1200 per term.

Banks had checked when he first arrived in town, but soon found he couldn't afford to send his daughter, Tracy, there.

Banks cadged some evidence bags from one of the SOCOs and, holding the satchel by its edges, tipped the contents inside one of them. All he found were a couple of exercise books with the name "Deborah Catherine Harrison" written on the cover, a portable chess set, a few cosmetic items and three loose tampons in cellophane wrappers. But why had the satchel been open? he wondered. The buckles seemed strong enough, so he doubted it came open during a struggle. Had someone been looking for something?

Glendenning directed one of his underlings to take oral, vaginal and anal swabs and comb the pubic hair. Then he groaned and got to his feet. "I'm getting old, Banks," he said, massaging his knees. "Too old for this sort of thing." He jerked his head towards the body. Tall and white-haired, with a nicotine-stained mustache, the doctor was probably in his late fifties, Banks guessed.

They moved away, letting the screen block their view of the victim. Every so often, Peter Darby's flash exploded, creating a strobe-light effect in the fog. Banks accepted one of Glendenning's Senior Service. Normally he smoked Silk Cut tipped, but he had cut down drastically on his smoking over the last few months and wasn't even carrying a packet with him. Well, he thought, as Glendenning proffered a gold, initialled lighter, cutting down had been easy enough to do in a lazy summer with no murders to investigate. Now it was November and there was a body at his feet. He lit up and coughed.

"Ought to get that cough seen to, laddie," said Glendenning. "Might be a touch of lung cancer, you know."

"It's nothing. I'm just getting a cold, that's all."

"Aye . . . Well, I don't suppose you dragged me out here on a mucky night like this just to talk about your health, did you?"

"No," said Banks. "What do you make of it?"

"I can't tell you much yet, but judging by her color and

the marks on her throat, I'd say asphyxia due to ligature strangulation."

"Any sign of the ligature?"

"Off the record, that satchel strap fits the bill pretty nicely."

"What about time of death?"

"Oh, come off it, laddie."

"Vaguely?"

"Not more than two or three hours ago. But don't quote me on that."

Banks looked at his watch. Eight o'clock. Which meant she was probably killed between five and six. Not on her way home from school, then. At least not directly.

"Was she killed here?"

"Aye. Almost certainly. Hypostasis is entirely consistent with the position of the body."

"Any sign of the rest of her underwear?"

Glendenning shook his head. "Only the brassiere."

"When can you get her on the table?"

"First thing in the morning. Coming?"

Banks swallowed; the fog scratched his throat. "Wouldn't miss it for the world."

"Fine. I'll reserve you the best seat in the house. I'm off home. You can get her to the mortuary now."

And with that, Glendenning turned and faded into the fog.

Banks stood alone for a moment trying to forget the girl he had just seen spread-eagled so cruelly before him, trying desperately not to see Tracy in her place. He stubbed out his cigarette carefully on the side of the Inchcliffe Mausoleum and pocketed the butt. No point leaving red herrings at the crime scene.

A couple of yards away, he noticed a light patch on the grass. He walked over and squatted to get a closer look. It looked and smelled as if someone had been sick. He could also make out the stem and fragments of a wineglass, which seemed to have smashed on the stone edging of a grave. He picked up one of the slivers carefully between thumb and forefinger. It was stained with blood or wine; he couldn't be certain which.

He saw DI Stott within hearing range and called him over.

"Know anything about this?" he asked.

Stott looked at the glass and vomit. "Rebecca Charters. Woman who discovered the body," he said. "Bit of an oddball. She's in the vicarage. WPC Kemp is with her."

"Okay. I'll talk to her later." Banks pointed to the mausoleum. "Anyone had a look in there yet?"

"Not yet. I sent PC Aiken to see if he could come up with a key from the vicar."

Banks nodded. "Look, Barry, someone's got to break the news to the girl's parents."

"And seeing as I'm the new lad on the block . . ."

"That's not what I meant. If you're not comfortable with the job, then get someone else to do it. But get it done."

"Sorry," said Stott, taking his glasses off and wiping them on a white handkerchief. "I'm a bit . . ." He gestured towards the body. "Of course I'll go."

"Sure?"

"Yes."

"Okay. I'll join you there soon. Before you go, call in DC Gay and DS Hatchley and tell them to get down here. Someone might have to drag Jim out of The Oak."

Stott raised his eyebrows. Banks noticed his little moue of distaste at the mention of Detective Sergeant Hatchley. Well, he thought, that's *his* cross to bear.

"And get as many officers out on the streets as you can. I want every house in the area canvassed as soon as possible. It's going to be a long, busy night, but we'd better work fast. People forget quickly. Besides, by tomorrow the vultures will be here."

"Vultures?"

"Press, TV people, sightseers. It's going to be a circus, Barry. Prepare yourself."

Stott nodded. PC Aiken turned up with the key to the mausoleum. Banks borrowed a torch from one of the search team, and he and Stott trod carefully down the weed-covered steps.

The heavy wooden door opened after a brief struggle with the key, and they found themselves in the dark with the dead; six sturdy coffins rested on trestles. A few tentacles of fog slid down the stairs and through the door after them, wreathing around their feet.

The small tomb didn't smell of death, only of earth and mold. Fortunately, there were no fresh Inchcliffes buried there; the family had left Eastvale fifty years ago.

All Banks could see on his first glance around were the spider-webs that seemed to be spun in the very air itself. He gave a little shudder and shone his torch over the floor. There, in the corner furthest from the entrance, lay two empty vodka bottles and a pile of cigarette ends. It was hard to tell how recent they were, but they certainly weren't fifty years old.

They found nothing else of interest down there, and it was with great relief that Banks emerged into the open air again; foggy as it was, it felt like a clear night after the inside of the tomb. Banks asked the SOCOs to bag the empty bottles and cigarette ends and search the place thoroughly.

"We'll need a murder room set up at the station," he said, turning to Stott again, "and a van parked near the scene; make it easy for people to come forward. Exhibits Officer, phone lines, civilian staff, the usual thing. Get Susan Gay to see to it. Better inform the Chief Constable, too," Banks added with a sinking feeling.

At the moment, Banks was senior man in Eastvale CID, as Detective Superintendent Gristhorpe had broken his leg while fixing his drystone wall. Technically, Detective Chief Superintendent Jack Wormsley, from North Yorkshire Regional HQ at Northallerton, was supposed to be in charge of a murder investigation. However, Banks knew from experience not to expect much beyond the occasional phone call from DCS Wormsley; he was rumored to be far too close to finishing his scale matchstick model of the Taj Mahal to be bothered with a mere murder. If it came from anywhere, Banks knew, the main hindrance would come from the new chief constable: Jeremiah "Jimmy" Riddle, a high-flier of the pushy, breathe-down-your-neck school of police management.

"We'll also need a thorough ground-search of the graveyard," Banks went on, "but we might be better doing that in daylight, especially if this fog disperses a bit during the night. Anyway, make sure the place is well secured." Banks looked around. "How many entrances are there?"

"Two. One off North Market Street and one off Kendal Road, just by bridge."

"Should be easy to secure, then. The wall looks high enough to deter any interlopers, but we'd better have a couple of men on perimeter patrol, just to make sure. The last thing we need is some intrepid reporter splashing crime-scene photos all over the morning papers. Is there any access from the riverside?"

Stott shook his head. "The wall's high there, too, and it's topped with broken glass."

"Welcoming sort of place, isn't it?"

"I understand they've had a bit of vandalism."

Banks peered through the fog at the lights in the vicarage. They looked like disembodied eyes. "You're a bit of a churchman, aren't you, Barry?"

Stott nodded. "Yes. St. Cuthbert's, though, not St. Mary's."

Banks nodded towards the vicarage. "Do you know who the vicar is here?"

"Father Daniel Charters."

Banks raised his eyebrows. "I thought so. I don't know all the details, but isn't he the one who's been in the news a bit lately?"

"He is," Stott said through gritted teeth.

"Interesting," said Banks "Very interesting." And he wandered off towards the vicarage.

III

The woman who answered Banks's knock at the back door was in her mid-thirties, he guessed, with a lustrous cascade of auburn hair spilling over her shoulders, an olive complexion, large hazel eyes and the fullest, most sensuous lips he had ever seen. She also had a stunned, unfocused look on her face.

"I'm Rebecca Charters," she said, shaking his hand. "Please come through."

Banks followed her down the hall. A tall woman, she was wearing a heavy black shawl draped over her shoulders and a loose, long blue skirt that flowed over the swell of her hips almost down to the stone flags of the hallway. Her feet were bare and dirty, with blades of grass stuck to her ankles and instep. There was also a fresh cut by the Achilles tendon of her right foot. As she walked, her hips swayed just a little more than he would have expected in a vicar's wife. And was it his imagination, or did she seem a little unsteady on her pins?

She led him into a living-room with a high ceiling and dull, striped wallpaper. WPC Kemp stood by the door, and Banks told her she could leave now.

Bottle-green velour curtains were drawn across the bay window against the fog. An empty tiled fireplace stood directly across from the door, and in front of it lay a huge bundle of brown-and-white fur that Banks took to be a large dog of some kind. Whatever it was, he hoped it stayed there. Not that he disliked dogs, but he couldn't stand the way they slobbered and fussed over him. Cats were much more Banks's kind of animal. He liked their arrogance, their independence and their sense of mischief, and would have one for a pet were it not that Sandra, his wife, was violently allergic.

The only heat was provided by a small white radiator against the far wall. Banks was glad he hadn't taken off his raincoat yet; he was thankful for the extra layer of warmth.

A three-piece suite upholstered in worn brown corduroy ranged around the coffee-table, and in one of the armchairs sat a man with thick black eyebrows that almost met in the middle, a furrowed brow, a long, pale face and prominent cheekbones. He had the haunted look of a troubled young priest from an old movie.

As Banks came in, the man stood up, a maneuver that resembled some large, long-limbed animal uncurling from its lair, and reached out his slender hand.

"Daniel Charters. Would you like some coffee?"

Shaking his hand, Banks noticed the carafe on the table and nodded. "Love some," he said. "Black, no sugar."

Banks sat on the sofa, Rebecca Charters next to him. Also on the coffee-table stood an empty bottle of Sainsbury's Romanian Pinot Noir.

As Daniel Charters poured the coffee, Rebecca walked over to a glass-fronted cabinet, brought out a bottle and a brandy balloon and poured herself a large one. Banks noticed her husband gave her an angry look, which she ignored. The coffee was good. Almost as soon as he sipped it Banks felt the scratchiness in his throat ease up a little.

"I realize you've had a terrible shock," Banks said, "but do you think you could answer a few questions?"

Rebecca nodded.

"Good. Did you report finding the body immediately?"

"Almost. When I saw the shape, what it was, I . . . I was sick first. Then I ran back here and telephoned the police."

"What were you doing in the graveyard at that time, on such a miserable night?"

"I went to see the angel."

Her voice was such a low whisper, Banks didn't believe he could have heard right. "You what?" he asked.

"I said I went to see the angel." Her large, moist eyes held his defiantly. They were red-rimmed with crying. "What's wrong with that? I like graveyards. At least I did."

"What about the glass?"

"I had a glass of wine. I dropped it, then I fell. Look." She lifted her skirt as far as her knees. Both of them were bandaged, but the blood was already seeping through.

"Perhaps you should see a doctor?" Banks suggested.

Rebecca shook her head. "I'm all right."

"Did you disturb the body in any way?" Banks asked.

"No. I didn't touch anything. I didn't go near her."

"Did you recognize her?"

"Just that she was a St. Mary's girl."

"Did you know a girl called Deborah Catherine Harrison?"

Rebecca put her hand to her mouth and nodded. For a moment, Banks thought she was going to be sick again. Her husband didn't make a move, but Banks could tell from his expression that he recognized the name, too.

"Is that who it was?" Rebecca asked.

"We think so. I'll have to ask you not to say anything to anyone until the identity has been confirmed."

"Of course not. Poor Deborah."

"So you knew her?"

"She sang in the choir," Daniel Charters said. "The school and the church are very closely linked. They don't have a chapel of their own, so they come here for services. A number of them also sing in the choir."

"Have you any idea what she might have been doing in the graveyard around five or six o'clock?"

"It's a short cut," Rebecca said. "From the school to her house."

"But school finishes at half past three."

Rebecca shrugged. "They have clubs, societies, activities. You'd have to ask Dr. Green, the head." She took another gulp of brandy. The dog on the hearth hadn't moved. For a moment Banks thought it might have died, then he noticed the fur moving slowly as it breathed. Just old, most likely. The way he was feeling.

"Did either of you see or hear anything outside earlier this evening?" he asked.

Daniel shook his head, and Rebecca said, "I *thought* I did.

When I was in the kitchen opening the wine. It sounded like a stifled cry or something."

"What did you do?"

"I went over to the window. Of course, I couldn't see a damn thing in this fog, and when I didn't hear anything else for a couple of minutes I decided it must have been a bird or a small animal."

"Can you remember what time that was?"

"Around six o'clock, maybe a few minutes after. The local news was just starting on television."

"And even though you thought you heard a cry, you still went out into the dark, foggy graveyard alone forty minutes later?"

Rebecca cast her eyes on the empty wine bottle. "I'd forgotten all about it by then," she said. "Besides, I told you, I assumed it was an animal."

Banks turned to Daniel Charters. "Did you hear anything?"

"He was in his study until I came back screaming about the body," Rebecca answered. "That's the other room at the front, the far side. He couldn't have heard a thing from there."

"Mr. Charters?"

Daniel Charters nodded. "That's right. I was working on a sermon. I'm afraid my wife is correct. I didn't hear anything."

"Have either of you seen any strangers hanging around the area recently?"

They both shook their heads.

"Has anyone been inside the Inchcliffe Mausoleum lately?"

Charters frowned. "No. As far as I know no-one's been in there for fifty years. I just gave the key to one of your men."

"Where do you usually keep it?"

"In the church. On a hook in the vestry."

"So it's accessible to anyone?"

"Yes. But I can't see—"

"Someone's been down there recently. We found vodka bottles and cigarette ends. Have you any idea who it might be?"

"I can't . . ." Then he stopped and turned pale. "Unless . . ."

"Unless what, Mr. Charters?" Banks drank some more coffee.

"As you probably know," Charters said, "I've been under a bit of a cloud these past two months. Do you know the details?"

Banks shrugged. "Only vaguely."

"The whole thing *is* only vague. Anyway, we employed a Croatian refugee here as a sexton. He turned out to be a complete mistake. He drank, he was abusive and he frightened people."

"In what way?"

"He used to leer at the schoolgirls, make lewd gestures. One girl even saw him urinating on a grave." Charters shook his head. "That sort of thing. He never actually touched anyone as far as we know, but some of the girls complained to Dr. Green, and she and I had a long talk. The upshot was, I decided to get rid of him. As soon as he'd gone, he went to the church authorities and claimed that I fired him because he refused to have sex with me."

"And the church authorities believed him?"

"It doesn't matter what they believed," said Charters, with a bitter glance at his wife. "Once the accusation is made, the wheels start to grind, inquiries have to be made. And the accused is put immediately on the defensive. You ought to know how it works, Chief Inspector."

"Like 'when did you stop beating your wife?' "

"Exactly."

"And you think he might have been in the mausoleum?"

"He's the only one I can think of. And he had better access to the key than most. Also, as I remember, vodka was his drink of preference because he believed people couldn't smell it on his breath."

"What do you think of all this, Mrs. Charters?"

Rebecca shook her head, looked away and drank more brandy.

"My wife, as you can see," said Charters, "has been a pillar of strength."

Banks decided to leave that one well alone. "What's he called, this man you fired?"

"Ive Jelačić."

"How do you spell that?"

Charters told him, explaining the diacritical marks. Banks wrote it down.

"What does he look like?"

"He's tall, about my height, solidly built. He has black hair, which always needed cutting, a dark complexion, a slightly hooked nose." He shrugged. "I don't know what else to say."

"Where is he now?"

"Leeds."

"Has he ever threatened or bothered you at all since you fired him?"

"Yes. He's been back a couple of times."

"Why?"

"To offer me a deal. He suggested that he would drop the charges if I gave him money."

"How much?"

Charters snorted. "More than I can afford, I'm afraid."

"And how would he get the charges dropped?"

"Say he misinterpreted my gesture. Cultural differences. I told him to go away. The man's a liar and a drunk, Chief Inspector. What difference does it make?"

"It might make a lot of difference," said Banks slowly, "if he had a reputation for bothering the St. Mary's girls and he had a grudge against you. Do you know his address?"

Charters went over and opened a sideboard drawer. "I ought to," he muttered, flipping through a pile of envelopes. "There's been enough correspondence on the matter. Ah, here it is."

Banks looked at the address. It was in the Burmantofts area of Leeds, but he didn't recognize the street. "Mind if I use your phone?" he asked.

"Go ahead," said Charters. "There's an extension in my study, if you want some privacy. It's just across the hall."

Banks went into the study and sat at the desk. He was impressed how tidy it was—no papers scattered all around, no chewed pencils, no reference books open face down, no errant paperclips or rubber bands, the way his own desk usually looked when he was working on something. Even the ruler was lined up parallel with the edge of the blotter. A neat man, the Reverend Charters. So neat that he had even tidied his desk *after* his wife came in screaming about a murder in the graveyard?

Banks consulted his notebook and phoned Detective Inspector Ken Blackstone at home. Blackstone, a good friend, worked for West Yorkshire CID out of Millgarth, Leeds. Banks explained what had happened and asked Blackstone if he could arrange to have a couple of officers go around to the address Charters had given him. First, he wanted to know if Jelačić was at home, and secondly, whether he had an alibi for this evening. Blackstone said it would be no problem, and Banks hung up.

When he went back into the living-room he obviously interrupted Daniel and Rebecca Charters in the midst of a hissed argument. Rebecca, he noticed, had refilled her brandy glass.

Banks had nothing more to ask, so he knocked back the rest of his lukewarm coffee and headed out into the graveyard.

IV

As soon as Banks had gone, Daniel Charters looked disgustedly at the empty wine bottle and the remains of the brandy, then at Rebecca. "I asked you why you did that," he said. "Why on earth did you lie to him?"

"You know why."

Daniel leaned forward in his chair, hands clasped between his knees. "No, I don't. You didn't even give me a chance to answer. You just jumped right in with your stupid lie."

Rebecca sipped her brandy. "I didn't notice you rushing to correct me."

Daniel reddened. "It was too late by then. It would have looked suspicious."

"Shpicious? Oh, that's a good one, Daniel. And how do you think it looks *already?*"

Daniel's face contorted in pain. "Do you think I did it? Do you really believe *I* killed that girl out there?" He pointed a long, bony finger towards the graveyard. "Is that what you think you were protecting me from? Giving me an alibi for?"

Rebecca turned away. "Don't be silly."

"Then why did you lie?"

"To make things easier."

"Lies never make things easier."

Oh, don't they? Rebecca thought. Shows what you know. "We've got enough problems," she said with a sigh, "without having you as a suspect in a murder investigation."

"Don't you want to know where I was?"

"No. I don't care where you were."

"But you lied for me."

"For us. Yes." She ran her hand through her hair. "Look, Daniel, I saw something horrible out there in the graveyard. I'm tired, I'm upset and I feel sick. Can't you just leave me alone?"

Daniel remained silent for a moment. Rebecca could hear the clock ticking on the mantelpiece. Ezekiel stirred briefly then settled down to sleep again.

"You think I did it, don't you?" Daniel persisted.

"Please, Daniel, just let it drop. Of course I don't think you did it."

"Not the murder. The other business."

"I don't think anything of the kind. I told you. Haven't I

stuck by you? Do you think I'd still be here if I thought you did it?"

"*Here?* You're not *here.* You haven't been *here* since it happened. Oh, you may actually be physically present in this room. Yes, I'll admit that. But you're not really *here,* not with me. Most of the time you're in the bottle, the rest you're . . . God knows where."

"Oh, right, and we all know you're such a bloody saint you haven't touched a drop throughout all our troubles. Well, maybe I'm not as *strong* as you, Daniel. Maybe we're not all so bloody *devout.* Some of us might just show a little human *weakness* every now and again. But you wouldn't know about that, would you?"

Rebecca topped up her brandy with a shaking hand. Daniel reached forward and knocked the glass out of her hand. The brandy spilled on the coffee-table and the sofa, and the glass bounced on the carpet.

Rebecca didn't know what to say. Her breath caught in her throat. It was the first time since she had known him that Daniel had shown even the slightest sign of violence.

His face was red, and his frown knitted his thick dark eyebrows together at the bridge of his nose. "You have your doubts don't you?" he insisted. "Go on. Admit it. I'm waiting."

Rebecca bent down, picked up the glass and poured herself another shot with shaking hands. This time Daniel did nothing.

"Answer me," he said. "Tell me the truth."

Rebecca let the silence stretch, then she took a long sip of brandy and said, in a parody of a prostitute's tone, "Well, you know what they say, don't you, ducky? There's no smoke without fire."

V

Banks left his car parked on North Market Street, outside St. Mary's, and set off on foot to Hawthorn Close. The fog appeared less menacing on the main road than it had in the unlit graveyard, though the high amber street-lights and the flashing Belisha beacons at the zebra crossing looked like the Martian machines out of *War of the Worlds*.

Why had Rebecca Charters lied for her husband? She *had* lied, of that Banks was certain, even without the evidence of the tidy desk. Was she giving him an alibi? Perhaps tomorrow he would call on them again. She was certainly an odd one. *Going to see the angel,* indeed!

Banks looked at his watch. Luckily, it was just after nine o'clock, and he still had time to nip into the off-license at the corner of Hawthorn Road and buy twenty Silk Cut.

After he had walked about two hundred yards down Hawthorn Road, he took Hawthorn Close to the right, a winding street of big, stone houses that traditionally housed Eastvale's gentry.

He found number 28, stubbed out his cigarette and walked up the gravel drive, noting the "O" registration Jaguar parked outside the front door. On impulse, he put his hand on the bonnet. Still a little warm.

Barry Stott answered the door, looking grim. Banks thanked him for doing the dirty work and told him he could return to the station and get things organized; then he walked down the hall alone into a spacious white room, complete with a white grand piano. The only contrasting elements were the Turkish carpets and what looked like a genuine Chagall on the wall over the Adam fireplace, where a thick log burned and crackled. A white bookcase held Folio Society editions of the classics, and French windows with white trim led out to the dark garden.

There were three people in the room, all sitting down, and all, by the looks of it, in a state of shock. The woman wore a gray skirt and a blue silk blouse, both of a quality you'd be hard-pushed to find in Eastvale. Her shaggy blonde hair was the expensive kind of shaggy, and it framed an oval face with a pale, flawless complexion, pale blue eyes and beautifully proportioned nose and mouth. All in all, an elegant and attractive woman.

She got up and floated towards him as if in a trance. "Has there been a mistake?" she asked. "Please tell me there's been a mistake." She had a hint of a French accent.

Before Banks could say anything, one of the men took her by the elbow and said, "Come on, Sylvie. Sit down." Then he turned to Banks. "I'm Geoffrey Harrison," he said. "Deborah's father. I suppose it's too much to hope there *has* been a mistake?"

Banks shook his head.

Geoffrey was about six foot two, with the long arms and broad shoulders of a fast bowler. In fact he looked a bit like a famous test cricketer, but Banks couldn't put a name to him. He was wearing gray trousers with sharp creases and a knitted green V-neck sweater over a white shirt. No tie. He had curly fair hair, with some gray visible around the ears, and a strong, cleft chin, a bit like Kirk Douglas. Everything about his movements and features spoke of power, of someone used to getting his own way. Banks put his age at about forty-five, probably a good ten years older than his wife.

All of a sudden, the realization hit Banks like a bucket of cold water. Christ, he should have known. Should have been able to add it all up. This damn cold must be addling his brain. The man in front of him was Sir Geoffrey Harrison. *Sir.* He had been knighted for services to industry—something to do with leading-edge computers, electronics, microchips and the like—about three years ago. And Deborah Harrison was his daughter.

"Do you have a recent photograph of your daughter, sir?" he asked.

"Over there on the mantelpiece. It was taken last summer."

Banks walked over and looked at the photograph of the

young girl posing on the deck of a yacht. It was probably her first year in a bikini, Banks guessed, and while she hardly had the figure to fill it out, it still looked good on her. But then anything would probably have looked good on such youth, such energy, such potential.

Deborah was smiling and holding the mast with one hand; with the other she held back a long strand of blonde hair from her face, as if the wind were blowing it out of place. Even though the girl in the picture glowed with health and life, it was the same one who now lay in Eastvale mortuary.

"I'm afraid it's not a mistake," he said, glancing at the photograph beside it. It showed two smiling young men in cricket whites, one of them unmistakably Sir Geoffrey, standing together in a quadrangle. The other man, who had his arm casually draped over Sir Geoffrey's shoulder, could easily have been the other person in the room about twenty-five years ago. Even now, he was still slim and good-looking, though the sandy hair above his high forehead was receding fast and thinning on top. He was wearing what looked like very expensive casual clothes—black cords and a rust-colored cotton shirt—and a pair of gold-rimmed spectacles hung around his neck on a chain. "Michael Clayton," he said, getting up and shaking Banks's hand.

"Michael's my business partner," said Sir Geoffrey. "And my oldest friend. He's also Deborah's godfather."

"I live just around the corner," said Clayton. "As soon as Geoff heard the news . . . well, they phoned me and I came over. Have there been any developments?"

"It's too early to say," said Banks. Then he turned to Sir Geoffrey and Lady Harrison. "Did you know if Deborah was planning on going anywhere after school?"

Sir Geoffrey took a second to refocus, then said, "Only the chess club."

"Chess club?"

"Yes. At school. They meet every Monday."

"What time is she usually home?"

Sir Geoffrey looked at his wife. "It's usually over by six,"

Lady Harrison said. "She gets home about quarter past. Sometimes twenty past, if she dawdles with her friends."

Banks frowned. "It must have been after eight o'clock when Detective Inspector Stott came to break the bad news," he said. "But you hadn't reported Deborah missing. Weren't you worried? Where did you think she was?"

Lady Harrison started to cry. Sir Geoffrey gripped her hand. "We'd only just got in ourselves," he explained. "I was at a business reception at the Royal Hotel, in York, and the damn fog delayed me. Sylvie was at her health club. Deborah has a key. She *is* sixteen, after all."

"What time did you get back?"

"About eight o'clock. Within minutes of each other. We thought Deborah might have been home and gone out again, but that wasn't like her, not without letting us know, and certainly not on a night like this. There was no note, no sign she'd been here. Deborah's not . . . well, she usually leaves her school blazer over the back of a chair, if you see what I mean."

"I do." Banks's daughter Tracy was just as untidy.

"Anyway, we were worried she might have been kidnapped or something. We were just about to phone the police when Inspector Stott arrived."

"Have there ever been any kidnap threats?"

"No, but one hears about such things."

"Could your daughter have been carrying anything of value? Cash, credit cards, anything?"

"No. Why do you ask?"

"Her satchel was open. I was just wondering why."

Sir Geoffrey shook his head.

Banks turned to Michael Clayton. "Did you see Deborah at all this evening?"

"No. I was at home until I got Geoff's phone call."

Sir Geoffrey and Lady Harrison sat on the white sofa, shoulders slumped, holding hands like a couple of teenagers. Banks sat on the edge of the armchair and leaned forward, resting his hands on his knees.

"Inspector Stott says Deborah was found in St. Mary's graveyard," Sir Geoffrey said. "Is that true?"

Banks nodded.

Anger suffused Sir Geoffrey's face. "Have you talked to that bloody vicar yet? That pervert?"

"Daniel Charters?"

"That's him. You know what he's been accused of, don't you?"

"Making a homosexual advance."

Sir Geoffrey nodded. "Exactly. If I were you, I'd—"

"Please, Geoffrey," Sylvie said, plucking at his sleeve. "Calm down. Let the chief inspector talk."

Sir Geoffrey ran his hand through his hair. "Yes, of course. I apologize."

Why such animosity towards Charters? Banks wondered. But that was best left for later. Sir Geoffrey was distraught; it wouldn't be a good idea to press him any further just now.

"May I have a look at Deborah's room?" he asked.

Sylvie nodded and stood up. "I'll show you."

Banks followed her up a broad, white-carpeted staircase. What a hell of a job it would be to keep the place clean, he found himself thinking. Sandra would never put up with white carpets or upholstery. Still, he didn't suppose the Harrisons did the cleaning themselves.

Sylvie opened the door to Deborah's room, then excused herself and went back downstairs. Banks turned on the light. It was bigger, but in much the same state of disarray as Tracy's. Clothes lay tossed all over the floor, the bed was unmade, a mound of rumpled sheets, and the closet door stood open on a long rail of dresses, blouses, jackets and jeans. Expensive stuff, too, Banks saw as he looked at some of the designer labels.

Deborah's computer, complete with CD-ROM, sat on the desk under the window. Beside that stood a bookcase filled mostly with science and computer textbooks and a few bodice-rippers. Banks searched through all the drawers but found nothing of interest. Of course, it would have helped if he had known what he was looking for.

Arranged in custom shelving on a table by the foot of the bed were a mini-hi-fi system, a small color television and a video—all with remote controls. Banks glanced through some of the CDs. Unlike Tracy, Deborah seemed to favor the rough, grungy style of popular music: Hole, Pearl Jam, Nirvana. A large poster of Kurt Cobain was tacked to the wall next to a smaller poster of River Phoenix.

Banks closed the door behind him and walked back down the stairs. He could hear Sylvie crying in the white room and Sir Geoffrey and Michael Clayton in muffled conversation. He couldn't hear what they were saying, and when he moved close, they saw him through the open door and asked him back in.

"I have just one more question, Sir Geoffrey, if I may?" he said.

"Go ahead."

"Did your daughter keep a diary? I know mine does. They seem to be very popular among teenage girls."

Sir Geoffrey thought for a moment. "Yes," he said, "I think so. Michael bought her one last Christmas."

Clayton nodded. "Yes. One of the leather-bound kind, a page per day."

Banks turned back to Sir Geoffrey. "Do you know where she kept it?"

He frowned. "I'm afraid I don't. Sylvie?"

Sylvie shook her head. "She told me she lost it."

"When was this?"

"About the beginning of term. I hadn't seen it for a while, so I asked her if she'd stopped writing it. Why? Is it important?"

"Probably not," said Banks. "It's just that sometimes what we don't find is as important as what we do. Trouble is, we never really know until later. Anyway, I won't bother you any further tonight."

"Inspector Stott said I'd have to identify the body," Sir Geoffrey said. "You'll make the arrangements?"

"Of course. Again, sir, my condolences."

Sir Geoffrey nodded, then he turned back to his wife. Like a butler, Banks was dismissed.

VI

What with one thing and another, it was after two in the morning when Banks parked the dark-blue Cavalier he had finally bought to replace his clapped-out Cortina in front of his house. After Hawthorn Close, it was good to be back in the normal world of semis with postage-stamp gardens, Fiestas and Astras parked in the street.

The first thing he did was tiptoe upstairs to check on Tracy. It was foolish, he knew, but after seeing Deborah Harrison's body, he felt the need to see his own daughter alive and breathing.

The amber glow from the street-lamp outside her window lit the faint outline of Tracy's sleeping figure. Every so often, she would turn and give a little sigh, as if she were dreaming. Softly, Banks closed her door again and went back downstairs to the living-room, careful to bypass the creaky third stair from the top. Despite the late hour, he didn't feel at all tired.

He turned on the shaded table lamp and poured himself a stiff Laphroaig, hoping to put the image of Deborah Harrison spread-eagled in the graveyard out of his mind.

After five minutes, Banks hadn't succeeded in getting his mind off the subject. Music would help. "Music alone with sudden charms can bind / The wand'ring sense, and calm the troubled mind," as Congreve had said. Surely it wouldn't wake Sandra or Tracy if he played a classical CD quietly?

He flipped through his quickly growing collection—he was sure that they multiplied overnight—and settled finally on Richard Strauss's *Four Last Songs*.

In the middle of the second song, "September," when Gundula Janowitz's crystaline soprano was soaring away with the melody, Banks topped up his Laphroaig and lit a cigarette.

Before he had taken more than three or four drags, the door opened and Tracy popped her head around.

"What are you doing up?" Banks whispered.

Tracy rubbed her eyes and walked into the room. She was wearing a long, sloppy nightshirt with a picture of a giant panda on the front. Though she was seventeen, it made her look like a little girl.

"I thought I heard someone in my room," Tracy muttered. "I couldn't get back to sleep so I came down for some milk. Oh, Dad! You're smoking again."

Banks put his finger to his lips. "Shhh! Your mother." He looked at the cigarette guiltily. "So I am."

"And you promised."

"I never did." Banks hung his head in shame. There was nothing like a teenage daughter to make you feel guilty about your bad habits, especially with all the anti-smoking propaganda they were brainwashed with at school these days.

"You did, too." Tracy came closer. "Is something wrong? Is that why you're up so late smoking and drinking?"

She sat on the arm of the sofa and looked at him, sleep-filled eyes full of concern, long blonde hair straggling over her narrow shoulders. Banks's son, Brian, who was away studying architecture in Portsmouth, took after his father, but Tracy took after her mother.

They had come a long way since the bitter arguments over her first boyfriend, long since dumped, and too many late nights over the summer. Now Tracy had determined not to have a boyfriend at all this year, but to put all her efforts into getting good A-level results so she could go to university, where she wanted to study history. Banks couldn't help but approve. As he looked at her perching so frail and vulnerable on the edge of the sofa his heart swelled with pride in her, and with fear for her.

"No," he said, getting up and patting her head. "There's nothing wrong. I'm just an old fool set in his ways, that's all. Shall I make us both some cocoa?"

Tracy nodded, then yawned and stretched her arms high in the air.

Banks smiled. Gundula Janowitz sang Hermann Hesse's words. Banks had listened to the songs so many times, he knew the translation by heart:

> *The day has tired me,*
> *and my spirits yearn*
> *for the starry night*
> *to gather them up*
> *like a tired child.*

You can say that again, thought Banks. He looked back at Tracy as he walked to the kitchen. She was examining the small-print CD liner notes with squinting eyes trying to make out the words.

She would find out soon enough what had happened to Deborah Harrison, Banks thought. It would be all over town tomorrow. But not tonight. Tonight father and daughter would enjoy a quiet, innocent cup of cocoa in the middle of the night in their safe, warm house floating like an island in the fog.

Chapter 2

I

Chief Constable Jeremiah Riddle was already pacing the lino when Banks arrived at his office early the next morning. Bald head shining like a new cricket ball freshly rubbed on the bowler's crotch, black eyes glowing like a Whitby jet, clean-shaven chin jutting out like the prow of a boat, uniform sharply creased, not a speck of fluff or cotton anywhere to be seen, and a poppy placed ostentatiously in his lapel, he looked alert, wide-awake and ready for anything.

Which was more than Banks looked, or felt for that matter. All told, he had got no more than about three hours' uneasy sleep, especially as an early telephone call from Ken Blackstone had woken him up. Though the fog was quickly turning to drizzle this morning, he had walked the mile to work simply to get the cobwebs out of his brain. He wasn't sure whether he had succeeded. It didn't help that his cold was getting worse, either, filling his head with damp cotton wool.

"Ah, Banks, about bloody time," said Riddle.

Banks removed his headphones and switched off the Jimi Hendrix tape he had been listening to. The breakneck arpeggios of "Pali Gap" were still ringing in his stuffed-up ears.

"And do you have to go around with those bloody things stuck in your ears?" Riddle went on. "Don't you know how silly you look?"

Banks knew a rhetorical question when he heard one.

"I suppose you're aware who the victim's father is?"

"Sir Geoffrey Harrison, sir. I talked to him last night."

"In that case you'll realize how important this is. This . . . this . . . terrible tragedy." Never at a loss for a cliché wasn't Jimmy Riddle, Banks reflected. Riddle slid his hand over his head and went on. "I want a hundred per cent on this one, Banks. No. *Two* hundred per cent. Do you understand? No shirking. No dragging of feet."

Banks nodded. "Yes, sir."

"Now what about this Bosnian fellow? Jurassic, is it?"

"Jelačić, sir. And he's Croatian."

"Whatever. Think he's our man?"

"We'll certainly be talking to him. Ken Blackstone has just reported that Jelačić's known to the Leeds police. Drunk and disorderly, one charge of assault in a pub. And he didn't get home until after two this morning. They've got his prints, so we should be able to compare them if Vic gets anything from the vodka bottle."

"Good." Riddle grinned. "That's the kind of thing I like to hear. I want a quick arrest on this one, Banks. Sir Geoffrey's a personal friend of mine. Do you understand?"

"Yes, sir."

"Right. And take it easy on the family. I don't want you pestering them in their time of grief. Am I clear?"

"Yes, sir."

Riddle straightened his uniform, which didn't need it, and brushed imaginary dandruff from his shoulders. Wishful thinking, Banks guessed. "Now I'm off to give a press conference," he said. "Anything I ought to know to stop me looking a prize berk?"

Nothing could stop you from looking like a prize berk, Banks thought. "No, sir," he said. "But you might like to drop by the murder room and see if there's anything fresh come in."

"I've already done that. What do you think I am, a bloody moron?"

Banks let the silence stretch.

Riddle kept pacing, though he seemed to have run out of things to say for the present. At last he headed for the door. "Right, then. Remember what I said, Banks," he said, pointing a finger. "Results. Fast."

Banks felt himself relax and breathe easier when Riddle had gone, like a Victorian lady when she takes her corsets off. He had read about "Type A" personalities in a magazine article—all push and shove, ambition and self-importance, and bloody exhausting to be in the same room with.

Banks lit a cigarette, read the reports on his desk and looked at the *Dalesman* calendar on his wall. November showed the village of Muker, in Swaledale, a cluster of gray limestone buildings cupped in a valley of muted autumn colors. He walked over to the window where the early morning light was leaking through the cloud cover like dirty dishwater.

The market square, with its Norman church to his left, bank, shops and cafés opposite and Queen's Arms to the right, was a study in slate-gray, except for one bright red Honda parked by the weathered market cross. Banks watched a bent old lady hobble across the cobbles under a black umbrella. He checked his watch with the church tower clock: five to eight, time to gather his papers and head for the morning meeting.

DI Stott was already waiting and raring to go in the "Boardroom," so called because of its well-polished oval table, ten matching stiff-backed chairs and dark-burgundy wallpaper above the wainscoting.

Detective Constable Susan Gay arrived two minutes later. Her make-up almost hid the bags under her eyes, the gel made her short curly hair look as if it were still wet from the shower, and her subtle perfume brought a whiff of spring to the room.

Detective Sergeant Jim Hatchley, big and heavy, like a rugby prop-forward gone to seed, came in last. He hadn't freshened up. His face looked like a lump of dough with

tufts of stubble sticking out of it, his eyes were bloodshot
and his strawy hair uncombed. His navy-blue suit was
creased and shiny.

"Okay," said Banks, shuffling the papers in front of him,
"we've got two new pieces of information to deal with. I'd
hesitate to call them leads, but you never know. First off, for
what it's worth, one of our diuretically challenged constables found the missing underwear while nipping behind a
handy yew to drain the dragon. They're with the rest of her
clothing at the mortuary. The second item might be even
more significant," he went on. "Some of you may already
know that a Croatian refugee called Ive Jelačić was recently
fired by Daniel Charters, vicar of St. Mary's, and subse-
quently brought charges of sexual harassment against him.
By the sound of it, this Jelačić's an unsavory character. According to West Yorkshire CID, Mr. Jelačić didn't get home
until after two o'clock last night, plenty of time to get back
from committing a murder in Eastvale, even in the fog. He
said he'd been playing cards with some fellow countrymen
at a friend's house."

Hatchley grunted. "These foreigners would lie as soon as
look at you," he said. "Especially to cover up for one another."

"West Yorkshire CID are already checking it out," Banks
went on, "but I'm afraid Detective Sergeant Hatchley has, in
his inimitable fashion, probably put his finger on the truth of
the matter. So we'll take this alibi with a large pinch of salt.
DI Blackstone said they'll sit on Jelačić until we get there. I
think we'll let him sweat for a couple more hours.

"Now we don't have anything in from the lab yet, but
from my observations of the scene, what we've got here
looks like a sex murder. There was an *arranged* quality to it
all. But I want to stress *looks like*. Right now, we just don't
know enough. There are several other avenues we simply
can't afford to overlook." He counted them off on his fingers. "School, family, Jelačić, boyfriends and the couple at
the vicarage, for starters. Rebecca Charters lied to me last
night when I asked where her husband had been at the time

of the crime. She gave him a false alibi and I'd like to know why he needed it, especially given the recent scandal involving him. We also need to know a lot more about Deborah Harrison's life. Not just her movements yesterday, but her interests, her activities, her sex life, if she had one, and her past. We need to know what made her tick, what kind of person she was. Any questions?"

They all shook their heads.

"Good. Barry, I'd like you and Sergeant Hatchley to spend the morning going through the records of all known sex offenders in the county. You know the procedure. If anyone sounds likely, make inquiries. After that, ask around at some of the restaurants and cafés in the St. Mary's area, places that might have been closed after eight or nine last night, when the uniforms did their house-to-house. You never know, our man might have stopped off for a cup of tea on his way to the graveyard."

Stott nodded.

"And, I'd also like you to try and find out anything you can about Jelačić from records, immigration, wherever. Does he have form back home? Has he ever committed a sex offense of any kind there?"

Stott scribbled notes on his pad.

"Susan, I'd like you to team up with me and check out a few things closer to home. For a start we've got to find out exactly what Deborah's movements were yesterday, who saw her last. Okay?"

"Yes, sir."

"So if there's nothing else," Banks said, "let's get on with it. Everyone check in with the murder room at regular intervals."

Given their tasks, they drifted away. Except DC Susan Gay, who topped up her milky coffee and sat down again.

"Why me, sir?" she asked.

"Pardon?"

"Why am I teamed up with you on this? I'm only a DC. By rights it should—"

"Susan, whatever your rank, you're a good detective.

You've proved that often enough. Think about it. Taking Jim Hatchley around to a girls' school, a vicarage and Sir Geoffrey Harrison's . . . It would be like letting a bull loose in a china shop."

Susan's lips twitched in a smile. "What exactly will we be doing?"

"Talking to the family, friends, teachers. Trying to find out if this isn't just the sex murder it seems, and if someone had a *reason* to want Deborah Harrison dead."

"Are you going to check her parents' alibis?"

Banks paused for a moment, then said, "Yes. Probably."

"The chief constable won't like it, will he?"

"Won't like what?"

"Any of it. Us going around poking our noses into the Harrison family background."

"Maybe not."

"I mean, it's pretty common knowledge around the station that they're in the same funny-handshake brigade, sir. The chief constable and Sir Geoffrey, that is."

"Oh, is it?"

"So rumor has it, sir."

"And you're worried about your career."

"Well, I've passed my sergeant's exam, as you know. I'm just waiting for an opening. I mean, I'm with you all the way, sir, but I wouldn't want to make enemies in the wrong places, not just at the moment."

Banks smiled. "Don't worry," he said, "it's my balls on the chopping-block, not yours. I'll cover you. My word on it."

Susan smiled back. "Well, that's the first time not having any balls has ever done me any good."

II

When she woke up shortly after eight o'clock on Tuesday morning, Rebecca Charters felt the hammering pain behind her eyes that signaled another hangover.

It hadn't always been like this, she reminded herself. When she had married Daniel twelve years ago, he had been a dynamic young cleric. She had loved his passionate faith and his dedication just as she had loved his sense of humor and his joy in the sensual world. Lovemaking had always been a pleasure for both of them. Until recently.

She got up, put on her dressing-gown against the chill and walked over to the window. When they had first moved to St. Mary's six years ago, her friends had all said how depressing and unhealthy it would be living in a graveyard. Just like the Brontës, darling, they said, and look what happened to them.

But Rebecca didn't find it at all depressing. She found it strangely comforting and peaceful to consider the worms seething at their work just below the overgrown surface. It put things in perspective. It also reminded her of that Marvell poem Patrick had quoted for her just on the brink of their affair, when things could have gone either way:

> *But at my back I always hear*
> *Time's wingèd chariot hurrying near;*
> *And yonder all before us lie*
> *Deserts of vast eternity.*
> *Thy beauty shall no more be found;*
> *Nor, in thy marble vault, shall sound*
> *My echoing song; then worms shall try*
> *That long preserv'd virginity:*
> *And your quaint honor turn to dust;*
> *And into ashes all my lust.*
> *The grave's a fine and private place,*
> *But none I think do there embrace.*

What an easy seduction it had been, after all. The poem worked. Marvell would have been proud of himself.

Rebecca pulled back the curtain. Some fog still drifted around the yew trunks and the heavy gray headstones, but the drizzle seemed to have settled in now. From her window, she could see uniformed policemen methodically searching the ground around the church in a grid pattern.

Deborah Harrison. She had often seen Deborah taking a short cut through the churchyard; she had also seen her in church and at choir practice, too, before the trouble began.

Deborah's father, Sir Geoffrey, had deserted St. Mary's at the first hint of a scandal. The school had stuck with Daniel, but Sir Geoffrey, to whom appearances were far more important than truth, had made a point of turning his back, taking his family and a number of other wealthy and influential members of the congregation with him. And St. Mary's was the wealthiest parish in Eastvale. Had been. Now the coffers were emptying fast.

Rebecca rested her forehead against the cool glass and watched her breath mist up the window. She found herself doodling Patrick's name with her fingernail and felt the need for him burn in her loins. She hated herself for feeling this way. Patrick was ten years younger than she was, a mere twenty-six, but he was so ardent, so passionate, always talking so excitedly about life and poetry and love. Though she needed him, she hated her need; though she determined every day to call it off, she desired nothing more than to lose herself completely in him.

Like the drinking, Patrick was an escape; she had enough self-knowledge to work that out, at any rate. An escape from the poisoned atmosphere at St. Mary's, from what she and Daniel had become, and, as she admitted in her darkest moments, an escape from her own fears and suspicions.

Now this. It didn't make sense, she tried to convince herself. Daniel couldn't possibly be a murderer. Why would he want to murder someone as innocent as Deborah Harrison? Just because you feared a person might be guilty of one thing, did that mean he had to be guilty of something else, too?

As she watched the policemen in their capes and Wellingtons poke through the long grass, she had to face the facts: Daniel had come home only *after* she had gone to see the

angel; he had gone out *before* she thought she heard the
scream; she hadn't known where he was, and when he came
back his shoes were muddy, with leaves and gravel stuck to
their soles.

III

The mortuary was in the basement of Eastvale General Infirmary, an austere Victorian brick building with high drafty
corridors and wards that Susan had always thought were
guaranteed to make you ill if you weren't already.

The white-tiled post-mortem room, though, had recently
been modernized, as if, she thought, the dead somehow deserved a healthier environment than the living.

Chilled by the cooling unit rather than by the wind from
outside, it had two shiny metal tables with guttered edges
and a long lab bench along one wall, with glass-fronted cabinets for specimen jars. Susan had never dared ask about the
two jars that looked as if they contained human brains.

Dr. Glendenning's assistants had already removed Deborah Harrison's body from its plastic bag, and she lay, clothed
as she had been in the graveyard, on one of the tables.

It was nine o'clock, and the radio was tuned to "Wake up
to Wogan." "Do we have to listen to that rubbish?" Banks
asked.

"It's *normal,* Banks," said Glendenning. "That's why we
have it on. Millions of people in houses all around the country will be listening to Wogan now. People who aren't just
about to cut open the body of a sixteen-year-old girl. I suppose you'd like some fancy classical concert on Radio 3,
wouldn't you? I can't say that the thought of performing a
post-mortem to Elgar's *Enigma Variations* would do a hell
of a lot for me." Glendenning stuck a cigarette in the corner
of his mouth and pulled on his surgical gloves.

Susan smiled. Banks looked at her and shrugged.

The girl on the slab wasn't a human being, Susan kept

telling herself. She was just a piece of dead meat, like at the butcher's. She remembered June Walker, the butcher's daughter, from school in Sheffield, and recalled the peculiar smell that always seemed to emanate from her. Odd, she hadn't thought of June Walker in years.

The smell—stale and sharp, but sweet, too—was here, all right, but it was buried under layers of formaldehyde and cigarette smoke, for both Glendenning and Banks were smoking furiously. She didn't blame them. She had once seen a film on television in which an American woman cop rubbed some Vick's or something under her nose to mask the smell of a decomposing body. Susan didn't dare do such a thing herself for fear the others would laugh at her. After all, this was Yorkshire, not America.

Still, as she watched Glendenning cut and probe at the girl's clothing, then remove it for air-drying and storage, she almost wished she were a smoker. At least that smell was easier to wash away than the smell of death; that seemed to linger in her clothes and hair for days after.

Deborah's panties lay in a plastic bag on the lab bench. They weren't at all like the navy-blue knickers, the "passion-killers," that Susan had worn at school, but expensive, silky and rather sexy black panties. Maybe such things were *de rigueur* for St. Mary's girls, Susan thought. Or had Deborah been hoping to impress someone? They still didn't know if she'd had a boyfriend.

Her school blazer lay next to the panties in a separate bag, and beside that lay her satchel. Vic Manson, the fingerprints expert, had sent it back early that morning, saying he had found clear prints on one of the vodka bottles but only blurred partials on the smooth leather surface of the satchel. DI Stott had been through Deborah's blazer pockets and found only a purse with six pounds thirty-three pence in it, an old chewing-gum wrapper, her house keys, a cinema ticket stub and a half-eaten roll of Polo mints.

After one of his assistants had taken photographs, Glendenning examined the face, noting the pinpoint hemorrhages in the whites of the eyes, eyelids and skin of the cheeks. Then he examined the weal on the neck.

"As I said last night," he began, "it looks like a clear case of asphyxia by ligature strangulation. Look here."

Banks and Susan bent over the body. Susan tried not to look into the eyes. Glendenning's probe indicated the discolored weal around the front of the throat. "Whoever did this was pretty strong," he said. "You can see how deeply the strap bit into the flesh. And I'd say our chappie was a good few inches taller than his victim. And she was tall for her age. Five foot six." He turned to Susan. "That's almost 168 centimeters, to the younger generation. See how the wound is deeper at the bottom, the way it would be if you were pulling a leather strap upwards?" He moved away and demonstrated on one of the assistants. "See?" Banks and Susan nodded.

"Are you sure the satchel strap was the weapon?" Banks asked.

Glendenning nodded. He picked it up and held it out. "You can see traces of blood on the edge here, where it broke the skin. We're having it typed, of course, but I'd put money on this being your weapon."

Next, he set about removing the plastic bags that covered the hands. Gently—almost, Susan thought, like a manicurist—he held up each hand and peered at the fingernails. Deborah's nails had been quite long, Susan noticed, not the bitten-to-the-quick mess hers had been when she was at school.

When Glendenning got to the middle finger of her right hand, he murmured to himself, then took a shiny instrument from the tray and ran it under the top of the nail, calling to one of his assistants for a glassine envelope.

"What is it?" Banks asked. "Did she put up a fight?"

"Looks like she got at least one good scratch in. With a bit of luck we'll be able to get DNA from this."

Passing quickly over the chest and stomach, Glendenning next picked up a probe and turned his attention to the pubic region. Susan looked away; she didn't want to witness this indignity, and she didn't care what anyone said or thought of her.

But she couldn't shut out the sound of Glendenning's voice.

"Hmm. Interesting," he said. "No obvious signs of sexual interference. No bruising. No lacerations. Let's have a look behind."

He flipped the body over; it slapped against the table like meat on a butcher's block. Susan heard her heart beating fast and loud during the silence that followed.

"No. Nothing," Glendenning announced at last. "At least nothing obvious. I'm waiting for the test results on the swabs but I'd bet you a pound to a penny they'll turn up nothing."

Susan turned back to face the two of them. "So she wasn't raped?" she asked.

"Doesn't look like it," Glendenning answered. "Of course, we won't know for sure until we've had a good look around inside. And in order to do that . . ." He picked up a large scalpel.

Glendenning bent over the body and started to make the Y incision from shoulders to pubes. He detoured around the tough tissue of the navel with a practiced flick of the wrist.

"Right," said Banks, turning to Susan, "We'd better go."

Glendenning looked up from the gaping incision and raised his eyebrows. "Not staying for the rest of the show?"

"No time. We don't want to be late for school."

Glendenning looked at the corpse and shook his head. "Can't say I blame you. Some days I wish I'd stayed in bed."

As they left Glendenning to sort through the inner organs of Deborah Harrison, Susan had never felt quite so grateful to Banks in her life. Next time they were in the Queen's Arms, she vowed she would buy him a pint. But she wouldn't tell him why.

Chapter 3

I

St. Mary's School wasn't exactly Castle Howard, but it certainly looked impressive enough to be used as a location in a BBC classic drama.

Banks and Susan turned through the high, wrought-iron gates and drove along a winding driveway; sycamores flanked both sides, laying down a carpet of rust and gold leaves; double-winged seeds spun down like helicopter blades in the drizzle.

Through the trees, they first glimpsed the imposing gray stone building, with its central cupola, high windows and columns flanking the front entrance. Statues stood on the tops of the columns, against a frieze, and double stairs curled out at the front like lobster claws.

St. Mary's School for Girls, Banks had read, was founded in 1823 on forty acres of woodland by the River Swain. The main building, completed in 1773, had been intended as a country house but had never been lived in. Rumor had it that Lord Satterthwait, for whom the house had been built, lost much of his fortune in an ill-advised business venture abroad, along with the money of a number of other county luminaries, and was forced to flee the area in disgrace for America.

The grounds were quiet this morning, but a group of girls

in maroon blazers saw Banks pull up and started whispering among themselves. The car was unmarked, but Banks and Susan were strangers, and by now everyone must know that Deborah Harrison had been murdered.

Banks asked one of the girls where they might find the head, and she directed him through the front door, right down to the back of the building, then along the last corridor to the right. Inside, the place was all high, ornate ceilings and dark, polished wainscoting. Susan's footsteps echoed as they walked. It was certainly a far cry from the institutional gloom of Eastvale Comprehensive, or from Banks's old redbrick school in Peterborough, for that matter.

They walked along the narrow corridor, noting the gilt-framed paintings of past heads on the walls. Most of them were men. When they reached the door marked "Dr. J.S. Green: Principal," Banks knocked sharply.

Expecting to be asked into an anteroom and vetted by a secretary first, Banks was surprised when he and Susan found themselves in the head's office. Like the rest of the building, it had a high ceiling with elaborate cornices, but there its ancient character ended.

The wainscoting, if there had been any, had been removed and the walls were papered in an attractive Laura Ashley print. A shaded electric light hung from the old chandelier fixture, and several gunmetal filing cabinets stood against the wall. The bay window dominated the room, its window seat scattered with cushions that matched the wallpaper. The view through the trees to the river, Banks noticed, was magnificent, even on a drizzly November morning. Across the river was St. Mary's Park, with its pond, trees, benches and children's playground.

"What do you think?" Dr. Green asked, after they had introduced themselves and shaken hands.

"Pardon?" said Banks.

She took their raincoats and hung them on a rack in the corner. "I couldn't help but notice that you were 'casing the joint' as they say," she said.

"Hardly," said Banks. "That's what the bad guys do."

She blushed slightly. "Oh, dear. My gaffe. I suppose criminal parlance is not my forte."

Banks smiled. "Just as well. Anyway, it's very nice."

The tall, elegant Dr. Julia Green looked every bit as Laura Ashley as her walls. The skirt and waistcoat she wore over her white blouse were made of heavy cloth; earth colors dominated, browns and greens, mixed with the odd flash of muted pink or yellow, like wildflowers poking their way through the undergrowth.

Her ash-blonde hair lay neatly piled and curled on her head, with only one or two loose strands. She had a narrow face, high cheekbones and a small nose. There was also a remote, unattainable quality about her that intrigued Banks. She might be one of the pale and distant beauties, but there was no mistaking the sharp glint of intelligence in her apple-green eyes. Right now, they also looked red from crying.

"This is a terrible business," she said. "Though I suppose you have to deal with it all the time."

"Not often," said Banks. "And you never get used to it."

"Please, sit down."

Banks and Susan sat in the two chairs opposite the small, solid desk. Susan took her notebook out.

"I don't know how I can help you," Dr. Green went on, "but I'll do my best."

"Maybe you could start by telling us what kind of a girl Deborah was."

She rested her hands on the desk, tapered fingers laced together. "I can't tell you very much," she said. "Deborah is . . . was . . . a day-girl. Do you know how the system works?"

"I don't know much about public schools at all."

"*Independent* school," she corrected him. "Public school sounds so Victorian, don't you think? Well, you see, we have a mix of day-girls and boarders. The actual balance changes slightly from year to year, but at the moment, we have 65 day-pupils and 286 boarding. When I say that Deborah was a day-girl I don't describe her status in any way, just note the simple fact that she came and went each day, so one didn't develop any special relationship with her."

"Relationship?"

"Yes. Well, when you live in such close proximity to the pupils, you're bound to get to know more about them, aren't you?"

"In what way?"

"In any number of ways. Whether it be the crisis of Elizabeth's first period, Meredith's parents' divorce or Barbara's estrangement from her mother. These things can't help but come out from time to time with the boarding pupils."

"So you'd soon find out who's a troublemaker, for example?"

"Yes. Not that we have any troublemakers. Nothing serious, anyway. We did catch one girl smoking marijuana in the dorm last year, and some years ago one of our upper-sixth girls got pregnant. But these are extremes, you understand, quite rare."

"Have you ever had any inkling of widespread problems here?"

"Such as what?"

"Drugs, perhaps, or pornography."

"Chief Inspector, this isn't a comprehensive, you know."

"Perhaps not. But girls will be girls."

"I don't know what you mean by that, but to answer your question, no, there's been nothing of that nature at St. Mary's."

"Do *you* live on the school grounds?"

Dr. Green nodded. "There's a small block of flats for members of staff—for some of us, anyway—and I live there."

"Alone?"

"Yes. Alone."

"So what can you tell me about Deborah Harrison?"

Dr. Green shrugged. "Just superficial things, really. She was a bright girl. Very intelligent. I don't think there's much doubt she would have ended up at Oxford or Cambridge, had she lived."

"Where did her strengths lie?"

"She was something of an all-rounder, but she excelled in the sciences—maths and physics, in particular. She was also good at modern languages. She had just entered the lower sixth this year. The school offers twenty-three subjects at A-level. Deborah was taking four: mathematics, French, German and physics."

"What about her personality?"

Dr. Green leaned back and put her hands on the arms of her chair. "Again, I can only be fairly superficial."

"That's all right."

"She always seemed cheerful and lively. You know, some girls can get very moody and withdrawn in the lower sixth—they go through a very difficult period in their lives—but Deborah seemed to be outgoing. She was an outstanding athlete. Swimming, tennis, running, field events. She was a good equestrian, too."

"I understand she belonged to the chess club?"

"Yes. She was a fine player. A superb strategist."

"You sound as if you play, yourself."

She smiled. "Moderately well."

"I'd appreciate it if you could provide me with a list of the other members."

"Of course." Dr. Green searched through one of the filing cabinets and handed Banks a sheet of paper with ten names on it. Then she paused, scratched her cheek, and said, "I must admit, Chief Inspector, the questions you're asking surprise me."

"They do? Why?"

"Well, I know nothing of police work, of course, but I fail to understand why you should require *my* impressions of Deborah in order to apprehend the criminal who attacked and murdered her."

"What kind of questions do you think I should be asking?"

She frowned. "I don't know. About strangers in the area, that sort of thing."

"Have you noticed any suspicious strangers hanging around the area lately?"

"No."

Banks blew his nose. "Sorry. Well, that covers that one, doesn't it? Now, what about Deborah's faults?"

"Faults?"

"Yes, was she mischievous, disobedient, dishonest, willful?"

"No more than any other child of her age. Less than most, actually." She thought for a moment. "No, I'd say if Deborah did have a fault it was that she tended to show off her abilities to some extent. She could sometimes make the other girls feel small, or awkward and clumsy. She had a tendency to belittle people."

"Was she boastful?"

"Not at all. No, that's not what I mean. She never *boasted* about her abilities, she just used them to the full. She wasn't the kind to hide her light under a bushel. Half the time it was as if she didn't even realize she was so much brighter and more fortunate than many. She liked the way her quickness with figures impressed people, for example, so she would add up or multiply things in her head quicker than some of the other girls could do it with a calculator."

"That's one good way to make enemies." Banks remembered his own school math reports: *Could do better than this; Harder work needed; Watch that arithmetic!*

"It was hardly serious," Dr. Green went on, shrugging. "Simply a matter of girlish exuberance, a young woman taking full joy in her talents." Her eyes sparkled for a moment. "Have you forgotten what it was like to be young, to be popular, gifted?"

"I don't know that I was ever gifted or popular," Banks said, with a sidelong glance at Susan, who was smiling down into her notebook. "But I do remember what it was like to be young. I thought I would live forever."

After the awkward silence that followed, Banks asked, "Was Deborah popular with the other girls?"

"What do you mean?"

"She sounds like a right little madam to me, a proper pain in the neck. I was wondering how she got on with her classmates?"

"Really, Chief Inspector," Dr. Green said through tight lips. "These were very minor faults I'm talking about. Mostly, Deborah was friendly, cheerful and helpful."

"Was there any friend in particular?"

"Yes. Megan Preece. Her name's on the list I gave you."

"I understand from Daniel Charters," Banks went on, "that there was some trouble with Ive Jelačić, the sexton."

"Yes." Julia Green rubbed her cheek. "He'd been bothering the girls. Saying things, making lewd gestures, that sort of thing."

"Had Deborah, in particular, complained about him?"

"I believe she had."

"Did she continue going to the church after Mr. Jelačić made his accusations against Daniel Charters? It was my impression that her father seemed more upset about what Charters had been accused of, rather than what Jelačić *did*."

Julia Green paused for a moment, then said, "Yes, yes he was. I don't understand it myself. The school stands one hundred per cent behind Father Charters, but Sir Geoffrey forbade Deborah from singing with the choir or attending any services."

"Why do you think he did that?"

"I don't know. Some people are just . . . well, very funny about any hint of homosexuality in the ministry."

"Did Deborah obey him?"

"As far as I know she did. I never saw her there, anyway."

"Did Deborah keep any of her belongings here at school?"

"All the girls have desks."

"No lockers or anything?"

She shook her head. "Not the day-girls. They bring what they need from day to day, mostly."

"Might we have a look?"

"Of course. We've canceled classes for the day, so the room should be empty."

She led them through a maze of high corridors to a small room. It wasn't like any classroom Banks had ever seen before, with its well-polished woodwork and nicely spaced desks.

"This one," said Dr. Green, pointing to a desk.

Banks lifted the hinged flap. He hadn't expected much—school desks are hardly the most private of places—but he was disappointed by how little there was: a couple of school exercise books, a computer magazine, textbooks, pens and pencils. There was also a tattered paperback Jeffrey Archer. Deborah's intelligence obviously hadn't stretched as far as her literary taste.

Under the flap, Deborah had taped a photograph of a scruffy pop star Banks didn't recognize.

Dr. Green saw it and said, with a smile, "We discourage such things, but what can you do?"

Banks nodded. Then he examined the desk surface to see if Deborah had carved any initials, the way he had at school. Again, nothing. Strongly discouraged, no doubt.

"Thanks," he said to Dr. Green. "Can we have a word with Megan Preece now? Is she here?"

Dr. Green nodded. After stopping back at her office for their raincoats and her umbrella, she led them outside.

"Where are we going?" Banks asked.

"The school infirmary. That's where Megan is. I'm afraid she had rather a nasty turn when I broke the news in assembly this morning."

II

The brick shattered the vicarage window at nine-thirty that morning, waking Rebecca from the uneasy doze she had slipped into after taking three aspirin and a glass of water.

At first she lay there terrified, fearing that someone had broken in. Then, slowly, so as not to make the bedsprings creak, she sat up, ears pricked for any sounds. But nothing came.

She put on her dressing-gown and looked out of the bedroom window. Nothing but the drizzle on the trees and graves, and policemen in capes searching the grounds. She tiptoed downstairs, and when she got to the front room she saw the damage.

Shards of glass lay all over the floor, and some had even got as far as the sofa and coffee-table. The brick had clearly been thrown from the river path, beyond the small garden, an area that was unguarded because it didn't provide access to the graveyard.

The brick had bounced off the coffee-table and ended up in the far corner by the sideboard. It had a piece of paper wrapped around it, fixed by a rubber band. Slowly, Rebecca bent, picked up the brick and unfolded the paper:

Once you let the devil into your heart he will corrupt every cell in your body and this is what has happened it is clear. You must confess your sins. It is the only way. Or else we must take things into our own hands.

Someone knocked at the back door. Crumpling the note in her pocket, Rebecca gathered her dressing-gown around her and went to see who it was.

"Is everything all right, ma'am?" asked one of the uniformed constables who had been searching the graveyard. "I thought I heard breaking glass."

"You did," Rebecca said. "But everything's fine. Just a little domestic accident."

"Are you sure?"

"Yes." Rebecca started closing the door on him. "Thank you, everything's fine." When she had shut the door she leaned her back against it and listened. In a few seconds, she heard his footsteps going along the path.

She took out a dustpan and broom and busied herself sweeping up the glass, wondering what she could use to cover the broken window before she caught a chill and died. Maybe that would be best for everyone, she thought. It would be very fitting, too. Hadn't Emily Brontë died after catching a chill at her brother's funeral? But no. She wasn't going to give the miserable, mean-spirited bastards the satisfaction.

Just as she was trying to tape up a piece of cardboard over the window, the phone rang.

"Can you talk?" the familiar voice asked.

"Patrick. Yes. Yes, I can."

"We've been given the day off, pupils and staff. That terrible business with the girl. It must have been especially awful for you. How are you bearing up?"

"Oh, not bad, I suppose."

"Is Daniel . . . ?"

"He's out. Meeting in York. Said he couldn't get out of it."

"Could we see one another? I could come over."

"I don't know," Rebecca said, feeling herself flush with desire like a silly schoolgirl as she spoke. "No, I don't think we should. Not the way things are around here."

"But I want you."

Rebecca put her hand over the mouthpiece and took a deep breath.

"Don't you want me?" he went on.

"Of course I want you, Patrick. You know I do. It's just . . . there's police all over the place."

"We could go for a drive."

Rebecca paused and looked around her. She couldn't stay here, not with this mess, not after the threatening note; she would go insane. And she couldn't deal with the police, either. On the other hand, the very thought of Patrick made her tingle. God, how she hated herself, hated the way her body could so easily betray her morality and her good intentions, how her defective conscience found ways of rationalizing it all.

"All right," she said. "But you mustn't come here. I mean it about the police. We shouldn't be seen together."

"I'll pick you up at the—"

"No. Let's meet at the hotel." She looked at her watch. "There's a bus at ten-fifteen."

"All right. I'll be waiting for you."

III

"These are the dormitories for the boarding pupils," Dr. Green pointed out as they walked through the school grounds. The two large buildings ahead were of far more recent construction than the main school building, redbrick for the most part, with some stone at their bases, functional rather than aesthetically pleasing. "As I said earlier, we have 286 boarders. They have showers, central heating, all the comforts the modern child requires. You'll also notice we have installed a number of lamps along all the major pathways. They're kept on until ten o'clock every night, by which time all the girls are expected to be in bed. This isn't Lowood or Dotheboys, you realize. Parents spend a lot of money to send their children here."

"Television?"

She smiled. "Yes, that too."

"What's that building over there?" Banks pointed through the trees to a three-storey rectangular building that seemed to be made of some sort of prefabricated concrete the color of porridge.

"That's the staff residence, I'm afraid," said Dr. Green. "Ugly isn't it? Actually, it's quite nice inside. The flats are quite spacious: living-room, bedroom, storage heaters. Luxury."

"Who lives there, apart from you?"

"At the moment, six of the flats are occupied. It all depends. We have thirty members of staff, a very good ratio, and some of our teachers live in or near town. The flats are essentially for single members of staff who have recently moved into the area, or, as in my case, single teachers who want to maintain close contact with the school." She tilted her umbrella and gave Banks a challenging glance from under the rim. "You asked me rather impertinently not so long ago whether I lived alone. The school is my life, Chief Inspector. I have neither the inclination nor the time for anyone or anything else."

Banks nodded. Then he sneezed. Susan blessed him.

"Here we are," Dr. Green went on, stepping under the porch of the dormitory and lowering her umbrella. She shook it carefully before rolling it up. "The infirmary is on the ground floor. We have one full-time nurse on staff and a local doctor on call."

They walked down the hall and entered the infirmary. It smelled of disinfectant. After a brief word with the nurse, Dr. Green directed Banks and Susan towards a row of curtained cubicles, in one of which Megan Preece lay on a narrow bed.

"Megan's fine, nurse says," Dr. Green whispered. "But she's had a terrible shock and she's been given a mild tranquillizer, so please go slowly."

Banks nodded. There clearly wasn't room for all of them in the cubicle, yet Dr. Green seemed to want to stay.

"It's all right," Banks said, ushering Susan to Megan's bedside chair. "We'll find our own way out when we've finished."

Dr. Green stood for a moment and frowned, then she nodded, turned on her heel and clicked away down the corridor.

When Banks found a chair for himself, Susan was already talking to Megan, reassuring her that everything would be all right. From what Banks could see of the head poking above the gray blanket, Megan was a slight, thin girl of about Deborah Harrison's age, with dark curly hair and a tanned complexion.

But Megan's features lacked whatever cohesion or symmetry it took to make her conventionally pretty, unlike her friend Deborah, who had been beautiful in that lissom, blonde, athletic sort of way. Megan's nose was a little too big, and slightly crooked; her lips were too thin, and her mouth was too small for her teeth. But her big, serious earth-brown eyes were striking; they seemed to capture you at first glance and draw you to her.

Banks introduced himself, noting that Megan seemed comfortable enough in the presence of a male policeman, and said he wanted to ask her a few questions about Deborah. Megan nodded, eyes turning a little glassy at the mention of her friend's name.

"Were you very close friends?" he began.

She nodded. "We're both day-girls and we've known each other for years. We both live in the same area."

"I thought you must be boarding," said Banks. "Why aren't you at home?"

"I had a dizzy spell at assembly, then I . . . I got all upset. Nurse says I should rest here for a while, then I can go home at lunch-time. There'll be nobody there, anyway. Mummy's away in America and Daddy's at work."

"I see. Now can you tell me what happened yesterday after the chess club. Go as slowly as you want, there's no hurry."

Megan chewed her lower lip, then began. "Well, when we'd put all the boards and pieces away in the cupboard and made sure the room was tidy, we left the school—"

"Was this the main building?"

"Yes. We hold the chess club in one of the upstairs class-rooms."

"What time?"

"Just before six o'clock."

"How many attended last night?"

"Only eight. Lesley and Carol are doing a play with the theatre department, so they had rehearsals. The others are all boarders."

"I see. Was there anyone else around?"

"A few people, coming and going, as usual. The school is always well lit and there are always people around."

"Okay. Go on."

"Well, we walked down the drive to Kendal Road. There's only one main gate, you see. The school's surrounded by woods, and there's the river on the west side. It was so foggy we could hardly see the trees around us. I must admit I was getting a bit scared, but Debs seemed to be enjoying herself."

"What do you mean?"

"Oh, she liked things like that. Spooky things. She liked to tell ghost stories in graveyards, just for fun."

"Do you know if she ever went inside the Inchcliffe Mausoleum?"

"She never said anything to me about it if she did."

"Okay. Go on."

"We crossed the road. I live on St. Mary's Hill, behind the shops, so Debs and I always said goodbye at the bridge." She put her hand over her eyes.

"Take it easy," Susan said. "Take your time." When Banks looked down, he noticed that Megan was gripping Susan's hand at the side of the bed.

Megan took a deep breath and went on. "That's all," she said. "We said goodbye. Debs was running backwards, just showing off, like, then she disappeared into the fog." She frowned.

"Was there something else?" Banks asked. "Did you notice anyone else around?"

"Well, like I said, it was so foggy you couldn't really see more than a few feet, but I saw a shape behind her. I remember thinking at the time there was something odd about it, but I put it down to the way Debs had been scaring me with her stories of ghosts taking shape from the fog."

"You mean you thought you were imagining it?"

"Yes. Seeing things. But I know I wasn't, if that makes any sense."

"You're doing fine, Megan. What kind of shape was it?"

"It was a man's shape. A tall man."

"What was he doing?"

"Nothing. He was just standing on the bridge looking down the river towards the town." She paused and her eyes lit up. "That's it. That's what was strange. He was looking over the bridge towards the town, but he couldn't possibly see anything, could he, because of the fog. So why was he standing there?"

"Did you think that at the time?"

"No. It just came to me."

"Did you see what he looked like?"

"Not really, because of the fog. I mean, he was like a silhouette, a dark figure. His features weren't clear, and he was in profile. He did have a bit of a big nose, though."

"Could you see what he was wearing?"

"An anorak, I think. A bright color. Orange or red, maybe."

"Did you see him approach Deborah?"

"No. He was just behind her. I don't think she'd seen him because she was still running backwards and waving good-bye. I remember thinking if she wasn't careful she'd bump into him and that would give her a shock, but I really didn't think much of it. I mean, it wasn't the only person we'd seen."

"Who else did you see?"

"Just ordinary people, you know, crossing the road and such. I mean, life goes on, doesn't it? Just because it's foggy you can't stop doing everything, can you?"

"That's true," said Banks. "Can you remember anything else?"

Megan squeezed her eyes shut. "I think he had dark hair," she said. "Then I turned away and went home. I never thought anything of it. Until . . . until this morning, when I heard . . . I should have known something was going to happen, shouldn't I?"

"How could you?"

"I just should. Poor Debs. It could have been me. It *should* have been me."

"Don't be silly, Megan."

"But it's true! Debs was so good, so wonderful and pretty and talented. And just look at me. I'm nothing. I'm not pretty. She should have lived. I'm the one who should have died. It's not fair. Why does God always take the best?"

"I don't know the answer to that," Banks replied softly. "But I do know that *every* life is important, every life has its value, and *nobody* has the right to decide who lives and who dies."

"Only God."

"Only God," Banks repeated, and blew his nose in the ensuing silence.

Megan took a tissue from the box on the table beside her and wiped her eyes. "I must look a sight," she said.

Banks smiled. "Just like me first thing in the morning," he said. "Now, when we found Deborah, she had about six pounds in her purse. Did she ever have a lot of money to flash around?"

"Money? No. None of us ever carried more than a few pounds."

"Do you know if she kept anything valuable in her satchel?"

Megan frowned. "No. Just the usual stuff. Exercise books, textbooks, that sort of thing."

"Did she say if she was intending to meet anyone after the chess club or go anywhere else before she went home?"

"No. As far as I know, she was going straight home."

"Can you tell us anything else about her?"

"Like what?"

"You were her best friend, weren't you?"

"Yes."

"Did you ever fall out?"

"Sometimes."

"Why?"

"Nothing, really. Maybe Debs would tease me about a lad she thought I liked, or something, or about not being good at arithmetic, and I'd get mad. But it wouldn't last long."

"Is that all?"

"Yes. She can be quite a tease, can Debs. She gets her little needle in where she knows it hurts and just keeps pushing." She put her hand to her mouth. "Oh, I didn't mean that to sound as bad as it did, honest I didn't. All I mean is that she had an eye for a weakness and she could be a bit nasty about it. It was never anything serious."

"Do you know if anything had been bothering her lately?"

"I don't think so. She'd been a bit moody, that's all."

"Since when?"

"The beginning of term."

"Did she say why?"

"No. We have a lot on our minds. A lot of work. And she's been moody before."

"She didn't mention any problems, anything that might have been worrying her?"

"No."

"Did she have any enemies, anyone who might have wanted to harm her?"

"No. Everyone loved Debs. It must have been a stranger."

"Did she ever mention Mr. Jelačić, the sexton at St. Mary's?"

"The man who got fired?"

"That's the one."

"She said he was gross, always sticking his tongue out and licking his lips when she went past."

"Did he ever bother you?"

"I never went in the churchyard. I live this side of the river, over Kendal Road. It was a short cut for Debs."

"Are you sure Deborah didn't have any other problems, any worries? Maybe at home?"

"No. She didn't complain about anything in particular. Only the usual stuff. Too much homework. That sort of thing."

Banks realized that Deborah Harrison would probably have fewer practical causes for concern than his own daughter, Tracy, who, at one time anyway, had been constantly moaning about some new style of jacket or jeans she just had to have because everyone else was wearing it, and the Doc Martens that were just *essential* these days.

Banks had been like that himself, and he gave Tracy the same answer his mother and father gave him when they bought him a pair of heavy workboots for school instead of the thin-soled winkle-pickers he had asked for. "We can't afford it. You'll just have to make do. These will last a lot longer."

But Deborah Harrison had wanted for nothing, at least nothing that had a monetary value.

"What about boyfriends?" Banks asked.

Megan blushed. "We don't have time, not in the lower sixth. And Debs was always involved in some school event: equestrian, sports or quizzes or whatever."

"So she didn't have a boyfriend?"

"I'm not saying she *never* had one."

"When was the last one?"

"In the summer."

"What was his name?"

"She told me his name was John, that's all. They didn't go out together for long. She said he was really cool but too thick, so she chucked him."

"Did she tell you anything else about him?"

Megan blushed. "No."

"Are you sure?"

"Yes. That's all I know. His name was John and he was a thickie."

"Where did she meet him?"

"I don't know. She didn't say. I was away in America all summer with my parents, so I didn't see her until school started. By then she'd already chucked him."

"Was he her first boyfriend?"

"I don't think so, but there was never anyone serious."

"How do you know?"

"She would have told me."

"Does she tell you everything?"

Megan considered the question seriously for a moment or

so, then said, "No, I don't think so. She can be secretive, can Debs. But she'd tell me if she had a boyfriend. Or I'd just *know*."

"Was she being secretive about anything recently?"

Megan frowned. "Yes, she was. I was getting fed up of it."

"Did she tell you anything about it?"

"No. It wouldn't be a secret then, would it?"

"Did she tell you who or what it concerned?"

Megan shook her head. "No."

"Did she say *anything* about it?"

"Just that she thought it was time to tell someone, and then to watch what happened when the sh—. Just to see what happened."

"When did she tell you this?"

"Just as she was leaving, on the bridge."

"While she was running backwards?"

"Yes. It's . . . it was the last thing she said." Her eyes filled with tears. "I'm tired."

"All right," said Banks. "I'm sorry, Megan. You're doing really well. I'll try not to be much longer. But you must realize how important it is. If it was a secret about somebody who didn't want it known . . . And if that somebody knew that Deborah knew . . . Do you see what I mean?"

Megan nodded.

"How long had she been talking about this secret?"

"Since the beginning of term."

"That's quite a long time."

"Yes. She'd let it drop for a week or two, then bring it up again."

"Would she have told anyone else?"

"No. I'm her *best* friend."

"Is there anything else you can tell us, Megan? Anything at all."

Megan shook her head. "I don't think so."

Banks and Susan stood up. "Get some rest now," Banks said. "And believe me, we'll be doing our best to find out who did this."

They said goodbye to the nurse, picked up their raincoats and headed out into the drizzle.

"What did you think?" Banks asked Susan as they walked back to the car.

"About Megan? I think she told us pretty much all she knew."

"Notice the way she blushed and turned her eyes away when I pushed her about the boyfriend? I'd say there's more to that relationship than she's told us."

"Well, sir," said Susan, "from my experience I'd say Deborah probably said he had his uses but he was thick."

"You think Deborah might have slept with this John?"

"She might have, but that's not what I mean. What I mean is, she'd say that, or hint that she had, the way kids do. It doesn't mean they actually *did* anything."

"And Megan was embarrassed by it?"

"Yes. I'd guess Megan is a bit shy around boys."

"Would you agree she was the ugly one in that relationship?"

"I wouldn't put it quite that way, sir."

Banks smiled. "I'm sorry. It must be something to do with being on school grounds again. It takes me back. But when you were a teenager and you met two girls, one of them was bound to be the ugly one."

"And when you met two boys, one of them was certain to be a drip and the other an octopus. If you were really lucky, you got a combination of the two."

Banks laughed.

"I'm sorry, sir," Susan went on, "I don't get your point. Surely you're not suggesting that Megan Preece had anything to do with Deborah's murder?"

"No. Of course not. Just thinking out loud, is all."

They got in the unmarked police car. When it started up, Vaughan Williams's *Suite for Viola and Orchestra* was playing on the radio: the beautiful, melancholy "Ballad." It suited the falling leaves and the November drizzle perfectly, Banks thought.

"I'm just trying to understand the relationship so that I can understand the way Deborah related to people," he said. "The way I see it is that Megan was the less attractive of the two friends. That would probably make her adoring and resentful in equal measures. She knew she was overshadowed and outclassed by Deborah's looks and talent, and for the most part she was probably content to bask in the glory of being the chosen one, best friend of the goddess. Are you with me so far?"

"Yes, sir. Megan was the kind of friend who could only make Deborah look even better."

"Right. But it also sounded as if Deborah could twist the knife, too, could be cruel. If she could annoy her best friend the way she did, then she could have angered a more dangerous enemy, don't you think?"

"It's possible, sir. But a bit far-fetched, if you don't mind me saying so. I still say we're looking for a stranger. And from what we know already, that stranger on the bridge could have been Ive Jelačić."

"True," said Banks. "It could also have been a figment of Megan's imagination, at least in part. But we'll sort out Mr. Jelačić later. He's not going anywhere. Ken Blackstone's got him under surveillance. What do you think about the secret?"

"Not much. A lot of schoolkids are like that. As Megan said, it probably didn't mean anything."

"Not to her, perhaps. But maybe to someone else. Look, isn't that . . ." He pointed.

As they were turning left onto North Market Street, Banks noticed a woman in a long navy raincoat standing at the bus-stop over the road.

"Isn't it who?" Susan asked.

"Oh, I forgot. You haven't met her. Rebecca Charters, the vicar's wife. I'm sure it was her. I wonder where she's going?"

"Curioser and curioser," said Susan.

Chapter 4

I

"Well, sir," said Sergeant Hatchley, looking at his watch. "Don't you think we might as well have a spot of lunch?"

Barry Stott sighed. "Oh, all right. Come on."

This was the detective inspector's first major case after his promotion and transfer, and he intended to make the most of it. The only thorn in the ointment was this idle, thick lump of Yorkshire blubber beside him: Detective Sergeant Hatchley.

Stott would have preferred DC Susan Gay. Not because she was prettier than Hatchley—he didn't find her attractive in that way—but because she was smarter, keener and a lot less trouble.

Like now. Left to himself, Stott would have skipped lunch, or bought a take-away from one of the cafés on North Market Street. The morning had been a waste of time; they had found no leads in the sex offender files, and all Stott could find out from immigration about Jelačić was that he was an engineer from Split, who had come to England two years ago. And since then, he had worked at a variety of odd jobs, never lasting long in any one place. Short of going to Croatia himself, Stott thought, it didn't look as if it would be an easy task getting hold of a criminal record, if there was one.

At least out here, near the crime scene, he felt he had a good chance of scoring some success. *Somebody* had to have noticed a stranger in the area, fog or no fog. Or a car parked where it shouldn't be. St. Mary's was, after all, an upper-crust area, and people who could afford to live there were very wary of strangers. And Stott was sure that a stranger had murdered Deborah Harrison.

They were standing in the rain outside the Nag's Head at the north-west corner of Kendal Road and North Market Street, diagonally across from St. Mary's Church, and Stott was ready to do just about anything to shut Hatchley up.

It wasn't the kind of pub you'd expect in such a wealthy area, Stott thought: no thick carpet, polished brass and gleaming wood, pot of mulled wine heating on the bar. In fact, it looked distinctly shabby. He guessed it was probably a traveler's pub, being situated at such an important junction. In one form or another, Kendal Road ran all the way from the Lake District to the east coast and Market Street was a major north-south route. The locals would have their own tasteful pubs hidden away in the residential streets. Either that or they drove out to the country clubs.

There were about six people in the lounge bar. Stott noted with distaste that the room smelled of smoke and beer. This certainly wasn't his kind of pub, if there were such a place. He far preferred churches. Pubs, as far as Stott was concerned, were simply breeding grounds for trouble.

Pubs were where fights started—and he had a couple of scars from his beat days to prove that—they were where crooked deals took place, dodgy goods traded hands, places where drugs were openly sold, where prostitutes plied their filthy trade, spreading disease and misery. Close all the pubs and you'd force the criminals into the open, right into the waiting arms of the police. At least that was what DI Barry Stott thought as he turned up his nose in the Nag's Head that lunch-time.

Sergeant Hatchley, on the other hand, looked quite at home. He rubbed his ham-like hands together and said, "Ah, this is better. Nowt like a bit of pub grub to take away the chill, don't you think, sir?"

"Let's make it quick, Sergeant."

"Yes, sir. Alf! Over here, mate. Let's have a bit of service. A person could die of thirst."

If there were a landlord Hatchley didn't know by name in all of the Eastvale—nay, all of Swainsdale—Stott would have been surprised.

When Alf finally turned up, Stott waited while he and Hatchley exchanged a few pleasantries, then ordered a ham and cheese sandwich and a cup of tea. Alf raised his eyebrows but said nothing.

"I'll have one of those bloody great big Yorkshire puddings full of roast beef, peas and gravy," said Hatchley. "And a pint of bitter, of course."

This seemed to please Alf more.

Pint in hand, Hatchley marched over to a table by the window. Through the streaked glass, they could see the rain-darkened trees in the park and the walls of St. Mary's church across the intersection, square tower poking out above the trees.

The drizzle hadn't kept the ghouls away. Here and there along the six-foot stone wall, people would jump up every now and then and hold themselves up by the fingertips for a glimpse into the graveyard.

A group of about ten people stood by the Kendal Road entrance. Journalists. One of them, a woman, stood talking into a microphone and looking into a video camera wrapped in a black plastic bag to protect it from the rain. Someone else held a bright light over her head. Yorkshire Television, Stott thought. Or BBC North. And newspaper reporters. Pretty soon they'd be doing re-enactments for "Crimewatch." Banks was right; the vultures had come.

"We haven't had much of a chance to get to know one another since you got here, have we, sir?" said Hatchley, lighting a cigarette. "And I always find it helps to know a bit about one another if you're going to work together, don't you?"

"I suppose so," said Stott, inwardly grimacing, trying to sit downwind of the drifting smoke. It didn't work. He thought it must be one of those laws, like Sod's and Murphy's: wherever a non-smoker sat, the smoke was going to come his way, no matter which way the draft was blowing.

"Where are you from, sir?" Hatchley asked.

"Spalding, Lincolnshire."

"I'd never have guessed it. Not from the accent, like."

"We moved away when I was just a boy."

"Where?"

"All over the place. Cyprus, Germany. My father was in the army." Stott remembered the misery of each move. It seemed that as soon as he had made friends anywhere, he had to abandon them and start all over again. His childhood had consisted of a never-ending succession of new groups of strangers to whom he had to prove himself. Cruel strangers with their own initiation rights, just waiting to humiliate him. He remembered the beatings, the name-calling, the loneliness.

"A squaddie, eh?"

"Major, actually."

"Pretty high up, then?" Hatchley swigged some beer. "Where does he live now?"

"Worthing. He retired a few years ago."

"Not a dishonorable discharge, I hope, sir."

"No."

"Look, sir," said Hatchley, "I've been wondering about this here inspector's exam. I've been thinking of giving it a go, like. Is it easy?"

Stott shook his head. All promotional exams were tough and involved several stages, from the multi-choice law test and the role-playing scenarios to the final oral in front of an assistant chief constable and a chief superintendent. How Hatchley had even passed the sergeant's exam was a mystery to Stott.

"Good luck," he muttered as a pasty-faced young woman delivered their food and Stott's pot of tea, which was actually just a pot of lukewarm water and a teabag on a string to dunk in it. And they were stingy with the ham, too. "About one in four get through," he added.

How old was Hatchley? he wondered. He couldn't be older than his mid-thirties. Maybe five or six years older than Stott himself. And just look at him: unfit, a bulky man with hair like straw, piggy eyes, freckles spattered across his fleshy nose, tobacco-stained teeth. He also seemed to own only one suit—shiny and wrinkled—and there were egg stains on his tie. Stott could hardly imagine Hatchley going up before the chief for his formal promotion dressed like that.

Stott prided himself on his dress. He had five suits—two gray, two navy blue and one brown herring-bone—and he wore them in rotation. If it's Thursday, it must be herring-bone. He also wore his father's old striped regimental tie and, usually, a crisply laundered white shirt with a starched collar.

He always made sure that he was clean shaven and that his hair was neatly parted on the left and combed diagonally across his skull on each side, then fixed in place with spray or cream if need be. He knew that the way his ears stuck out still made him look odd, especially with his glasses hooked over them, just as they had when he was a young boy, and that people called him names behind his back. There was an operation you could have for sticking-out ears these days, he had heard. Maybe if it wasn't too late he'd have his ears done soon. A freakish appearance could, after all, be detrimental to one's career path. And Barry Stott felt destined for the chief constable's office.

Hatchley tucked into his Yorkie with great relish, adding a gravy stain to the egg on his tie. When he had finished, he lit another cigarette, inhaled deeply and blew out the smoke with a sigh of such deep satisfaction as Stott had never encountered before over a mere physical function—and an unpleasant one at that. One of nature's true primitives, Sergeant Hatchley.

"We'd better be getting along, Sergeant," he said, pushing his plate aside and standing up.

"Can't I finish my fag first, sir? Best part of the meal, the cigarette after, if you know what I mean." He winked.

Stott felt himself flush. "You can smoke it outside," he said rather harshly.

Hatchley shrugged, slurped down the rest of his pint, then followed Stott towards the door.

"Bye, Alf," he said on the way to the door. "I hope our lads didn't catch you serving drinks after hours last night."

"What lads?" said Alf.

Hatchley turned and walked towards the bar. "Police. Didn't they come and ask you questions last night? Whether you'd seen any strangers, that sort of thing?"

Alf shook his head. "Nah. Nobody in last night. I shut up at ten o'clock. Filthy weather."

By the time Stott got to the bar, Hatchley seemed to have magically acquired another pint, and his cigarette had grown back to its original length.

Stott swallowed his anger.

"Were you open earlier?" Hatchley asked.

Alf snorted. "Aye, for what it were worth."

"Any strangers?"

"We get a lot of strangers," he said. "You know, commercial travelers and the like. Tourists. Ramblers."

"Aye, I know that," said Hatchley. "But how about yesterday, late afternoon, early evening?"

"Nah. Weather were too bad for driving."

"Anyone at all?"

Alf scratched his stubbly cheek. "One bloke. He had nobbut two pints and a whisky and left. That were it."

"A regular?"

"Nah. Don't have many regulars. People round here are too stuck-up for the likes of this place."

Stott was beginning to feel frustrated. This Alf was obviously a moron; they would get nothing useful out of him. "But you said you hadn't had any strangers in lately," he said.

"He weren't a stranger, either."

"Who was he, then?"

"Nay, don't ask me."

"But you said you knew him."

Alf looked over at Hatchley and gave a sniff of disgust before turning back to Stott and answering. "No, I didn't," he said. "I said he weren't a regular, but he weren't exactly a stranger, either. Different thing."

"So you've seen him before?"

Alf spat on the floor behind the bar. "Well, of course I bloody have. Stands to reason, doesn't it? He'd have been a stranger if I hadn't seen him before, wouldn't he?"

Hatchley took over again. "All right, Alf," he said. "You're right. Good point. How often have you seen him?"

"Not often. But he's been in three or four times this past year or so. Used to come in with a lass. A right bonnie lass, and all. But not the last few times."

"Do you know who he is?"

"No. He always stuck to himself."

"Any idea where he lives?"

"Could be bloody Timbuktu, for all I know."

"Are you saying he was African-English?" Stott cut in.

Alf gave him a withering look. "It's just a saying, like. Summat me mother used to say."

"What did he look like?" Hatchley asked.

"Well, he were a tall bloke, I remember that. A bit over six foot, anyroad. Thick black hair, a bit too long over t'collar, if you ask me. Bit of a long nose, too."

"Did you talk to him?"

"No more than to serve him and make a few remarks about the weather. He didn't seem to want to talk. Took his pint over by the fire and just sat there staring into his glass. Muttered to himself now and then, too, as I recall."

"He talked to himself?"

"Well, not all the time. And not like he was having a conversation or anything. No, he'd just say something once in a while, as if he were thinking out loud, like you do sometimes."

"Did you hear anything he said?"

"Nay. He were too far away."

"Did he have any sort of an accent?" Stott cut in.

"Couldn't say."

"Did you know Ive Jelačić, the sexton over the road at St. Mary's?"

"Nah. He drank at t'Pig and Whistle."

"How do you know?"

"Landlord, Stan, told me, after it was in t'papers, like, about him and that dodgy vicar."

"Did you ever see Mr. Jelačić?"

"Only from a distance."

"Could this have been him?"

"Could've been, I suppose. Same height and hair color."

"Do you know if this customer had a car?"

"How would I know that?" Alf rubbed his chin. "Come to think of it, he looked more like he'd been walking. You know, a bit damp, short of breath."

"What time was this, Alf?" Hatchley asked.

"About five o'clock."

"What time did he leave?"

"Just afore six. Like I said, he had nobbut two pints and a double whisky. One for the road, he said, and knocked it back in one, then he was out the door." Alf mimicked the drinking action.

Stott pricked up his ears. The timing worked, assuming the girl had been killed on her way home from the school chess club. Was that the way a person might act before raping and murdering a sixteen-year-old schoolgirl in a foggy graveyard? Stott wondered. A dram of Dutch courage? He tried to remember what he'd learned in the criminal psychology course.

The trouble was, you could justify just about any sort of behavior if you were talking about a psycho. Some of them liked to sit and have a beer and a fag before a nice little dismemberment; others liked to buy a box of chocolates or bunch of flowers for their mothers. You could never predict.

So maybe the killer would have dropped in at the Nag's Head. Why not? Maybe he just needed to sit there for a while, have a little chat with himself about what he was going to do?

"Did you see which direction he went?" Stott asked.

"Nay. You don't expect me to chase outside after my customers and see which way they're going, do you?"

"What was he wearing?" Stott asked.

"Orange anorak. Expensive type, by the looks of it. That Gore-Tex stuff. Lots of pockets and zips."

"Can you remember anything else about his appearance?"

"I'm not good at describing people. Never was."

"Do you think you could work with a police artist?"

"Dunno. Never tried it."

"Will you give it a try?"

Alf shrugged.

"Sergeant," Stott said, "go and see if you can get a police artist out as soon as possible, will you? I'll wait here."

It was almost worth suffering the stale smoke and booze atmosphere of the Nag's Head for another hour or so to see the expression on Sergeant Hatchley's face as he trudged out into the rain.

II

They had made love in every position imaginable: sideways, backwards, forwards, upside down. They had also done it in just about every place they could think of: her bed, his bed, hotels, a field, his cramped Orion, up against a wall, under the kitchen table. Sometimes, it seemed to last forever; other times, it was over almost before it began. Sometimes, the foreplay went on so long Rebecca thought she would burst; other times, they were overtaken by a sense of urgency and didn't even have time to get all their clothes off.

This time, it had been urgent. Afterwards, Rebecca lay on the bed of a hotel room in Richmond panting for breath, covered by a film of sweat. Her skirt was bunched up around her waist, her knickers down, still hanging around one bare ankle; her blouse was open at the front, a couple of the buttons torn off in the heat of the moment, and her bra was pushed up to expose her breasts.

Patrick's head lay against her shoulder. She could feel his breath warm against her skin. Both their hearts were beating fast. Rebecca rested one hand over his broad, strong shoulders, and with the other she stroked the hair over his ear, felt the stubbly down at the back of his neck, where it had been recently cut. It wasn't love—she knew enough to realize that—but it was one hell of a fine substitute.

But all too soon the sense of shame and melancholy that always came to her after sex with Patrick began to descend like a thick fog, numbing the nerve-ends that, only minutes before, had thrilled to such exquisite pleasure, and guilt began to overwhelm the vestiges of her joy.

Patrick moved away and reached for a cigarette. It was the one thing she disliked, his smoking after sex, but she didn't have the heart to tell him not to. He also put his glasses on. She knew he couldn't see a thing without them, but sometimes she laughed because he looked so funny naked except for his glasses.

"What is it?" Patrick asked, clearly sensing something was wrong. "Didn't you enjoy it?"

"Of course I did. You know that. I always do . . . with you. No . . . it's just that I feel so . . . so damn guilty."

"Then leave him. Come and live with me."

"Don't be foolish, Patrick. Just imagine the scandal. Schoolteacher shacks up with minister's wife. You'd lose your job, for a start. And where would we live?"

"Oh, don't be so practical. We'd manage. We'll get a flat in town. I can get another job. We'll move away."

Rebecca shook her head. "No. No. No."

"Why not? Don't you love me?"

Rebecca didn't answer.

"You do love me, don't you?" he persisted.

"Of course I do," Rebecca lied. It was easier that way.

"Then leave him."

"I can't."

"You don't love him."

"I . . . I . . . don't know." Rebecca *did* love Daniel. Somewhere inside her, the feeling was still there, she knew: battered, bruised, half-evaporated, but still there. She couldn't explain that to Patrick.

"I shouldn't tell you this, but . . ."

Rebecca felt a tingle run up her spine at the words, nothing to do with sex. "Yes?" she prompted him. "Go on."

"Yesterday evening your husband came to see me."

"Daniel went to see you? Why?"

"He came to talk to me."

Rebecca sat up. She quickly slipped her bra down and rearranged her skirt to cover herself, holding the front of her blouse together as best she could. "What about?" she asked, feeling awkward and stupid.

"About us." Patrick flicked his ash into the ashtray on the bedside table. It was a small room, with the curtains drawn, and Rebecca already felt claustrophobic.

"But he doesn't know about us."

"Oh, but he does. He says he's known for a while. He suspected something, then he watched you. He's seen us together."

"My God."

"He told me not to tell you he'd been to see me."

"What did he want?"

"He asked me to stop seeing you."

"What did you say?"

"I told him the truth. That we were in love. That you were discovering for the first time your true erotic nature. And that as soon as we could manage it you were going to leave him and we were going to live together."

Rebecca couldn't believe what she was hearing. Daniel knew? Had known for ages? "You bloody fool." She swung her legs over the side of the bed and pulled up her knickers.

Then she buttoned her blouse, put on her jacket over it and went to the wardrobe where her raincoat was hanging. "You bloody fool," she muttered again under her breath. "Daniel. I must go to him."

Patrick sat up and stubbed out his cigarette. "What do you mean? It *is* the truth, isn't it?"

"You idiot. You've ruined everything."

He got up and walked over to her. She thought he suddenly looked ridiculous with his glasses on, the limp penis hanging between his thin, hairy legs.

"Rebecca," he said, grasping her arms. "He's only concerned about how it looks. With appearances. Don't you see? He wants everything to seem normal, for you to act like the dutiful vicar's wife. But it's not you. It's really not you. I *know* you, Rebecca. I know your true nature. We've discovered it together. You're a wild, passionate, sensual creature, not a bloody dried-up vicar's wife."

"Let me go!"

She tore herself out of his grasp, finished putting her raincoat on and grabbed the door-handle.

"Don't do this, Rebecca," he said. "Stay with me. Don't be afraid of finding out who you really are. Follow your passion, your *feelings*."

"Oh, shut up, you pompous bastard. It was just a fuck, that's all. You don't know a bloody thing, do you?"

"Wait. I'll drive you," he called out as she walked through the door.

"Don't bother," she said over her shoulder. "I'll catch a bus." And she slammed the door behind her.

III

A couple of uniformed policemen kept the press away from Sir Geoffrey's house. When Banks and Susan got there early in the afternoon, there were only about six reporters hanging around at the end of the driveway. They fired off a few questions, but Banks ignored them. Too early to start giving statements to the press. Unless you were Chief Constable Riddle, of course.

The only new information Banks had was that the swabs taken from Deborah had revealed no traces of semen, and he certainly wasn't going to tell the media that. He had also discovered that Sir Geoffrey's reception at the Royal Hotel in York had ended at four o'clock, plenty of time to get back home by six, even in the fog. Lady Harrison had, indeed, been at the health club; but she hadn't arrived there until almost six-thirty.

Banks hadn't noticed in the fog last night, but the house had a large lawn and beautiful flower-beds, clearly the work of a gardener. Even keeping the lawn trimmed would have been a full-time job. The house itself was an ostentatious pile of Victorian stone, complete with gables, probably built for one of the get-rich-quick wool merchants in the last century.

Sir Geoffrey himself answered Banks's ring and beckoned the two of them in. Banks introduced Susan.

"Is there any news?" Sir Geoffrey asked.

Banks shook his head. "Not yet, sir. Sorry."

Sir Geoffrey looked drawn and stooped, and he had large bags, like bruises, under his eyes. Banks followed him through to the white room with the bookcases, the Chagall and the grand piano. Michael Clayton was sitting in one of the armchairs, also looking as if he had gone without sleep for a week.

"Michael, I believe you met Detective Chief Inspector Banks last night," Sir Geoffrey said.

"Yes," said Clayton, "and I know Detective Constable Gay, too. I don't know if I ever thanked you."

Susan smiled. "All part of the service, sir."

Banks gave her a quizzical look.

"Mr. Clayton had his car and a valuable notebook computer stolen in August," she explained. "We got them back for him. Someone was trying to sell the computer at Eastvale market."

"I don't think I explained last night," Sir Geoffrey went on, "but in addition to being a dear friend, Michael's the scientific genius behind HarClay Industries. I simply provide the sales and marketing strategies." He clapped Clayton on the shoulder. "I don't know what we'd do without him. Please, sit down."

"Where's your wife, sir?" Banks asked.

"Sylvie's resting. She . . . we didn't get much sleep last night. She's exhausted. Me, too. Look, we . . . er . . . I'm sorry. Things are a bit of a mess around here. How can I help you?"

"We won't keep you long. Just a couple of questions."

Sir Geoffrey nodded wearily. "I'll do the best I can."

"Thank you," said Banks. "We've talked to a few people at Deborah's school, and everyone seems to agree that Deborah was a cheerful and talented girl."

Sir Geoffrey nodded. "Sylvie and I are very proud of her."

"But even the best of people make enemies," Banks went on. "Often inadvertently. Can you think of any enemies Deborah might have made?"

Sir Geoffrey closed his eyes and thought for a moment, then shook his head. "No. She got along well with her schoolfriends and teachers—I'm sure they'll all bear that out—and there wasn't really anyone else in her life aside from family."

"I heard that she had a tendency to show off at times. Would you say that's fair?"

Sir Geoffrey smiled. "Yes, Deborah can be a show-off, and a bit of a devil at times. But what child can't be?"

Banks smiled, thinking of Tracy. "And Deborah *was* still a child in some ways," he said. "She might not always have realized the effects of her actions on others. Do you see what I mean?"

Sir Geoffrey nodded. "But I can't see us getting anywhere with this," he said. "Unless you're implying that someone at the school had something to do with her death. Or that bloody minister at St. Mary's."

"Daniel Charters?"

"That's the one."

"Why do you dislike him so?"

"The man's a pervert. He abused his power."

Banks shook his head. "But nothing's been proved against him. Isn't he entitled to be presumed innocent until proven guilty?"

"In theory, perhaps. But a man in his position should be above suspicion."

"The man who accused Father Charters is called Ive Jelačić. Would it surprise you to know that he made lewd gestures towards your daughter, and that she complained to Dr. Green, the head of St. Mary's?"

"She never told me that. If she had, I'd have broke his bloody neck."

Banks turned to Clayton. "Did Deborah ever confide in you about anything?"

Clayton raised his eyebrows. "Me? Good heavens, no. I suppose I was just as uncool as her parents as far as she was concerned."

"Uncool?"

"You know teenagers, Chief Inspector. We're ancient and decrepit creatures to them."

"I suppose we are." Banks took a deep breath and turned back to Sir Geoffrey. "This is a little delicate, I'm afraid, but I have to ask where you went after the Royal Hotel reception ended at four o'clock yesterday."

"Good God, man! You can't poss—"

"Geoff, he has to ask. He's just doing his job," said Michael Clayton, putting his hand on Sir Geoffrey's arm. "Offensive though it may be."

Sir Geoffrey ran his hand over his hair. "I suppose so. I had a private meeting with a client, if you must know. A man from the government called Oliver Jackson. It's a very confidential matter, and I don't want *anyone* else to know about the meeting. Things like this can have an effect on share prices and any number of market factors. Not to mention international affairs. Do you understand?"

Banks nodded. "There is just one more thing. . . ."

Sir Geoffrey sighed. "Go ahead, if you must."

"I was wondering about any boyfriends Deborah might have had."

"Boyfriends?"

"Yes. It would be perfectly natural for a girl of sixteen to have an interest in the opposite sex. Perfectly innocent things, like going to the pictures with a boy, maybe. She did have a ticket stub from the Regal in her blazer pocket."

Sir Geoffrey shook his head. "She used to go to the pictures with her mother a lot. The two of them . . . Deborah didn't have any boyfriends, Chief Inspector. You're barking up quite the wrong tree there. She didn't have time for boys."

"Had she never had a boyfriend?"

"Only Pierre, if that counts at all."

"Pierre?"

"In Bordeaux, or rather at Montclair. My wife's family owns a chateau in the country near Bordeaux. We often spend holidays there. Pierre is a neighbour's son. All quite innocent, of course."

"Of course," Banks agreed. "And a long way away."

"Yes . . . well. Look, about this Jelačić character. That's a disturbing piece of news. Are you going to bring him in?"

"We're pursuing inquiries in a number of directions," Banks said as he and Susan walked to the door, annoyed at himself for sounding as if he were talking to the press.

Outside, they ducked through the reporters beyond the gate and got back into Banks's car out of the rain.

"Interesting, don't you think?" Banks said. "About the boyfriend."

"Yes, sir. Either he really didn't know, or he was lying."

"But why lie?"

"Perhaps Deborah really did keep it a secret from him? If he's a strict father, I could see her doing that."

"Possibly. What about his alibi?"

"Very plausible," said Susan. "I noticed you didn't ask his wife for hers."

"One at a time, Susan. One a time. Besides, I hardly think Sylvie Harrison murdered her own daughter. She's not tall or strong enough, for a start."

"If she goes to a health club, she's probably strong enough," Susan pointed out. "Maybe she stood on a stone?"

Banks sneezed into his handkerchief.

"Bless you, sir," Susan said.

They headed towards North Market Street. "You know," said Banks, "I think there's a lot more to Deborah's life than people know, or are saying. I'd like to have another talk with her mother, alone if possible. Michael Clayton was right, teenagers don't have a lot of time for adults, but daughters do sometimes confide in their mothers. And I'd like to find this John, if he exists."

"Oh, I'm sure he does, sir. Deborah was an attractive girl. And she was sixteen. I'd be very surprised indeed if she had nothing at all to do with boys."

Banks's car phone beeped. He picked it up.

"DI Stott here."

"What's up, Barry?"

"I think we should meet up back at the station. We've got a description of a possible suspect in the Deborah Harrison murder, and it could be Jelačić. Vic Manson called, too. Jelačić's prints are all over the vodka bottles."

"We're on our way." Banks switched off the phone and put his foot down.

IV

All the way home on the rickety bus, Rebecca chewed her nails. She didn't look once at the fading autumn scenery beyond the rain-streaked windows: the muted gold, russet and lemon leaves still clinging to the roadside trees, fragile and insubstantial as the moon's halo; the soft greens and browns of the fields; the runic patterns of the drystone walls. She didn't notice the way that the dale to her west, with its gradually steepening valley sides, was partially lost in mist and drizzle, making it look just like a Chinese water-color.

Rebecca just chewed her nails and wished that tight, tearing, churning feeling inside her would go away. She felt constantly on the verge of screaming, and she knew if she started she could never stop. She took deep breaths and held them to calm herself. They helped.

By the time the bus lumbered into Eastvale, she had regained some control of her emotions, but she still felt devastated, as if her world had been suddenly blown apart. She supposed it had to happen, that she had been living a lie, living on borrowed time, or whatever other cliché she could come up with to describe the last few months of her life.

Looking at it now, her life had simply become one hangover after another; either from booze or infidelity, it didn't seem to make any difference. What pleasures she had found in getting drunk or having sex were so fleeting and so quickly overwhelmed by the pains—headaches, stomachache, guilt, shame—that they no longer seemed worthwhile. But was it too late now? Had she lost Daniel?

Almost there.

She pushed the bell and felt the driver and other passengers giving her strange looks as she waited for the bus to stop. What could they sense about her? Could they smell sex on her? She hadn't washed before leaving Patrick in Richmond; she had simply pulled her clothes on as quickly as possible and left. But her raincoat covered the torn blouse. God, what could she do about that? If Daniel were home, he would notice. But what did it matter now? He knew anyway. Even so, she couldn't stand the thought of his knowing she had been with Patrick this afternoon.

As the bus approached the stop, she saw the knot of reporters hanging about by the church walls and knew why the passengers were looking at her. She was getting off at St. Mary's, the scene of the most horrible crime Eastvale had experienced in decades.

The bus came to a sharp halt and Rebecca would have

tumbled forwards if she hadn't been holding onto the metal pole. When the doors opened, she jumped off and dashed past the policeman at the gate, then ran through the church-yard to the vicarage.

When she got there she flung open the door and called out for Daniel. Silence. Thank God, he wasn't home. Pulling off her torn blouse, she ran upstairs to the bathroom to wash the smell of sex from her body. Then she would be ready to face Daniel. She would have to be.

V

Ive Jelačić lived on the sixth floor of a ten-story block of flats in Burmantofts, off York Road. In the gray November drizzle, the maze of tall buildings reminded Banks of a newspaper picture he'd seen of workers' quarters in some Siberian city.

"Charming, isn't it?" said Detective Inspector Ken Black-stone, waiting for them outside. He looked at his watch. "Do you know, the council had to put slippery domes on all the roofs to stop kids climbing down on the upper balconies and breaking in through people's windows?"

Immaculately dressed as usual, Blackstone made Banks aware that his top collar button was undone and his tie a lit-tle askew. Blackstone looked like an academic, with his wire-rimmed glasses, bookworm's complexion and thinning sandy hair, a little curly around the ears, and he was, in fact, something of an expert on art and art fraud. Not that there was often much call for his area of expertise in Leeds. No-body had knocked off any Atkinson Grimshaws recently, and only an idiot would try to fake a Henry Moore sculpture.

"Jelačić's alibi checks out," Blackstone said as they walked towards the entrance. "For what it's worth. And we've had a poke about his flat. Nothing."

"What do *you* think it's worth?" Banks asked.

Blackstone pursed his cupid's-bow lips. "Me? About as

much as a fart in a bathtub. There were three of them—all Croatian. Stipe Pavič, Mile Pavelič and Vjeko Batorac. They'd probably swear night was day to protect one another from the police. Here it is. Take my word, the lift doesn't work."

Banks looked through the open sliding doors. The walls of the lift were covered in bright, spray-painted graffiti, and even from where he stood he could smell glue and urine. They took the stairs instead, surprising a couple of kids sniffing solvent on the third-floor stairwell. The kids ran. They knew the only people dressed like Blackstone in that neighborhood were likely to be coppers.

There were a few times when Banks regretted smoking, and the climb to the sixth-floor flat was one of them. Puffing for breath and sweating a little, he finally arrived at the outside walkway that went past the front doors.

Number 604 had once been red, but most of the paint had peeled off. It also looked as if it had been used for knife-throwing practice. Jelačić answered on the first knock, wearing jeans and a string vest. His upper body looked strong and muscular, and tufts of thick black hair spilled through the holes in the vest. With his height, longish hair and hooked nose, he certainly resembled the descriptions of the man seen in St. Mary's yesterday evening.

"Why you bother me?" he said, standing aside to let them in and letting his eyes rest on Susan for longer than necessary. "I tell you already, I have done nothing."

Inside, the flat was small enough to feel crowded with four people in it and tidy enough to surprise Banks. If nothing else, Ive Jelačić was a good housekeeper. An ironing board stood in one corner, with a shirt spread over it, and there was a small television set in the opposite corner. No video or stereo equipment in sight. The only other furniture in the room consisted of a battered sofa and a table with three chairs. Family photographs and a couple of religious icons stood on the mantelpiece over the electric fire.

"How are you making a living now, Mr. Jelačić?" Banks asked.

"Dole."

"Do you own a car?"

"Why?"

"Just answer the question."

"*Da*. Is old Ford Fiesta."

"Did you drive it to Eastvale yesterday?"

Jelačić looked at Blackstone. "*Ne*. I tell him already. I play cards. Vjeko tells you. And Stipe and Mile."

Jelačić sat down on his sofa, taking up most of it, and lit a cigarette. The room quickly began to fill with smoke. Blackstone stood with his back against the door, and Banks and Susan sat on the wooden chairs. Banks soon noticed the way Jelačić was sliding his eyes over Susan's body, and he could tell Susan noticed it too, the way she made sure her skirt was pulled down as far over her knees as it would go and the way she kept her knees pressed tight together. But still Jelačić ogled.

"The thing is," Banks said, "that people will often lie to cover for their friends, if they think a friend is in trouble."

Jelačić leaned forward aggressively, muscles bulging in his arms and shoulders. "You call my friends liars! *Jebem ti mater!* You tell that to their face. Fascist police. *Šupak*."

Banks held out a photograph of Deborah Harrison. "Did you know this girl?"

Jelačić glared at Banks for a moment before glancing towards the photo. He shook his head.

"Are you sure?"

"*Da*."

"She went to St. Mary's, sang in the church choir, used to walk through the graveyard on her way home."

He shook his head again.

"I think you're lying, Mr. Jelačić. You see, she complained about you. She said you used to make lewd, sexual comments and gestures towards her. What do you think about that?"

"Is not true."

"Father Charters said you were drunk most of the time,

you didn't do your job properly and you bothered the girls. Is that true?"

"*Ne*. He is liar. All St. Mary's people lie, get Ive in trouble, make him lose job."

"Did you ever enter the Inchcliffe Mausoleum."

"*Nikada*. Is always locked."

Banks looked at Ken Blackstone and rolled his eyes. "Oh, come on, Ive. We found your fingerprints all over the empty vodka bottles in there."

"*Vrag ti nosi!*"

"We know you went down there. Why?"

Jelačić paused to sulk for a moment, then said, "All right. So I go down there sometime in summer when it get too hot. Just for cool, you understand? Maybe I have a little drink and smoke. Is not crime."

"Did you ever take anyone else down there? Any girls?"

"*Nikada*."

Banks waved the photograph. "And you swear you didn't know this girl?"

Jelačić leaned back on the sofa. "Maybe I just see her, you know, if I am working and she walk past."

"So you do admit you might have seen her?"

"*Da*. But that is all."

"Mr. Jelačić, what were you wearing last night?"

Jelačić pointed towards a coat-hook by the door. A red windcheater hung on it.

"Shoes?"

Frowning, Jelačić got to his feet and picked up a pair of old trainers from the mat below the hook. Banks looked at the soles and thought he could see gravel trapped in the tread and, perhaps, bits of leaves. There was also mud on the sides.

"How did your shoes get in this state?" he asked.

"I walk back from Mile's."

"You didn't drive?"

Jelačić shrugged. "Is not far."

"We'd like to take your shoes and windcheater in for testing," Banks said. "It would be easiest if you gave us permission. You'll get a receipt."

"If I do not?"

"Then we'll get a court order."

"Is okay. You take them. I have nothing to hide."

"Were you standing on the Kendal Road bridge around six o'clock yesterday evening?"

"*Ne.* I go to Mile's house. We play cards until late."

"Did you have two pints of beer and a double whisky in the Nag's Head, opposite St. Mary's Park?"

"I tell you. I go to Mile's and we play cards and drink."

"Daniel Charters told us you'd been back to Eastvale to extort money from him. Is that true?"

"*Vražje!* I tell you, that man, he is Satan's tool, an evil liar."

"So it's not true that you offered to withdraw the charges in exchange for money?"

"Is not true. *Ne.* And I have nothing more to say." Jelačić looked at Susan again, letting his eyes travel slowly from her feet all the way up to her breasts, where they lingered. He didn't exactly lick his lips, but he might as well have done. Banks saw Susan flush with embarrassment and rage.

"Well, let me just get clear what you *have* told us," Banks said. "Last night, you were playing cards with friends who will vouch for you, right?"

Jelačić nodded.

"You didn't know the girl in the photograph, though you might have seen her in passing."

"*Da.*"

"But you certainly didn't leer at her or make any suggestive gestures."

"*Ne.*"

"And after you were unjustly fired you never went back to Eastvale and tried to extort money out of Father Daniel Charters."

"*Nikada.*"

"Fine, then," said Banks, standing up. "That'll be all. We'll be off now."

Jelačić looked surprised. "You leave now?"

"Don't worry, we'll take good care of the clothing and get it back to you as soon as we've run our tests. Thank you for your cooperation, Mr. Jelačić. Good day."

And they left him gaping after them.

"Biggest load of bollocks I've ever heard in my life," said Ken Blackstone as they walked down the stairs. A dog went on pissing nonchalantly against the wall as they passed by.

Banks lit a cigarette. "Yes, it was, wasn't it? What do you think Susan?"

"Whether he did it or not," Susan Gay said between gritted teeth, "I think the bastard should be hung over the balcony by his balls. Sir."

Chapter 5

I

*I*t was after six and Daniel still wasn't back. Rebecca paced. She should make a start on dinner. At least it would take her mind off things. Had all this happened just a couple of days ago, she would have gone to see the angel, blabbed her fears and feelings out to its marble heaven-ward gaze, but the Inchcliffe Mausoleum was soured for her now by what she had seen there.

She put on her striped butcher's apron—a birthday present from Daniel, when he still had his sense of humor—and searched in the fridge for the remains of the weekend's roast. She would make shepherd's pie. There was a bottle of Marks and Sparks Sauvignon Blanc in the fridge, lying on its side near the front. After a moment's hesitation, Rebecca opened it and poured herself a generous glass before setting about grinding the leftover meat.

She was halfway through her second glass, and had just put the potatoes on, when she heard the door open. Daniel. Her legs turned to water. Suddenly she couldn't face him, didn't know what to say. He called out her name and she managed to tell him she was in the kitchen. Quickly, she knocked back the rest of the wine and poured herself another glass. Her hand was shaking so much she spilled some of it on the table. Sometimes you just couldn't get drunk enough quick enough.

"What happened to the front window?" Daniel asked when he came through.

Rebecca stared down at the potatoes in the pan, waiting for the water to boil. "Someone chucked a brick through it," she said. She didn't tell him about the note.

"Where were the police?"

"Up around the Inchcliffe Mausoleum."

"Isn't it marvelous? Police all over the place but still a crime gets committed." Daniel rested the backs of his thighs against the solid wood table.

"Daniel, a young girl's been killed. And I found her."

Daniel rubbed his brow. "I know. I'm sorry. I wasn't thinking clearly. Bad day."

"How was the meeting?"

"At least they're resolved on not kicking me out for the present," Daniel said. Over the past month, he had developed a tic beside his left eye. It was jumping now. "But the bishop is very upset about the murder, especially about its happening on church property. That's another nail in my coffin. Things could hardly get much worse."

"Don't tempt providence."

"Providence? Hah. I don't know if I still believe in providence any more. Or in anything, for that matter. I'm hungry." He went to the fridge, found some old Cheddar and cut himself a chunk. "How about you?"

Rebecca shook her head. The way her stomach felt, she thought she might never be able to eat again. The potatoes came to a boil. She turned down the heat and wiped her hands on her apron. The tension inside her had built so high that she felt like a volcano about to erupt. She couldn't stand it any longer.

"Daniel?" She turned to face him.

"What?"

"I . . . I don't . . . Today. I—"

The front doorbell rang.

"Damn!" Rebecca banged her fist on the table. "Who could that be?"

"I'll go and see." Daniel went off to answer it.

Rebecca grasped the edge of the table. She could feel the room spinning around her, and it wasn't the booze this time.

"Becky!" The note of concern in his voice brought her back "Are you all right?"

She closed her eyes and shook her head. Not so bad. "I'm fine. Sorry. I just came over a bit funny, that's all." When she opened her eyes, she saw Daniel standing next to the detective who had visited them last night.

He was smaller than you'd expect for a policeman, she noticed, compact, lean and wiry, with an aura of pent-up strength. His closely cropped black hair showed just a little gray at the temples, and his blue eyes danced and sparkled with energy. There was a little crescent scar beside his right eye.

"Detective Chief Inspector Banks is back," Daniel said. "He wants to ask us some more questions."

Rebecca nodded, took off her apron and followed them through to the living-room. She left the glass of wine on the kitchen table. Another postponement. Maybe she could drink herself through yet another night of guilt and misery.

"I'm sorry to intrude again," Banks said when they had all sat down. He sneezed, took out a large handkerchief and blew his nose. "Sorry. I seem to be catching a cold. Look, I'll come straight to the point. I can see you were busy getting dinner ready. I was just wondering if maybe you'd decided to tell me the truth about last night?"

For a moment, Rebecca was stunned by the matter-of-fact way Banks spoke. "The truth?" she echoed.

"Yes. You're a poor liar, Mrs. Charters. And you can take that as a compliment." He glanced towards Daniel. "When I asked your husband where he had been at the time you said you heard a cry, you jumped in a bit too quickly and answered for him."

"I did?"

"Yes. Then he felt duty-bound to lie to cover for you. It's all very admirable in some ways, but it won't do. Not when there's a sixteen-year-old girl lying dead in Eastvale mortuary."

Rebecca felt completely tongue-tied. What the hell was going on? Her mind whirled, searching for things to say, but before she could say anything a voice far calmer than her own cut in.

"Chief Inspector," Daniel Charters said. "I'm afraid that's my fault. I should have corrected Rebecca rather than let the deceit stand. Believe me, there was no need for a lie. I have nothing to hide."

Banks nodded. He seemed to be waiting for something else.

Daniel sighed and went on. "Yes, I was out at the time my wife heard the cry, but I can assure you that my whereabouts had absolutely nothing at all to do with the poor girl's murder."

"Where were you?" Banks asked.

Rebecca noticed Daniel's lips tighten for a moment as he tensed in thought. "I'd rather not say."

"It would help us a lot if we could verify your story."

Daniel shook his head. "I'm afraid I wouldn't be able to prove my alibi, even if I told you."

"You could let *us* try."

He smiled sadly. "It's a kind offer, but—"

The doorbell rang again.

"I'll go," said Rebecca.

"Whoever it is," Daniel told her, "get rid of them."

Leaving them in silence, Rebecca went to open the front door. Patrick Metcalfe was standing there. He looked as if he had been walking around in the rain without a raincoat for hours.

"Oh, my God," Rebecca cried, trying to shut the door against his shoulder. "Please, go away. Can't you see you've caused enough trouble already?"

"Let me in, Rebecca. I want to come in. I must come in. I want to talk to both of you. You must listen to me."

He kept pushing at the door and Rebecca wasn't strong enough to hold him back. Suddenly, Banks's calm voice behind her said, "Why don't you let him in, Mrs. Charters? Whoever he is. The more the merrier."

II

Even Barry Stott was almost ready to call it a day by six-thirty. The drizzle that, at one time, had looked like ending, had turned into a much harder downpour as darkness fell, and now both he and Sergeant Hatchley were soaked to the skin. Even the best raincoat and shoes, which Stott's were, could only take so much without springing leaks. If only Jelačić had broken down and confessed instead of stubbornly protesting his innocence, the way Banks said he had, how much easier life would have been.

They were showing the police artist's impression, based on Alf's description—and what a lengthy and frustrating experience getting that done had been—along the rather twee row of shops set back from Kendal Road opposite the school. The newsagent hadn't seen anyone, the grocer was closed and the hairdresser gave a lengthy opinion as to the sorry state of the suspect's locks, but said she was closed on Mondays, and no, she hadn't noticed anyone strange hanging around on any other days.

The teashop was also closed, the way most Yorkshire teashops close at teatime, but the Peking Moon, the Chinese restaurant next door, had just opened. It was, as Hatchley explained, a rather pricey, up-market sort of Chinese restaurant, not the kind of place that yobbos go for a quick chop suey after a skinful of ale on a Friday night.

"I wonder why they don't change the name," Sergeant Hatchley said as they approached the door. "Isn't Peking called Beijing now? A real Chinaman wouldn't have a clue where he was if he saw this."

Stott turned to Hatchley before he pushed the door open. "I know what you're thinking, Sergeant. And you can forget it. We're not staying here for dinner. Definitely not. Got it?"

Hatchley looked hurt. "Furthest thing from my mind, sir. I don't even like Chinese food. It's got no sticking power. I'm always hungry again ten minutes after I've eaten it."

"Right. Just as long as we understand each other. . . ."

The bell at the top of the door jingled as they went in. Like many Chinese restaurants, its decor was simple and relaxing, with a series of ancient Chinese landscapes—tiny human figures dwarfed by evergreen-covered mountains—on the walls, and plain red tablecloths. Soft, tinkling music played in the background. So soft that Stott couldn't even figure out whether it was pop or classical. Or Chinese. Not that he cared much for music.

A waiter in a white jacket walked towards them. "Jim, me old mate. What can I do you for?" he asked in a cockney accent you could cut with a knife, despite the oriental eyes and complexion.

"DI Stott," Hatchley introduced them, "This is Well Hung Low." He laughed, and the waiter laughed with him.

Stott seethed inside, his rage, as it always did, crystallizing quickly from fire to ice.

"Just a joke, sir," Hatchley went on. "His name's Joe Sung. Deserted the bright lights of Whitechapel for the greener pastures of Eastvale. Joe wanted to be a copper once, too, sir, but I managed to persuade him he was better off where he was. His father owns this place. It's a little gold-mine."

"Perhaps you should reconsider," Stott said with a smile, shaking Joe's hand. "We need more . . . a more ethnically diverse police force. Especially in Yorkshire."

"Aye," said Hatchley. "I told him he wouldn't know what was worse, the prejudice or the patronizing."

Joe laughed.

Again, Stott felt his anger boil up and freeze. Oafs like Hatchley symbolized all that was wrong in today's police force. His type's days were numbered. "I wonder if we might ask you a few questions?" he said to Joe Sung.

"Fire away, mate." Joe gestured to the empty restaurant.

"See how busy we are. Here, take the weight off." He beck-oned them to join him at one of the tables.

"Remember what I said, Sergeant," Stott hissed in Hatch-ley's ear as they followed. "This isn't another meal break."

"No, sir." But Hatchley took the ashtray on the table as an invitation to light up.

"What is it, then?" Joe asked when they'd sat down. "Of-ficial business? About that murder?"

"Yes," said Stott.

Joe shook his head. "Terrible business. I knew the girl, too, you know."

"Knew her?"

"Well, not in the real sense of the word. Not to talk to, like. I mean she'd eaten in here with her mates, that's all. I couldn't believe my eyes when I saw that photo in the *Evening Post*."

Stott couldn't understand how it happened, but a tray of appetizers suddenly appeared on the table in front of them: spring rolls, garlic shrimp, chicken balls. All Stott noticed was the retreating back of another waiter. He hadn't heard a thing. Hatchley picked up a shrimp and popped it in his mouth between drags on his cigarette.

"When did she eat here?" Stott asked.

"They come here every now and then. A bunch of girls from the school, that is. Maybe when one of their daddies sends the monthly check. Anyway, they generally keep quiet, don't cause any trouble, and they don't expect to be served beer. She was with them once or twice, that Deborah Harrison who got killed. I recognized her."

"Do you remember anything about her?"

"Nah, not really. 'Cept that she was a good-looking girl. That's why I remembered her in particular."

"Ever noticed anyone take an unusual interest in her, or the other St. Mary's girls?"

"Well, they've caught the odd eye or two. There's a couple of right corkers among them, and there's always something about a girl in a school uniform. Sorry. That was in bad taste."

"Not at all, Joe," said Hatchley. "I know what you mean, and I'm sure the inspector does, too."

Stott said nothing. Three bottles of beer materialized with three glasses on the table before them, as if by magic.

"Somefink to wash the food down," Joe said with a grin. "My treat."

Stott ignored the beer. Hatchley grabbed a bottle and ignored the glass. Well, let him drink it, Stott thought. Fine. He wasn't going to touch any, himself. Give Hatchley enough rope and he'll surely hang himself. If only he didn't have a strong ally in Chief Inspector Banks. Stott couldn't understand that relationship at all. Banks seemed like an intelligent, civilized sort of copper. What could he possibly see in a boor like Hatchley?

Right now, though, there were more important things to think about than Hatchley's eating and drinking habits. "So you noticed nothing unusual about the girl and nobody taking any undue interest in her or her friends?" Stott asked.

"That's right," said Joe. "Noffink out of the ordinary."

"Did she ever meet anyone here? Anyone other than her schoolfriends?"

"No. They always came and left together as a group. Never had any boys with them, if that's what you mean. Too close to the school, if you ask me. You never know when one of the teachers might drop in and catch them. They eat here, too, sometimes."

Stott glanced over at Hatchley, who took out the artist's impression of the stranger in the Nag's Head. "Ever seen this man?" he asked.

Joe stared at the picture, shaking his head. "It doesn't look much like him, except for the hair," he said, "but we had a bloke looked a bit like that in here just last night."

Stott's pulse began to race. "What was he wearing?"

"An orange anorak."

"Tall?"

"Yeah, tall-ish. Bit over six feet, anyway."

"What time did he come in?"

"About half six. I remember because he was the only one in at that time. Miserable night."

The time fit, Stott thought, feeling his excitement rise. The killer had a couple of drinks at the Nag's Head, murdered Deborah Harrison, and then he came here for dinner.

"Did he do or say anything unusual?"

"He seemed a bit restless. I saw him muttering to himself once or twice."

"Hear what he said?"

"Sorry."

"Who waited his table?"

"I did. We were short-staffed because of the fog. He was certainly hungry, I'll say that. First he had spring rolls, then he ordered orange beef *and* Szechuan shrimp, a bowl of rice and a pint of lager. Ate it all, too."

"Did you talk to him?"

"Only to take his order. He didn't seem communicative, so I didn't push it. You learn how to behave in this business, who wants to chat and who just wants to be left alone. This bloke wanted to be left alone."

Stott saw his bottle of beer disappear into Hatchley's hand. He let it pass. "Did you notice anything else about him?"

"Yeah. He had a little cut, just up there, high on his left cheek." Joe touched the spot on his own cheek.

Stott could hardly contain his excitement. The postmortem had reported skin and tissue under the middle fingernail of Deborah Harrison's right hand. She had scratched her attacker. It had to be Jelačić. "How long did he stay?" Stott asked.

"Just as long as it took to order and eat. About three-quarters of an hour."

"Did he have a car?"

"If he did, I didn't see it. Somehow, I got the impression he was on foot. I mean, who'd take the car out by himself on a night like that, just to go out alone for a Chinese meal? Fine as the food here is. Me, I'd order a take-away and let some other poor bugger do the driving."

"Good point," said Stott. "See where he went?"

"Afraid not."

From the corner of his eye, Stott noticed the last spring roll disappear between two sausage-like fingers.

"Had you ever seen him before?" he asked.

Joe shook his head.

Stott smiled. "I don't suppose he happened to mention his name, did he?"

Joe grinned back. "Sorry. Didn't mention his address, either. No. Like I said, some of them are chatty, this one wasn't." He paused. "I'll tell you what, though."

"What?"

Joe stood up. "If my memory serves me right, he paid by card. You might be able to get his name from that. I haven't done the returns yet. Shall I go get it for you?"

Stott sent up a silent prayer of thanks to God.

Joe came back with a sheaf of Visa slips in his hand and started going through them. "Not this one. Not that . . . no . . . no. Yeah. Right, this is the one." And he passed it over.

Anxiously, Stott grabbed the slip of paper, but as soon as he looked at it, his spirits sank. He couldn't read the signature—that was just a mess of loops and whirls—but the name was printed clearly enough in the top left corner. And it *wasn't* Ive Jelačić.

Beside him, he heard the glug of an emptying beer bottle followed by a resonant burp.

III

"Right," said Banks, "now that we've all calmed down a bit, maybe we can play truth or consequences. And I'm telling you, the consequences will be bloody severe if you don't play. Got it?"

The three pale, miserable-looking people in the chilly vicarage living-room nodded in unison. The brown-and-white bundle of fur on the hearth scratched and fell still again.

As soon as Banks had appeared in the hall, Patrick Metcalfe had tried to make a break for it. Perhaps he believed that the power of his love could vanquish unhappy husbands, but he must have known it didn't stand a chance against the long arm of the law. As he turned to run away, he slipped on the doorstep and fell down three stone steps onto the garden path, sprawling in the rain on the worn pavingstones, holding his knee and cursing. Banks helped him inside with a firm hand and sat him down in one of the armchairs.

Now he sat there, hair plastered to his skull, looking sullen. The "consumptive" look wasn't hard for him to cultivate, given his lanky frame and hollow cheeks. He kept giving Rebecca Charters significant stares with his soulful eyes, but she averted her gaze.

By this time, Rebecca had brought the bottle of wine from the kitchen and topped up her glass. She was beginning to look a little blurred around the edges. Daniel Charters, permanent frown etched in his high brow, muscle twitching beside his left eye, just sat there, long legs crossed, his face growing steadily paler, looking like a man old before his time.

"Now, then, Mr. Charters," Banks said. "You were trying to tell me where you were last night before we were so rudely interrupted."

"He was with me," the newcomer burst out.

"And you are?"

"Patrick Metcalfe. I'm the history teacher at St. Mary's."

"So you knew Deborah Harrison?"

"I wouldn't say I *knew* her. I taught her history last year."

"And you say Mr. Charters was with you yesterday evening?"

"He was."

"What time did he arrive?"

Metcalfe shrugged. "About a quarter to six. I was just thinking about putting something in the microwave for dinner, and I usually eat at about six."

"Does that time sound right to you, Mr. Charters?"

Charters nodded glumly.

Banks turned back to Metcalfe. "Where do you live?"

"One of the school flats. On St. Mary's grounds."

"Alone?"

"Yes. Alone." Metcalfe looked longingly at Rebecca Charters, who stared down into her wineglass.

"What time did Mr. Charters leave?" Banks asked.

"Around ten to six. He didn't stay more than five minutes. He could see I wasn't interested in what he had to say."

Which meant that Charters was unaccounted-for during the crucial period around six o'clock. Banks could see Rebecca frowning at this information. She had lied for her husband, only to have someone give him what seemed like an alibi, then immediately snatch it away again. Did *she* know where he had been between ten to six and whenever he got back home?

And, Banks realized, this also left Patrick Metcalfe without an alibi. Rebecca, too, for that matter; he only had her word that she had heard something like a cry around six o'clock.

"What were you wearing?" Banks asked Charters.

"Wearing? A raincoat."

"Color?"

"Beige."

"May I see it."

Charters went and brought the raincoat in from the hall closet. Banks examined it closely but could see no traces of blood or earth. "Do you mind if I take this for further testing?" he asked. "I'll give you a receipt of course."

Charters looked alarmed. "Should I call my lawyer?"

"Not if you've got nothing to hide."

"I've got nothing to hide. Go ahead. Take it."

"Thank you."

"Where did you go after you left Mr. Metcalfe?"

"Nowhere in particular. I just walked."

"Where?"

"In the school grounds. By the river."

"Did you see anyone?"

"There were a few people about, yes."

"What about on or near the bridge?"

He thought for a moment, then said, "Yes, come to think of it, I did see someone. When I came out of the main school gate and crossed the road, there was a man in front of me walking along Kendal Road towards the bridge."

"Did you get a good look at him?"

"No. He stopped on the bridge and I walked past him. He was about my height—six foot two—and he was wearing an orange anorak. I could see that much from behind. His hair was dark and rather long."

"Are you sure it was a man?"

"Certain. Even in the fog I could tell by the way he walked. There's something . . . I don't know how to explain it . . . but I'm *certain* it was a man."

Another sighting of the mysterious stranger that Stott and Hatchley had unearthed in the Nag's Head. Interesting. "Can you tell me anything more about him?"

"I'm afraid not," said Charters. "I had other things on my mind."

"Could it have been a red windcheater rather than an orange anorak?"

Charters frowned. "I suppose it *could* have been. I wasn't paying really close attention."

"I hope you realize, Mr. Charters, that if you'd continued lying to us you would also have been withholding what could be an important piece of evidence."

Charters said nothing.

"Where did you go next?" Banks asked.

"I walked up to North Market Street, carried along there for a while, then took Constance Avenue back down to the river path and home." He looked at Rebecca, then looked away again. "But when I got here I . . . I . . . didn't want to go in and . . . Not just yet. So I kept on walking for a good ten minutes or so, then turned back and came home."

"Is that everything?"

"Yes."

"Did you go into the churchyard at any time?"

"No. I wish I had. I might have been able to prevent the poor girl's murder."

"What time *did* your husband get home, Mrs. Charters?"

"He was home when I got back from the graveyard."

"And that was about a quarter to seven?"

"Yes."

"And what did you do after Mr. Charters left your flat?" Banks said to Metcalfe.

"Nothing much. Heated up my dinner. I considered coming over here and putting an end to the ridiculous charade, but decided against it."

"What ridiculous charade?"

They were all silent for a moment, as if someone had finally gone too far and they were deciding how to cover up, then Daniel Charters spoke up. "I went to talk to Metcalfe," he said, "to try to persuade him to stop seeing my wife."

Banks looked at Metcalfe. "Is this true?"

"Yes."

"And what was your response?"

Metcalfe sneered at Charters. "I told him I wasn't interested, that it was too late. Rebecca and I are in love and we're going away together."

Banks looked towards Rebecca. She had lowered her head, so he couldn't see her expression, only the mass of auburn hair hanging down to her knees. Her glass of wine had sat untouched for several minutes on the table.

"Tell him," Metcalfe urged her. "Go on, Rebecca. Tell him it's true. Tell him how this marriage is a sham, how it's stifling you, destroying your true nature. Tell him you don't love your—"

"No!"

"What?"

Rebecca Charters held her head up and stared directly at Metcalfe. Her dark eyes flashed with angry tears. "I said no,

Patrick." She seemed to gain control of the situation; the welling tears remained at the edges of her eyes. She spoke quietly: "I tried to tell you before, but you wouldn't listen. You didn't want to understand. I'm not defending myself. What I've done is wrong. Terribly wrong." She looked at her husband, who showed no expression, then back at Metcalfe. "But it's *my* guilt, *my* sin. If I wasn't strong enough to stand by my husband when he needed me most, if I let a hint of scandal and suspicion poison our marriage, then it's my mistake, my fault. But I won't compound it with lies."

She turned to Banks. "Yes, Chief Inspector, I had an affair with Patrick. I met him at a social evening we put on for the staff and upper sixth of St. Mary's School around the middle of last month. He was charming, interesting, passionate, and I became infatuated with him. Daniel and I were already going through a difficult time, as I think you know, and when I should have been strong, I was weak. I'm not proud of myself, but I want you to know that's why I lied to you, because I was afraid that too many questions would lead to exactly this kind of situation. Now it's happened, I'm glad, believe me, though I've been trying to avoid it at all costs. There's been far too much distrust and suspicion around this house lately. I can't believe that my husband had anything to do with this murder, any more than I can believe he's capable of doing what that vile man accused him of."

She turned back to Metcalfe, tears still hanging on the rims of her eyes, dampening the long, dark lashes. "I'm sorry, Patrick, if I misled you. I didn't intend to. Just put it down to a foolish woman seeking temporary escape. But you were only a distraction. I didn't mean for you to fall in love with me. And, if you're honest with yourself, I think you'd have to admit that you're not in love with me at all. I think you're in love with the idea of being in love, but you're far too self-absorbed to ever love anyone but yourself."

Metcalfe stood up. "It's not true, Rebecca. I do love you. Can't you see how you're blinding yourself? If you stay, you'll wither up and die before your time, before you've even—"

A harsh sound came from one of the armchairs, and Banks saw Daniel Charters bend forward, cup his head in his hands and start to cry like a child. Rebecca jumped up and went over to him, putting her arm around his shoulder.

"He doesn't even like women," Metcalfe went on. "You can't possibly—"

Banks picked up Charters's raincoat, grasped Metcalfe by the back of the collar and shoved him towards the front door. Even though Metcalfe was a few inches taller than Banks, he didn't put up much of a struggle, just muttered something about police brutality.

Once outside, Banks shut the door behind them, guided Metcalfe down the path and tossed him out of the gate onto the river path. "On your bike," he said.

Still muttering, Metcalfe walked towards the school. Banks glanced back as he closed the gate and saw Rebecca and Daniel framed in the window. Rebecca was cradling her husband's head against her breast, like a baby's, stroking his hair. Her mouth was opening and closing, as if she were uttering soothing words.

Banks had unfinished business at the vicarage—they weren't off the hook yet—but it could wait. He looked up into the dark sky, as if searching for enlightenment, but felt only the cool raindrops on his face. He sneezed. Then he pulled his collar up and set off along the river path for the Kendal Road bridge.

Chapter 6

I

*O*wen Pierce had just opened a bottle of wine and taken the heated remains of last week's beef stew out of the oven when the doorbell rang.

Muttering a curse, he put his stew back in the oven to keep warm and trotted to the front door. At the end of the hall, he could make out two figures through the frosted glass: one tall and heavy-set, one shorter and slim.

When he opened the door, he first thought they were Jehovah's Witnesses or Mormons—who else came to the door in pairs, wearing suits? But these two didn't quite look the part. True, one of them did look like a bible salesman—sticking-out ears, glasses, not a hair out of place, freshly scrubbed look—but the other looked more like a thug.

"Mr. Pierce? Mr. Owen Pierce?" asked the bible salesman.

"Yes, that's me. Look, I was just about to eat my dinner. What is it? What do you want? If you're selling—"

"We're police officers, sir," the man went on. "My name is Detective Inspector Stott and this is Detective Sergeant Hatchley. Mind if we come in?" They flashed their warrant cards and Owen stood back to let them in.

As soon as they got into the living-room, the big one started poking around.

"Nice place you've got," Stott said, while his partner

prowled the room, picking up vases and looking inside them, opening drawers an inch or two, inspecting books.

"Look, what is this?" Owen said. "Is he supposed to be going through my things like that? There are no drugs here, if that's what you're looking for."

"Oh, don't mind Sergeant Hatchley. He's just like that. Insatiable curiosity."

"Don't you need a search warrant or something?"

"Well, Owen" said Stott, "the way it works is like this. We *could* go to a magistrate, and we *could* apply for a warrant to search your premises, but it takes a lot of time. Sergeant Hatchley would have to stay here with you while I took care of the formalities. I think this way is much better all round. Anyway, you've nothing to hide, have you?"

"No, no, it's not that. It's just . . ."

"Well," said Stott with a smile. "That's all right, then, isn't it?"

"I suppose so."

"Mind if I sit down?"

"Be my guest."

Stott sat in the chair by the fake coals and Owen sat opposite him on the sofa. A mug of half-finished coffee stood between them on the glass-topped table beside a couple of unpaid bills and the latest *Radio Times*.

"Look," Owen said, "I'm afraid you've got me at a disadvantage here. What's it all about?"

"Just routine inquiries, sir. That's a nasty scratch on your face. Mind telling me where you got it?"

Owen put his hand up to his cheek. "I've no idea," he said. "I woke up this morning and there it was."

"Were you in the St. Mary's area of Eastvale yesterday evening?"

"Let me think . . . Yes, yes, I believe I was." He glanced at Hatchley, who seemed fascinated by the print of Renoir's *Bathers* over the fireplace.

"Why?"

"What? Sorry."

"Look, just ignore Sergeant Hatchley for the moment," Stott said. "Look at me. I asked you *why* you were in St. Mary's."

Owen shrugged. "No particular reason. I was just walking."

"Walking? On a miserable night like that?"

"Well, if you let the weather dictate it, you wouldn't get much walking done in Yorkshire, would you?"

"Even so. St. Mary's is quite a distance from here."

"No more than three miles each way. And it's a very pleasant walk along the river. Even in the fog."

Hatchley fished a copy of *Playboy* out of the magazine rack and held it up for Stott to see. Stott frowned and reached over for it. The cover showed a shapely blonde in skimpy pink lace panties, bordered in black, a flimsy slip, stockings and suspender belt. She was on her knees on a sofa, and her round behind faced the viewer. Her face was also turned towards the camera: glossy red lips, eyes an impossible shade of green, unfocused, as if she had just woken from a deep sleep. One thin strap had slipped over her upper right arm.

"I bought it because of one of the stories I wanted to read," Owen said, immediately feeling himself turn red. It wasn't so much that he had been caught with something warped and perverted, but with something sub-literary, something beneath his intelligence and dignity. "It's not illegal, you know. You can buy it at any newsagent's. It's not pornography."

"That's a matter of opinion, sir, isn't it?" said Stott. He handed the magazine back to Hatchley as if he were dropping something in a rubbish bin, holding it between his thumb and forefinger.

"And there's a video tape full of what sounds like sexy stuff to me, sir, judging by the titles," said Hatchley. "One of them's called *School's Out*. And you should have a butcher's at some of the poses in these here so-called art books."

"I'm an amateur photographer," Owen said. "It's my hobby. For Christ's sake, what do you expect? Is that what all this is about? Pornography? Because if it is—"

Stott waved his hand. "No," he said. "It's of no matter, really. It might be relevant. We'll have to see. Do you live here by yourself, Mr. Pierce?"

"Yes."

"What kind of work do you do?"

"I'm a lecturer at Eastvale College. English."

"Ever been married?"

"No."

"Girlfriends?"

"Some."

"But not to live with?"

"No."

"Videos and magazines enough to satisfy you, eh?"

"Now just a min—"

Stott held up his hand. "Sorry," he said. "Sorry, I shouldn't have said that. Tasteless of me. Out of line."

Why couldn't Owen quite believe the apology? He sensed very strongly that Stott had made the remark on purpose to nettle him. He hoped he had passed the test, even though he couldn't be sure what the question was. Feeling more like Kafka's Joseph K. every minute, he shifted in his chair. "Why do you want to know all this?" he asked again. "You said you were going to tell me what it's all about."

"Did I? Well, first, would you mind if we had a quick look around the rest of the place? It might save us coming back."

"Go ahead," Owen said, and accompanied them as they did the rounds. It wasn't a thorough search, and Owen felt that by granting them permission he had probably saved himself a lot of trouble. He had seen on television the way search teams messed up places. They gave the bedrooms, one of which was completely empty, a cursory glance, poked about in his clothing drawers and wardrobe. In the study, Stott admired the aquarium of tropical fish and, of course, Hatchley rummaged through some of Owen's photo files and found the black-and-white nude studies of Michelle. He showed them to Stott, who frowned.

"Who's this?" Stott asked.

Owen shrugged. "Just a model."

"What's her name?"

"I'm sorry. I don't remember."

"She looks very young."

"She was twenty-two when those were taken."

"Hmm, was she now?" muttered Stott, handing the photos back to Hatchley. "Must be artistic license. Notice any resemblance, Sergeant?" he asked Hatchley.

"Aye, sir, I do."

"Resemblance to who?"

"Mind if we take these, too?" Stott asked.

"As a matter of fact, I do. They're the only prints I've got, and I've lost the negatives."

"I understand, sir. You want to hang onto them for sentimental reasons. We'll take good care of them. Wait a minute, though . . . didn't you say she was just a model?"

"I did. And I didn't say I wanted to keep them for sentimental reasons. They're part of my portfolio. For exhibitions and such like."

"Ah, I see. Might we just take one of them, perhaps, then?"

"Oh, all right. If you must."

Hatchley leafed through some more art books on a shelf over the filing cabinet. One of them dealt with Japanese erotic art, and he opened it at a charcoal sketch of two young girls entwined together on a bed. They had either shaved off their pubic hair, or they were too young to have grown any. It was difficult to tell. He shoved it under Stott's nose.

"A bit like those books in the other room, sir," he said.

Stott turned up his nose.

"And some of them novels he reads have been on trial," Hatchley went on. "*Lady Chatterley's Lover, Naked Lunch, Ulysses, Delta of Venus,* a bit of De Sade . . ."

"For Christ's sake!" Owen cut in. "I can't believe this. I'm an English teacher, you fucking moron. That's what I do for a living."

"Now, you look here, mate," said Hatchley, squaring up to

him. "The last bloke used that kind of language with me had a nasty accident on his way down the police station steps."

"Are you threatening me?"

Hatchley thrust his chin out. "Take it any way you want."

"Stop it, Sergeant!" Stott cut in. "I'll not have you talking to a member of the public this way. Apologize to Mr. Pierce at once."

"Yes, sir," said Hatchley. He looked at Pierce and said, "Sorry, sir."

"If you ask me," Owen said, "you're the ones who are sick. Like witch-hunters, seeing the devil's work everywhere."

"Maybe it is everywhere," Stott said calmly. "Have you ever thought about that?"

"It's just hard to believe there's someone who still thinks *Lady Chatterley's Lover* and *Ulysses* are dirty books, that's all."

They sat down in the living-room again. "Now why don't you tell me all about what you did in St. Mary's yesterday evening," Stott said. "Sergeant Hatchley will take notes. No hurry. Take your time."

Owen told them about his walk, the drinks at the Nag's Head, the meal at the Peking Moon and the walk home. As he spoke, Stott looked directly at him. The stern, triangular face showed no expression; and the eyes behind the lenses seemed cool. The man's ears almost made Owen want to laugh out loud, but he restrained himself. The big one, Hatchley, scribbled away in a spiral-bound notebook. Owen was surprised he could even write.

"Are you in the habit of talking to yourself, Mr. Pierce?" asked Stott when he had finished.

Owen reddened. "I wouldn't say *talking* to myself exactly. Sometimes I get lost in thought and I forget there are people around. Don't you ever do that?"

"No," said Stott, "I don't."

Finally, after they had asked him to go over one or two random points again, Hatchley closed his notebook and Stott got to his feet. "That'll be all for now," he said.

"For now?"

"We might want to talk to you again. Don't know. We have to check up on a few points first. Would you mind if we had a look in your hall cupboard on the way out?"

"Why?"

"Routine."

"Go ahead. I don't suppose I can stop you."

Stott and Hatchley searched through the row of coats and jackets and pulled out Owen's new orange anorak. "Is this what you were wearing last night?"

"Yes. Yes, it is. But—"

"What about these shoes?"

"Yes, those too. Look—"

"Mind if we take them with us, sir?"

"But why?"

"Purposes of elimination."

"You mean it might help clear this business up?"

Stott smiled. "Yes. It might. We'll let you have them back as soon as we can. Do you think you could get me a plastic bag while the sergeant here writes out a receipt?"

Owen fetched a bin-liner from the kitchen and watched Stott put the shoes and anorak inside it while Hatchley wrote out the receipt. Then he accepted the slip of paper and signed a release identifying the items as his.

Stott turned to Hatchley. "I think we'd better be off, then, Sergeant," he said. "We've already taken up enough of Mr. Pierce's valuable time."

Hatchley took the plastic bag while Stott slipped the photograph into his briefcase, then they walked towards the door.

"Aren't you going to tell me what it's all about?" Owen asked again as he opened the front door for them. It was still raining.

Stott turned and frowned. "That's the funny thing about it, Owen," he said. "That you don't know." Then he shook his head slowly. "Anybody would think you don't read the papers. Which is odd, for an educated man like yourself."

II

Tracy Banks's bedroom, lit by a shaded table lamp, was a typical teenager's room, just like Deborah Harrison's, with pop-star posters on the wall, a portable cassette player, a narrow bed, usually unmade, and clothes all over the floor.

Tracy also had a desk against one wall and perhaps more books on her shelves than many girls her age. They ran the gamut from *The Wind in the Willows* to the *Pelican History of the World*. A row of dolls and teddy bears sat on the bookcase's lowest shelf; they always reminded Banks that his daughter wasn't that far away from childhood things yet. One day, they would disappear, as had most of his own toys: the fort with its soldiers, the Hornby train set, the Meccano. He had no idea where they had gone. Along with his childhood innocence.

Tracy herself sprawled on the bed in black leggings and a sloppy sweatshirt. She looked as if she had been crying. When Banks had got the message from his wife, Sandra, at his office, saying that Tracy was upset and wanted to talk to him, he had hurried straight home.

Now Banks sat on the edge of the bed and stroked his daughter's hair, which was tied back in a ponytail. "What is it, love?" he asked.

"You didn't tell me," Tracy said. "Last night."

"Are you talking about the murder?"

"Yes. Oh, it's all right. I know *why* you didn't tell me." She sniffled. "You wanted to spare my feelings. I don't blame you. I'm not mad at you or anything. I wish you had told me, though. It wouldn't have been such a shock when all the girls at school started talking about it."

"I'm sorry," said Banks. "I knew you'd find out eventually and it would upset you. I suppose I was just trying to give you one more night of peace before you had to deal with it. Maybe it was selfish of me."

"No. Really. It's all right."

"So what *is* wrong?"

Tracy was silent a moment. Banks heard laughter and music from downstairs. "I knew her," she said finally.

"Knew who?"

"Deborah Harrison. I knew her."

Apart from both being attractive blonde teenagers, Tracy and Deborah Harrison were about as far apart as you get in background and class. Deborah went to the expensive, élite St. Mary's School, where she was carefully groomed for Oxford or Cambridge, and Tracy went to Eastvale Comprehensive, where she had to fight her way through overcrowded classes, massive apathy and incompetent teaching to get decent enough A-levels to get into a redbrick university. Now here was Tracy saying she *knew* Deborah.

"How?" he asked.

Tracy shifted on the bed and sat cross-legged. She pulled the duvet over her shoulders like a shawl. "You won't get mad at me, will you, Dad? Promise?"

Banks smiled. "I've a feeling I'm not going to like this, but you've got my word."

Tracy took a deep breath, then said, "It was in the summer. A few times I hung around with the crowd at the Swainsdale Center down by the bus station."

"You hung around with those yobs? Jesus Christ, Tracy, I—"

"See! I knew you'd be mad."

Banks took a deep breath. "Okay. I'm not mad. Just surprised, that's all. How could you *do* that? Those kids are into drugs, vandalism, all sorts of things."

"Oh, we didn't do any harm, Daddy. It was just somewhere to go, that's all. And they're not so bad, really. I know some of them look pretty weird and frightening, but they're not really. What did you used to do when you were a kid with nowhere to go?"

Banks would like to have to answered, "Museums, art galleries, long walks, books, classical concerts." But he couldn't. Mostly he and his friends had hung around on street corners, on waste ground or in empty schoolyards.

Sometimes they had even broken into condemned houses and played there.

"Okay," he said. "We'll let it pass for now. Carry on."

"Deborah Harrison was down there shopping one day and one of the girls in the group knew her vaguely from dressage or swimming competitions or something, and they got talking. She came down a couple of days later—dressed down a bit—and started to hang out. I think she was bored with just staying at home and studying so she thought she'd slum it for a while."

"What about her own friends?"

"I don't really think she had any. She said most of her schoolfriends were away for the summer. Most of the boarders had gone home, of course, and the day-girls had all jetted off to exotic places like America and the south of France. Why can't we go to places like that, Dad?"

"You were in France earlier this year."

She slapped his arm. "I'm only teasing. It wasn't a serious question."

"When did Deborah first start joining in with the group?"

"Early August, I think."

"And how did the others treat her?"

"They'd tease her about being a bit lah-de-dah, sometimes, but she took it well enough. She said somebody had to be, and besides, it wasn't all it was cracked up to be."

"What did she mean by that?"

"It was just her way of talking about things."

"Did she ever flaunt her wealth, flash it about?"

"No. Not that I saw."

"How long did she hang around with the group?"

"About three weeks, on and off."

"Have you seen her since then?"

Tracy shook her head. "Well, she wouldn't want to be seen dead with the likes of us now, would she? Not now she's back at St. Mary's." Then she put her hand over her mouth. "I'm sorry, Dad. I just haven't got used to the idea that she's dead yet."

Banks patted her arm. "That's all right, love. It takes time. How well did you know her?"

"Not very well, but we chatted once or twice. She wasn't so bad, you know, when you got to know her a bit. I mean, she wasn't so snobbish. And she was quite bright."

"Did you ever talk about school?"

"Sometimes."

"What did she think of St. Mary's?"

"She thought it was all right. At least the teachers were pretty good and the classes weren't too big. She said they had a staff to pupil ratio of one to ten. It must be more like one to five hundred where I go."

"Did she mention any teachers in particular?"

"Not that I can remember."

"Patrick Metcalfe. Does that name sound familiar?"

Tracy shook her head. "No."

"What kind of things did she say about school?"

"Nothing much, really. Just like, 'You'd be surprised if you knew some of the things that go on there.' That sort of thing. Very melodramatic."

"What did you think she meant?"

Tracy looked down and rubbed her hand against her knee. "Well, there's a lot of girls live in, you know, all together in the dormitories. I thought she meant, like, lesbians and stuff."

"Did she imply that any of the teachers had any sort of sexual relations with the pupils?"

"No, Dad. Honest, I don't know. I mean, she never really *said* anything. Not specific. She just implied. Hinted. But she was like that about everything."

"Like what?"

"As if she knew more than she let on. And as if we were poor fools who saw only the surface, and she knew what *really* went on underneath. Like, *we* all swallowed the illusion, but she knew the underlying truth. I'm not trying to paint her in a bad way. She was really nice, but she just had this sort of tone, like, as if she knew more than everyone else."

"Did she ever speak about her family?"

"She mentioned her father's business now and then."

"What did she say about that?"

"I said once that it must be interesting having a father as famous as Sir Geoffrey Harrison, being knighted and all that."

So much for having a mere detective for a father, Banks thought, swallowing his pride. "What did she say?"

"The usual. Something like, 'Oh, you'd be shocked if you knew some of the things I know.' "

"And she didn't elaborate?"

"No. I just shrugged it off. I thought she meant the bad side of technology, all the war stuff, missiles and bombs and that. We all know Sir Geoffrey Harrison's companies are involved in things like that. It's in the papers nearly every day."

"And she didn't say any more about it?"

"No."

"Did she ever mention Father Daniel Charters or Ive Jelačić?"

"The people from St. Mary's church?"

"Yes."

"Not to me. If you ask me, she was more interested in boys than anything else."

"Boys? Anyone in particular."

"Well, she sort of took up with John Spinks." Tracy pulled a face. "I mean, of all the boys . . ."

Banks leaned forward. The bedsprings creaked. "Tell me about John Spinks," he said.

Chapter 7

I

*E*astvale College of Further Education was a hodgepodge of ugly redbrick and concrete buildings on the southern fringe of the town, separated from the last few houses by a stretch of marshy waste ground. There was nothing else much around save for the Featherstone Arms across the road, a couple of industrial estates and a large riding stable, about half a mile away.

The college itself was a bit of a dump, too, Owen thought over his lunch-time pint and soupy lasagna, and he wouldn't be teaching there if he could get anything better. The problem was, with only a BA from Leeds and an MA from an obscure Canadian university, he *couldn't* get anything better. So he was stuck teaching the business, secretarial and agriculture students how to spell and write sentences, skills they didn't even want to know. It was a long way from the literary ambitions he had nursed not so many years ago.

But he had more immediate problems than his teaching career: he had lied to the police, and they probably suspected as much.

It wasn't much of a lie, admittedly. Besides, it was none of their business. He had said he never lived with a woman, but he had. With Michelle. For five years. And Michelle was the woman in the black-and-white nude photographs.

So Owen wasn't exactly surprised when Stott and Hatchley walked into the pub and asked him if he would mind going to the station with them to clear up a few points. Nervous, yes, but not surprised. They said the department head had told them where they were likely to find him, and they had walked straight over.

Nobody spoke during the first part of the journey. Sergeant Hatchley drove the unmarked Rover, and Inspector Stott sat beside him. Owen could see the sharp line of his haircut at the back of his neck and the jug-handle shape of his ears, glasses hooked over them. As they approached the market square, Owen looked out of the window at the drab, shadowy figures hurrying from shop to shop, holding onto their hats.

"I wonder if you'd mind very much," Stott said, turning slightly in his seat, "if we arranged to take a couple of samples?"

"What kind of samples?"

"Oh, just the usual. Blood. Hair."

"Do I have to?"

"Let me put it like this. You're not under arrest, but the crime we're investigating is very serious indeed. It would be best all around if you gave your permission and signed a release. For elimination purposes."

"And if I refuse? What will you do? Hold me down, pull my hair out and stick a needle in me?"

"Nothing like that. We could get the superintendent to authorize it. But that wouldn't look good, would it? Especially if the matter ever went to court. Refusing to give a sample? A jury might see that as an admission of guilt. And, of course, as soon as you're eliminated from the inquiry, the samples will all be destroyed. No records. What do you say?"

"All right."

"Thank you, sir." Stott turned to face the front again and picked up his car phone. "I'll just take the liberty of calling Dr. Burns and asking him to meet us at the station."

It was all handled quickly and efficiently in a private office at the police station. Owen signed the requisite forms, rolled up his sleeve and looked away. He felt only a sharp, brief pricking sensation as the needle slid out. Then the doctor pulled some hair out of his scalp. That hurt a little more.

The interview room they took him to next was a desolate place: gray metal desk; three chairs, two of them bolted to the floor; grimy windows of thick wired glass; a dead fly smeared against one institutional-green wall; and that was it.

It smelled of stale smoke. A heavy blue glass ashtray sat on the desk, empty but stained and grimy with old ash.

Stott sat opposite Owen, and Sergeant Hatchley moved the free chair and sat by the wall near the door, out of Owen's line of vision. He sat backwards on the chair, wrapping his thick arms around its back.

First, Stott placed the buff folder he'd been carrying on the desk, smiled and adjusted his glasses. Then he switched on a double-cassette tape recorder, tested it, and gave the date, time and names of those present.

"Just a few questions, Owen," he said. "You've been very cooperative so far. I hope we don't have to keep you long."

"So do I," said Owen, looking around the grim room. "Shouldn't I call my lawyer or something?"

"Oh, I don't think so," said Stott. "Of course, you can if you want. It's your right." He smiled. "But it's not as if you're under arrest or anything. You're free to leave anytime you want. Besides, do you actually have a solicitor? Most people don't."

Come to think of it, Owen didn't have a solicitor. He knew one, though. An old university acquaintance had switched from English to law after his first year and now practiced in Eastvale. They hadn't seen each other in years, until Owen had bumped into him in a pub a few months back. Gordon Wharton, that was his name. Owen couldn't remember what kind of law he specialized in, but at least it was a start, if things went that far. For the moment, though, Stott was right. Owen hadn't been arrested, and he didn't see why he should have to pay a solicitor.

"Let me lay my cards on the table, Owen. You have admitted to us that you were in the area of St. Mary's on Monday evening. Is that true?"

"Yes."

"Why?"

"I told you. I went for a walk."

"Shall we just go over it again, for the record?"

Owen shrugged. "There's really nothing to go over." He could see the sheet of paper in front of Stott, laid out like an appointment book. Some of the times and notes had question marks in red.

"What time did you set off on this walk?"

"Just after I got back from work. About four. Maybe as late as half past."

"How far is it to St. Mary's?"

"Along the river? About three miles from my house. And the house is about half a mile from the river."

"About seven miles there and back, then?"

"Yes. About that."

"Now, before you ate at the Peking Moon you drank two pints of bitter and a Scotch whisky at the Nag's Head, right?"

"I wasn't counting, but yes, I had a couple of drinks."

"And you left the pub at about a quarter to six?"

"I wasn't especially aware of the time."

"That's what the landlord told us."

"I suppose it must be true, then."

"And you ate at the Peking Moon at approximately six-thirty, is that correct?"

"About then, yes. Again, I didn't notice the actual time."

"What did you do between a quarter to and half past six?"

"Walked around. Stood on the bridge."

"Did you go into St. Mary's graveyard?"

"No, I didn't. Look, if you're trying to tie me in to that girl's murder, then you're way off beam. Why would I do something like that? Perhaps I *had* better call a solicitor, after all."

"Ah!" Stott glanced over Owen's shoulder towards Sergeant Hatchley. "So he *does* read the papers, after all."

"I did after you left. Of course I did."

Stott looked back at him. "But not before?"

"I'd have known what you were talking about, then, wouldn't I?"

Stott straightened his glasses. "What made you connect our visit with that particular item of news?"

Owen hesitated. Was it a trick question? "It didn't take much," he answered slowly, "given the kind of questions you asked me. Even though I know nothing about what happened, I know I was in St. Mary's that evening. I never denied it. And while we're on the subject, what led you to me?"

Stott smiled. "Easy, really. We asked around. Small, wealthy neighborhood like St. Mary's, people notice strangers. Plus you were wearing an orange anorak and you used your Visa card in the Peking Moon."

Owen leaned forward and slapped his palms on the cool metal surface. "There!" he said. "That proves it, then, doesn't it?"

Stott gave him a blank look. "Proves what?"

"That I didn't do it. If I *had* done it, what you seem to be accusing me of, I would hardly have been so foolish as to leave my calling card, would I?"

Stott shrugged. "Criminals make mistakes, just like everybody else. Otherwise we'd never catch any, would we? And I'm not accusing you of anything at the moment, Owen. You can see our problem, though, can't you? Your story sounds thin, very thin. I mean, if you were in the area for some real, believable reason . . . Maybe to meet someone? Did you *know* Deborah Harrison, Owen?"

"No."

"Had you been watching her, following her?"

Owen sat back. "I've told you why I was there. I can't help it if you don't like my reason, can I? I never thought I'd have to explain myself to anyone."

"Did you see anyone acting suspiciously?"

"Not that I remember."

"Did you see Deborah Harrison?"

"No."

"About that scratch on your cheek," Stott said. "Remember yet where you got it?"

Owen put his hand to his cheek and shrugged. "Cut myself shaving, I suppose."

"Bit high up to be shaving, isn't it?"

"I told you. I don't remember. Why?"

"What about the nude photos, Owen? The ones we found at your house?"

"What about them? They're figure studies, that's all."

Sergeant Hatchley spoke for the first time, and the rough voice coming from behind startled Owen. "Come on lad, don't be shy. What's wrong with you? Don't you like looking at a nice pair of tits? You're not queer, are you?"

Owen half-twisted in his seat. "No. I didn't say I didn't like looking at naked women. Of course I do. I'm perfectly normal."

"And some of the girls in that magazine seemed very young to me," said Stott.

Owen turned to face him again. "Since when has it been a crime to buy *Playboy?* You people are still living in the middle ages. For Christ's sake, they're models. They get paid for posing like that."

"And you like videos, too, don't you, Owen? There was that one in your cabinet, your own private video to keep, to watch whenever you want. Including *School's Out.*"

"A friend gave me it, as a sort of joke. I told him I'd never seen any porn—any sexy videos before, and he gave me that, said I'd enjoy it."

"Well, I'll tell you, Owen," said Stott. "I've got to wonder about a bloke who watches stuff like that and likes the sort of art books and pictures you like. Especially if he takes nude photos of young girls, too."

"It's a free country. I'm a normal single male. I also hap-

pen to be an amateur photographer. And I have a right to
watch whatever kind of videos I want as long as they're
legal." Owen felt himself flushing with embarrassment.
Christ how he wished Chris Lorimer at the college hadn't
given him the bloody video.

"School's Out," Hatchley said quietly from behind him.
"A bit over the top, that, wouldn't you say?"

"I haven't even watched that one."

"You can see what Sergeant Hatchley's getting at, though,
can't you, Owen?" said Stott. "It looks bad: the subject-
matter, the image. It all looks a bit odd. Distinctly fishy."

"Well, I can't help that. It's not fishy. I'm perfectly innocent, and that's the truth."

"Who's the girl in the photographs? The one who looks
about fifteen."

"She was twenty-two. Just a model. It was a couple of
years ago. I can't remember her name."

"Funny, that."

"What is?"

"That you remember her age but not her name."

Owen felt his heart pounding. Stott scrutinized him
closely for a few seconds, then stood up abruptly. "You can
go now," he said. "I'm glad we could have our little chat."

Owen was confused. "That's it?"

"For the moment, yes. We'll be in touch."

Owen could hardly stand up quickly enough. He banged
his knee on the underside of the metal desk and swore. He
rubbed his knee and started to back towards the door. His
face was burning. "I can really go?"

"Yes. But stay available."

Owen was shaking when he got out of the police station
and turned down Market Street towards home. Could they
really treat you like that when you went along with them of
your own free will? He had a feeling his rights were being
trampled on and maybe it *was* time to look up Gordon
Wharton.

The first thing he did when he got into the house was tear

up the copy of *Playboy* and burn the pieces in the waste-bin, Cormac McCarthy story and all. Next, he took the video that Chris Lorimer had given him, pulled the tape out, broke the plastic casing and dumped it in the rubbish bin to burn too. At least they couldn't use it as evidence against him now.

Finally, he went into the spare room and took the rest of the nude photographs of Michelle from his filing cabinet. He held them in his hands, ready to rip them into tiny pieces and burn them along with the rest, but as he held them he couldn't help but look at them.

They were simple, tasteful chiaroscuro studies, and he could tell from the way Michelle's eyes glittered and her mouth was set that she was holding back her laughter. He remembered how she had complained about goose-bumps, that he was taking so long setting up the lighting, then he remembered the wine and the wild lovemaking afterwards. She had liked being photographed naked; it had excited her.

His hands started to shake again. God, she looked so beautiful, so perfect, so young, so bloody innocent. Still shaking, he thrust the photos back in the cabinet and turned away, tears burning in his eyes.

II

While Stott and Hatchley were interviewing Owen Pierce, Banks drove out to St. Mary's to see Lady Sylvie Harrison. He would have liked Susan with him, for her reactions and observations, but he knew he was risking Chief Constable Riddle's wrath by having anything more to do with the Harrisons, and he didn't want to get Susan into trouble.

She was right; she had worked hard and passed her sergeant's exam, all but the rubber stamp, and he wouldn't forgive himself easily if he ruined her chances of a quick promotion. He would be sad to lose her, though. Detective constables were rarely promoted straight to the rank of detective sergeant, and almost never in the same station; they usually went back in uniform for at least a year, then they had to reapply to the CID.

Before setting off, Banks had phoned the Harrison household and could hardly believe his luck. Sir Geoffrey was out with Michael Clayton, and Lady Harrison was at home alone. No, she said, with that faint trace of French accent, she would have no objections to talking to Banks without her husband present.

As he drove along North Market Street past the tourist shops and the community center where Sandra worked, Banks played the tape of Ute Lemper singing Michael Nyman's musical adaptations of Paul Celan's poems. It was odd music, and it had taken him some time to get used to it, but now he adored them all, found them pervaded by a sort of sinister melancholy.

It was a chilly day outside, gray and windy, skittering the leaves along the pavements. But at least the rain had stopped. Just as "Corona" was coming to an end, Banks pulled up at the end of the Harrisons' drive.

Lady Harrison must have heard him coming because she opened the large white door for him as soon as he got out of the car. She wore jeans and a blue cashmere pullover. She hugged herself against the cold as she stood in the doorway.

She had done her best to cover up the marks of misery and pain on her face, but they were still apparent through the make-up, like distant figures looming in the fog.

This time, instead of heading for the white room, she hung up his overcoat and led him to the kitchen, which was done in what Banks thought of as a sort of rustic French style: lots of wood paneling and cupboards, copper-bottomed pots and pans hanging on hooks on the wall, flower-patterned mugs on wooden pegs, a few potted plants, a vase of chrysanthemums on the table and a red-and-white checked tablecloth. The room smelled of herbs and spices, cinnamon and rosemary being the two most prominent. A kettle was just coming to the boil on the red Aga.

"Please sit down," she said.

Banks sat on a wooden chair at the kitchen table. Its legs scraped along the terracotta floor.

"Tea? I was just going to make some."

"Fine," said Banks.

"Ceylon, Darjeeling, Earl Gray or Lapsang Souchong?"

"Lapsang, if that's all right."

She smiled. "Exactly what I was going to have."

Her movements were listless and Banks noticed that the smile hadn't reached her eyes. It would probably be a long time before one did.

"Are you sure you're all right here alone, Lady Harrison?" he asked.

"Yes. Actually, it was *my* idea. I sent Geoffrey out. He was getting on my nerves. I needed a little quiet time to . . . to get used to things. What would be the point of us both moping around the house all day? He's used to action, to doing things. And please," she added with a fleeting smile, "call me Sylvie."

"Fine," he said. "Sylvie it is."

She measured out the leaves into a warmed pot—a rather squat, ugly piece with blue squiggles and a thick, straight spout—then sat down opposite Banks and let it brew.

"I'm sorry to intrude on your grief," Banks said. "But there are still a lot of questions need answering."

"Of course," said Sylvie. "But Geoffrey told me this morning that you already have a suspect. Is it true?"

Interesting, Banks thought. He hadn't realized there was a lodge meeting last night. Of course, as soon as Stott had tracked down Owen Pierce and sent his anorak off to the lab for analysis, Banks had let the chief constable know what was happening, and Riddle obviously hadn't wasted much time in reporting to Sir Geoffrey. Ah, privilege.

"Someone's helping us with our inquiries, yes," he said, immediately regretting the trite phrase. "I mean, last night we talked to someone who was seen in the area on Monday evening. Detective Inspector Stott is interviewing him again now."

"It's not that man from the church, the one who was fired?"

"We don't think so, but we're still keeping an open mind about him."

"Do you think this other person did it?"

"I don't know. I haven't talked to him yet. We're playing it very cautiously, very carefully. If he is the one, we want to be certain we don't make any mistakes that will come back to haunt us when the case goes to court."

"Sometimes," mused Sylvie, "it seems that the system favors the criminal rather than the victim. Don't you think?"

Tell me about it, thought Banks wearily. If they did think they'd got their man, next they would have to convince the Crown Prosecution Service they had a case—not always an easy job—then, after they had jumped through all the hoops, as often as not they could look forward to watching the accused's lawyer tear the evidence to shreds. "Sometimes," he agreed. "Did Deborah ever mention anyone called Owen Pierce?"

Sylvie frowned. "No. I've never heard the name before."

Banks described Pierce, but it meant nothing to her.

She poured the tea, tilting her head slightly and biting the end of her tongue as she did so. The Lapsang smelled and tasted good, its smoky flavor a perfect foil for a gray, cold November day. Outside, the wind whistled through the trees and rattled the windows, creating dust devils and gathering the fallen leaves into whirlwinds. Sylvie Harrison put both hands around her mug, as if keeping them warm. "What do you want to know from me?" she asked.

"I'm trying to find out as much as I can about what Deborah was like. There are still a few gaps."

"Such as?"

"Boyfriends, for example."

"Ah, boyfriends. But Deborah was far too busy at school for boys. There was plenty of time for that later. After she finished her education."

"Even so. There was the summer."

Sylvie held his gaze. "She didn't have a boyfriend."

Banks paused, then said slowly, feeling as if he were digging his career grave with every word, "That's not what I heard. Someone told me she had a boyfriend in August."

Sylvie paled. She pressed her lips so tight together they almost turned white.

"*Did* she have a boyfriend?" Banks asked again.

Sylvie sighed, then nodded. "Yes. In the summer. But she finished with him."

"Was his name John Spinks?"

She raised her eyebrows. "How did you know that?"

"You knew about him?"

She nodded. "Yes. He was a most unpleasant character."

"Why do you think a bright, pretty girl like Deborah would go out with someone like that?"

A distant look came into her eyes. "I don't know. I suppose he was good-looking, perhaps exciting in a way. Sometimes one makes mistakes," she said, with a shrug that Banks thought of as very Gallic. "Sometimes one makes a fool of oneself, does something with the wrong person for all the wrong reasons."

"What reasons?"

She shrugged again. "A woman's reasons. A young woman's reasons."

"Was Deborah having sex with John Spinks?"

Sylvie paused for a moment, then nodded and said with a sigh, "Yes. One day I came home unexpectedly and I caught them in Deborah's bedroom. I was crazy with anger. I shouted at him and threw him out of the house and told him never to come back."

"How did he react?"

She reddened. "He called me names I will not repeat in front of you."

"Was he violent?"

"He didn't hit me, if that's what you mean." She nodded in the direction of the hall. "There was a vase, not a very valuable vase, but a pretty one, a present from my father, on a stand by the door. He lifted it with both hands and threw it hard against the wall. One small chip of pottery broke off and cut my chin, that's all." She fingered the tiny scar.

"Did he leave after that?"

"Yes."

"Did you tell Sir Geoffrey about him?"

"No."

"Why not?"

She paused before answering. "You must understand that Geoffrey can be very Victorian in some ways, especially concerning Deborah. I hadn't even told him she was seeing the boy in the first place. He would have made things very uncomfortable for her if he'd known, given Spinks's character and background. I . . . well . . . I'm a woman, and I think in some ways I understood what she was going through, more than Geoffrey would have, anyway. I'm not saying I approved, but it was something she had to get out of her system. Stopping her would only have made her more determined. In the long run it would probably have resulted in even more damage. Do you know what I mean?"

"I think so. Did Deborah go on seeing Spinks?"

"No. I don't think so. Not after he threw the vase. She was very upset about what happened and we had a long talk. She said she was really sorry, and she apologized to me. I like to think that she understood what I was telling her, what a waste of time seeing this Spinks boy was. She said she realized now what kind of person he was and she would never go near him again. She'd heard him curse me in the most vile manner. She'd seen him throw the vase at the wall, seen the sliver cut me, draw blood." Sylvie touched the small scar again. "I think it truly shocked her, made her see him in a new light. Deborah is a good girl inside, Chief Inspector. Stubborn, willful, perhaps, but ultimately sensible too. And like a lot of girls her age, she is very naïve about men."

"In what ways?"

"She didn't understand the way they use women, manipulate them, or the power of their lust. I wanted her to learn to value herself. In sex, when the time came, as much as in everything else. Unless a woman respects her sexual self, she's going to be every man's victim all her life. Giving herself away to that . . . that *animal* was a bad way for her to start. You men don't always understand how important that time of a woman's life is."

"Was she a virgin before she met Spinks?"

Sylvie nodded and curled her lip in disgust. "She told me all about it that night after the row. He stole a car, like so many youths do these days. They went for a ride out on the moors. . . ." Her fists clenched as she talked. "And he did it to her in the back of the car."

"Had you met him before that time?"

She nodded. "Just once. It was two or three weeks earlier. Deborah brought him to the house. It was a sunny day. They were out making a barbecue when I got back from shopping in Leeds."

"What happened?"

"That time? Oh, nothing much. They were drinking. No doubt at the boy's instigation, Deborah had taken a bottle of my father's estate wine from the cellar. I was a little angry with them, but not too much. You must remember, Chief Inspector, that I grew up in France. We had wine with every meal, taken with a little water when we were children, so drinking under age hardly seems the great sin it does to you English."

"What was your impression of John Spinks?"

"He was very much a boy of single syllables. He didn't have much to say for himself at all. I'll admit I didn't like him right from the start. Call me a snob, if you like, but it's true. After he'd gone, I told her he wasn't good enough for her and that she should consider breaking off with him."

"How did she react to that?"

Sylvie smiled sadly. "The way any sixteen-year-old girl would. She told me she'd see who she wanted and that I should mind my own business and stop trying to run her life."

"Exactly what my daughter said in the same situation," said Banks. "Is there anything else you can tell me about Spinks?"

Sylvie sipped some tea, then she went to fetch her handbag. She slipped her hand inside and pulled out a packet of Dunhill. "You don't mind if I smoke, do you?" she asked. "Why I should ask permission in my own house, I don't know. It's just, these days . . . the anti-smoking brigade . . . they get to you. It's only in moments of stress I revert to the habit."

"I know what you mean," said Banks, pulling his Silk Cut out with a conspiratorial smile. "May I join you?"

"That would be even better. Geoffrey will go spare, of course. He thinks I've stopped."

The phrase "go spare" sounded odd with that sight French lilt to it; such a Yorkshire phrase, Banks thought.

"Your husband told me you're from Bordeaux," Banks said, accepting a light from her slim gold lighter.

Sylvie nodded. "My father is in the wine business. A *négociant.* One of *la noblesse du bouchon.*"

"I'm afraid my French is very rusty."

"Literally, it means 'the bottle-cork nobility.' It's a collective term for the *négociants* of a great wine center, like Bordeaux."

"I suppose it means he's rich?"

She wrinkled her nose. "Very. Anyway, I met Geoffrey when he was on a wine-tasting tour of the area. It must have been, oh, seventeen years ago. I was only nineteen at the time. Geoffrey was thirty."

"And Sir Geoffrey fell in love with the *négociant's* daughter? How romantic."

Sylvie dredged up another sad smile. "Yes, it was romantic." Then she drew deep on her cigarette and let the smoke out of her nose. "You asked if there was anything else about Spinks, Chief Inspector. Yes, there was. Things had been going missing from the house."

"Missing? Like what?"

She shrugged. "A silver snuffbox. Not very valuable, though it might look antique to the untrained eye. Some foreign currency. A pair of silver earrings. Little things like that."

"Since Deborah had been seeing Spinks?"

She nodded. "Yes. I'm almost certain of it. Deborah wouldn't do anything like that. I'm not saying she was a saint—obviously not—but at least she was honest. She was no thief."

"Did you challenge her about the stolen articles?"

"Yes."

"And what did she say?"

"She said she didn't know about the missing things but she would talk to him."

"Did she tell you what he said?"

"She said he denied it."

"Did Spinks ever bother either of you after that day you threw him out?"

Sylvie frowned and stubbed out her cigarette. She rubbed the back of her hand over her lips as if to get rid of the taste. "He made threats. One day, he came to the house when both Deborah and Geoffrey were out."

"What did he do?"

"He didn't *do* anything. Nothing physical, if that's what you mean. If he had, I wouldn't have hesitated to call the police. I tried to close the door on him, but he pushed his way in and asked for money."

"Did you give him any?"

"No."

"What did he say?"

"He said if I didn't give him money, he would keep on seeing Deborah, and that he would get her pregnant, make himself part of the family." She shuddered. "He was disgusting."

"And you still didn't give him anything?"

"No. Then he said if I didn't give him money he would start spreading the word around that he had deflowered Sir

Geoffrey Harrison's daughter. That she was nothing but a slut. He said he would spread it around St. Mary's and get her expelled, and he would make sure people in the business community knew so that they would all laugh at Geoffrey behind his back."

"What did you do?"

"Nothing. I was too shocked. Luckily, Michael was here at the time. He handled it."

"What did he do?"

"I don't know. You'll have to ask him. I was so upset I went upstairs. All I can say is that I heard nothing more of the matter after that. Spinks disappeared from our lives just as if he had never been there in the first place. Not without leaving some damage, of course."

"Did he ever threaten to harm Deborah physically?"

Sylvie shook her head. "Not that I heard."

"But he certainly seemed capable of acting violently?"

She touched her scar again. "Yes. Do you think . . . ?"

"I honestly don't know," said Banks. "But anything's possible. Did Mr. Clayton know about Spinks from the start?"

"Yes. He dropped by the house that time when they were having the barbecue. He said something to Spinks about the drinking and Spinks was very rude. Michael agreed with me then that Deborah was wasted on the boy. And I told him about . . . when I found them together in bed. I had to tell someone."

Clayton seemed to be dropping by Sir Geoffrey's house an awful lot, Banks thought. Especially when Sir Geoffrey wasn't there but Sylvie was.

"Does Mr. Clayton have any family of his own?" he asked.

"Michael? No. He and his wife, Gillian, split up three years ago. It was a childless marriage." She smiled. "I think part of the problem was that Michael is married to his work. Sometimes I think he has his computers wired directly to his brain. He has a girlfriend in Seattle now, and that seems ideal for him. Long-distance romance. He travels there quite often on company business."

"How long have he and Sir Geoffrey known one another?"

"Since Oxford. They've always been inseparable. In fact, Michael was with Geoffrey when we met."

Banks paused for a moment and sipped some lukewarm tea. "Do you know any of the teachers at St. Mary's?" he asked.

"Some of them. When you pay as much money to send your child to school as we do, you tend to have some say in the way the place is run."

"And?"

"And St. Mary's is an excellent school. Wonderful facilities, good staff, a healthy atmosphere . . . I could go on."

"Did you ever get the sense there was anything unpleasant going on there?"

"Unpleasant?"

"I'm sorry I can't be any more precise than that. But if anyone, or any group, was up to something at school—something illegal, such as drugs—and if Deborah found out about it. . . . She was attacked on her way home from school, after all. Someone could have followed her from there."

Sylvie shook her head slowly. "The things you policemen dream up. No, I never heard the slightest hint of a rumor of anything wrong at St. Mary's. And I believe one *does* hear about these things, if they are going on."

"Did you have any reason to think John Spinks or anyone else might have introduced Deborah to drugs?"

She sighed. "I can't say I didn't worry about it." Then she shook her head. "But I don't think so. I never saw any signs. Deborah was a very active girl. She valued her physical health, her athletic prowess, far too much to damage it with drugs."

"Do you know Patrick Metcalfe?"

"I've met him, yes."

"Did Deborah ever talk about him?"

"No, not that I recall."

"Did she like him?"

"She didn't say one way or the other. She did quite well at history, though it wasn't her best subject. But why do you ask?"

"He's just part of the tapestry, that's all. Maybe not an important part. Did Deborah have any contact with the church after you and your husband stopped going?"

"I don't think so. Geoffrey was quite adamant that we all stay away. But the school and the church remained close. She may have had some contact." She rubbed her eyes and stood up. "Please excuse me, Chief Inspector, but I'm feeling very tired. I think I've told you all I can for the moment. And I hope you'll be discreet. I'd prefer it if you didn't let Geoffrey know about what I've told you today."

Banks smiled. "Of course not. Not if you don't tell him I've been here. I'm afraid my boss—"

But before he could get the words out, the front door opened and shut and Sir Geoffrey shouted out, "I'm home, darling. How is everything?"

III

At the back of Eastvale bus station, past the noise of revving engines and the stink of diesel fumes, a pair of heavy glass doors led past the small newsagent's booth to an escalator that rarely worked.

At the top of the staircase, a shop-lined corridor ended in an open, glass-roofed area with a central fountain surrounded by a few small, tatty trees in wooden planters. The Swainsdale Center.

Several other corridors, leading from other street entrances, also converged like spokes at the hub. There were shops all around—HMV, Boots, W.H. Smith, Curry's, Dixon's—but at six-thirty that Wednesday evening, none of them were open. Only the small coffee shop was doing any business at all—if you could call two cups of tea and a Penguin biscuit in the last two hours "business."

The teenagers hung out around the fountain, usually leaning against the trees or sitting on the benches that had been put up for little old ladies to rest their feet. No little old ladies dared go near them now.

A number of pennies gleamed at the bottom of the pool into which the fountain ran. God knew why people felt they had to chuck coins in water, Banks thought. But the small pool was mostly full of floating cigarette ends, cellophane, Mars bar wrappers, beer tins, plastic bags containing traces of solvent, and the occasional used condom.

Banks experienced a brief flash of anger as he approached, imagining Tracy standing there as one of this motley crowd, smoking, drinking beer, pushing one another playfully, raising their voices in occasional obscenities or sudden whoops, and generally behaving as teenagers do.

Then he reminded himself, as he constantly had to do these days, that he hadn't been much different himself at their age, and that as often as not, beneath the braggadocio and the rough exteriors, most of them were pretty decent kids at heart.

Except John Spinks.

According to Tracy, Spinks was a hero of sorts among the group because of his oft-recounted but never-detected criminal exploits. She thought he made most of them up, but even she had to admit that he occasionally shared his ill-gotten gains with the others in the form of cigarettes and beer. As he didn't work and couldn't have got very much from the dole, he clearly had to supplement his income through criminal activities. And he never seemed short of a few quid for a new leather jacket.

He lived with his mum on the East Side Estate, a decaying monument to the sixties' social optimism, but he never talked much about his home life.

He had boasted of going to an "Acid House" party in Manchester once, Tracy said, and claimed he took Ecstasy there. He had also tried glue-sniffing, but thought it was kids' stuff and it gave you spots. He was proud of his clear complexion.

Spinks, standing a head taller than the rest, was immediately recognizable from Tracy's description. His light-brown hair was short at the back and sides, and long on top, with one long lock half-covering the left side of his face. He wore jeans, trainers with the laces untied and a mid-length flak jacket.

When Banks and Hatchley approached, showed their warrant cards and asked for a private little chat, he didn't run, curse them or protest, but simply shrugged and said, "Sure," then he gave his mates a sideways grin as he went.

They went into the coffee shop, took a table, and Hatchley fetched three coffees and a couple of chocolate biscuits. The owner's face lit up; it was more business than she'd done in ages.

In a way, Tracy was right; Spinks did resemble someone from "Neighbors." Clean cut, with that smooth complexion, he had full lips, perhaps a shade too red for a boy, brown eyes that could probably melt a young girl's heart, and straight, white teeth, the front ones stained only slightly by tobacco. He accepted the cigarette Banks offered and broke off the filter before smoking it.

"You Tracy Banks's dad, then?" he said.

"That's right."

"She said her father were a copper. Nice bit of stuff, Tracy is. I've had my eyes on her for a while. Come to think of it, I haven't seen her for a few weeks. What's she up to, these days?"

Banks smiled. It hadn't taken long to get past the good looks to the slimy, vain and cocky little creep underneath. Now he knew he wouldn't feel bad, no matter what he had to do to get Spinks to talk.

When Banks didn't answer, Spinks faltered only slightly before saying, "Why don't you ask her to drop by one evening? She knows where I am. We could have a really good time. Know what I mean?"

"One more remark like that," Hatchley cut in, "and you'll be mopping blood from your face for the rest of our little chat."

"Threats now, is it?" He shrugged. "What's it matter, anyway? I've already had the little bitch and she's not—"

The woman behind the counter looked over just after Spinks's face bounced off the table, and she hurried over with a cloth to stem the flow of blood from his nose.

"That's police brutality," Spinks protested, his words muffled by the cool, wet cloth. "Broke my fucking nose. Did you see that?"

"Me?" said the woman. "Didn't see nothing. And there's no call for that sort of language in here. You can keep the cloth." Then she scurried back behind the counter.

"Funny," said Banks, "I was looking the other way, too." He leaned forward. "Now listen you little arse-wipe, let's start again. Only this time, I ask the questions and you answer them. Okay?"

Spinks muttered a curse through the rag.

"Okay?" Banks asked again.

Spinks took the cloth away. The flow of blood seemed to have abated, and he only dabbed at it sulkily now and then throughout the interview. "You've broken my tooth," he whined. "That'll cost money. I was only joking, anyway, about your—"

"Deborah Harrison," Banks said. "Name ring a bell?"

Spinks averted his eyes. "Sure. It's that schoolkid from St. Mary's got herself killed the other day. All over the news."

"She didn't 'get herself' killed. Someone murdered her."

"Whatever." The lock of hair kept slipping down over Spinks's eye, and he had developed the habit of twitching his head to flick it back in place. "Don't look at me. I didn't kill her."

"Where were you on Monday around six o'clock?"

"Was that the day it was really foggy?"

"Yes."

"I was here." He pointed to the group outside. "Ask anyone. Go on, ask them."

Banks nodded at Sergeant Hatchley, who went out to talk to the youths.

"Besides," Spinks went on, "why would I want to kill her?"

"You went out together over the summer and you parted on bad terms. You were angry with her, you wanted revenge."

He probed his tooth and winced. "That's a load of old knob-rot, that is. Besides, they wasn't supposed to tell you that."

"Who wasn't?"

"*Them.* The French tart and that bloody Clayton. They went to enough trouble to stop *me* from telling anyone, now they go and tell you themselves. Bloody stupid, it is. Doesn't make sense. Unless they just wanted to drop me in it." He dabbed at his red nose.

Hatchley came back inside and nodded.

"They telling the truth?" Banks asked.

"Hard to say. Like Jelačić's mates, they'd probably say black was white if young Lochinvar over here told them to."

Banks studied Spinks, who showed no emotion, but kept dabbing at his nose and probing his tooth with his tongue. "What did Michael Clayton do to stop you from talking?" he asked.

Spinks looked down into the bloodstained rag. "Imagine how it would sound if some newspaper got hold of the story that an East Side Estate yobbo like me had been sticking it to Sir Geoffrey Harrison's daughter."

"That's *why*. I asked you *what*."

"Gave me some money."

"Who did?"

"Clayton."

"Michael Clayton gave you money to stay away from Deborah?"

"That's what I said."

"How much?"

"Hundred quid."

"So you admit to blackmailing Lady Harrison?"

"Nothing of the sort. Look, if you sell a story to the papers, they pay you for it, don't they? So why shouldn't you get paid if you *don't* sell the papers a story?"

"Your logic is impeccable, John. I can see you didn't waste your time in school."

Spinks laughed. "School? Hardly ever there, was I?"

"Was Deborah there when you went to ask for money?"

"Nah. Just the two of them. Clayton and the old bag." He put on a posh accent. "It was Deborah's day for riding, don't you know. *Dressage.* Got a horse out Middleham way. Always did like hot flesh throbbing between her legs, did Deborah."

"So the two of them had a talk with you?"

"That's right."

"And after Lady Harrison had gone upstairs, Michael Clayton hit you and gave you a hundred pounds."

"Like I said, we came to an arrangement. Then her ladyship came back and said if she ever heard I'd been talking about her daughter, she *would* tell Sir Geoffrey and he'd probably have me killed."

"You blackmailed her and she threatened you with murder?"

"Yeah. Get away with anything, those rich fuckers. Just like the pigs."

"You've been listening to too many Jefferson Airplane records, John. They don't call us pigs now."

"Once a pig, always a pig. And it's compact discs now, not *records.* Jefferson Airplane, indeed. You're showing your age."

"Oh, spare us the witty repartee. Did you see Deborah again after that?"

"No."

"Did you ever have anything to do with St. Mary's Church, with Daniel Charters and his wife, or with Ive Jelačić?"

"Church? Me? You must be fucking joking."

"Did Deborah ever mention an important secret she had?"

"What secret?"

"You're not being very co-operative, Johnny."

"I don't know anything about no secret. And my name's John. What you gonna do? Arrest me?"

Banks took a sip of coffee. "I don't know yet. If you didn't kill Deborah, who do you think did?"

"Some psycho."

"Why are you so sure?"

"I saw it on telly. That's what they said."

"You believe everything you hear on telly?"

"Well if it wasn't a psycho, who was it?"

Banks sighed and lit another cigarette. This time he didn't offer Spinks one. "That's what *I'm* asking *you*." He snapped his fingers. "Come on, wake up, John boy."

Spinks dabbed at his nose; it had stopped bleeding now. "How should I know?"

"You knew her. You spent time with her. Did she have any enemies? Did she ever talk to you about her life?"

"What? No. Mostly we just fucked, if you want to know the truth. Apart from that, she was boring. Always on about horses and school. And always bloody picking on things I said and the way I said them."

"Well, she was an educated woman, John. I realize it would have been hard for you to keep up with her intellectually."

"Like I said, she was only good for one thing."

"I understand you once stole a car and took Deborah for a joyride?"

"I . . . Now, hang on just a minute. I don't know who's been spreading vicious rumors about me, but I never stole no car. Can't even drive, can I?" He took a pouch of Drum from his flak-jacket pocket and rolled a cigarette.

"What about drugs?"

"Never touch them. Stay clean. That's my motto."

"I'll bet if we had a look through his pockets," said Sergeant Hatchley, "we'd probably find enough to lock him up for."

Banks stared at Spinks for a moment, as if considering the idea. He saw something shift in the boy's eyes. Guilt. Fear.

"No," he said, standing up. "He's not worth the paperwork. We'll leave him be for the moment. But," he went on,
"we'll probably be back, so don't wander too far. I want you
to know you're looking good for this, John. You've got quite
a temper, so we hear, and you had every reason to hold a
grudge against the victim. And one more thing."

Spinks raised his eyebrows. Banks leaned forward, rested
his hands on the table and lowered his voice. "If I ever catch
you within a mile of my daughter, you'll think that bloody nose
Sergeant Hatchley gave you was a friendly pat on the back."

IV

At home later that evening, after dinner, when Tracy had
gone up to her room to do her homework, Banks and Sandra
found a couple of hours to themselves at last. With Elgar's
first symphony playing quietly on the stereo, Banks poured
himself a small Laphroaig and Sandra a Drambuie with ice.
He wouldn't smoke tonight, not at home, he decided, even
though the peaty bite of the Islay almost screamed out for an
accompaniment of nicotine.

First, Banks told Sandra about John Spinks and his visit
to Sylvie Harrison.

"I thought the chief constable ruled the family off-limits,"
she said.

"He did." Banks shrugged. "Actually, I just escaped by the
skin of my teeth. Sir Geoffrey came in and caught me talking to her. A word in Jimmy Riddle's ear and my name
would be mud. Luckily, Lady Harrison didn't want him to
know we'd been talking about Deborah's boyfriend, so she
told him I'd just dropped by to give them a progress report.
He was more annoyed that she'd been smoking than he was
about my presence."

"This Spinks," Sandra said. "He sounds like a bad character. Do you think Tracy had anything to do with him?"

Banks shook his head. "He was part of the crowd, that's all. She's got more sense than that."

"Deborah Harrison obviously didn't have."

"We all make mistakes." Banks stood up and walked towards the hall.

"Oh, go on," Sandra said with a smile. "Have a cigarette if you want one. It's been a tough day at the gallery. I might even join you." Sandra had stopped smoking some years ago, but she seemed able to cheat occasionally without falling back into the habit. Banks envied her that.

As it turned out, Banks hadn't been going for his cigarettes but for the photograph that Stott and Hatchley had got from Owen Pierce. Still, not being one to look a gift horse in the mouth, he weakened and brought the Silk Cut from his overcoat pocket.

Once they had both lit up and the Elgar was moving into the adagio, Banks slid the photograph out of the envelope and passed it to Sandra.

"What do you think?" he asked.

"Very pretty. But not your type, surely. Her breasts are too small for your taste."

"That's not what I meant. And I've got nothing against small breasts."

Sandra dug her elbow in his side and smiled. "I'm teasing."

"You think I didn't know that? Seriously, though, what do you think? Professionally."

Sandra frowned. "It's not *her,* is it? Not the girl who was killed?"

"No. Do you see a resemblance, though?"

Sandra shifted sideways and held the photo under the shaded lamp. "Yes, a bit. The newspaper photo wasn't very good, mind you. And teenage girls are still, in some ways, unformed. If they've got similar hair color and style, and they're about the same height and shape, you can construe a likeness easily enough."

"Apparently she's not a teenager. She was twenty-two when that was taken."

Sandra raised her dark eyebrows. "Would we could all look so many years younger than we are."

"What do you think of the style?"

"As a photograph, it's good. Very good in fact. It's an excellent composition. The pose looks natural and the lighting is superb. See how it brings out that hollow below the breasts and the ever-so slight swell of her tummy? You can even see where the light catches the tiny hairs on her skin. And it has a mood, too, a unity. There's a sort of secret smile on her face. A bit Mona Lisa-ish. A strong rapport with the photographer."

"Do you think she knew him?"

Sandra studied the photograph for a few seconds in silence, Elgar playing softly in the background. "They were lovers," she said finally. "I'll bet you a pound to a penny they were lovers."

"Women's intuition?"

Sandra gave him another dig in the ribs. Harder this time. Then she passed him the photo. "No. Just look at her eyes, Alan, the laughter, the way she's looking at him. It's obvious."

When he looked more closely, Banks knew that Sandra was right. It *was* obvious. Men and women only looked like that at one another when they had slept together, or were about to. He couldn't explain why, certainly couldn't offer any proof or evidence, but like Sandra, he *knew*. And Barry Stott had said that Pierce denied knowing the woman. The next job, then, was to find her and discover why. Banks would wait for the initial forensic results, then he'd have a long chat with Owen Pierce himself.

Chapter 8

I

The man who sat before Banks in the interview room at two o'clock that Saturday afternoon looked very angry. Banks didn't blame him. He would have been angry, himself, if two hulking great coppers had come and dragged him off to the police station on his day off, especially with it being Remembrance Day, too.

But it couldn't be helped. Banks would rather have been at home listening to Britten's *War Requiem* as he did every November 11, but it would have to wait. New information had come in. It was time for him to talk to Owen Pierce in person.

"Relax, Owen," said Banks. "We're probably going to be here for a while, so there's no point letting your blood pressure go right off the scale."

"Why don't you just get on with it," Owen said. "I've got better things to do with my time."

Banks sighed. "Me, too, Owen. Me too." He put new tapes in the double-cassette recorder, then he told Owen that the interview was being taped, and, as before, stated the names of everyone in the room, along with the time, place and date.

Susan Gay was the only other person present. Her role was mostly to observe, but Banks would give her the chance to ask a question or two. They were taking a "fresh team" approach—so far only Stott and Hatchley had interviewed Pierce—and Banks had already spent a couple of hours that morning going over the previous interview transcripts.

"Okay," Banks began, "first let me caution you that you do not *have* to say anything, but if you do not mention now something which you later use in your defense, the court may decide that your failure to mention it strengthens the case against you. A record will be made of anything you say and it may be given in evidence if you are brought to trial."

Owen swallowed. "Does this mean I'm under arrest?"

"No," said Banks. "It's just a formality, so we all know what's what. I understand you've been informed about your right to a solicitor?"

"Yes."

"And you've waived it?"

"For the moment, yes. I keep telling you, I haven't done anything. Why should I have to pay for a solicitor?"

"Good point. They can be very expensive. Now then, Owen, can we just go over last Monday evening one more time, please?"

Owen sighed and told them exactly the same as he had told Stott the last time and the time before that.

"And you never, at any time that day, had contact with the victim, Deborah Harrison?"

"No. How could I? I had no idea who she was."

"You're quite sure you didn't meet her?"

"I told you, no."

"Why were you in the area?"

"Just walking."

"Oh, come on. Do you think I was born yesterday, Owen? Hey? You had a meeting with Deborah, didn't you? You knew her."

"Don't be ridiculous. How could I know someone like her?"

Banks reached down into his briefcase and pushed the photograph across the desk. "Who's this?" he asked.

"Just a model."

"Look at it, Owen. Look closely. You *know* her. Any idiot can see that."

Banks watched Owen turn pale and lick his lips. "I don't know what you mean," he said. "She was just a model."

"Bollocks she was just a model. Have you noticed her resemblance to the murdered girl?" Banks set a photograph of Deborah Harrison next to it.

Owen looked away. "I can't say I have."

"Look again."

Owen looked and shook his head. "No."

"And you still maintain that you've never met Deborah Harrison?"

"That's right." He looked at his watch. "Look, when is this farce going to end? I've got work to do."

Banks glanced over at Susan and nodded. She leaned forward and placed two labeled packages on the desk. "The thing is, Owen," Banks said, "that this evidence shows otherwise."

"Evidence? What evidence?"

"Hair, Owen. Hair." Banks tapped the first envelope. "To cut a long story short, this envelope contains samples of hairs taken from those we found on the anorak you were wearing on Monday evening when you went for your walk, the one you gave us permission to test. There are a number of hairs that our experts have identified as coming from the head of Deborah Harrison."

Owen grasped the edge of the desk. "But they can't be! You must be mistaken."

Banks shook his head gravely. "Oh, I could bore you with the scientific details about the medulla and the cortex and so on, but you can take my word for it—they match."

Owen said nothing. Susan pushed the other package forward. "Now this," Banks said, "contains hair samples taken from Deborah Harrison's school blazer. Oddly enough, some of these hairs have been positively identified as yours, again matched with the samples you freely allowed us to take the other day." Banks sat back and folded his arms. "I think you've got quite a bit of explaining to do, haven't you, Owen?"

"You're trying to set me up. Those hairs aren't mine. They can't be. You're lying to get me to confess, aren't you?"

"Confess to what, Owen?"

Owen smiled. "You're not going to catch me out as easily as that."

Banks leaned forward and rested his palm on the desk. "Read my lips, Owen," he said. "We're not lying. The hairs are yours."

Owen ran his hand through his hair. "Wait a minute. There must be some simple explanation for this. There's got to be."

"I hope so," said Banks. "I'd really like to hear it."

Owen bit his lip and concentrated. "The only thing I can think of," he said after a few moments, "is that when I was on the bridge, someone bumped into me. It all happened so fast. I was turning from looking over the river, and she knocked the wind out of me. I didn't get a really good look because she disappeared into the fog and I only saw her from behind, but I think she had long fair hair and wore a maroon blazer and skirt. It could have been her, couldn't it? That *could* have been how it happened, couldn't it?"

Banks frowned and looked through the notes in front of him. "I don't understand, Owen. When you talked to DI Stott and DS Hatchley you didn't say anything about this."

"I know." Owen looked away. "At first I just forgot, then, well . . . when I remembered, when I'd seen the paper and knew why they'd been questioning me . . . Well, I'd already not said anything, so I suppose I was worried it would look bad if I spoke up then."

"Look bad? But how could it, Owen? How could it look bad if you simply said the girl might have bumped into you? What were you afraid of?"

"Yes, but I mean, if it really *had* been Deborah Harrison . . . I don't know. Besides, I couldn't be *sure* it was her.

It just seemed like the best thing to do at the time. Keep quiet. It didn't seem important. I'm sorry if it caused you any problems."

"Caused *us* any problems? Not really, Owen. But it has caused you quite a few. It's funny you should mention it now, though, isn't it, now we've matched the hair samples?"

"Yes, well . . . I told you. Look, you can check, can't you? Didn't her friend see me? I could just see her through the fog."

Banks tapped the two envelopes. "What if she did see you? That doesn't help your case at all, does it? In fact, it makes things worse."

"But I never denied being on the bridge."

"No. But you led us to believe you didn't see Deborah Harrison. Now you're changing your story. I'd like to know why."

"I was confused, that's all."

"I understand that, Owen. But why didn't you tell the detectives who first interviewed you that you'd seen Deborah that night?"

"I told you. It slipped my mind. After all, I had no idea *why* the detectives were talking to me. Then later, when I knew . . . well, I was worried that this was exactly the kind of thing that would happen if I did tell you, that you would misconstrue it."

"Misconstrue?"

"Yes. Misinterpret, distort, misunderstand."

"I know what the word means, Owen," said Banks. "I don't need a bloody thesaurus, thank you very much. I just don't see how it applies in your case."

"I'm sorry. Just put it down to an English teacher's pedantry. What I mean is, I thought you'd read more into it, that's all. When you get right down to it, it's not very much in the way of evidence, is it? You have to admit." Owen attempted a smile, but it came out crooked. "I mean, a couple of hairs. Hardly enough to stand up in court, is it?"

"Don't get clever with me, sonny."

"I . . . I wasn't. I was just pointing out, that's all."

"But we don't know *how* the hairs got where they did, do we?"

"That's what I'm saying. Maybe it happened when she bumped into me."

"If it was her who bumped into you."

"I can't think of any other explanation."

"But I can. See, you've lied to us before, Owen. To DI Stott and DS Hatchley. Why should we believe you now?"

Owen swallowed. His Adam's apple bumped up and down. "Lied?"

"Well, you never told us about seeing Deborah, or about bumping into her for that matter. That's a lie of a kind, isn't it? You might call it a lie of omission. And you also said you didn't know the girl in the photo, but you do know her, don't you?"

"No. I—"

Banks sighed. "Look, Owen, I'm giving you a chance to dig yourself out of this hole before it's too late. We've talked to the landlord of the Nag's Head again, showed him the picture of this 'model.' He says you've been in the pub with her on a number of occasions. He's *seen* you together. What do you have to say about that?"

Banks noticed the sweat start beading on Owen's forehead. "All right, I know her. Knew her. But I don't see how it's relevant in any way. She was my girlfriend. We lived together. Does that satisfy you?"

"Who is she? Where is she now? What happened to her?"

Owen put his hands over his ears. "I don't believe I'm hearing this. Surely you can't think that I've killed Michelle, too?"

"Too? As well as who?"

"For Christ's sake. It's a figure of speech."

"I'd have thought a pedantic English teacher like yourself would be more careful with his figures of speech."

"Yes, well, I'm upset."

"This Michelle, what happened?"

"We lived together for nearly five years, then we split up over the summer. Simple as that."

"And where is she now?"

"She lives in London. In Swiss Cottage."

"Why did you split up?"

"Why does anyone split up?"

"Irreconcilable differences?" Banks suggested.

Owen laughed harshly. "Yes. That'll do. Irreconcilable differences. You could call it that."

"What would *you* call it?"

"It's none of your business. But there is something else. It's got nothing to do with this at all, but if it'll help . . ."

"Yes?"

"Well, it's the reason I was out walking. It was the anniversary. The anniversary of the day we met. I was a little down, a bit sad. We used to go for walks by the river, as far as St. Mary's, or even further, and we'd sometimes drop in at the Nag's Head to wet our whistles. So I just went for that long walk to get it out of my system."

"You were upset?"

"Of course I was upset. I loved her."

"And did you get it out of your system?"

"To a certain extent."

"How did you get it out of your system?"

"Oh, this is absurd. You've got a one-track mind. There's no point talking to you any more."

"Maybe not, Owen. But you've got to admit things are looking pretty bleak. You lied to us *four* times." He counted them off on his fingers. "Once about why you were out walking, once about never meeting Deborah Harrison, once about not knowing the girl in the photo and once again about never having lived with anyone. All lies, Owen. You see what a position it puts me in?"

"But they were all so . . . such small lies. Yes, all right, I lied. I admit it. But that's all. I haven't harmed anyone."

At that point came the soft knock at the door that Banks had arranged earlier. He turned off the tape recorders and told the person to come in. DI Stott entered, nodded quickly at Owen Pierce and apologized for disturbing them. Then he handed a report to Banks and stood by the door.

Banks glanced over the sheets of paper, taking his time, pretending he didn't already know the information they contained. When he had finished, he passed them to Susan. All the time, he was aware of Owen's discomfort and restlessness. Susan read the report and raised her eyebrows. Banks thought they were overacting a bit, behaving like doctors who had just looked at the X-rays and found out their patient had an inoperable tumor. But it was working. Pierce was really sweating now.

Banks turned the tape recorders on again, explaining briefly why he had turned them off and adding that DI Stott was now also in the room. "Results of the blood tests," he said to Owen.

"What blood tests?"

"Remember, we took samples the other day?"

"Yes, but . . ."

"With your permission."

"I know, but—"

"Well, we also found a small dried bloodstain on your anorak, and according to this report, Owen, it's Deborah Harrison's blood group, not yours. Can you explain that?"

"I . . . I . . ."

The three detectives remained silent for a few moments as Owen struggled for an explanation. Then Banks spoke up again. "Come on, Owen," he said. "Tell us about it. It'll do you good."

Owen slammed his fist on the table. "There's nothing to tell! I saw a girl. She bumped into me. Then she ran off. She *might* have been Deborah Harrison. It was foggy. I didn't get a clear enough look. That's all that happened. I don't know how her blood got there. You're trying to frame me. You're planting evidence."

"You're starting to sound a bit desperate now, Owen,"

Banks said. "Clutching at straws. Why don't you calm down and tell us all about it?"

"But *why* would I have killed the girl? What possible reason could I have? Why don't you believe me?"

"Because you didn't tell us the truth. That means you had something to hide. And there's something else, too."

"What?"

"We found your blood under Deborah Harrison's fingernails. What do you have to say to that?"

"Nothing," Owen said, "I want a solicitor. Now. I'm not saying another word until I get a solicitor."

"That's your right," said Banks. "But just hear me out for a moment before you do or say anything else. You'll feel much better if you just tell us what happened. And it'll go better for you in the long run. When you saw Deborah Harrison on the bridge, she reminded you of this Michelle, didn't she? The girl you were upset about. Were you punishing Michelle through Deborah, Owen? Is that what all this was about? What did she do to you?"

Owen broke off eye contact. "Nothing," he said. "This is all just speculation. It's rubbish."

"You followed her into the graveyard and you approached her, didn't you?" Banks went on, resting his elbows on the desk and speaking softly. "Maybe you offered her a fiver to toss you off so you could pretend it was Michelle doing it. Whatever. It doesn't matter. But she reacted badly. She got scared. You dragged her off the path, behind the Inchcliffe Mausoleum. It was dark and foggy and quiet there. You were going to give her what for, weren't you? Give it to her good and proper just to show her she couldn't do what she did to you and get away with it? All your anger burst out, didn't it, Owen? What happened? Couldn't you get it up? What did Michelle do to you? It *was* her you were strangling, wasn't it? Why did you lie about knowing her?"

Owen put his head in his hands and groaned. Banks packed up his papers, stood and nodded to Stott, who said,

"Owen Pierce, you have already been cautioned and now we're going to put you under arrest. I'm going to ask you to come with me to the custody officer. Do you understand me, Owen?"

II

Stott had called it the "custody suite" on the way down, and the sign on the door said "Charge Room," but to Owen it resembled nothing less than the entrance to hell. Abandon all hope . . .

It was a cavernous room in the basement of the old Tudor-fronted Eastvale Regional HQ, full of noise and activity. Saturday afternoon was one of the busiest times in the Eastvale custody suite. Today, in addition to the usual Saturday bouts of shoplifting, hooliganism and drunkenness, Eastvale United were playing at home to arch-rivals, Ripon, and there had already been plenty of violence both on and off the field.

The flaking paint had obviously once been an attempt at a cheerful lemon color; now it looked like a nicotine stain. Owen sat between Stott and Hatchley on a hard bench opposite elevated, joined desks, screwed to the floor, that ran the whole length of the room like a counter. Behind the desks, about six or seven uniformed police officers typed, bustled about, shouted, laughed, filled in forms and questioned people, presided over by the custody sergeant himself. The contrast between the real smell of fear and this slick, bureaucratic activity brought, for Owen, its special brand of terror, like a hospital casualty department where ripped flesh bleeds and pristine machines hiss and beep.

At the moment, a drunk with a bloody face leaned over the desk singing "Danny Boy" at the custody sergeant, who was trying to get his personal details. On the benches near Owen sat a couple of gloomy skinheads, laces missing from their bovver boots; a man who resembled nothing more than a bank clerk, perhaps an embezzler, Owen thought; and a nervous-looking young woman, smartly dressed, biting her lip. A kleptomaniac?

Another man at the desk started arguing with one of the officers about being picked on because he was black. The drunk paused in his song to look over and shout, "Bloody right, too. Ought to go back to the bloody jungle where you came from, Sambo," then he emitted a technicolor whoosh of vomit all over the desk and sank to his knees on the floor to clutch his stomach and whimper. The sergeant swore and jumped backwards, but he wasn't quick enough to prevent some of the vomit from spattering the front of his uniform.

"Get that bastard out of here!" he yelled. In the room's eerie acoustics, his voice rose, echoed wildly, then fell dead.

Adrenalin pumped through Owen's system. He took a couple of deep breaths to calm himself and almost gagged on the stink of vomit and ammonia cleaning fluid that permeated the stale air.

An officer filled in names, numbers, charges and times with a black marker on a white board. Posters covered the walls: one gave a graphic warning about the possible consequences of driving while drunk; one informed prisoners of their rights; a third showed sign language; another advised officers to wear gloves when dealing with vomit and blood due to possible AIDS and Hepatitis B exposure.

Two officers dragged the drunk out and another started clearing up the mess with a mop, cloth and a bucket of Lysol. He was wearing plastic gloves. Blood had dripped on the pale green linoleum. Even the skinheads looked cowed by it all.

Owen kept trying to convince himself that the nightmare would end any moment and he would wake up and find himself out shopping with the rest of the Saturday crowd. Perhaps he would go to HMV in the Swainsdale Center and buy the new Van Morrison CD. Then, maybe a pint or two and a nice dinner out, Chinese or Indian, just to celebrate. Alone, the way he liked it best.

Or perhaps the policemen would rip off their uniforms to

reveal clowns' costumes underneath, and Stott would break into a song and dance number, like characters out of a Dennis Potter play.

As soon as the custody sergeant was free, Stott went over and had a brief word, then gestured for Owen to approach the desk. Stott disappeared through the far door.

"Empty your pockets, please, sunshine," said the sergeant, after taking Owen's personal details.

Owen emptied his pockets onto the desk. There wasn't much in them: keys, wallet, three pounds sixty-eight pee in change, check book, bank machine and credit cards, a few crumpled shopping lists and old bus tickets that had been through the washer and dryer a couple of times, his gold Cross fountain-pen, the small Lett's appointment diary-cum-address book with the pencil tucked down the spine, three pieces of Dentyne chewing-gum and a few balls of fluff.

The sergeant flipped through Owen's diary. It was empty apart from a few addresses. Next he looked through Owen's wallet. "Nothing much there," he said, placing it in the plastic bag with the other items. He held the pen between thumb and forefinger and said, "Gold-looking fountain-pen."

"It *is* gold," Owen said. "It's not just gold-looking."

"Well we're not going to get a bloody appraiser in, mate, are we?" the sergeant said. "Gold-looking." He dropped it in the bag.

Before they sealed the bag, a constable patted Owen down to see if he had anything else hidden.

"Shall we have a look up his arse, sir?" he asked the custody sergeant when he had finished.

The sergeant looked at Owen, then back at the constable, as if he were seriously considering the proposition. "Nah," he said. "I never did like rectal searches, myself. Messy business. Never know what you might find. Take him to the studio."

Jesus Christ, thought Owen, they're enjoying this! They don't need to be rude, violent and brutal; they get their kicks better this way, the vicious tease, the cruel joke. They had already judged and condemned him. In their minds, he was guilty, and the rest would be mere formality. And if they believed it, wouldn't everyone else?

When they put him jail, he thought with a stab of fear, it would be even worse. He had heard about the things that went on, how people like the Yorkshire Ripper and Dennis Nilsen had to be kept in solitary for their own good, how Jeffrey Dahmer had been murdered in prison and Frederick West had hanged himself.

Solitary confinement would probably be better than a poke up the bum from a three-hundred-pound Hell's Angel with tattoos on his cock, Owen thought. But could he stand the loneliness, the feeling of being hopelessly cut off from everything he held dear, abandoned by the whole civilized world? He liked the solitary life, but that was his choice. Could he stand it when it was imposed on him?

The constable led him into another room for fingerprinting and mug shots taken by a mounted camera. The "studio." Another cruel joke.

"Now then, mate," the constable said, "let's have your belt and shoelaces."

"What? Why on earth—"

"Regulations. So's you don't top yourself, see."

"But I'm not going to do away with myself. I've told you all. I'm innocent."

"Aye. Well, it doesn't matter. It's more than my job's worth. We'd have your tie too if you were wearing one. Saw a fellow once topped himself with his tie. Polka-dot tie it was. A nice one. You should've seen him, eyes all bulging and his tongue sticking out. And the pong, you wouldn't believe it! Aye, nasty business, it was. Don't worry, mate, you'll get your things back—that's if you're ever in a position to need them again."

He had a good laugh at that while Owen took the belt off his jeans and the long white laces from his trainers.

Back at the desk, the custody sergeant gave Owen a pamphlet on legal aid and sheet of paper that advised him of his rights: to call a solicitor, to inform a friend, and to consult the Codes of Practice. Then he went over to scrawl details on the board.

"I want to call my solicitor," Owen said.

The sergeant shrugged and gestured to the constable again, who escorted Owen to a telephone. He felt in his inside pocket for his address-book, where he had politely jotted down Wharton's number, but realized it had been taken away along with all his other possessions. He turned to the constable.

"The phone number," he said. "It's in my diary. Can I get it back for a minute?"

"Sorry," the constable replied. "Against regulations. It's all been entered and bagged."

"But I can't remember my solicitor's number."

"Best try this, then." He pulled a dog-eared telephone directory from the desk drawer. "It usually works."

Owen flipped through and managed to find Gordon Wharton's office number. He got an answering machine, and even though it was late on Saturday afternoon, left an urgent message anyway, just in case. Then he tried the listed home number, but got no answer. "What now?" he asked the constable.

"Cells." Another constable appeared beside them. They took Owen gently by the elbows and led him back into the corridor. "Nothing to worry about," the first officer said. "Quite comfortable really. More like a hospital ward. Most modern part of the whole building."

Police boots echoed from the greenish-blue walls and high ceiling as the three of them walked down the hallway. At the end, the constable took out a key and opened a heavy, hinged door.

True, the cell wasn't the dank, dripping dungeon Owen had imagined; it was actually very clean, all white tiles, like a public urinal, and bright light from bulbs covered by wire mesh.

It contained a narrow bed, fixed to the wall and floor, with a thin mattress, a washstand and a seatless toilet made of molded orange plastic. There was only one window, set high and deep in the wall, about a foot square and almost as thick. The door had a flap for observation. A faint odor of dead skin and old sweat lurked under the smell of disinfectant.

"Sorry there's no telly," said one of the jailers, "but you can have something to read if you like. A book, maybe, or a magazine?" He turned to his companion. "Jock here's probably got an issue or two of *Playboy* hidden away at the back of his desk."

Owen ignored the taunt. He simply shook his head and stared around in amazement at the cell.

"Owt to eat?" the jailer asked.

When he thought about it, Owen realized that he *was* hungry. He said yes.

"The special's steak and kidney pud today. Or there's fish and chips, sausage and—"

"Steak and kidney pud sounds just fine," Owen said.

"Mug of tea? Milk and sugar?"

Owen nodded. This is bloody absurd, he thought, almost unable to contain his laughter. Here I am, sitting in a cell in the bowels of the Eastvale police station putting in an order for steak and kidney pudding and a mug of tea!

"You won't be here long," said the jailer. "And if it wasn't a weekend we'd have you up before the beak tomorrow. Anyway, just so's you know, you'll be well treated. You'll get three square meals a day, a bit of exercise if you want it, reading material, pen and paper if you want—"

"We can't give him a pen, Ted," said Jock. "He might . . . you know . . . Remember that bloke who . . . ?" He drew his forefinger across his throat and made a gurgling sound.

"Aye, you're right." Ted turned back to Owen. "We had a bloke once tried to cut his throat with a fountain-pen. Messy. And another jabbed a pencil right through his eye socket. A yellow HB, if I recollect it right." He shook his head slowly. "Sorry lad, you'll have to wait for writing privileges. It's our responsibility, see. Anything else you want, though, just let us know. As I always say, just ring the bell and ask for room service."

They laughed and walked out into the corridor. The heavy door slammed shut behind them.

III

"So what do you think, sir?" Susan Gay asked over the noise, handing Banks the pint she had just bought him.

"Thanks. Looks like I was wrong, doesn't it?" Banks said, with a shrug.

The Queen's Arms was buzzing with conversation and ringing with laughter that Saturday evening. Rumors had leaked out that the "Eastvale Strangler" was in the holding cells and all was well with the world. Parents could once again rest easy in their beds; just about every phone, fax and modem in town was tied up by the press; and those police who were off duty were celebrating their success. The only things missing were the fireworks and the brass band.

Banks sat next to Susan Gay, with Hatchley and Stott not far away. Stott looked like the cat that got the cream.

Chief Constable Riddle had visited the station earlier, patting backs and bragging to the media. He hadn't wasted the opportunity to admonish Banks for pestering the Harrisons; nor had he neglected to praise Stott for his major role in what was probably the quickest arrest of a sex murderer ever.

This time, Riddle was going to go and tell the Harrisons personally that he had a man in custody for Deborah's murder, largely due to the efforts of a new member of Eastvale CID, DI Barry Stott. Of course, Riddle wouldn't be seen dead drinking in a pub with the common foot-soldiers, even if he didn't have a couple of TV interviews lined up. Thank God for small mercies, Banks thought.

As he sipped his pint and let the conversation and laughter ebb and flow around him, Banks wondered why he felt so depressed. Never one to shy away from self-examination, he considered professional jealousy first.

But was that really true? Banks had to admit that it would only look that way to the chief constable and one or two others who had it in for him. As far as the media were concerned, Detective Chief Inspector Alan Banks had headed the most successful investigation in the history of Eastvale Divisional Headquarters. *His* troops had won the battle. He was the general. So why did he feel so depressed?

"The evidence is pretty solid, isn't it, sir?" Susan shouted in his ear.

Banks nodded. It was. Nothing on the shoes that Pierce couldn't have picked up on the river path, but positive blood and hair matches both ways. His and hers. Suspect a bit of an oddball. A liar, to boot. Seen in the area, with no good reason, around the time of the murder. Oh, yes, Banks admitted, even the Crown Prosecution Service should have no trouble with this one. What could be better? And if the DNA results were positive when they came through . . .

He looked at Susan. Earnest expression on her round face, with its peaches and cream complexion; short, slightly up-turned nose; tight blonde curls. She had a glass of St. Clement's in front of her.

Banks smiled, trying to shake off his gloom. "Let me buy you a drink, Susan," he said. "A *real* drink. What would you like?"

"I shouldn't, sir, really . . ." Susan said. "I mean, you know, officially . . ."

"Bugger *officially.* You're off duty. Besides, this is your senior officer telling you it's time you had a real drink. What's it to be?"

Susan blushed and smiled, averting her blue-gray eyes. "Well, in that case, sir, I'll have a port and lemon."

"Port and lemon it is."

"Let me go, sir."

"No, stay there. Save my seat."

Banks got up and edged his way through the crowd, nodding and smiling a hello here and there. One or two people clapped him on the back and congratulated him on the speed with which he had caught the killer.

With his pint in one hand and Susan's port and lemon in the other, he excuse-me'd his way back. Before he had got halfway he felt a tap on his shoulder and turned around to see Rebecca Charters standing there, long auburn hair framing her pale face.

Banks smiled. "A bit off the beaten track, aren't you?" he said.

"I dropped by the police station first. The man on the front desk said you were all over here celebrating. I've heard that you've got someone under arrest for Deborah Harrison's murder. Is it true?"

Banks nodded. "Yes. A suspect, at least."

"Does that mean you'll be leaving us alone now? Things can get back to normal?"

"Whatever that is," Banks said. "Why? What are you worried about?"

"I'm not worried about anything. It would just be nice to know we could get on with our lives in private now rather than sharing every significant emotional event with the local police."

"That was never my intention, Mrs. Charters. Look, it's a bit silly just standing here like this. Would you like a drink?"

He could see Rebecca consider the offer seriously, needily. She eyed the bottles ranged behind the bar, then suddenly she shook her head. "No. No thank you. That's another thing I'm trying to put behind me."

"Good," said Banks. "Good for you."

"How the hell would *you* know?" she said, and stormed out.

Banks shrugged and headed back to the table, where everyone, even DI Stott, was laughing at one of Hatchley's jokes. Banks didn't mind missing it; he had heard them all before, at least five times.

When he slid into his seat again, Susan thanked him for the drink. "What was all that about?" she asked.

"I'm not sure," said Banks. "I think I offended her. Or maybe abstinence has made her irritable."

"As long as she doesn't complain to the chief constable. What next, sir?"

"Next, I think we've got to find out a bit more about what makes Pierce tick. We've still got no motive, have we? He asked us why he should have committed such a crime, and I think we have a duty to try and answer that. If not for his sake, then for a jury's."

"But, sir, if it was a sex murder we don't really need a motive, do we? We wouldn't expect a rational one."

"Did Owen Pierce seem mad to you?"

"That's a very difficult question," Susan said slowly. "The kind of thing experts argue about in court."

"I'm not asking for an official statement. This is off the record. Your personal observations, your copper's intuition."

Susan sipped her port and lemon. "Well, to start with, he was nervous, edgy, hostile and confused."

"Isn't that how you would feel if you were accused of murder and subjected to an interrogation?"

Susan shrugged. "I don't know, sir. I've never been in that position. I mean, if you've got nothing to hide . . . If you're telling the truth . . . Why get upset?"

"Because everyone *thinks* you did it. And they've got all the power. We have the power. We basically bullied Pierce until he was so confused he acted like a guilty man."

"Are you saying you still don't think he did it, sir?"

Banks scratched the scar beside his right eye. It was itching; sometimes that meant something, sometimes not. He wished he knew which was which. "No. All I'm saying is that everyone's got *something* to hide. Everyone starts to feel guilty when they're stopped and questioned by the police, whether they've done anything or not. Almost anyone

would react the way Pierce did under that sort of pressure."
Banks lit a cigarette and blew out the smoke slowly, careful
to blow it away from Susan, then he took a long swig of
beer.

"But you still have doubts?"

Banks clicked his tongue. "I shouldn't, should I? I mean, I
did arrest him. This is just perfect: signed, sealed and delivered. I'm still confused, that's all. All this business with Pierce
has happened so quickly. There are still too many loose ends.
There was so much going on around Deborah. Remember?
Jelačić's alibi still doesn't really hold water. Then there's that
triangle of Daniel and Rebecca Charters and Patrick Metcalfe.
That's a pretty volatile combination if ever I've seen one.
There's John Spinks, another character capable of violence.
Add to that the open satchel, Michael Clayton spending half
his time with Sylvie Harrison while her husband is out, and
you've still got a lot of unanswered questions."

"Yes, sir, but are any of them relevant now we've got
Pierce with the hair and blood?"

Banks shrugged. "Hair and blood aren't infallible. But
you're probably right. Sometimes I wish I could just accept
the official version."

"But you agree Pierce *could* have done it?"

"Oh, yes. He probably *did* do it. We found no trace evidence at all on either Charters's or Jelačić's clothing. And
Pierce *was* in the area. There's also something about him
that *harmonizes* with the crime in an odd sort of way. I don't
know how to put it any better than that."

"You struck a nerve in him there, sir. I must admit, he
gives me the creeps."

"Yes. There's a part of him that has some sort of imaginative sympathy with what happened to Deborah Harrison.
What I tried to do in that room was make contact with his
dark side." Banks gave a little shudder.

"What is it, sir?"

"Everyone has a dark side, Susan. Doesn't Owen Pierce
make you wonder about your own?"

Susan's eyes widened. "No, sir. I don't think so. I mean, we've done our job. We've got the evidence, we've got a suspect in custody. I think we should just let it lie and move on."

Banks paused, then smiled. "You're right, of course," he said. "But we've still a fair bit of work to do. How do you fancy a trip to London on Monday?"

"London? Me, sir?"

"Yes. I'd like to pay this Michelle a visit, see what her story is. He did his best to keep their relationship from us, so there has to be something in it. Besides, I'd like your impressions, woman to woman, if that's not a terribly sexist thing to say."

"It isn't, sir. Of course. I'd love to come."

"Good." Banks looked at his watch and finished his pint. "I'd better get home. Have a nice lie-in tomorrow. You'll enjoy it."

Susan smiled. "I think I will, sir, good-night."

Banks put his overcoat on, said farewell to everyone and acknowledged a few more pats on the back as he walked through the crowd to the door. He stood for a moment on Market Street by the cobbled square watching his breath plume in the clear, cold air.

So much had happened today that he had hardly had time to notice the clear blue sky, the autumn wind stripping leaves from the trees. Now it was dark and the stars shone for the first time in days. A line from last month's Eastvale Amateur Dramatic Society production tripped through his mind: "The fault, dear Brutus, is not in our stars, / But in ourselves." Again, Banks thought of that foggy night in the graveyard and wondered what had really happened there. Perhaps he would never know.

It was a cold night to walk home, but he had drunk three pints, too much for driving, and he decided he wanted to clear his head anyway. With numb hands, he managed to put on his headphones and flip the switch of the Walkman in his pocket. After a second or two of hiss, he was shocked by the assault of a loud, distorted electric guitar. He had forgotten about the Jimi Hendrix tape he had put in earlier in the week to wake him up on his way to work. He hadn't listened to it since then. Then he smiled and started walking home. Why not? "Hear My Train a' Coming" would do just fine; he would listen to Britten's *War Requiem* later.

Chapter 9

I

*T*he 9:36 InterCity from York pulled into London King's Cross at 12:05 on Monday, November 13, twenty minutes late. A problem with points outside Peterborough, the conductor explained over the PA system. Not for the first time, Banks regarded the bleak, post-industrial landscape of his hometown with a mixture of nostalgia and horror. *Peterborough.* Of all the places to come from. Even if the football team he had supported as a teenager had recently edged about halfway up the second division.

As forecast, the rain came. Not a shower or a storm, but steady November drizzle that looked as if it would keep falling forever from a leaden sky. It was raining in Eastvale when Banks and Susan drove out to York that morning; it was raining in York when they caught the train; and it was raining in London when they got off the underground at Oxford Circus. At least it was a little warmer than the weekend: raincoat weather, not heavy overcoat.

To make it easy all around, Michelle Chappel had suggested over the telephone that she talk to them during her lunch-hour, which started at 12:30, in a small pasta restaurant off Regent Street, near where she worked as office administrator for a quality stationery company.

As the questioning was to be informal, and Michelle herself certainly wasn't suspected of any crime, Banks agreed. It meant they could get the job done and be back in Eastvale by late afternoon if they were lucky.

As usual, Regent Street was crowded, even in the rain, and Banks found he had to dodge many an eye-threatening umbrella spoke as he and Susan made their way to the rendezvous in a side-street not far from Dickins & Jones.

They got there about five minutes late, and Banks spotted Michelle Chappel at a window table. With a skill that Peterborough United could have used the previous weekend, he managed to sidestep the waiter, who was blocking the way, holding out large menus and muttering about a fifteen- to twenty-minute wait.

The restaurant was unpretentious in appearance—rickety tables and chairs, plenty of scratched woodwork, gilt-framed water-colors of Venice and Florence, stained white tablecloths—but when Banks looked at the list of specials chalked on the blackboard, he soon realized it was the kind of London unpretentiousness you pay for through the nose.

The small dining-room was crowded, but Michelle had saved two places for them. Waiters scurried around, sweaty-browed; carafes of wine appeared on tables; and the smell of garlic, tomatoes and oregano permeated the air. Despite the bustle, though, it wasn't unduly noisy, and when they had introduced themselves and sat down, they didn't have to shout to be heard.

"I've told Mr. Littlewood I might be a few minutes late getting back," Michelle said. "He said he didn't mind."

"Good," said Banks. "We'll certainly try not to take up too much of your time."

"That's all right."

Physically, Michelle resembled her photograph very closely except for her hair, which was now cut short, razor-sculpted around her delicate ears, and hung in a ragged fringe. The strong bone structure was still apparent in her cheeks and jaw, the pale, almost translucent skin still flawless, and although she was sitting, it was clear that she main-

tained her slim, athletic figure. She wore a tailored red
jacket over a black silk blouse buttoned up to the hollow of
her long, swan-like neck. From her tiny, pale ears two silver
angel earrings danced every time she moved her head.

"You said on the telephone that you would recognize me
from one of Owen's photographs," Michelle said to Banks,
clearly aware of his scrutiny. "That was two years ago. Have
I changed very much?"

Banks shook his head.

"It was one of the nudes, I suppose."

"Yes."

"Then I'm afraid you'll have to take my word on the rest."
She smiled, and the humor flickered in her eyes for a moment just as Owen Pierce had captured it on film. She
touched her hair. "I had this cut six months ago. Just for a
change. Would you like to eat?"

Both Banks and Susan had skipped the train food and
were starving. After much study and some consultation,
Banks decided on the gourmet pizza with goat cheese,
olives, sun-dried tomatoes and Italian sausage. It was London, after all, he thought, and London prices, so why not?
Susan went for the cannelloni. They ordered a half-liter of
red wine for the two of them. Michelle was already drinking
white. She ordered linguine with clam sauce.

That done, they settled back to talk. Customers came and
went, more leaving than arriving as it got close to one
o'clock, and the drizzle continued to streak the window behind the slightly dirty white lace curtains.

"I'm not sure what you want from me," Michelle said.
"You didn't tell me very much on the telephone."

"I'm not certain myself, Miss Chappel," said Banks. "I
just hope I'll know it when I hear it."

"Call me Michelle. Please."

Banks nodded.

"You said Owen has been arrested?"

"That's right"

"On what charge?"

"You mean you don't know?"

"Well, his name's not been in the papers, and you didn't tell me over the phone. How could I know?"

"Of course not." Banks looked at Susan and nodded.

"I'm afraid it's very serious, Michelle," Susan said. "Owen's been arrested for murder. I'm sorry."

"Murder? But who . . . Wait a minute . . . Not that schoolgirl?"

"Deborah Harrison. Yes."

"I read about it." Michelle shook her head slowly. "Bloody hell. So he's . . ." She looked back at Banks. "And what do you think I can do for you?"

"We'd like to know what you can tell us about him. He didn't seem willing to admit he knew you, or tell us who you were."

"I'll bet he didn't."

"Did something happen between you?"

Michelle frowned. "What do you know already?"

"Not much. Given the nature of the crime, we need to get some sort of grasp on what kind of person he is. We understand already that he's a bit of a loner, something of an odd-ball, according to some people."

"Is he? He wasn't always, you know. Not at first. He could be fun, could Owen. For a while, anyway, then . . ." her eyes darkened.

"Then what?"

"Oh, just . . . things change. People change. That's all."

"Well, you can see our problem, can't you?" Banks said. "He's got no close family, and no-one in Eastvale seems to know him very well. We were hoping you might be able to throw some light on his character."

"Is he going to plead insanity?"

"It's nothing like that. Why do you ask?"

"I mean, what do you want to know about him for?"

"Look, don't worry. We're not going to drag you into court or anything."

"Oh, I don't mind that."

"Then what?"

Michelle leaned forward and rested her elbows on the table. "In fact," she said, lowering her voice, "I'd be more than happy to go into court."

Banks frowned. "I don't understand, Michelle. What happened between you? All we know is that the two of you split in the summer and that Owen seemed reluctant to admit he knew you. In fact he tried to tell us the photographs were of some anonymous model."

Michelle snorted. "I'll bet he did."

"Why would he do that?"

"Why? I'll tell you why. Because he tried to kill me, too, that's why."

II

It was less than a mile from the police station to the Town Hall, and Owen would have appreciated the walk after being cooped up in a cell all weekend. But two officers escorted him straight to a van in front of the station. Before they went out of the doors, one of them threw a musty old raincoat over his head.

It was no distance from the front doors to the van, either, but on the way Owen had the awful sensation of being swallowed up by a huge mob, and he had to struggle to stop his bowels from loosening.

He could hear people shouting questions, yelling insults and cursing him. One group, all women by the sound of them, were chanting, "Hang him! Hang him!" Owen had always feared crowds, had never been able to attend a football match or a music concert in comfort. To Owen, crowds weren't really human; they were a mindless beast with the power of an elemental force. The raincoat over his head smelled of other people's fear.

Luckily the jostling didn't last. Before Owen actually lost control of his bowels and made a fool of himself, he felt himself pushed into the back of a van and heard the door slam. The shouts and chants were muffled now, and the van's engine soon drowned them out completely.

Things weren't quite as bad at the other end, where he was hustled through a smaller crowd, then taken to an antechamber. When Owen was finally able to remove the raincoat, the first person he saw was Gordon Wharton. Not the prettiest sight in the world, but a welcome one under the circumstances.

Wharton leaned back in his chair, plucked up the crease of his pinstripe trousers and crossed his legs. It was a prissy sort of gesture, Owen thought, and one that went with his supercilious expression, the pink, well-scrubbed cheeks and the way he wore his few remaining strands of oily hair combed across his gleaming skull. Though he was probably about the same age as Owen, he looked much older. It was partly the fat, Owen thought, and the baldness, and maybe the strain of overwork. Why did the only solicitor he knew turn out to be *Wharton?*

He had been the university swot, never time for a drink in the local or a film in town, and Owen had never much liked him. He sensed the feeling was mutual. The only reason they had first come into contact at all was a shared subsidiary subject in their first year, and then they had both ended up working in Eastvale and met by chance that day.

Wharton had finally arrived to see Owen on Sunday morning, having been out of town on Saturday, and had been unable to get him out on police bail.

"All right?" Wharton asked.

Owen took a few deep breaths. "I suppose so. What are they trying to do, get me torn to pieces?"

Wharton shrugged.

"What nobody seems to realize is that I'm *innocent*."

Wharton made a steeple of his fingers and looked down. "Owen, you're not the first innocent man to be arrested for some offense or other, and you won't be the last. That's why we have the law. Everyone's innocent until they're proven guilty. The police are only concerned with whether they can prove a case. It's up to the courts to decide now. Trust in justice."

Owen snorted. "The British justice system? It hasn't done me a lot of good so far, has it?"

"Carp all you may, Owen, but it *is* the best justice system in the world. In many other countries you'd be on your way to the executioner already, or languishing forever in some smelly cell. Look, I suggest that you accept your situation. Complaining will do you no good at all in your present circumstances. It will only lead to self-pity. Now let us see if there's anything else we need to consider."

Pompous bastard, Owen thought. "It's all very well advising me not to complain," he said. "You're not the one who's in jail. Will I get bail at court this morning?"

Wharton shook his head. "I doubt it. Not on a charge like this one."

"Look, I'm sure if you could persuade the police to do a bit more digging around, they'll come up with the real killer."

Wharton leaned forward and rested his hands on the desk. Owen noticed the gold cufflinks flash in the light. "Owen," he said, pausing for emphasis, "you still don't seem to realize the gravity of your situation. You have been arrested for the most serious crime there is: murder. Nobody's going to let you simply walk away."

"Whose side are you on?"

Wharton held his hand up. "Let me finish. As far as the police are concerned, they have already got their man. Why would they waste their time looking for an alternative? You'll have to face up to the facts, Owen, you've been arrested for murder, you're being held, in a week or two the Crown Prosecution Service will start building a case against you, and you're going to be tried in court. I will do everything in my power to help you, including engaging the services of the best barrister I can find to represent you, but you *must* accept the situation. Do you understand me?"

Owen wasn't sure that he did, but he nodded anyway.

"Good," said Wharton.

"So what *will* happen in court? What's the point of coming here if they're only going to send me back to jail?"

"For remand. They'll either grant it or release you. As I've already said, I wouldn't depend on the latter. Then they'll set a date for the preliminary hearing."

"How long will I have to wait before that?"

"Hmm. It's hard to say. There's supposed to be a time limit of fifty-six days." Wharton gave a twisted smile. "Unfortunately, you're not the only alleged criminal in the system. We get backlogs."

Owen felt his chest tighten. "Are you saying I could be in jail until February before I even get a preliminary hearing?"

"Oh, at least. Not in Eastvale nick, though. No. Probably somewhere like Armley. And don't worry, they know well enough to keep the other prisoners away from you. Everyone knows how moral criminals get when sex crimes are involved. You'll be isolated. But don't worry about that now. Take things as they come, Owen. One day at a time. That's my advice. I'll be working for you, never fear."

Why didn't that thought comfort Owen as much as it should have? he wondered.

A clerk popped his head around the door. "Time, gentlemen."

Wharton smiled and picked up his black leather briefcase. "Come on then, Owen," he said. "Better gird up your loins."

III

The food arrived just after Michelle's remark about Owen Pierce trying to kill her, and they kept silent as the waiter passed them the hot plates and refilled the baskets of bread. It was after one o'clock now. Michelle was going to be late back for work, Banks knew, but she didn't seem to mind. She clearly wanted to tell them the worst about Owen Pierce.

Banks waited until they had all sampled their food and commented on its quality, then went on. "There was something you said earlier, about Owen being fun at first, then changing. How did he change? Was that anything to do with what happened? Did he become violent?"

"No. Well, not really *violent*. Not until the end, that is."

"The end?"

"The day I left him. The night before, rather."

"If he wasn't violent before that, then what *was* wrong? How did he change?"

"He was just becoming impossible, that's all. Bad-tempered. Complaining. Irrational. Jealous." She paused and took a mouthful of her linguine, following it with a sip of white wine.

"Did he have a violent temper?"

Michelle nodded. Her angel earrings danced. "He started developing one. It got worse towards the end. He just became so possessive, so jealous. He'd fly into rages over nothing."

"Is that why you left him? Fear of violence?" Susan cut in. "Were you frightened he'd hurt you?"

Michelle looked at Susan. "No," she said. "Well, not really. It *was* frightening, especially the last night, but . . . how can I make you understand?"

"We're listening." Susan watched Banks nibble at his pizza out of the corner of her eye. "What happened? Will you tell us?"

Michelle gulped a little more wine, looked at her, then nodded. When she spoke, she looked back and forth between the two of them. "All right. Yes. I'd been out late with a friend. Owen was waiting up for me. And he'd been drinking."

"Did he usually drink much?" Banks asked.

Michelle speared some linguine and twisted it on her fork. "No, not usually, though he had been doing more lately. Especially if he was brooding about something, which he always seemed to be. Anyway, I could definitely smell the whisky on his breath that night."

Banks sipped his red wine. It tasted watery. "Had you been drinking much, too?" he asked.

"Only a couple of glasses of wine."

Banks nodded. "What happened next?"

"He started calling me terrible names and accusing me of all kinds of disgusting things and then he . . . he . . ."

"He what, Michelle?"

"Oh, bugger it. Get it out, Michelle." She took a deep breath and rubbed the back of her hand across her eyes. "He tried to force himself on me, that's what he did."

"He tried to rape you?"

"Yes. He tried to rape me." She wasn't crying, but her eyes glittered with anger.

"Was this the first time he had ever tried such a thing?"

"Of course it was. Do you think I'd willingly stay a moment longer than I had to with anyone who did that to me?" She hadn't finished her meal, but she pushed her plate aside and sipped some more wine.

"I don't know what your situation was," Banks said. "Sometimes people, women especially, get stuck in abusive situations. They don't know what to do."

"Yes, well, not me. I'm not like that. Oh, I'd done my best, tried to please him, given in to his . . . but it was getting impossible. I was at my wits' end. His demands were getting too much for me. This was the last straw. And I was especially upset by the names he called me and the dirty things he accused me of."

"So you resisted him?"

"Yes. I thought it was awful that someone would say such horrible things to me, call me such vile names and then want to do it to me . . . you know . . . like animals."

"Did you struggle?"

Michelle nodded.

"Then what happened?"

"It's not very clear after that. I know he hit me at least once and then everything went dark."

"He hit you when you refused to have sex with him?"

"Yes. I just remember falling and my head hurting and everything going dark for . . . I don't know . . . maybe only a few seconds."

"What happened next?"

"I felt his hands around my neck."

"Owen was trying to strangle you?"

"Yes. He had his hands on my throat and he was pressing."

"How did you stop him?"

"I didn't. I hadn't the strength. I must have passed out again."

"Then what?"

"I woke up. It was light, early morning, and I was still on the floor, where I'd fallen. I felt all stiff and my head hurt. My clothes were torn. I had an awful headache."

"Where was Owen?"

"He was in bed asleep, or passed out. I heard him snoring and went to look."

"Had he interfered with you sexually in any way?"

"Yes. I think he'd had sex with me."

"You can't be certain?"

"No. I wasn't conscious. But I'm pretty sure he had."

"How did you know?"

She looked directly at Banks. He couldn't detect any strong emotion in her eyes now, despite the events she was relating. She wasn't exactly being cold and clinical about it all, but she wasn't overly agitated, either. The few remaining diners would never have guessed what horrors the trio near the window were talking about.

"A woman can tell about those things," she said, then she turned to Susan. "I felt sore . . . you know . . . down there."

Susan nodded and touched her arm.

Banks finished his pizza and looked around to see if anyone was smoking. Miraculously, one or two people were. The restaurant had quietened down a lot, and when Banks beckoned the waiter to bring him an ashtray, he did.

"What did you do next?" Banks asked Michelle.

"I packed up my things, what little I had, and I left."

"Where did you go?"

"I just walked and walked. I had nowhere *to* go. At least it was summer. And it wasn't raining. I remember sleeping in the sun in a park."

"And that night?"

"I tried to sleep at the railway station, but the police kept moving me on. I went in shop doorways, wherever I could find shelter. I was scared."

"And the next day?"

"I swallowed my pride, went back to my parents and faced the music. A month later I got the job down here."

"What did you tell them?" Susan asked.

"I couldn't tell them the truth, could I? I was too ashamed. I couldn't tell anyone that. I made up a story about just not, you know, being happy with Owen, and they believed it. It was what they wanted to hear. They'd only met him once and didn't like him anyway. Thought he was too old for me. All I had to do was tell them what they wanted to hear and eat enough crow. They always believed what I told them."

"Why didn't you report the incident to the police?" Banks asked.

"I told you. I was too ashamed. I'm sure Detective Constable Gay will understand that."

Susan nodded. "Yes."

"Oh, I know what I *should* have done," Michelle went on. "Especially now, after what's happened to that poor schoolgirl. In a way, I feel terribly guilty, almost responsible. But you can't really predict what a person will do, can you, how far he will go? I knew Owen was a bit unbalanced, that he could be dangerous. I should have known just *how* dangerous, and I should have reported him to the police. But I was scared." She looked at Susan again. "And I'd heard such awful things about what they do, you know, in court, to girls who make such complaints. How they make out you're the guilty one, that you're just a slut, and how they get all sorts of doctors and . . . I . . . I just didn't think I could go through with it. I mean, I *was* living with Owen, wasn't I? And I had given in to him willingly before. What would they have said about that? They'd have said I led him on, that's what."

"The courts aren't so easy on rapists these days, Michelle," said Susan. "It wouldn't have been like that."

"But how was I to know?"

"Was that the only reason you didn't report the incident?" Banks asked. "Fear of the police and the courts?"

"Well, mostly. But there was Owen, too, wasn't there? I mean, after someone's done something like that to you, something violent, you have to wonder, don't you, whether they're capable of anything. You hear about men stalking women and all the things they do to them. I was ashamed, but I was scared as well. Scared of what he might do." She looked at her watch. "My God, it's after two," she said. "Look, I really must go now. Mr. Littlewood is only liberal to a degree."

"In the light of what you've just told us," Banks said, "we'd like to get a full statement from you. We can do it after you've finished work this evening, if you've got no objection."

Michelle bit her lip and thought for moment.

"No," she said. "I've got no objection. Yes. Let's do it. Let's get it over with. I finish at five-thirty."

"We'll be waiting."

They watched her go, then Banks lit another cigarette and they each ordered a cappuccino. "Well," said Banks, "it looks like we're stuck in the big city for the afternoon. Want to see the crown jewels? Maybe tour the Black Museum? Or we could always do some early Christmas shopping."

Susan laughed. "No thanks, sir. Perhaps we could give Phil Richmond a call at the Yard? He might be able to sneak away for an hour or so."

"All right," said Banks. "Why don't you phone him?"

"Yes, sir. Got a ten-pee piece?"

IV

Armley Jail loomed ahead like a medieval fortress. Owen could only see part of it through the mesh window between himself and the van's driver, but he knew the building well enough; he'd seen it many times when he was at Leeds University.

Standing on a hill to the west of the city center, it was an enormous, sprawling Victorian edifice of black granite, complete with battlements and towers and newer sections that seemed constantly under construction. The place was practically a tourist attraction. They had kept Peter Sutcliffe, the "Yorkshire Ripper" on remand there for a while in 1981.

At least the van driver had a sense of humor. Elvis Presley belted out "Jailhouse Rock" as the van passed through the huge gates with its load of prisoners shackled in heavy cuffs. Owen wondered if he did that every trip, the way tour guides always made the same jokes.

In a low-ceilinged reception room, the cuffs were removed, and Owen found himself signed over from the police to the jailers. He might easily have been a cow or pig sold at market. Next he was given a number he made no attempt to memorize, then, after his belongings had been catalogued and placed in a box, much as in the charge room at the police station, he was taken to a cubicle and strip-searched.

After that, the governor explained that as Owen was regarded as a Category A inmate, he would spend twenty-three and a half out of twenty-four hours alone in his cell, the other half-hour being set aside for supervised exercise. He would be allowed to purchase as many cigarettes as he wanted—not that this appealed to Owen at all—and given access to writing paper and books.

The whole thing reminded Owen of the scene from Kubrick's film, *A Clockwork Orange,* where Alex is inducted into jail. This room had the same gray inhuman feel, a perfect setting for humiliation. He was now a number, no longer a man.

After a cursory medical ("Ever suffered from palpitations, shortness of breath?") no doubt required to protect the authorities should he drop dead tonight in his cell, he was ordered to take a bath in about six inches of lukewarm water. The tub was an old, Victorian model, with stained sides and claw feet. When he had dried off, he was given his prison uniform: brown trousers and a blue striped shirt that felt coarse and scratchy next to his skin.

After this, he was handed his equally rough bedding and escorted to his cell. It was in a special wing of the prison with black metal stairs and catwalks like something out of an M.C. Escher print. The walls were covered in flecked institutional-green paint, and high ceilings echoed every footstep.

His cell was slightly larger than the one in Eastvale police station, but a lot more gloomy. The whitewashed walls had turned gray with age and dirt; the floor was cold stone. The only window stood high in the wall. About as big as a handkerchief, it seemed to be made of reinforced glass. Light shone from a low wattage bulb hanging from a ceiling outlet; the shade was covered by wire mesh. Though a washstand, soap and a towel stood in the corner behind the door, there was no toilet. Looking around, Owen located a bucket and some toilet paper beside his bed.

One added feature was the table and chair. They were so small that he could hardly get his knees underneath comfortably. The scored table was a bit rickety, but a couple of sheets of toilet paper, folded and wadded beneath one of the legs, soon fixed that.

He had asked for paper and books from the prison library—science fiction if possible, to let him escape, at least in mind from his dreary surroundings. Sci-fi had been a passion during his adolescence, though he hadn't read any since. Now, curiously, he felt an urge to start reading it again. Wharton would also be bringing him his Walkman and a few cassettes as soon as possible.

He paced for a while, then tried to take approximate

measure of his cell. He concluded that it was about eight feet by ten. Next he slouched on his hard, narrow mattress and stared at the cracks on the ceiling. He had expected to find days crossed off all over the walls, just like he had seen in films, but there were none. There wasn't even a trace of graffiti, a name scratched by fingernail, to show who had been here last.

Perhaps it had been the Ripper himself. Owen shivered. That was a foolish thought, he told himself. It was years ago that Sutcliffe had been held here. Dozens of people must have been in and out since then. Still . . . a haunted cell, that would just about make his day.

It was time to keep his imagination in check and take stock of his situation. Certainly he was aware of what *could* happen to him, the "worst case scenario" as Wharton had put it earlier that morning, and that didn't bear thinking about.

Wharton had already been right about the Magistrates' Court; the whole thing had been over in a couple of minutes and Owen found himself on remand awaiting trial for the crime of murder. So much for truth and justice.

What worried him most now were the practical things: his job, the house, the fish, his car. Wharton had taken his keys and said he would take care of things, but still . . . Had anyone let the department at college know? If so, what had the chairman done? It wouldn't be too difficult to share out his classes among his colleagues until a temporary lecturer could be brought in, but what if this thing dragged on for months? He didn't have tenure, so the college could let him go whenever they felt like it. If he lost his job because of this farce, this absurd mistake, he wondered if he could seek any kind of compensation.

The house would remain his as long as his bank account could stand the strain of the standing payment order for his mortgage, and that should be long enough. After all, he had been making fairly decent money for some time and had very little in the way of expenses. He hoped that his neighbor Ivor, who also had a key, would take good care of the fish.

The sound of footsteps disturbed his train of thought, then he heard the key turn in the lock. It was meal-time already. The warder had also brought him a felt-tipped pen, writing pad and envelopes, a surprisingly well-thumbed copy of Wordsworth's *Collected Poems* and Isaac Asimov's *Foundation* trilogy.

When he had finished his meal and the door closed again behind the warder, Owen picked up the pen and sat at the desk. He had no-one to write to, but he could certainly pass time on a journal of his experiences and impressions. Maybe someday someone would want to publish it.

Fifty-six days or longer, Wharton had said. Well, there was nothing he could do about it, was there, so he might as well just get used to it.

Chapter 10

I

The offices of the Eastvale Crown Prosecution Service were located on the top floor of a drafty old three-story building on North Market Street, straddling two shops between the community center and the Town Hall. The lower floor was taken up by a clothes boutique catering to oversize people and a shop that sold imported Belgian chocolate. Somewhere else in the building, a dentist had managed to squeeze in his surgery. Sometimes you could hear the drill while discussing a case.

The chief CPS lawyer assigned to the Pierce file was Stafford Oakes, a shabby little fellow with elbow patches, greasy hair, a sharp nose and eagle eyes. Banks had worked with Oakes before on a number of occasions and had developed great respect for him.

Banks was with DI Stott, and beside Oakes sat Denise Campbell, his colleague, whose expensive and stylish designer clothes stood in stark contrast to Oakes's off-the-peg bargain items. Denise was an attractive and ambitious young lawyer with short black hair and pale skin. Banks had never once seen her smile, and she seemed far too stiff, prim and proper for her age.

In general, the police were wary of the CPS because of its negative attitude towards bringing cases to court, and indeed

Banks had had more than one argument with Oakes on this subject. On the whole, though, Oakes was a fair man, and he didn't usually—like so many Crown Prosecutors—do more damage to the case than the defense did. Banks had even had a pint with him on a couple of occasions and swapped stories of life in the trenches of London, where they had both spent time.

Oakes's office was as untidy as the man himself, briefs and files all over the place. Many of them bore his trademark—linked coffee-rings, like the Olympic games symbol—for Oakes was a caffeine addict and didn't care where he rested his mug. Today it sat on top of the post-mortem report on Deborah Harrison.

It was already only a couple of weeks before Christmas, more than two weeks since they had first consulted by telephone. DNA tests had confirmed that it was, indeed, Deborah's blood on Owen's anorak and Owen's tissue under her fingernail. Banks had sent over all the witness statements and forensic test results collected in the Initial Case File. Owen Pierce's defense team would also have copies of them by now.

"I like this," Oakes was saying, tapping the foot-thick heap of files on his desk. "I particularly like this DNA analysis. Something I can really get my teeth into. No confession, you say?"

"No," Banks answered.

"Good." He slurped some coffee. "Nothing but trouble, confessions, if you ask me. You're better off without them. What do you think, Denise?"

"We've had *some* success with confessions. Limited, I'll admit. As often as not they'll retract, say the police falsified it or beat it out of them." She gave Banks a stern look. "But even scientific evidence isn't entirely problem-free. Depends very much on how it was gathered and who's presenting it."

"Oh, I know that," said Oakes, waving his hand in the air. "Remember that dithering twit in the Innes case we did in

Richmond?" He looked at Banks and Stott and rolled his
eyes. "Open and shut. Or should have been. Simple matter
of bloodstains. By the time the defense had finished with
this chap, he was a nervous wreck, not even sure any more
that two and two made four. But what I mean is, a good,
solid case rests on facts. Like DNA. That's what judges like
and that's what juries like. Facts. Indisputable. Beautiful.
Facts. Am I right, Denise?"

Denise Campbell nodded.

"Now," Oakes went on after another slug of coffee, "I
trust that Mr. Pierce gave his permission for the blood and
hair samples to be taken?"

"Yes," said Banks. "They were taken by a registered police surgeon. You should have copies of the signed consent
forms."

Oakes frowned and dug around deeper in the pile. "Ah,
yes," he muttered, pulling out a few coffee-ringed sheets.
"Here they are. Good. Good. And I trust his anorak was
legally obtained in the first place?"

Banks looked at Stott, who said, "Yes. He gave us his permission to take it in for tests and we gave him a receipt."

"But you didn't go into his home with a search warrant?"

"No," said Stott. "At that stage in our inquiries we merely
wanted to talk to Mr. Pierce. Then, when I saw the orange
anorak, having heard descriptions of a man in a similar orange anorak in the vicinity of the crime scene, I took the ini-
tiative and—"

Oakes flapped his hand again. "Yes, yes, yes, Inspector.
All right. You're not giving evidence in court. Spare me the
formalities. It's a bit flimsy, but it'll have to do."

Stott sat stiffly in his chair, red-faced, mouth tight. Banks
couldn't resist a smile. It was the new lad's first taste of
Stafford Oakes.

Oakes went on, thumbing through the pile on his desk.
"Good stuff, most of this," he said. "DNA, hair, blood analysis. Good stuff. Can't understand a word of it myself, of
course, but get the right man in the box and we'd even be

able to sell it to your average *Sun* reader. That's the key, you know: plain language, without talking down." He put a thick wad of papers aside and flapped a few statements in the air. "And this," he went on. "Not so bad, either. Your vicar, what's his name . . . Daniel Charters . . . places our man on the bridge around the right time." He touched his index finger to the side of his nose. "Must say though, Banks, there's a hint of moral turpitude about the fellow."

"Daniel Charters was accused of making a homosexual advance to a church worker," said Banks. "A Croatian refugee called Ive Jelačić, who was also a suspect in this case, until we turned up Pierce. If it's of any interest, I don't believe Charters did it."

"Doesn't matter what *you* believe. Does it, Denise?"

"No," said Denise.

"See, my learned colleague agrees. No, what matters, Banks, is what the jury believes. Vicar with a whiff of scandal lingering around the dog-collar like a particularly virulent fart." He shook his head and tut-tutted. "Now, there, they say to themselves, goes a true hypocrite, a man who preaches the virtue of chastity, a man who belongs to a church that won't even ordain homosexual ministers, caught with his hand up the choirboy's surplice, so to speak. Well, you see what I mean? It's tabloid scandal-sheet material, that's what it is."

"The point is academic, anyway," Banks said, "as Owen Pierce openly admits to being on the bridge at the time."

"Ah-hah," said Oakes, raising a finger. "I wouldn't take too much notice of that. It's about as useful as a confession. And remember, that's what he said *before* he talked to his solicitor. A lot can change between now and the trial. Believe me, we need as much evidence as we can get."

"Charters isn't the only one who can place Pierce on the bridge around the right time. Deborah's friend Megan Preece saw him, too."

Oakes shook his head. "I've read her statement. She's not entirely *sure* it was him. Damn good thing, too. Nothing worse than children in the box. Oh, we'll use your vicar. Don't worry about that. Just playing devil's advocate. Have to anticipate all eventualities." He glanced at more statements. "The landlord of the Nag's Head places Pierce in the pub a short while before, too, I see. He's reliable, I suppose?"

Banks looked at Stott again. "Well," the latter said stiffly. "He seems a bit slow to me, but given that it wasn't a busy night and Pierce seems to have been about his only customer, I think we can rely on him, yes."

"Good. And what's this other place now. . . . Ah, the Peking Moon. A Chinese restaurant." He wrinkled his nose. "Chinaman, I suppose?"

"Born and bred in Whitechapel," said Stott.

"Chinaman with a cockney accent, then?"

"Yes."

Oakes shook his head. "Juries don't like Chinamen. Don't trust them. Still think of the old Fu Manchu image, you know, inscrutable, yellow peril and all that. Don't go for it myself, but you can't seem to get these racist attitudes out of people's minds as quickly as you'd like, and you certainly can't legislate them away. Still, we'll do our best. Bright fellow, is he?"

"He's very articulate," said Stott.

"Good, that'll help. Unless he seems too bright, of course. Juries don't like people who come across as being *too* clever. Especially foreigners. They expect it of the boffins, of course, but not of your common-or-garden sort of restaurateur. Well, can't be helped." He got up and refilled his coffee mug from the machine on the filing cabinet. "Now what really bothers me," he went on, "is this other stuff here." He reached into the pile again and pulled out more papers. "You took a statement from a woman called Michelle Chappel, an ex-girlfriend of Pierce's. It's all above board, of course, but the whole issue's dodgy." He clicked his tongue and rested his hand on the papers, as if ready to swear on the Bible. "Dodgy in the extreme."

"In what way?" asked Banks.

Oakes sat back in his chair, linked his hands behind his head and quoted at the cracked ceiling. " 'A trial judge in a criminal trial has always a discretion to refuse to admit evidence if in his opinion its prejudicial effect outweighs its probative value.' Lord Diplock, Regina v. Sang, 1979."

"And do you think this is the case with Michelle Chappel's statement?" Banks asked.

"I'm saying it could be a problem. 'There should be excluded from the jury information about the accused which is likely to have an influence on their minds prejudicial to the accused which is out of proportion to the true probative value of admissible evidence conveying that information.' Same source. And it usually relates to evidence of similar fact. You're implying here, by trying to introduce the woman's statement as evidence, that Pierce was just the kind of person who would commit such a crime. Freudian mumbo-jumbo, and juries don't like it, except on television. And, more to the point, a lot of judges don't like it, either."

Banks shrugged. "I'm aware of the similar fact rule," he said, "but what we're trying to establish here is a history of violence against women. And there's a marked physical similarity between the two victims. We're trying to get at a motive."

Oakes's eyebrows shot up. "Ah, yes, that's all very well and good, Banks. But then you're an imaginative sort of chap, kind who reads a lot of fiction, aren't you? If you understand the problem of similar fact evidence, then you must see that what you're doing is saying that Pierce was the sort of person who would commit such a crime because he once acted in a way *similar* to the perpetrator of the crime under consideration. And, what's more, it's an unreported crime based purely on the evidence of a woman who no doubt despises the man for rejecting her." He tut-tutted again and drank some coffee. "Still," he mused, "stranger things have happened."

"So what's your conclusion?" Banks asked.

"My conclusion?" He slapped the stack of coffee-stained files. "Oh, we'll give it a try. Why not? At worst, her evidence can only be declared inadmissible." He chuckled. "It used to be that the definition of inadmissible evidence was anything that might help the defense. That was in the good old days. Sometimes, depending on the judge, you can get a bit of leeway on these matters, especially in a case as serious as this one. I've seen similar fact evidence admitted more than once. What the rule actually states is that the *mere fact* that the accused has previously acted in a similar way to the crime he is standing trial for is not relevant. However, if there's a *very close* similarity, something that links the two events in a convincing way as part of a whole system of actions, an emerging *pattern,* so much so that it becomes more than a matter of mere coincidence, then such evidence may be admissible. Do you follow me?"

"I think so," said Banks.

"If we attempt to show that the two assaults are part of such a pattern," Oakes continued, "then we might just be able to squeeze it in. Depending on the judge, of course. Have you got a psychologist you can consult on this? What about that young woman I've seen you with in the Queen's Arms? Pretty young thing. Redhead. Isn't she a psychologist?"

"Jenny Fuller?"

"That's the one."

"Yes. But Jenny's still teaching in America. She won't be back until after Christmas."

"That'll do fine. No hurry, dear boy, no hurry. We've got enough for committal already. Just need something to beef up the admissibility quotient, if we can."

"Are you going to prosecute, then?"

Oakes drank more coffee, looked at the papers and sniffed a few times. "Oh, I think so," he said, after what seemed like an eternity. Then he nodded. "Yes, yes, I think we've got a good case. What about you, Denise?"

Denise Campbell nodded. "Let's nail the bastard," she

said. Then she blushed and put her hand over her mouth as if she had just burped.

II

Owen's committal proceeding occurred in early February. The whole affair was about as exciting as a damp squib, more reminiscent of a college faculty meeting than an affair at which grave matters were decided. Nobody was even wearing wigs and robes.

He appeared before three JPs one bitter cold morning, and on Wharton's advice, they heard the "new-style committal." That is, they read all the prosecution's statements and the defense offered no case. It was basically committal by consent. And just as Wharton had guaranteed, the JPs agreed there was *prima facie* case and Owen was bound over for trial in the Crown Court. A trial date was set for late March. There were a few spectators in court, and Owen's name was now known to the general public, but only the charges and bare details were made known to the press, not the actual evidence.

Luckily, Owen had quickly got used to the monotony of prison routine: lights on, slop out, lights out, sleep. After the first few weeks, he had lost track of time. He was allowed out of his cell only to exercise in the dreary yard for half an hour each day. He hardly saw another soul there but for his guards, and it was no pleasure walking around in circles alone.

The food reminded him of school dinners: bread-and-butter pudding, gray leathery beef, lumpy custard, Spam fritters. Usually he left most of it. Even so, he felt constipated most of the time.

The cells around him were all occupied. At night he heard voices, even crying sometimes, and one evening the person in the next cell tried to strike up a conversation, asking him what he'd done. But Owen didn't answer. What could the man possibly want to talk about? Compare notes on rape and mutilation?

Mostly, he listened to the tapes Wharton brought him and read poetry and science fiction. He had Wordsworth almost by heart after the first month.

Every few days, for some unknown reason, the prison authorities played musical cells with him. Only the smells were different. One place had a mattress acrid with spilled semen; one of the washstands seemed to breathe vomit fumes from its depths. But maybe that was his imagination. The predominating odor was of disinfectant and slops. In one cell, he discovered in the middle of night that there was no chamber pot or bucket. He called a warder, who told him to piss on the floor. He pissed down the sink. That wasn't his imagination.

As time went on, it was the little things that began to get him down: the rough feel of his prison clothes, the lack of cooking or tea-making facilities, the lousy coffee, the dreadful food. . . . The more he thought about them, the less petty they seemed. These were the essential parts of the tapestry of his liberty, things he took for granted normally. Now he had no access to them, they assumed greater importance in his mind.

It was all relative, of course. For a starving child in an Ethiopian village, for example, prison food would be a luxury and freedom might simply be defined as the hour or two's relief from the agony of hunger. When people are starving, they have no true freedom. But for someone like Owen—middle-class, reasonably well-off, well-educated, living in England—freedom was made up of myriad things, some more abstract than others, but it all came down to *having a choice*.

Locked in his small, lonely cell once again, Owen actually felt relieved to be left alone at last, to be shut away from the bureaucrats, the reporters and the women who stared at him with such naked hatred in their eyes. He was protected here from the crowds outside eager for his blood, and from the policemen so anxious to rip off the surface of his life and dig their hands deep into the slimy darkness below.

His cell was the only place he felt safe now; its routine and isolation sheltered him from the malevolent absurdity of the world outside.

III

Jenny Fuller dashed into the Queen's Arms ten minutes late, shucked off her black overcoat and folded it carefully over the back of the adjacent chair. She gave her head a shake to toss back her mass of flame-colored hair, then sat down and patted her chest. "Out of breath. Sorry I'm late. Are we on expenses?"

Dr. Jennifer Fuller was a lecturer in psychology at the University of York, and over the years her focus had shifted towards criminal and deviant psychology. Now, she had even started publishing in the field and was quickly making a name for herself. Hence the summer in America. Banks had worked with her on several cases before, and an initial attraction had transformed into an enduring friendship that delighted and surprised both of them.

Banks laughed. "Afraid not."

"Pity. I was getting sort of used to that in America. Everyone's on expenses there."

"Let me buy the first one, at least."

"How kind. I'll have a small brandy please, to take the chill off."

"And to eat?"

"Chicken in a basket."

On his way to the bar, Banks recognized one or two of the local shop-owners and the manager of the NatWest Bank on his lunch-break. Cyril had also got the coal fire going nicely. The closest table to it was already taken by a group of ramblers in hiking boots and waterproof gear, so Banks and Jenny sat off to one side, near the window. Rain spattered the red and amber diamonds and blurred the clear panes. Along with the drinks, Banks ordered Jenny's chicken and scampi and chips for himself.

Jenny rubbed her hands together and gave a mock shiver when Banks came back with the drinks, then she picked up her small glass and said, "Cheers." They clinked glasses. "Have a good Christmas?"

"The usual. My parents for Christmas Eve, Sandra's for Christmas Day and Boxing Day."

"And how is Sandra?"

"She's fine."

Jenny took another sip of brandy. "So," she said, "I see you've got your man under lock and key. Another notch in your truncheon."

Banks nodded. "It looks that way."

"I take it that's what you *do* want to pick my brains about, and this isn't just a ruse to secure the pleasure of my company?"

Banks smiled. "Yes to the first. Not that I'd be averse to the latter."

"Stop it, you sweet man. You'll make the lady blush. How can I help?"

Banks lit a cigarette. "I don't know if you can. Or if you will, rather. Just listen, first of all, and tell me if I'm going way off the tracks."

Jenny nodded. "Okay."

Banks told her what they knew about Owen Pierce and Michelle Chappel, stressing Owen's reluctance to admit to knowing Michelle, her resemblance to Deborah Harrison, and what she said Owen had done to her.

When he had finished, Jenny sat quietly for a moment, sucking her lower lip and thinking. Banks sipped some beer and said, "I've been trying to work up some sort of psychological scenario for this crime. Owen Pierce had means and opportunity, and the DNA evidence is pretty damning. I suppose I'm looking for a *motive*."

"You should know by now that you don't always get one

with crimes like this, Alan. Motiveless, stranger killings. At least not what you or I would regard as a logical or even a reasonable motive, like anger or revenge."

"True. But bear with me, Jenny. Say he's upset about the girl, Michelle, angry at her. He goes for a walk and there, out of the fog, this vision appears. Michelle. Well, maybe not *exactly* Michelle, but an approximation. A younger model, more innocent, perhaps more vulnerable, less threatening. So he follows her into the graveyard, approaches her, she says something and sparks his anger. He's already been violent towards Michelle, remember, so there's a precedent. Does it make sense?"

Jenny frowned. "It could do," she said. "Sometimes, we act out, we behave towards people as if they were someone else. It's called 'displacement,' an unconscious defense mechanism where emotions or ideas are transferred from one object or person to another that seems less threatening. I think Freud defined it as one of the neuroses, but my Freud's a bit rusty at the moment. What you're asking is whether I think Owen Pierce could have displaced his feelings for Michelle to Deborah because of some vague superficial resemblance—"

"And because of his mental state at the time."

"All right, that too. And that this led him to kill her. Really he was killing Michelle."

"Yes. What do you think?"

"I think you've got a point, or the beginnings of one."

"You don't think I'm way off beam?"

"Not at all." Their food came. "How about another drink to wash this down?"

"Please. I never argue when a woman wants to buy me a drink."

Banks watched Jenny walk to the bar. She moved well and had a superb figure: long legs, narrow waist and a bum like two plums in a wet paper bag. She had a new energy and confidence in her stride, too, and it looked as if the summer in California had done her good.

She was wearing tight black jeans and a jade-green jacket, made of raw silk, over a white shirt. Judging by the cut and the material of the jacket, the way it narrowed at her waist and flared slightly over the swell of her hips, it had probably cost her a small fortune on Rodeo Drive or some such place. But Jenny always had liked nice clothes.

Banks noticed her exchange a few words with a young man who looked like a trainee bank manager while she waited for Cyril to pour the pint. Poor fellow, Banks thought; he didn't stand a chance. But Jenny was smiling. Why did he feel a pang of jealousy when he saw her flirt with another man, even to this day?

She came back with a pint of bitter for Banks and a Campari and soda for herself. He thanked her. "Making a date?" he said, nodding towards the man.

Jenny laughed. "What do you think I am, a cradle-snatcher? Besides, he's not my type." Jenny was thirty-five in December; the young man about twenty-four. As yet, Banks knew, Jenny hadn't quite figured out what her "type" was.

When Jenny smiled, her green eyes lit up and the lines around them crinkled into a map of her humor. Her tan brought out the freckles across her nose and cheeks.

"How was California?" he asked.

"All sun and surf. Just like 'Baywatch.' "

"Really?"

She wrinkled her nose. "No, not really. You'd hate it," she said. "Can't smoke anywhere."

"And they call it the Garden of Eden. Is that where you developed a taste for fried chicken?"

"Not at all. I've always had a weakness for lean, relatively fat-free meat deep-fried in batter and cholesterol. It appeases both conflicting sides of my nature." She sliced off a chunk of deep-fried chicken breast and popped it in her mouth.

Banks laughed. They finished their meals in silence, then Banks lit a cigarette and said, "Back to Pierce. Look, I know I'm putting you on the spot, Jenny, but I'd like you to work something up for the CPS."

"Like what?"

"The kind of thing we were talking about. Displacement, for example. Tell me more."

Jenny sipped her Campari and soda. Banks still had half a pint left, and he wasn't allowing himself another drink this lunch-time.

"Okay," Jenny said, "let's say that he has poor control over his anger. It's pretty much a commonplace that people often respond to frustration by getting angry, and if their anger is really intense and their inner controls are weakened even further—say by alcohol or tiredness—then it can result in physical assault, even murder. That seems to be what happened with Michelle, but what about Deborah? Had he been drinking?"

"He'd had two pints and a whisky."

"Okay. Let's say, then, that we *are* dealing with displacement, which is a coping pattern. A defense mechanism, if you like."

"Defense against what?"

"Stress, basically. If a situation really threatens your sense of adequacy, your ego, your self-esteem, then your reactions become defense-oriented, you defend your *self* from devaluation."

"How?"

"Any number of ways. Denial. Rationalization. Fantasy. Repression. Things we all do. What it basically comes down to is ridding yourself of the anxiety and the tensions that are causing the pain."

"Sexual tension?"

"Could be. But that's just one kind."

"And displacement is one of these defense mechanisms?"

"Yes. You shift the strong feelings you have from the person or object towards which they were originally intended to another person or object. Often very difficult emotions are involved, like hostility and anxiety. It's an unconscious process."

"Are you suggesting he wasn't responsible?"

194 PETER ROBINSON

"Interesting point. But I don't think so. I don't know exactly what the law is, but I'm not saying a person suffering displacement isn't responsible for his actions, especially violent ones. Just that he might not know the inner processes that are leading him to want to do what he does."

"Which you can probably say for most of us most of the time?"

"Yes. In less extreme ways."

"Okay. Go on."

"Displacement is often combined with projection, where you put the blame for your own problems on someone else, or some group."

"Women?"

"Could be. In extreme cases it leads to a form of paranoia. People become convinced that forces or groups are working against them. He *could* have formed such a projection of his anxieties and hostilities against women in general. Plenty of men do. That French-Canadian who shot all those women at the college in Montreal, for example."

"And could he also have displaced his hostile feelings for Michelle onto Deborah, given the stress of the anniversary, the effect of alcohol and the resemblance between the two women?"

"Possibly. Yes. There's a study by a psychologist called Masserman, done in 1961, where he manages to show that under sustained frustration people become more willing to accept substitute goals."

"Deborah for Michelle?"

"Yes. Look, I'm a bit rusty on this. I'll need a few days to come up with something."

"How about next week?"

Jenny smiled. "I'll see what I can do."

"If there's anything else you want to know, give me a call."

"Can you get copies of the statements to me?"

"No problem."

"Okay. Now I really must go." She stood up and reached

for her raincoat. Then she leaned forward and gave Banks a quick peck on the cheek.

When she had gone, he lit another cigarette, vowing it would be his last for the day, and contemplated the remains of his pint. Another half wouldn't do any harm, he decided, so he went and got one, pouring it into the pint glass because he didn't like drinking beer from small glasses.

IV

One afternoon about three or four weeks after his committal—he was losing track of time—Owen was taken from his cell to a prison interview room, where he met for the first time the barrister Gordon Wharton had engaged to lead his defense.

In her early forties, Owen guessed, Shirley Castle, QC, was an attractive woman by any standards. She was also the first woman he had seen since his trip to the Magistrates' Court. She had glossy dark hair that fell over her shoulders and framed a pale, oval face. Her almond-shaped eyes were a peculiar shade of violet, so unusual that Owen wondered if she were wearing tinted contact lenses. She had on a gray pleated skirt and a pale pink blouse buttoned up to her chin. Her perfume smelled subtle and expensive.

Wharton sat beside her with a smug, proprietorial air about him, basking in the glory of her presence, as if to say, "Just look who I've got for you, my boy. What a treat!"

Shirley Castle took the cap off her Montblanc fountain-pen, shuffled some papers in front of her and began.

"It doesn't look very good, Owen," she said. "I don't want to give you any false hopes or illusions. We'll have an uphill struggle on our hands with this one."

"But all they've got is circumstantial evidence."

She looked at him. "The point is, that they can build a very good case on that. Look at it this way." She started to count off the points on her long fingers. "One, you had the opportunity. Two, motive in such crimes is so obscure, to say the least, that they don't really need to establish one. And, three, there's the DNA, hairs and blood."

"But I can explain it all. I have done. I never denied being in the area from the start, and I told them the girl bumped into me. Maybe that's how the hair and blood were exchanged."

"Maybe. But the police don't believe you," she said. "And quite frankly, I don't blame them, especially given that you only came up with that explanation at the eleventh hour. No, Owen, I'm afraid we're going to have to fight tooth and nail for this one."

"Are they still looking for the real murderer?"

"Why should they? They think they've already got him."

"So there's nobody out there trying to prove my innocence?"

"I'm afraid not."

"Can't you employ a private detective or someone?"

Shirley Castle laughed. It was a lighter, frothier, more vivacious sound than he would have imagined, given her overall gravity. But it was a nervous laugh, no doubt about that. "To do what?" she asked.

"Find the real murderer. Prove me innocent."

"Things don't work quite like that."

"Well, how *do* they work?"

She leaned back in her chair and frowned. "We go to court and we give them the best fight we can. There's no other way. It's only on 'Perry Mason' that the lawyer and the private eye get out on the mean streets and track down the *real* killer."

"Just let me tell them my story. I'm sure they'll believe me."

"I'm not sure yet if I'm going to put you in the witness box at all."

"Why not?"

Shirley Castle frowned. "Cross-examinations can be really tough."

"Is something bothering you?"

"Yes, as a matter of fact it is. The CPS file suggests an approach to the case that involves similar fact to try and establish a *motive* for the murder, too."

"But you said they didn't need one."

"Their case will be all that much stronger if they can come up with one."

"What are they saying?"

Shirley Castle rested her chin in her hand. "Tell me about Michelle Chappel, Owen."

Owen swallowed. His mouth felt dry. "What about her?"

"About your relationship. And why you lied to the police about the nude photographs, denied you knew her. You didn't want them to find her and talk to her, did you?"

"No, I can't say I did. Michelle . . . well, let's say we parted on bad terms. She'd have nothing good to say about me."

"As I understand it, there was violence, perhaps attempted murder?"

"That's absurd! Have you talked to her?"

"No," she said. "The police have. I've just been reviewing the statement, and it's very interesting. Read for yourself." She dropped a sheaf of papers in front of him.

Owen felt rising panic as he read the transcript of the taped interview with Michelle:

Q: Miss Chappel, could you tell us how and when you first met Mr. Pierce?
A: Yes. In class. He was my teacher. I was his student.
Q: How old were you at the time?
A: Seventeen.
Q: Was this at Eastvale College of Further Education?
A: Yes.
Q: How old was Owen Pierce when you met?
A: Thirty-two, thirty-three. I'm not exactly sure.
Q: So he was almost old enough to be your father?
A: Technically. I suppose a sixteen-year-old could be a father.

Q: Did you live at home?

A: Yes. Until I was eighteen.

Q: Where did you go then?

A: I moved in with Owen.

Q: How long did you live with him?

A: Five years.

Q: How did Mr. Pierce approach you?

A: He suggested a coffee after class, one day, then he asked me out to dinner.

Q: Were your marks good?

A: Yes.

Q: Did you start seeing one another regularly?

A: Yes. We went out together a few times for dinner, to the pictures or for a drink. Sometimes he took me out for a ride in the country in his car, and we'd find a little village pub somewhere.

Q: How soon did you become lovers?

A: Very soon after we first went out.

Q: Weeks? Days?

A: Days.

Q: And the relationship went well after you moved in with him?

A: At first it did, yes. Look, I mean, you have to realize, I was very young. A bit of a misfit, too, I suppose. I wasn't very happy at home, and I didn't really have any close friends. I found most people my own age immature. I was also very shy and Owen was nice to me. I suppose I was flattered, too, by the attention. When I talked about leaving home, he asked if I'd like to move in with him, and it seemed like a good idea. I felt safe with him.

Q: Were you still his student when you moved in with him?

A: I was in his business communications class, yes.

Q: Did you continue to do well in that course?

A: Very well.

Q: Deservedly?

A: I think so. Look, I'm not stupid, but I also admit it may have helped, sleeping with my teacher.

Q: Do you think there was a price to pay for your success?

A: What do you mean?

Q: Did Owen ever suggest or attempt to commit any unnatural acts?

A: Do you mean was he kinky?

Q: Something like that.

A: No, I wouldn't say that. I mean, he liked me to wear certain underclothes. You know, black silky things, thigh stockings, skimpy things. He liked me to keep them on when we . . . you know.

Q: During intercourse?

A: Yes.

Q: Was that all?

A: All? Was what all?

Q: The skimpy clothes. Did he ever make you do anything you didn't want to?

A: He wanted to do it to me from behind, like dogs. I didn't like that.

Q: But did you do as he wished?

A: Well, I . . . yes, at first I did. I wanted to please him.

Q: Because you were worried about your marks?

A: A bit, I suppose.

Q: Did he show any interest in pornography?

A: We watched a dirty video once. You know the sort of thing. I didn't really enjoy it. In fact, I thought it was dead gross, but it seemed to turn him on.

Q: How did he behave when you were watching the video?

A: Well, he was, you know, maybe a bit more ardent than usual. He wanted to try out things they were doing, you know, on the video.

Q: Against your will?

A: No, but I thought it was a bit weird.

Q: Did he ever resort to violence for the purpose of sexual stimulation?

A: He used to like to tie me up sometimes.

Q: How did you react to this?

A: What could I do? He was stronger than me. I wanted to

please him. It was uncomfortable and it frightened me a
bit, but it didn't really hurt. It was just a game, really. It
was something he'd seen in that silly film and it turned
him on.

Q: Did he beat you at all? Flagellation?

A: No.

Q: So apart from the tying up he wasn't violent?

A: No . . . not until the end. Then living with him became
sort of like being in prison. Every time I went out I had
to account for my movements. Some nights he wouldn't
even let me go out.

Q: How did he keep you in?

A: He just made such a fuss it wasn't worth it. I felt shut in,
always under observation. I couldn't breathe. I was
frightened of his temper. I started rebelling in small
ways, like seeing other friends and stuff, and it made
him more and more possessive.

Q: Is that why you left him? Fear of violence?

A: Partly . . . it was frightening, especially the last night,
but . . .

Q: Can you tell us about that last night, Michelle?

Michelle went on to tell about the night she claimed Owen
had raped and tried to strangle her. Pale, Owen shoved the
papers aside and looked at Shirley Castle.

"Well?" she asked. "What do you think of it?"

Owen shook his head slowly. "I don't know what to say."

"It's not true, then?"

"Some of it, maybe. But she even makes the truth sound
different, sound bad for me, the way she slants it."

"In what way?"

"Every way. The sex, for example. She makes me sound
like a pervert, but most of it was her idea. She loved it, the
tying up, the talking dirty. It really got her going. And she
liked the video."

"Did you hit her that last night?"

"I pushed her. I was protecting myself. She was berserk,

out of control. She'd have killed me if I hadn't pushed her away."

"And she hit her head as she fell?"

"Yes."

"Knocking her unconscious?"

"Yes, but . . . Oh, God." Owen held his head in his hands. "I know how it sounds, but I've never hurt anyone in my life, never on purpose."

"Did you have sex with her after she'd knocked herself out?"

"No, I didn't. That's a lie. What do you take me for?"

"I'm just trying to get at the truth, Owen. Did you try to force her to have sex at any time that evening?"

"No. I mean, yes. No, I didn't try to force her, but I suggested it. I just wanted to see how she would react. It was a test. I didn't force her."

Shirley frowned. "You made advances? I'm afraid I don't understand you, Owen. You'll have to explain it to me."

How could he tell her about that night? Still vivid in his mind, it was like watching a cartoon play, the gaudy colors, the exaggerated violence, the sense of being a spectator, unable to stop the film, unable even to walk out of the cinema.

"How did it start, Owen?"

Owen tried to explain. He had grown suspicious of Michelle over the last year or so, he said, suspected that she was seeing another man, or other men. That night, when she said she was going to meet a girlfriend, he followed her into Eastvale town center and watched her meet someone in a pub. As they talked and drank, rubbing close together, Owen sat, shielded by a frosted-glass partition and watched the shadows. At closing time, he followed them to a house not far from his own and watched outside as the bedroom light went on, then the curtains closed, and someone turned out the light.

He went home and paced and drank whisky until Michelle got in after two-thirty in the morning. Instead of challenging her immediately with what he'd found out, he made sexual advances to see how she would react.

She pushed him away and told him she was too tired, listening to her girlfriend's tales of woe till so late. He could smell the other man on her, the stale beer and smoke on her clothes, in her hair, mingled with the reek of sex. She hadn't even had the decency to take a shower afterwards.

Then he told her what he'd seen, what he had watched. She went wild, flew at him, screamed that he didn't own her and if he was no good in bed she had every damn right to find someone who was. It was like watching another person emerge from the shell of someone you thought you knew.

He called her a bitch, a whore, told her he knew she'd been at it all the time they'd been together, that she had just used him, had never really loved him. For a moment, she paused in her attack and a different look came into her eyes: hard, cold hatred. She picked up a pair of scissors from the table and lunged at him. He grabbed her hand and twisted until she dropped them.

Then she renewed the attack, kicking, scratching, flailing out wildly. He held his hands in front of his face to ward off the blows and tried to talk her down. But she wouldn't stop. Finally, out of desperation, he pushed her away, just to give himself some space to maneuver, and she fell over and hit her head on the chair leg.

He tried to tell Shirley Castle all this, as calmly as he could. He knew it sounded thin without the whole background of the relationship, from the early innocence to the bitter knowledge that it had all been a lie.

What he couldn't tell her, though, what he hardly dare even admit to himself, was that after Michelle had fallen on the floor, arms spread out, one leg crooked over the other, he had wanted her. Hating her even then, he had torn at her clothing, then, half-mad with jealousy and hatred, had put his hands around her throat and wanted to choke the life out of her for what she had done to him, for ruining, for defiling what he had thought was the love of a lifetime. He hated himself for wanting her, and he hated her for making him.

At that moment, the full power of his love turned to hate

and overwhelmed him, and he knew that everything, her words, her gestures, her lovemaking, her promises, had all been a lie. But he let go; he couldn't kill her. He stood up, steadied himself and went to collapse on the bed. She was still breathing; there was no blood; he hadn't raped her.

In the morning he found her sulking in the spare room, nursing the bump on her head. She tried to make up to him, told him she would do anything he wanted . . . *anything* . . . and started squirming around under the thin sheet. It had always worked before, but this time Owen had had more than enough.

He knew that if he took her back, if he lived with her for just one more day he would lose his self-respect forever. When he told her to go, she screamed and begged, but he threw her out in the street with only her suitcase. The next thing he knew, he got a letter with a Swiss Cottage address to send on the rest of her things. He did so.

Shirley Castle let the silence stretch after his explanation. Owen couldn't read the way she looked at him. He didn't know whether she believed him or not.

"Owen," she said finally. "Whatever the truth is, Michelle's is a very damning statement. You can imagine the case the Crown is trying to build up. A man obsessed with pornography, especially if it features young girls, capable of sexual violence against women . . . You see my point?"

"But it's not true!" Owen argued. "None of it. I'm not obsessed with pornography."

Shirley held up her hand. "I'm not attacking you, Owen. I'm simply trying to demonstrate the spin the prosecution will try and put on the facts, given the chance."

Owen laid his hands on the desk and stared at the veins in his wrists. "I don't know what you must think of me," he said, his voice hardly more than a whisper, "but I want you to know that I'm not the monster they say I am. It's a distortion. If I knew only *certain* facts about your life, or anyone's, if your fantasies were laid bare for all to see . . . well, I might form a picture, and it might be the wrong one. Do you know what I mean?"

He could have sworn there was an amused glint in her eyes, and perhaps a faint flush on her cheeks. "You don't need to please me, Owen," she said. "I'm here as a professional. It's not my place to make judgments about your private life, only to prove reasonable doubt. You don't need to seek my approval."

"But I want it," Owen said. "Damn it, I want it! You're not a machine, are you? You must have opinions, feelings."

Shirley Castle didn't answer. Instead, she shuffled the papers back towards her briefcase and said, "There's one more important question before I go, Owen. Why would Michelle do what she did? Why would she say all those things about you to the police if they're not true? What reason has she to want you to go to jail?"

"Don't you understand? Michelle's a user. She used me from the start, for her education, her escape from her overbearing parents, for her living-quarters, the good life. I was her passport through college. She threw me a few crumbs and I took them for love. Even now I have a hard time believing that you can live with someone for so long and not really see them for what they are, not know them at all. But it's true. Maybe I didn't *want* to see. All the time she was with me, she was going with other men, and I admit I got jealous and possessive. But she didn't care. She thought she could get away with everything, just take her clothes off for me and make it all right. At heart she's a cold, calculating monster. She has no conscience. Do you understand? Sometimes, it's only when the final piece falls into place that you see there was ever a pattern at all. That was what happened that last night. The final piece. She'd been doing it all along, lying to me, seeing other men, doing exactly what she wanted, using my home—*our* home—as a squat. I gave her all the freedom she wanted at first, before I started to suspect the truth. She was young after all. How can you keep the love of a younger woman if you try to put her in a cage? As soon as I became more vigilant, the cracks started to appear."

Shirley Castle shook her head. "I can accept all that,

Owen, but it doesn't really answer my question. Why does she wish you so much harm?"

"Why? Because I found her out," Owen answered, remembering that one calm moment in the final battle, when he had seen her for what she really was. "Because I saw through her. I saw her true face. And because I rejected her. I threw her out. Though she denied me the night before, just after she'd been with her boyfriend, she offered me her body the next morning. But I wouldn't take it. She begged me to forgive her and let her stay. But I threw her out. She was like a spiteful child if she didn't get her own way. She can't forgive me for seeing the truth and having the courage to throw her out before she dumped me."

Shirley Castle nodded slowly. "Well, Owen, that's all very well," she said. "But we'd just better hope, for your sake, that she doesn't get anywhere near the witness-box."

Chapter 11

I

Wood creaked as those present in court got to their feet one rainy April day. Judge Simmonds entered, resplendent in scarlet moire and white linen. He was a wizened old man with reptilian eyes buried deep in wrinkles and folds of flesh. His face was expressionless as he looked around the courtroom before sitting.

The benches groaned as everyone in the crowded room sat down. Owen noticed that the courtroom smelled of the same lemon-scented polish his mother used to use; it made him feel sad.

"The prisoner will stand."

So this was it. Owen stood.

"Is your name Owen Pierce?" asked the Clerk of the Court.

"It is."

The clerk then read out the indictment and asked Owen how he pleaded.

"Not guilty," Owen answered, as firmly and confidently as he could manage with all eyes on him.

He scrutinized the jury as he spoke: seven men and five women, all dressed for a day at the office. A pudgy man with a slack, flabby jaw looked at him with something like awe. A pursed-lipped young woman wouldn't meet his eyes at all, but looked down at her hands folded in her lap. Most of them at least glanced at him in passing. Some were nervous; others looked as if they had already made up their minds.

It was irrational, he knew, but he decided to pick one of them to be his barometer throughout the trial, one whose expressions he would chart to tell how the case was going— for or against him. Not the frowning woman in the powder-blue suit, nor the balding chap who reminded him of his insurance agent; not the conventionally pretty girl with the pageboy cut, nor the burly wrestler-type with his brick-red neck bulging out of his tight collar. It was difficult to find someone.

At last, he decided on a woman; for some reason, it had to be a woman. She was in her late thirties, he guessed, with a moon-shaped face and short mousy hair. She had a wide red slash of a mouth and large eyes.

But it wasn't her physical appearance so much as her aura that caused him to pick her out. For some reason, he decided, this woman was good and honest. What was more, she could tell the truth from lies. At the moment, she looked puzzled and confused to find herself in such a frightening role, but she would, he knew, as soon as the trial progressed, listen carefully, weigh, judge and decide. Her decision would be the right one, and he would be able to tell from her expression what it was. Yes, he would keep a close eye on her. He would call her "Minerva."

Almost before Owen realized it, Jerome Lawrence, QC, had launched into his opening address. Lawrence was a small, dark-complexioned man with beady, restless black eyes and a perpetual five-o'clock shadow, shiny as shoe-polish on his cheeks and chin. Somehow, he seemed to fit perfectly into his robes, looking even more like a bat ready to flap its wings and take off into the night than anyone else in the room. Like Shirley Castle, he spoke with his hands a lot, and his robe swished about in a most distracting way.

"The Crown shall seek to prove," Lawrence said in his

oiliest public-school voice, "that the accused is guilty of the most heinous, the most despicable, brutal, inhuman crime of all—the murder of a child, an innocent, a mere sixteen-year-old girl with her whole life before her."

And for the rest of the day, Owen could only listen, open-mouthed, to the depiction of himself as a barely human monster.

Though the parade of witnesses began dramatically enough, with Rebecca Charters tearfully recounting how she discovered Deborah Harrison's body, several things became clear to him in the first days. Probably the first and foremost of these was that you could be bored even at your own murder trial.

Witnesses came and went, people he had never met, people who didn't know him: vicars, shopkeepers, teachers, schoolgirls, policemen, pub landlords. Some of them seemed to spend hours in the box for no reason Owen could think of. Jerome Lawrence or Shirley Castle questioned most of them, but sometimes their juniors took over.

With unfailing regularity one lawyer or another would raise points of law that meant the jury had to be sent out, sometimes for hours, and all sides seemed to like nothing better than the kind of delay that meant an early adjournment for the day. Also, there were one or two days off due to illness of a jury member and another for a family bereavement. Every night, without fail, Owen was shipped back to his little cell at Armley Jail. He was becoming so used to it by now that he almost thought of it as home. He had forgotten what his real home looked like.

As far as Owen could tell, things seemed to be going quite well over the first few weeks. Shirley Castle made mincemeat of the policeman with the jug-ears for not explaining why he was visiting Owen in the first place. Detective Inspector Stott came out looking like a member of the Gestapo.

By the time Detective Chief Inspector Banks was called, Owen had lost track of the days.

II

"In the same situation, Chief Inspector, do you think you would bother to mention *everyone* you saw on the streets during a certain period?"

Banks shrugged. It was his second day giving evidence and Shirley Castle was cross-examining him. "I would hope I would do my duty and try to recall *everything* that happened around the crucial time," he answered finally.

"But you are a policeman, Chief Inspector. You have special training. Such facts and fine details are part of your job. I'm sure I wouldn't even remember most of the people I passed in the street. Nor, I imagine, would most members of the jury." And here, Shirley Castle paused long enough to look over at the jury. Most of them seemed to agree with her, Banks thought. "Yet you expect Mr. Pierce to remember every face, every detail," she went on. "I ask you again, Chief Inspector, do you really think this is reasonable?"

"Perhaps not on a busy thoroughfare at rush hour," said Banks, "but this was a foggy night in a quiet suburb. Yes, I think I would remember if I had seen a particular person. And Mr. Pierce remembered as soon as—"

"That's enough, Chief Inspector. You have answered my question."

Banks couldn't help but allow himself a slight feeling of satisfaction when he saw Shirley Castle reel from his answer. She had made a small mistake; she hadn't already known the answer to the question she asked.

She hurried on. "Now, as Mr. Sung, proprietor of the Peking Moon restaurant, has already testified, and as my learned friend brought out during his examination-in-chief, Mr. Pierce used his credit card to pay for his meal there. If the timing of events is correct—and I stress *if*—this would have occurred shortly *after* the murder of Deborah Harrison, would it not?"

"Yes."

"Now, in your professional experience, Chief Inspector,

would you not say that a criminal, someone who has just committed an attack of the most vile and brutal kind, would be a little more careful to cover his tracks?"

"Most criminals aren't that clever," said Banks. "That's why they get caught."

The members of the gallery laughed.

"But my client is *not* stupid," she went on, ignoring the interruption. "It is hardly likely that he would go and eat Chinese food and pay for it with a credit card after murdering someone, now, is it? Not to mention do it all wearing a bright orange anorak. Why would he be so foolish as to draw attention to himself in such an obvious way if he had committed the crime of which he is accused?"

"Perhaps he was distraught," Banks answered. "Not thinking clearly. Mr. Sung did say he was talking to—"

" 'Not thinking clearly,' " she repeated, with exactly the right tone of disdain. "Is it not a fact, Chief Inspector, that perpetrators of such random crimes are usually, in fact, thinking very clearly indeed? That they rarely get caught, unless by accident? That they take great care to avoid discovery?"

Banks fiddled with his tie. He hated having it fastened up and could only bear it if he kept the top button of his shirt undone. "There are certain schools would say that, yes. But a criminal's behavior is not easily predictable. If it were, we'd have an easier job on our hands." He smiled at the jury; one or two of them smiled back.

"Come on, Chief Inspector Banks, you can't have it both ways. Either they're stupid and easy to catch, as you said earlier, or they're unpredictable and impossible to catch. Which is it?"

"Some are stupid; some are not. As I said before, murderers don't always act rationally. This wasn't a rational crime. There's no way of predicting what the killer would do, or why he did things the way he did."

"But aren't you in the business of reconstructing crimes, Chief Inspector?"

"Nowadays we leave that to 'Crimewatch.' "

Laughter rose up from the gallery. Judge Simmonds admonished Banks for his flippancy.

"My point is," Shirley Castle went on without cracking a smile, "that you seem to know so very little of what went on in St. Mary's graveyard, or indeed, of what kind of criminal you're dealing with. Isn't that true?"

"We know that Deborah Harrison was strangled with the strap of her school satchel and that her clothing was rearranged."

"But isn't it true that you simply picked on the first person seen in the area whom you thought fit the bill, that Owen Pierce was unfortunate enough to be in the wrong place at the wrong time?"

"I'd say it was Deborah Harrison who was in the wrong place at the wrong time."

"Were there not certain elements of the crime scene that struck you as odd?"

"What elements?"

Shirley Castle consulted her notes. "As I understand it," she said, "the victim's school satchel was *open*. Doesn't that strike you as odd?"

"It could have come open during the struggle."

"Hardly," scoffed Shirley Castle. "It was fastened by two good-quality buckles. We've tested it, believe me, and it won't open unless someone *deliberately* unfastens it."

"Perhaps the murderer wanted something from her."

"Like what, Chief Inspector? Surely you're not suggesting robbery? From a schoolgirl's satchel?"

"It's possible. But I—"

"But what money could a schoolgirl have worth stealing? I understand Deborah Harrison had six pounds in her purse when she was found. If robbery were the motive, why not take that too? And wouldn't it make more sense to take the entire satchel? Why hang around the crime scene any longer than necessary?"

"Which question do you want me to answer first?"

Shirley Castle scowled. "Why would Deborah Harrison's killer remain at the scene and go through her satchel rather than take it with him?"

"I don't know. Perhaps he was looking for a trophy of some kind. Something personal to the victim."

"But was anything missing?"

"We don't know. No-one knew exact—"

"You don't know. We have heard a great deal of evidence," she went on, "placing Mr. Pierce in the vicinity of St. Mary's at the time of the crime, but let me ask you this, Chief Inspector: did anyone actually *see* Mr. Pierce enter St. Mary's graveyard?"

"He was seen—"

"A simple yes or no will suffice."

Banks was silent a moment, then said, "No."

"Is it not also possible, Chief Inspector, that Deborah went somewhere else first and returned to the graveyard later, after Mr. Pierce had gone to the Peking Moon?"

"It's possible. But—"

"And that Deborah Harrison was murdered by someone she knew, perhaps because of something she was carrying in her satchel?"

Exactly what I thought at first, Banks agreed. "I think that's a rather far-fetched explanation," he said.

"More far-fetched than charging Mr. Pierce here with murder?" She pointed at Pierce theatrically. "While you were busy harassing my client, did you pursue the investigation in other directions?"

"We continued with our inquiries. And we didn't har—"

She sniffed. "You continued with your inquiries. What does that mean?"

"We tried to find out as much about the victim and her movements as possible. We tried to discover, through talking to friends and family, if she had any enemies, anyone who would want to kill her. We collected all the trace evidence we could find and had it analyzed as quickly as possible. We found nothing concrete until we came up with Mr. Pierce."

"And after Mr. Pierce's name came up?"

Banks knew that most investigations tend to wind down once the police think they've got their man. And much as he would have liked to pursue other possibilities, there was other work to do, and there was also Chief Constable Riddle. "I continued other lines of inquiry until it became app—"

"You continued other lines of inquiry? As soon as you first interviewed him, you decided on Mr. Pierce's guilt, didn't you?"

"Objection!"

"Sustained. Ms. Castle, please stop insulting the witness."

Shirley Castle bowed. "My apologies, Your Honor, Chief Inspector Banks. Let me rephrase the question: what was your attitude to Mr. Pierce from the start?"

"We decided he was a definite suspect, and in the absence of any evidence to the contrary, we proceeded to build up our case against him in the usual, accepted manner."

"Thank you, Chief Inspector," Shirley Castle said, sitting down and trying to look bored. "No further questions."

"Then I suggest," said Judge Simmonds, "that we adjourn for the weekend. Court will be in session again at ten-thirty Monday morning."

III

On Monday morning, it happened: exactly what Owen had been fearing.

When he tried to reconstruct the sequence of events later, back in his cell, he couldn't be sure whether Jerome Lawrence had actually managed to call out Michelle's name before Shirley Castle jumped to her feet. Either way, Judge Simmonds listened patiently to the objection, then he dismissed the jury for yet another *voir dire*.

What followed was a legal wrangle that Owen, educated as he was, could only half follow, so mired was it in tortured

English and in citing of precedents. As far as he could
gather, though, both sides put their points of view to the
judge. Jerome Lawrence argued that Michelle's evidence
was relevant because it established a *pattern* of violent behavior that had its natural outcome in Deborah Harrison's
murder, and Shirley Castle countered that the proposed evidence was nothing but vindictive fantasy from an unreliable
witness, that it proved nothing, and that its prejudicial effect
by far outweighed any probative value it might have.

Owen held his breath as Judge Simmonds paused to consider the arguments; he knew that his entire future might be
hanging in the balance here. His mouth felt dry; his jaw
clenched; his stomach churned. If Simmonds disallowed the
evidence, Owen knew, there could be no reporting of what
had gone on in the jury's absence. Only a very few people
would ever know about what had happened between him
and Michelle. If Simmonds admitted it, though, the whole
world would know. And the jury. He crossed his fingers so
tightly they turned white.

Finally, Simmonds puckered his lips, frowned, and declared the evidence inadmissible.

Owen let out his breath. The blood roared in his ears, and
he felt his whole body relax: jaw, stomach, fingers. He
thought he was going to faint.

Shirley Castle flashed him a discreet thumbs-up sign and
a quick smile of victory. The jury was brought back in, and
Jerome Lawrence called his next witness.

Dr. Charles Stewart Glendenning made an imposing figure. Tall, with a full head of white hair and a nicotine-
stained mustache, the Home Office pathologist carried
himself erectly and had just the right amount of Scottish burr
in his accent to make him come across as a no-nonsense sort
of person. The serious expression on his face, which had
etched its lines over the years, added to the look of the con-
summate expert witness.

He entered the witness-box as if it were his second home
and spoke the oath. Owen noticed that he didn't rest his hand

on a copy of the New Testament and that the wording was slightly different from everyone else's. An atheist, then? Not surprising, Owen thought, given the evidence of man's inhumanity to man he must have seen over the years.

After spending what remained of the morning establishing Dr. Glendenning's credentials and responsibilities, Jerome Lawrence finally began his examination-in-chief after lunch.

"Rebecca Charters has already described finding the body and calling the police," he said. "Could you please describe, Doctor, the condition of the body at the scene?"

"The victim lay on her back. Her blouse was open, her brassiere torn and her breasts exposed. Her skirt had been lifted above her waist, exposing the pubic region, in the manner typical of a sex murder. Her underwear was missing. I understand it was later found nearby. On closer examination of the face, I noticed a reddish-purple color and traces of bleeding from the nose, consistent with death by asphyxia. There was also a small, fresh scratch by her left eye."

"Could you tell us what you discovered at the postmortem?"

"The girl was—had been—in good general health, to be expected in a girl of sixteen. There were no signs of toxicity in her organs. On further examination, I concluded as I had earlier, that death was caused by asphyxia due to strangulation."

"Would you care to elaborate on asphyxia for the members of the jury, Doctor?" Jerome Lawrence went on.

Glendenning nodded briefly. "Some strangulation victims die from vagal inhibition, which means heart stoppage caused by pressure on the carotid arteries in the neck." He touched the spot beside his jaw. "The victim in this case, however, died because of obstruction to the veins in her neck and the forcing of the tongue against the back of throat, cutting off her air intake. There are certain telltale signs. People who die from vagal inhibition are pale, those who die from asphyxia have reddish-purple coloring. There are also petechial hemorrhages, little pinpricks of blood in the whites of the eyes, eyelids, facial skin. Contrary to popular fiction, the tongue does not protrude."

Owen glanced over at Sir Geoffrey and Lady Harrison, the victim's parents, who had attended almost every day. Lady Harrison turned to her husband and let her head touch his shoulder for a moment. Both were pale.

Owen felt he glimpsed, at that moment, the cold-blooded logic of the prosecution's strategy, like the dramatic structure of a play or a novel, and it sent a chill up his spine.

After hearing Rebecca Charters's emotional account of finding the body and then Banks's solid, professional testimony about the police investigation, if things had gone according to plan the jury would next have heard Michelle's testimony. They would have seen only a sweet, innocent young girl in the witness box and heard how this monster in the dock had attempted to strangle her. (He was certain she would have touched her long, tapered fingers to her throat as she described the attack.) *Then* they would have heard the gruesome medical details of the effects of strangulation. And what would they have thought of Owen after all that?

"Thank you, Doctor," Lawrence went on. "Could you tell, in this case, *how* the victim was strangled?"

"Yes. With a ligature. A satchel strap, in fact."

"And was this found close to the scene?"

"Yes. It was still attached to the victim's satchel."

"In your expert opinion, do you have any reason to doubt it was used as the murder weapon?"

"None at all. We carried out a number of tests. The satchel strap matched the indentations in the victim's throat perfectly. It was angled slightly upwards, cutting into the skin at the bottom part, indicating that she had been strangled from behind and that her attacker was taller than her. There was also blood around the edge of the strap."

"How much taller was the killer?" asked Jerome Lawrence.

"The victim was five foot six, so I would put the attacker at least six inches taller, perhaps more."

"And the accused is six foot two, as has already been established?"

"So I believe, yes."

"Would it have required a great deal of strength?"

"A certain amount, yes. But nothing superhuman."

"Would the manner of attack make it difficult for the victim to fight off her attacker?"

"Almost impossible. There wouldn't be much she could do. She might manage a wild scratch, of course, or a backwards kick to the shins with her heel."

"You mentioned a 'wild scratch.' Would this be possible if she were strangled from behind?"

"Oh, yes. It's quite conceivable she might reach behind and scratch her assailant."

"Was it possible to tell whether she had been killed in St. Mary's churchyard or elsewhere?"

"Yes, by the extent of post-mortem lividity, such as it was. This—" he turned to explain to the jury without Lawrence's prompting, "means that when the heart stops, the blood simply obeys the force of gravity and sinks to the lowest part of the body. It gathers and stains at points where the flesh is not in contact with the ground. Parts of the body that do remain in contact with the ground will remain white, of course, because the pressure will not allow the blood to settle in the capillaries. In this case, the staining at the back of the neck, small of the back and backs of the legs indicated that the deceased had been lying in the same position since her death. Also, as lividity was in its early stages, she couldn't have been there for very long. It generally begins about thirty minutes to one hour after death, develops fully between three and four hours and becomes fixed between eight and ten hours. The lividity was still faint, and blanching still occurred."

"Could you explain blanching for the benefit of the court?"

"Certainly. Before the blood coagulates in the vessels, if

you touch an area of lividity it will turn white. When you re-move your fingertip, it will resume its lividity. After four or five hours the discoloration hardens, becomes clotted, and pressure will not cause blanching."

"And what does this tell you?"

"Amongst other things, it helps determine time of death. As I said, lividity had only just started and there was no sign of rigor mortis, which usually begins in the eyelids about two or three hours after death. I also took temperature read-ings, and based on a mathematical calculation, I came up with time of death somewhere between five o'clock and when she was discovered."

"No earlier?"

"In my opinion, that would be very unlikely indeed."

"And as the victim's friend Megan Preece reports parting with Deborah near the bridge at six o'clock, and the evi-dence of Daniel Charters places Owen—"

"Objection!"

"Sustained." Judge Simmonds pointed with a bony finger. "Mr. Lawrence, behave yourself. You ought to know better."

Lawrence bowed. "Your Honor. Thank you, Dr. Glenden-ning. I have no further questions."

Shirley Castle stood up to cross-examine. "I only have a couple of questions, Doctor," she said briskly. "Minor points, really. I shan't keep you long."

Dr. Glendenning inclined his head and smiled at her in a gentlemanly way.

"I assume you supervised the collection of oral, vaginal and anal swabs at the crime scene?" Shirley Castle began.

"I did."

"And did you find any traces of semen?"

"None."

"None at all?"

"That is correct."

"In your post-mortem examination, did you discover any signs of forcible intercourse?"

"I found no signs of any intercourse at all, forcible or otherwise."

Shirley Castle frowned. "Yet you referred to this as a 'sex crime' in your earlier testimony. Does that absence of evidence not strike you as unusual in such a crime?"

"Not really. There are many kinds of sex crimes. The way the clothing was disturbed was reminiscent, in my experience, of a sex-crime scene."

"And we have already heard your enviable credentials as an expert on such matters, Doctor. How accurate is your estimate of time of death?"

"It's always an approximate business," Glendenning admitted. "There are so many variables."

"Could you give the court an example of how you might determine time of death?"

"Certainly. As I have already indicated, there are a number of factors, such as rigor mortis, lividity and stomach contents, but body temperature is often the most accurate. If the temperature at the time of death is normal—thirty-seven degrees centigrade—and it takes the body twenty-four to thirty-six hours after death to fall to the temperature of the environment, then one can make a back-calculation to the time of death."

"Twenty-four to thirty-six hours," said Shirley Castle, frowning towards the jury. "That's between a day and a day and a half. That's a rather broad margin for error, isn't it?"

Glendenning smiled. "I did say it was an approximate business."

"Yes, but you didn't say how wildly inaccurate it was."

"Objection."

"Sustained, Mr. Lawrence."

Shirley Castle bowed. "My apologies. Doctor, how long would it have taken Deborah Harrison's body temperature to reach that of the environment?"

"Well, again it's hard to say precisely. She was healthy, normal, slim, partially unclothed, and it was a moist

evening, with a temperature of ten degrees centigrade. I'd
say quicker rather than later."

"Say twenty-eight hours? Twenty-six?"

"Around there."

"Around there. Very well. Does the body cool at an even,
steady rate?"

"As a matter of fact, no. It falls in a sigmoid curve."

"And how do you arrive at time of death from temperature?"

"Glaister's formula. In this case the victim's temperature
was thirty-five point five degrees centigrade. One subtracts
this from the normal temperature of thirty-seven degrees and
multiplies by one point one. The answer, in this case, is one
point six-five hours. Taking the temperature of the environment into account, that becomes between one and two hours
before I arrived on the scene."

"What might affect the rate at which temperature falls?"

"It's hard to say exactly. A number of factors."

Shirley Castle took a deep breath and leaned forward.
"But it is *not* hard to say, is it Dr. Glendenning, that thin
people cool *quicker* than fat ones, and Deborah Harrison
was thin. On the other hand, healthy people cool *more
slowly* than weak ones, and Deborah Harrison was healthy.
Naked bodies cool quicker than clothed ones, yet Deborah
Harrison was only *partially* clothed. Bodies cool quicker in
water than in air, yet in the humidity of the fog Deborah
Harrison was subject to both. Am I right?"

"These are all relevant factors," admitted Glendenning.

"According to evidence already given," Shirley Castle
went on, "Deborah was last seen alive at six o'clock, which
rules out her being murdered earlier, wouldn't you say?"

Glendenning raised his eyebrows. "I would say so, yes."

"But the body was discovered by Rebecca Charters at six
forty-five. Is that correct?"

"I understand so."

"And the first police officers arrived at six fifty-nine?"

"Objection."

"Yes, Mr. Lawrence?" Judge Simmonds asked.

"I'd like to know where Ms. Castle is going with this line of questioning, Your Honor."

"The defense requests Your Honor's indulgence. This will become clear in a short while."

"Make it fast, Ms. Castle."

"Yes, Your Honor. Deborah Harrison was last seen at about six o'clock, and her body was discovered in St. Mary's graveyard at six forty-five. That leaves forty-five minutes during which she could have been murdered. Now according to your evidence as regards time of death, Doctor, she *could* have been murdered later than six-thirty, couldn't she?"

Glendenning nodded. "Yes, she *could* have been."

"In fact, death *could* have occurred even as late as six-forty, couldn't it?"

"Yes. But I believe Rebecca Charters heard—"

"Please, Doctor. You should know better than that. Rebecca Charters has already admitted that what she heard could easily have been some animal or another. Now, given that nobody actually *saw* Owen Pierce enter St. Mary's graveyard, and given that time of death could have occurred as late as six-forty, when Mr. Pierce was already in the Peking Moon, there is no direct evidence placing him at the exact scene of the crime at the exact time the crime was committed, is there, Doctor?"

"This is not—"

"And as no-one saw either Deborah Harrison *or* Owen Pierce enter the graveyard," Shirley Castle charged on before anyone could stop her, "then it follows that Deborah could have gone somewhere else first, couldn't she?"

"It's not my place to speculate on such matters," said Glendenning. "I'm here to testify on matters of medical fact."

"Ah, yes," said Shirley Castle. "Facts such as time of death. It's a lot of leeway to give the definition of a fact, isn't it, Doctor?"

"Objection."

"Sustained. Will you get on with it, Ms. Castle?"

"I have no further questions, Your Honor," she said, and sat down.

Very clever, thought Owen, then he turned to watch the juror who looked like a wrestler try to scratch an egg stain off his club tie.

IV

A week later, after more legal arguments and a succession of dull, minor scientific witnesses, from the fingerprint man to the officer responsible for keeping track of the forensic exhibits, Owen watched Shirley Castle intimidate the hair expert, who ended up retreating into scientific jargon and admitting that it was virtually impossible to prove beyond a shadow of a doubt that hair found on a victim's or suspect's clothing could be positively matched to its source.

The final prosecution witness was Dr. Tasker, biologist and DNA expert, a thin-faced, thin-haired academic of about forty, Owen guessed. He seemed to know his stuff, but there was a tentativeness about his delivery that threw Jerome Lawrence off kilter occasionally.

Owen wondered if the jury were as bored as he was by the interminable descriptions of autorads and enzyme scissors, by the testimony as to the scientific validity of polymerase chain reactions and the meaning of short tandem repeats, by the seeming hours spent describing the extreme care taken against the possibility of contamination of laboratory samples.

When Shirley Castle stood up to cross-examine the next afternoon, Tasker seemed a little in awe of her, and if Owen were not mistaken, perhaps a mite smitten, too. Maybe she realized this. Her tone, as she began, was relaxed, friendly, a little flirtatious even.

"Dr. Tasker," she said with a smile, "I'm sure the court

was most impressed yesterday with your account of DNA analysis. You would seem to have proved, without blinding us all with science, that the DNA derived from the blood-stain on Mr. Pierce's anorak was indeed the DNA of Deborah Harrison. Is this true?"

Tasker nodded. "The DNA extracted from the dried bloodstain on Mr. Pierce's anorak was fifty million times *more likely to be hers* than anyone else's, and the DNA taken from the tissue sample discovered under the victim's finger-nail was fifty million times more likely to be Owen Pierce's than anyone else's. All we can say is how rare such a result is compared to the rest of the population."

"Still," smiled Shirley Castle. "Those are impressive odds, aren't they?"

"Oh, yes." Tasker beamed. "I certainly wouldn't bet against them."

"Almost beyond a shadow of a doubt," Shirley Castle said, "And that is, after all, what this is all about, isn't it? However, Dr. Tasker, there are one or two points you might be able to clarify for me."

Owen swore that Tasker almost flushed with pleasure. "Of course. It would be a pleasure."

Shirley Castle acknowledged the compliment with a slight tilt of her head. "How much of Deborah Harrison's blood did you find on my client's anorak?"

"A small amount."

"Could you please give the court some sense of how much that might be?"

Tasker smiled. "Well, not a great deal. But enough for polymerase chain reaction analysis, as I described earlier."

"Yes, but how much? A thimble full?"

"Oh, good heavens, no, not that much."

"As much, then, as might smear from a small cut or scratch?"

"Mmm. About that, yes."

"A pinprick?"

"Possibly."

"In other words, a spot of blood about the size of a pin-head. Am I right?"

"Perhaps a little bigger than—"

"*Approximately* the size of a pinhead?"

"I suppose so. About that, yes. But, as I said—"

"Now the court has already heard Dr. Glendenning testify that there was a small scratch beside Deborah Harrison's left eye. Is this the kind of wound that might produce a similar amount of blood if some fabric brushed against it?"

Tasker shifted in his seat. "Well, I didn't see the scratch so I can't say for certain, but it *was* a small amount, definitely commensurate with a minor injury such as the one you describe."

"Where did you find this blood?"

"On the accused's anorak."

"Where on the accused's anorak?"

"On the left arm. Near the shoulder."

"Now we have already heard that Deborah Harrison was five foot six inches tall and Owen Pierce is six foot two. Would this put Deborah Harrison's left eye in the region of his upper arm?"

Tasker shrugged. "I suppose so. I couldn't say exactly."

"If Your Honor would allow me," Shirley Castle addressed Judge Simmonds, "I would like the opportunity to demonstrate to the court that this is, in fact, so."

Owen could see her holding her breath. Most judges, she had told him, hate anything that smacks overly of theatrics. She must, however, have convinced him that she was following an important line of questioning, because he granted his permission after hardly any hesitation at all.

It was a simple enough thing to do. A man and a young girl were brought in—where Shirley had found them, Owen had no idea—the girl markedly shorter than the man. They were officially measured at five foot six and six foot two, then stood side by side. The girl's eye came level with the upper part of the man's arm. Shirley Castle thanked them and continued.

"Was that the only blood you discovered on my client's clothing?"

"Yes."

Shirley Castle called for Owen's anorak to be shown to the jury. One feature, she pointed out, was the zippered pocket at the outside top of the sleeve. "Did you, Dr. Tasker, find any of the girl's blood on or around this zip?"

"Yes. In the vicinity."

"Could you elaborate?"

"It was right at the end of the zip, actually."

"Would you point to the spot on the exhibit, please?"

Tasker did so.

"The edge of the metal teeth is fairly sharp there," Shirley Castle went on. "Does that not indicate to you that the girl may have scraped her cheek on the zip when she collided with Mr. Pierce after running backwards in the fog?"

"It could have got there in any number of ways."

"But it could have got there in the way I suggest?"

"Yes, but—"

"And that was *all* the blood you found?"

"I've already said that. I—"

"Not very much, is it?"

"As I said, it was enough for PCR analysis."

"Ah, yes: PCR, STR, DNA, 'genetic fingerprinting.' Magic words, these days. And what does that prove, Dr. Tasker?"

"That the blood on the defendant's anorak is fifty million times—"

"Yes, yes. We've already been through all that, haven't we? But the defense has *never denied* that it is Deborah Harrison's blood. She bumped into my client and scratched herself on the zip of his anorak. Would you admit that the *amount* and *location* of the blood you found bear out that explanation?"

"I suppose so."

"You suppose so. Did you find any traces of blood on the cuffs of the anorak?"

"No."

"Wouldn't you expect to if the victim were bleeding from the nose as the accused strangled her?"

"Perhaps."

"So he might be expected to get blood on his cuff if he did indeed strangle her from behind with the satchel strap?"

"Well, it's possible, yes, but—"

"And did you find any blood lower down his sleeve?"

"No. But she could have twisted side—"

"Thank you, Dr. Tasker. You have answered my question. Now, given the life-and-death struggle that must have taken place, it would have been difficult to avoid *some* close contact, wouldn't it?"

"Presumably."

"And did you test the rest of anorak for blood?"

"Yes. We carried out a thorough examination."

"But you found no blood other than this infinitesimal amount high on the sleeve, at the edge of the metal teeth on the zip?"

"No."

The infatuation seemed to be on the wane, Owen noticed. Tasker didn't even want to look Shirley Castle in the eye now. Owen glanced over at "Minerva," who was regarding the doctor sternly. No more would she believe the "scientific tests have proved" commercials, if, indeed, she ever had.

"Dr. Tasker, do you know where Deborah Harrison's hairs—what we have since learned only *might* in fact be Deborah Harrison's hairs—were found on Mr. Pierce's anorak?"

"No, that's not my—"

"Then let me tell you. They were found on the upper left arm and on the upper left arm *only*. In fact, all three of her hairs were found in the teeth of Mr. Pierce's zip, by the pinpoint bloodstain. What do you have to say to that?"

"I don't know. It's not my field."

"Not your field? But would you not say it's consistent with the scenario I just outlined for you? A minor collision?"

"I have already agreed that is a *possible* explanation."

"How much blood and skin did you find under the victim's fingernail?"

"A small amount. But enough for—"

"Consistent with what might be deposited from a light scratch?"

"Yes."

"If Deborah Harrison had been fighting for her life, wouldn't you have expected to find more, in your professional judgment?"

"Possibly. But again, it's not my—"

"I understand that, Dr. Tasker. But we can't have it both ways, can we? Either she did get the opportunity to defend herself by scratching, in which case she came away with a pitiful amount of skin, or she didn't. Which is it to be, in your opinion?"

Owen saw Lawrence on the verge of an objection, but he seemed to think better of it and sank down again.

"It could have been just a lucky strike," said Tasker. "I don't know."

"You don't know. Very well. Would you at least agree that the presence of a small amount of Mr. Pierce's skin under one of her fingernails could have got there during a minor collision, if she put out her hand to steady herself?"

"Yes."

"Then would you also agree that it is possible that Deborah Harrison's killer could have been someone other than my client?"

"Objection!"

"Overruled, Mr. Lawrence. Witness will please answer the question."

Tasker fiddled with his tie. "Well, theoretically, yes. Of course," he gave a nervous titter. "I mean, theoretically, anything's possible. I wasn't there, I can't tell you exactly what happened. The DNA was a good match to the defendant's, so he can't be excluded."

"I submit that the DNA match is irrelevant. Is your answer to my question yes?"

"I suppose so."

"Is it?"

"Yes."

Shirley Castle turned to the judge and threw her hands in the air. "Your Honor," she said, "I find myself exasperated that the prosecution's case is based on so little and such flimsy evidence. No further questions."

For the first time, Jerome Lawrence stood up to re-examine. It must be because it's his last witness, Owen thought. He wants to leave a positive impression.

"Just two questions, Dr. Tasker," he said. "You are fully aware of the nature of the crime, the nature of the victim's injuries. Would you say, in your expert opinion, that the amounts of the victim's blood left on the accused's clothing were in any way *too little* for him to have committed such a crime?"

"No, I wouldn't," said Tasker.

"And could the exchange of blood and tissue have taken place during a struggle for her life?"

"Indeed it could."

Jerome Lawrence gave an oily bow. "Thank you very much, Dr. Tasker."

Chapter 12

I

*N*othing could have prepared Owen for the shock of seeing Michelle sitting in the gallery when he glanced nervously around the courtroom before going into the witness-box.

His heart thudded against his ribcage. He felt as if a large bird had somehow found its way inside him and was scratching and plucking at his chest and throat, beating its wings, trying to get out. She was still beautiful; she still had the power to make his heart ache and yearn.

If anything, Owen thought, Michelle looked even younger than she had when they had been together: about fifteen or sixteen. She wore no make-up to mar her delicate, alabaster complexion, a maroon blazer and a simple white blouse, very much like the St. Mary's school uniform.

Her blonde hair—the same color and length as Deborah Harrison's—hung over her shoulders in exactly the same way Deborah's had in the newspaper photographs. Her lips, the color of the inside of a strawberry, were fixed in a childish pout. And the implication of innocence and immaturity permeated her entire bearing. Owen wondered if people knew who she was. She was sitting next to a man he had seen there often before: a reporter, Owen thought.

He tried to avoid looking at her. Why was she here? Had

the Crown lured her in to upset him? He had already realized that he was participating in a drama, a theatrical event more than anything else, and that the awards would be handed out in a few days' time. Did Michelle have a part to play, too? She wasn't going into the box—Shirley Castle had taken care of that—so what was she doing in court?

He was so distracted by her presence that he didn't hear Shirley Castle calling him to give evidence at first, then the judge called him to the box.

Shirley Castle spent more than a day taking him through the events of that fateful Monday in November, as smoothly as she had before in the interview room near his cell. He felt calm as he spoke, and he hoped the jury wouldn't interpret this as lack of emotion.

"Minerva," as far as he could tell, listened to him objectively, a slight furrow of concentration in her brow. Most of the others, he noticed, appeared to be paying attention too, but a couple had disbelieving sneers etched around their lips—that "come on, tell us another one" look he had become so adept at perceiving of late. Occasionally, he sneaked a glance at Michelle. Once in a while she turned and spoke behind her hand to the reporter next to her.

The next day, after Shirley Castle had finished eliciting a reasonable and believable account of events from Owen, or so he thought, Jerome Lawrence dragged himself to his feet. "There hardly seems any point," Lawrence's weary, long-suffering movements seemed to be saying, "in bothering with this, as you and I know he's guilty, ladies and gentlemen of the jury, but duty demands we go through the motions." Owen looked at the gallery and saw Michelle was in court again.

Lawrence asked what seemed a lot of dull questions for most of the morning, and after lunch he finally began to zoom in on the crime. "Mr. Pierce," he said, "you have told the jury that between the hours of about six and six-thirty on November 6 last year, you simply walked around the area of St. Mary's, Eastvale, in the fog, and stood on the bridge for some time. Is this so?"

"Yes."

"Were you intoxicated, Mr. Pierce?"

"Not at all."

"You drank, let me see, two pints of beer and a double Scotch at the Nag's Head, is that right?"

Owen shrugged. "I think so."

"And you weren't intoxicated?"

"I'm not saying I didn't feel the effects at all, just that I was perfectly in control. And I was walking, not driving."

"You had more to drink later, didn't you, at the Peking Moon?"

"Yes. With a large meal."

"Indeed. And can you tell the court why you spent so long standing on the bridge before a fine view that you *couldn't possibly see* because of the thick fog?"

"I don't know, really. It was just what I felt like doing. I had one or two problems to mull over and I find fog helps contemplation."

"What problems were these?"

Owen saw Shirley Castle making discreet warning signals. He looked Michelle in the eye. "Personal matters. Of no relevance."

"I see. And was it this same *personal matter* that led you to drink so much?"

"I didn't drink a lot. I've already told you, I wasn't drunk."

"And led you to hide yourself away in the corner of a restaurant and mutter to yourself?"

Owen felt himself flush with embarrassment. "That's just a habit, like when I'm adding up. I've always done it. Sometimes a thought just comes out loud, that's all. I forget that there are people around. It doesn't make me a maniac. Or a murderer."

"Are you sure you weren't muttering in the Peking Moon about what you'd just done? Murdered Deborah Harrison?"

"Of course not. That's totally absurd. I was just reasoning with myself, to calm down."

"Calm down?" There was no missing the verbal underlining in that repetition. "Why did you feel the need to calm down, Mr. Pierce? What made you so agitated in the first place."

"I wasn't agitated. There's a difference between being a little melancholy and being agitated, isn't there? I mean—"

"Would you please stick to answering my questions?" Lawrence butted in. "If I need lessons in the English language, believe me, I shall ask for them."

"I'm the one in the dock, aren't I? Why shouldn't my opinion count? You've asked everyone else's, haven't you? Why should I let you get away with distorting the meaning—"

"Mr. Pierce," Judge Simmonds grumbled. "Please answer Mr. Lawrence's questions as directly and as clearly as you can."

"I'm sorry, Your Honor," said Owen. He turned back to Lawrence. "The answer is no. I wasn't agitated; I was melancholy."

"Is it not true that you were upset and dejected about your break-up with a young lady some—"

"Objection!"

"Sustained. Mr. Lawrence!"

"I apologize, Your Honor."

What the hell was that little skirmish about? Owen wondered, his heart jumping. He glanced at Michelle again. Lawrence was trying it on; he knew damn well that evidence had been ruled inadmissible. The bastard was trying to slip it in regardless. He thanked his lucky stars Shirley Castle was so quick. Still, something had been lodged with the jury, no matter how much the judge might tell them to disregard it. He looked at "Minerva." She seemed puzzled. Owen's breath came a little quicker.

"Let us, then, move on to the scientific evidence," Lawrence continued. "You don't deny that Deborah Harrison's hair and blood were found on your clothing?"

"It's not for me to accept or deny," Owen said. "I'm not a

scientist. If your experts have identified these things, that's their business."

"And when faced with this fact by Detective Chief Inspector Banks, you gave him some story about bumping into the girl. Is this true?"

It was plain enough that Lawrence intended "cock and bull" to come before "story."

"I didn't bump into her," Owen said. "She bumped into me as I was turning from the wall."

"Answer the question."

"I would answer it if it were correctly posed."

Lawrence sighed and made a long-suffering gesture to the jury. "Very well, then, Mr. Pierce. You told the police that the girl bumped into you. Is this correct?"

"I told them exactly what happened."

"Why didn't you tell them earlier?"

"It didn't seem important."

"Come on, Mr. Pierce, the police had already told you how important everything that happened that day was the second time they interviewed you. You knew you were in a serious situation. Why didn't you tell them earlier?"

"I've already told you. I didn't tell them about the time I had to bend down and refasten my left shoelace, either, or about stopping at the newsagent's for an evening paper, which, by the way, they didn't have. It just *didn't seem important*."

"Yet you remembered it well enough later. In fact, as soon as you were challenged with evidence of your physical contact with the victim, you suddenly came up with an explanation." Lawrence laughed and flapped like a bat. "As if by magic. Really, Mr. Pierce. Do you expect the court to believe that?"

"Objection."

"Sustained. The witness's opinion on such matters of what the court should or should not believe is not required, as you well know, Mr. Lawrence."

"I am sorry, Your Honor. I submit to you, Mr. Pierce, that

you saw Deborah Harrison part from her companion, that you followed her into the graveyard, and that you—"

"No! I did nothing of the kind," Owen cut in.

"And that you strangled Deborah Harrison with her own school satchel strap!"

Owen clenched his fists and kept them out of sight. "I did not," he said quietly, with as much dignity as he could muster.

Lawrence held him with his black, beady eyes, then breathed, "No more questions," and sat down looking pleased with himself.

It was Friday afternoon, so Judge Simmonds adjourned for the weekend and Owen was escorted back to his cell.

II

Back in the dock on Monday, Owen tried to keep his eyes off Michelle and concentrate on Jerome Lawrence's final address to the jury. From what he heard, it wasn't much different from the opening remarks: Owen was a monster, hardly even human, who had brutally murdered a pure and innocent young girl. Most of the time he found himself looking towards Michelle. He sensed she knew he was staring at her, but she wouldn't catch his eye.

Lawrence went on for the best part of the day, piling atrocity on atrocity, outrage upon outrage, and it wasn't until Tuesday morning that Shirley Castle got to make her closing speech. Again, Owen found himself watching Michelle most of the time, and the next thing he knew, Shirley Castle was wrapping up.

"And, above all, remember the phrase *beyond reasonable doubt*," she said. "It is the very foundation upon which our justice system is built. The burden of proof lies with the Crown. Ask yourselves, has the Crown proven its case *beyond reasonable doubt?* Are you yourselves sure, beyond reasonable doubt, that this man before you is anything other than an innocent victim? Do you not harbor doubts your-selves? I think you will find that you do, and that you can honestly do no other than agree with me, and say *no,* the Crown has *not* proven its case. For you see in front of you a man who was in the wrong place at the wrong time, a man confused, worried and anxious by a police investigation he could not understand and which was not explained to him. But more than anything, you see in front of you an *innocent* man who has already been punished more than enough for a crime he did not commit. Look into your hearts, ladies and gentlemen, and I'm sure you will find there the certain knowledge that my client is innocent of all charges laid against him. Thank you."

After this carefully impassioned finale, Judge Sim-monds's summing up seemed perfunctory to Owen. At least he was fair, Owen had to admit. In a detached monologue, the judge reiterated the main points of the case, careful not to indicate any bias. As the old man talked, Owen kept switching his gaze between Michelle and "Minerva."

"Minerva" was clearly listening, but Owen could not help getting the impression that this final speech was superfluous to her, that she had already made up her mind. Once, she caught him looking at her for a second and turned away quickly, blushing. He could have sworn, though, that her eyes held no trace of accusation, of condemnation. When Michelle finally decided to return Owen's gaze, she smiled, and he couldn't mistake the cold, malicious glint in her eyes; it made him shiver.

III

While the jury was out, Owen sat in a cheerless room below the court with Shirley Castle and his guards drinking bitter coffee until his stomach hurt.

He had experienced anxious waiting before—after a job interview, for example, or those long nights at the window watching for Michelle to come home—but nothing as gut-wrenching as this. His stomach clenched and growled; he bit his nails; he jumped at every sound. He tried to imagine what it must have been like when the death penalty existed, but couldn't. Shirley Castle tried to make conversation but soon stopped after his terse and jumbled responses.

Hours, it seemed, went by. At last, someone came and said the jury hadn't reached a verdict yet, and as it was late, Owen was to spend the night back in his cell. He asked Shirley Castle about the jury taking so long, and she said it was a good sign.

That night, he hardly slept at all. Fear gnawed at him; the cell walls closed in. In that nether world between sleep and waking, where memories take on the aspect of dreams, he actually watched himself strangle Deborah Harrison in a foggy graveyard. Or was it Michelle? He had been told so often that he had done it that his subconscious mind had actually been tricked into believing it. He thought he screamed out in the night, but nobody came rushing to see what was wrong. When he woke from the dream, he noticed he had an erection and felt ashamed.

Morning came: slopping out, the stink of piss and shit that seemed to permeate the place, the supervised shave, breakfast. Then Owen sat around in his suit waiting to go back to the court and face the verdict. Still nothing. By mid-morning on Wednesday, he wasn't sure how much longer he could last without going mad. Just before lunch, his cell door opened and the warder said, "Come on, lad. It looks like they're back."

In court, Owen gripped the front of the dock until his knuckles turned white. The gallery was full: Michelle leaning forward, thumbnail between her front teeth, as she often did during thrillers or when she was concentrating hard; the Harrisons; two of the detectives, Stott and Banks; the vicar, Daniel Charters and his attractive wife, Rebecca; reporters; morbid members of the public. They were all there.

The jury filed back in. Owen looked at "Minerva." She

didn't glance in his direction. He didn't know what to make of that.

After the hush came the legal rigmarole about charges, then the question everyone had been waiting for: "Do you find the defendant Owen Pierce guilty or not guilty as charged?"

The split-second pause between question and answer seemed an eternity for Owen. His ears roared and he felt his head swimming. Then the spokesman, a drab-looking man Owen had guessed to be a banker, spoke the words: "We find the defendant not guilty, Your Honor."

There was more talk after that, but most of it was lost in the hubbub that raced through the courtroom like an explosive blast. Reporters dashed for phones. Owen swayed and clutched the dock for dear life. He couldn't seem to stop the ringing in his ears. He heard a woman yell, "It's a travesty!" Then everything went white and he fainted.

Owen came to in a room below the court, a cool, damp cloth pressed to his brow, with Shirley Castle and Gordon Wharton standing over him. As he recovered, he felt the stirrings of joy, like the first, tentative shoots of a new plant in spring, overtake the gnawing anxiety that had burdened him before. He was *free!* Surely it would sink in soon. Shirley Castle was talking to someone, but when she stopped and walked towards him, he could feel the muscles in his face form a smile for the first time in what seemed like years.

She smiled back, curled her fist and thumped the air triumphantly. "We did it!"

"You did it," Owen said. "I don't know how to thank you."

"Winning is thanks enough." She held out her hand. "Congratulations, Owen. And good luck."

He shook it, the first time he'd touched a woman in months, and he was conscious of the soft warmth under the firm grip. He felt her give a little tug and released her, embarrassed to realize he had held on too long. He wanted to kiss her. And not only because she had won his case. Instead, he turned to Wharton.

"What now?" he asked.

"What? Oh." The solicitor glanced away from the disappearing figure. "Wonderful woman, isn't she? I told you if anyone could do it, Shirley Castle could. It was a majority verdict, you know. Ten to two. That's what took them so long. What now? Well, you're free, that's what."

"But . . . what do I do? I mean, my stuff and . . ."

"Tell you what." Wharton looked at his watch. "I'll drive you back over to the prison, if you like, and you can pick your stuff up, then I'll take you back to Eastvale."

Owen nodded. "Thanks. How do we . . . I mean, do we just walk out of here?"

Wharton laughed. "Yes," he said. "Yes, that's exactly what we do. Hard to get used to, eh? But I think there'll be a bit of a mob out front, we'd better leave by the back way."

"A mob?"

Wharton frowned. "Yes. Well, you've seen the papers. Those sly innuendos about the 'evidence they couldn't present in court.' That not-guilty verdict won't have sunk in with them yet, will it? People lose all sense of proportion when they get carried away by chants and whatnot. Come on."

In a daze, Owen followed Wharton through the corridors to the back exit. The sun was shining on the narrow backstreet; opposite was a refurbished Victorian pub, all black trim and etched, smoked-glass windows; under his feet, the worn paving-stones looked gold in the midday light. Freedom.

Owen breathed the air deeply; a warm, still day. When he thought about it, he realized the trial had lasted almost two months, and it was now May, the most glorious month in the Dales. Back up near Eastvale, the woods, fields and hillsides would be a ablaze with wildflowers: bluebells, wild garlic, celandines, cowslips, violets and primroses; and here and there would be the fields of bright yellow rape-seed.

As they walked towards Wharton's car, Owen could vaguely hear the crowd outside the front of the courthouse: women's voices mostly, he thought, chanting, "Guilty! Guilty! Guilty!"

IV

"Fuck it," said Barry Stott loudly. Then he said it again, banging his fist on the arm of the bench for emphasis. *"Fuck it."* A couple standing by the pub door gave him a dirty look. "Sorry," he said to Banks, blushing right up to the tips of his jug-ears. "I just had to let it out."

Banks nodded in sympathy. It was the first time he had ever heard Barry Stott swear, and he had to admit he didn't blame him.

They were sitting on the long bench outside Whitelock's in the narrow alley called Turk's Head Yard, drinks and food propped on the upturned barrel that served as a table. Along with his pint of Younger's bitter, Banks had a Cornish pasty with chips and gravy, and Stott had a Scotch egg with HP Sauce, with a half of shandy to wash it down. They had just left Leeds Crown Court after the Owen Pierce verdict.

It was a beautiful May day; the pub had lured students from their studies and encouraged office workers to linger over their lunch-hours. Not much light penetrated Turk's Head Yard because of the high walls of the buildings on both sides, but the air was warm and full of the promise of summer. Men sat with their jackets off and shirtsleeves rolled up, while bare-legged women opened an extra button or two on their blouses.

Banks took a sip of beer before tucking into the pasty. He watched Stott pick at the Scotch egg, dip little pieces in the sauce, chew and swallow, too distracted to taste the food. It was obvious that he had no appetite. He had only eaten half when he pushed his plate away. Banks finished his own lunch quickly and lit a cigarette.

"I can't believe he got off," Stott said. "I just can't believe it."

"I'm just as pissed off as you are, Barry, but it happens," said Banks. "You get used to it. Don't take it personally."

"But I do. It was me who cottoned on to him, me who tracked him down. We build a solid case, and he just walks away."

Banks didn't bother reminding him how it was teamwork and hard procedural slog that had led them to Owen Pierce. "The case obviously wasn't solid enough," he said. "Dr. Tasker wasn't very good, for a start. Even Glendenning wasn't up to his usual form. Who knows? Maybe they were right?"

"Who?"

"The jury."

Stott shook his head. His ears seemed to flap with the motion. "No. I can't accept that. He did it. I know he did. I feel it in my bones. He murdered that poor girl, and he got away with it. You know, if we'd got the evidence from Michelle Chappel in, then we'd have got a conviction for certain. The judge made a hell of a mistake there."

"Perhaps. Did you see her there, by the way?"

"Where? Who?"

"Michelle Chappel. In court. I don't know if she's been there all along but she was in the public gallery for the verdict. She'd let her hair grow since last November, too. Looked more like Deborah Harrison than ever. She was even wearing a maroon blazer. She was talking to that reporter from the *News of the World*."

"See what I mean," said Stott. "If we'd been able to bring out that connection, her evidence of what he did to her, there's no jury in the country wouldn't have convicted Pierce."

"Maybe so, but that's not the point, Barry."

Stott flushed. "Excuse me, but I think it is. A guilty man has just walked out of that courtroom after committing one of the most horrible murders I have ever investigated, and you tell me that's not the point. I'm sorry, but—"

"I mean it's not the point I'm trying to make."

Stott frowned. "I don't follow."

"Why is Michelle Chappel so keen to stick the knife in Pierce?"

"Oh, I see. Well, maybe because he beat her up. Or perhaps because he tried to strangle her? Or could being raped by him after he knocked her out have upset her just a little a bit?"

Banks sipped some more beer. "All right, Barry, give it a rest. I catch your drift. Perhaps you're right. But why hang around after her evidence was declared inadmissible? Just to watch him suffer? Why take time off work?"

Stott frowned. "What makes you think there's a connection?"

"It's just odd, that's all." Banks stubbed out his cigarette and drank some more beer. "Her hair was short when we talked to her."

"Women's hair," said Stott with a shrug. "Who knows anything about that?"

Banks smiled. "Good point. Another pint? Half, rather?"

"Should we?"

"Yes, we damn well should. Jimmy Riddle's going to be out for our blood. Might as well put off the inevitable as long as possible."

"Oh, all right. I'll have another half of shandy. Then I'll have to be off."

Banks edged through the crowd to the bar, looking at his reflection in the antique mirror at the back while he waited. Not too bad for his early forties, he thought, still slim and trim, despite the pints and the poor diet; a few lines around the eyes, maybe, and a touch a gray at the temples, but that was all. Besides, they added character, Sandra said.

He intended to part company with Stott after the next drink and visit an old friend while he was in Leeds: Pamela Jeffreys, a violist with the English Northern Philharmonic orchestra. About a year ago, she had been badly hurt in an attack for which Banks still blamed himself. She wasn't back in the orchestra yet, but she was working hard and getting there fast, and this afternoon, she was playing a chamber concert at the university's music department. It might go some small way towards making up for the disappointment in court this morning.

He might also, while he was so close, drop in at the Classical Record Shop and see about the Samuel Barber song collection he had been wanting for a while. Listening to Dawn Upshaw singing "Knoxville: Summer of 1915" on the drive down had made him think about it.

On the other hand, the not-guilty verdict changed things. While he was in Leeds, he would also phone DI Ken Blackstone and see about having a chat with one of Jelačić's card-playing cronies. He might even have another word with Jelačić himself.

Though the Crown would probably appeal the verdict, as far as Banks was concerned it was back to the drawing-board for the time being, a drawing-board he was beginning to feel he should never have left in the first place. And Ive Jelačić was certainly high on his list of loose ends.

"Damn that judge," said Stott when he had thanked Banks for the drink. "Just thinking about it makes my blood boil."

"I'm not convinced Michelle Chappel's testimony would have helped as much as you think, Barry," Banks said.

"Why not? At least it proves he had homicidal tendencies towards young women of Deborah Harrison's physical type."

"It proves nothing of the kind," said Banks. "Okay, I'll admit, I was as excited about the psychological possibilities it opened up as you were. And, yes, I was bloody annoyed that Simmonds excluded it. But now I think about it, looking at her in court, I'm not so sure."

Stott scratched the back of his left ear and frowned. "Why not?"

"Because I think that defense lawyer, Shirley Castle, would have made mincemeat of her, that's why. In the final analysis, she'd have had the jury believing that Michelle Chappel was lying, that she did what she did out of pure vindictiveness towards Pierce, for revenge, because she harbored a grudge for the way he treated her."

"And rightly so, after what he did to her."

"But don't you see how it would discredit her testimony, Barry, make her seem like a lying bitch? Especially with such criticisms coming from another woman. That could be pretty damning. She's good is Ms. Castle. I've been up against her before. She'd have made sure that Pierce convinced them with *his* version of that night's events. And if they believed that he had simply been warding off the frenzied attack of a hysterical woman, then he could have gained their sympathy."

Stott took off his glasses and polished them with a spotless handkerchief. "I still think it would have helped us get a conviction."

"Well there's no way of knowing now, is there?"

"I suppose not," Stott said glumly. "What do we do now?"

"There's not much more we can do."

"Reopen the investigation?"

Banks sipped some beer. "Oh, yes. I think so, don't you? After all, Barry, someone out there killed Deborah Harrison, and according to all the hallmarks, it looks very much like someone who might do it again."

Chapter 13

I

Vjeko Batorac was out when Banks called in the afternoon, and a neighbor said he usually came home from work at about five-thirty. Ken Blackstone, who said Batorac was probably the most believable of Jelačić's three card-playing cronies, had given Banks the address.

Grateful for the free time, Banks played truant; he went up to the university and spent a delightful hour listening to Vaughan Williams's *String Quartet No. 2.*

And he was glad he did. As he watched and listened, all the stress and disappointment of the verdict, all his fears of having persecuted the wrong man in the first place, seemed to become as insubstantial as air, at least for a while.

As he watched Pamela Jeffreys play in the bright room, prisms of light all around, her glossy raven hair dancing, skin like burnished gold, the diamond stud in her right nostril flashing in the sun, he thought not for the first time that there was something intensely, spiritually erotic about a beautiful woman playing music.

It seemed, as he watched, that Pamela first projected her spirit and emotions into her instrument, the bow an extension of her arm, fingers and strings inseparable, then she became the music, flowing and soaring with its rhythms and melodies, dipping and swooping, eyes closed, oblivious to the world outside.

Or so it seemed. Though he had taken a few hesitant steps towards learning the piano, Banks couldn't actually play an instrument, so he was willing to admit he might be romanticizing. Maybe she was thinking about her pay-check.

Erotic fantasies aside, it was all perfectly innocent. They had coffee and a chat afterwards, then Banks headed back to Batorac's house.

Vjeko Batorac lived in a small pre-war terrace house in Sheepscar, near the junction of Roseville Road and Roundhay Road, less than a mile from Jelačić's Burmantofts flat. There was no garden; the front door, which looked as if it had been freshly painted, opened directly onto the pavement. This time, a few minutes before six o'clock, Banks's knock was answered by a slight, hollow-cheeked young man with fair hair, wearing oil-stained jeans and a clean white T-shirt.

"Molim?" said Batorac, frowning.

"Mr. Batorac?" Banks asked, showing his warrant card. "I wonder if I might have a word? Do you speak English?"

Batorac nodded, looking puzzled. "What is it about?"

"Ive Jelačić."

Batorac rolled his eyes and opened the door wider. "You'd better come in."

The living-room was sunny and clean, and just a hint of baby smells mingled with those of cabbage and garlic from the kitchen. What surprised Banks most of all was the bookcase that took up most of one wall, crammed with English classics and foreign titles he couldn't read. Serbo-Croatian, he guessed. The "Six O'Clock News" was on Radio 4 in the background.

"That's quite a library you've got."

Batorac beamed. *"Hvala lipo.* Thank you very much. Yes, I love books. In my own country I was a school-teacher. I taught English, so I have studied your language for many years. I also write poetry."

"What do you do here?"

Batorac smiled ironically. "I am a garage mechanic. Fortunately for me, in Croatia you had to be good at fixing your own car." He shrugged. "It's a good job. Not much pay, but my boss treats me well."

A baby started crying. Batorac excused himself for a moment and went upstairs. Banks examined the titles in more detail as he waited: Dickens, Hardy, Keats, Austen, Balzac, Flaubert, Coleridge, Tolstoy, Dostoevsky, Milton, Kafka . . . Many he had read, but many were books he had promised himself to read and never got around to. The baby fell silent and Batorac came back.

"Sorry," he said. "We have a friend takes care of little Jelena during the day, while we work. When she comes home she . . . how do you say this . . . she misses her mother and father?"

Banks smiled. "Yes, that's right. She has missed you."

"*Has* missed. Yes. Sometimes I get the tenses wrong. What is it you wanted to see me about? Sit down, please."

Banks sat. This didn't look or smell like the kind of house where one could smoke, especially with the baby around, so he resigned himself to refrain. It would no doubt do him good. "Remember," he asked, "a few months ago when the local police asked you about an evening you said you played cards with Ive Jelačić?"

Batorac nodded. "Yes. It was true. Every Monday we play cards. Dragica, my wife, she is very indulgent. But on Mondays only." He smiled. "Tuesday I do not have to go to work, so sometimes we talk and play until late."

"And drink?"

"Yes. I do not drink much because I drive home. The streets are not safe at night. But I drink some, yes. A little."

"And are you *absolutely* certain on that Monday, the sixth of November, you were playing cards with Stipe Pavic and Ive Jelačić at Mile Pavelic's house?"

"Yes. I swear on the Bible. I do not lie, Inspector."

"No offense. Please understand we have to be very thorough about these things. Was Jelačić there the whole time?"

"Yes."

"He said that he walked to Mr. Pavelic's house and back. Did he usually do that?"

"Yes. He only lives about five hundred meters away, over the waste ground."

"I'm curious, Mr. Batorac—"

"Call me Vjeko, please."

"Very well, Vjeko. I'm curious as to how the four of you got together. If you don't mind my saying so, you and Ive Jelačić seem very different kinds of people."

Vjeko smiled. "There are not many of my countrymen here in Leeds," he said. "We have clubs and societies where we meet to get news from home and talk about politics. What you English call a very good grapevine. Ive knew Mile from the old country. They are both from Split. I met Stipe here, in Leeds. He is from Zagreb and I am from Dubrovnik, long way apart. Have you ever visited Dubrovnik, Chief Inspector?"

Banks shook his head,

"It is a very beautiful city. Very much history, ancient architecture. Many English tourists came before the war. You have missed much. Perhaps forever."

"When did you come here?"

"In 1991, after the siege. I could not bear to see my home destroyed." He tapped his chest. "I am a poet, not a soldier, Chief Inspector. And my health is not strong. I have only one lung." Vjeko shrugged. "When Ive came from Eastvale, he came into contact with us. He told us his parents were both killed in the fighting. Many of us have lost friends and relatives in the war. I lost my sister two years ago. Raped and butchered by Serb soldiers. It gives us a common bond. The kind of bond that transcends—is that right? Yes?—that transcends personality. After that, we just started meeting to talk and play cards." He smiled. "Not for money, you understand. My Dragica would not be so indulgent about that."

Almost on cue, the front door opened, and a pretty, petite young woman with dark hair and sparkling eyes walked in. "What would your Dragica not be so indulgent about?" she asked with a smile, going over and kissing Vjeko affectionately before turning to glance curiously at Banks.

Vjeko told her who Banks was and why he was there. "I said you would not be indulgent if I played cards for money."

Dragica thumped him playfully on the shoulder and perched on the arm of the sofa. "Sometimes," she said, "I ask myself why you must stay up most of the night playing cards with those people instead of keeping your wife warm in bed and getting up when little Jelena cries. Ive Jelačić, particularly, is nothing but a useless *pijanac*."

"*Pijanac?*" Banks repeated. "What is that?"

"Drunk," said Vjeko. "Yes, Ive is . . . he does drink too much. He is not a pleasant man in many ways, Inspector. You must not judge my fellow countrymen by Ive's example. And I do not put forward the tragedy in his life as an excuse for his behavior. He lies. He boasts. Most of all, he is greedy. He often suggests that we play cards for money, and I know he cheats. With women he is bad, too. Dragica cannot bear him near her."

"That is true," Dragica told Banks, shuddering at the thought and hugging her slight frame. "He undresses you with his eyes."

Banks remembered Susan Gay's reaction to Jelačić's ogling and nodded.

"Please excuse me," Dragica said. "I must attend to Jelena." And she went upstairs.

"He is rude, too," Vjeko went on. "Ill-mannered. And I have seen him behave violently in pubs, picking fights when he is drunk." He laughed. "When I put it like that, I wonder why I do spend time with him. It is a mystery to me. But one thing I can tell you is that Ive wouldn't kill a young girl that way. Never. Perhaps in a fight, in a pub, he could kill, but not like that, not someone weaker than himself. It is a joke with us that Ive always picks on people bigger than himself, and he usually comes off worst."

"Do you know why Mr. Jelačić left Eastvale?" Banks asked.

"He told us that a *svecenik,* a man of God, made homosexual advances towards him."

"You said he was a liar. Do you believe his story?"

Vjeko shook his head. "No. I do not think it is true. I have listened to him talk about it, and I think he did what he did to get revenge for losing his job."

"If that's so," said Banks, "then he's caused Daniel Charters an awful lot of grief."

Vjeko spread his hands. "But what can anyone do? I did not know Ive back in Eastvale, when all this happened, and I do not know this Father Daniel Charters. Perhaps he is a good man; perhaps he is not. But I do think that Ive is tired with his revenge. He has had enough. The problem is that he is mixed up with lawyers and human-rights campaigners among our own people. It is not so easy for him to turn around and say to them it was all a lie, a mistake or a joke. He would lose face."

"And face is important to him?"

"Yes."

Dragica returned carrying a sleeping Jelena in her arms and said something in Croatian; Vjeko nodded, and she went into the kitchen.

"Dragica asked if dinner is nearly ready," he said. "I told her yes."

Banks stood up. "Then I won't use up any more of your time. You've been very helpful." He stuck out his hand.

"Why don't you stay for dinner?" Vjeko asked. "It is not very much, just *sarma.* Cabbage rolls. But we would be happy if you would share with us."

Banks paused at the door. It was almost six-thirty and he hadn't had anything since lunch at Whitelock's. He would have to eat sometime. "All right," he said. "Thanks very much. Yes, I'd love to stay."

II

Instead of continuing along Roundhay Road towards Wetherby and the A1, Banks cut back down Roseville Road and Regent Street, then headed for Burmantofts. He had dined well with the Batoracs, and conversation had ranged from books and teaching to the Balkan war and crime. After their goodbyes, it was a quarter to eight on a fine May evening, and dusk was slowly gathering when Banks pulled up near Jelačić's flat. In the failing, honeyed light, the shabby concrete tower blocks looked as eerie as a landscape on Mars.

There were plenty of people around in the recreation areas between the buildings, mostly teenagers congregated in little knots here and there, some of them playing on swings and roundabouts.

Banks managed to climb the six flights of graffiti-scarred concrete without incident, apart from a little shortness of breath, and rapped on Jelačić's door.

He could already hear the television blaring "Coronation Street" through the paper-thin walls, so when no-one answered the first time, he knocked even harder. Finally Jelačić answered the door, grubby shirt hanging out of his jeans, and scowled when he recognized Banks.

"You," he said. "*Šupak.* Why you come here? You already have killer."

"Things change, Ive," said Banks, gently shouldering his way inside. The place was as he remembered, tidy but overlaid with a patina of stale booze and cigarette smoke. Here he could light up with impunity. He turned down the sound on one of Jack and Vera Duckworth's loud public arguments.

Jelačić didn't complain. He picked up a glass of clear liquid—probably vodka, Banks guessed—from the table and flopped down on the settee. It creaked under his weight. Jelačić had put on quite a few pounds since they had last met, most of it on his gut. He looked about eight months pregnant.

"You'll be glad to hear," Banks said, "that your alibi still seems to hold water."

Jelačić frowned. "Water? Hold water? What you mean?"

"I mean we believe you were playing cards at Mile Pavelič's house at the time Deborah Harrison was killed."

"I already tell you that. So why you come here?"

"To ask you some questions."

Jelačić grunted.

"First of all, when exactly did you come here from East-vale?"

"Was last year. September."

"So the St. Mary's girls would have been back at school for a while before you left?"

"Yes. Two weeks."

Banks leaned forward and flicked his ash into an over-flowing tin ashtray, which looked as if it had been stolen from a pub. "Now the last time we talked," he said, "you swore blind you'd never seen Deborah Harrison, or at most that you might just have *seen* her once or twice, in passing."

"Is true."

"Now I'm asking you to rethink. I'm giving you another chance to tell the truth, Ive. There's no blame attached to this now. You're not a suspect. But you might be a witness."

"I saw nothing."

Banks nodded towards the TV set. "I don't suppose you watch the news," he said. "But for your information Owen Pierce was found not guilty and released earlier today."

"He is free?" Jelačić stared open-mouthed, then began to laugh. "Then you failed. You let the guilty man go free. Always that happens here." He shook his head. "Such a crazy country."

"Yes, well at least we don't shoot them first and ask questions later. But that's beside the point. He may or may not have committed the crime, but officially he didn't and we're reopening the case. Which is why I'm here. Now why is trying to get the tiniest scrap of help from you like getting blood out of a stone, Ive? Can you tell me that?"

Jelačić shrugged. "I know nothing."

"Don't you care what happened to Deborah Harrison?"

"Deborah Harrison. Deborah Harrison. Silly little English rich girl. Why I care? More girls killed in my homeland. Who cares about them? My father and mother die. My girl-friend is killed. But to you that means nothing. Nobody cares."

" 'Any man's death diminishes me.' John Donne wrote that. Have you never heard it, Ive? Have you never heard of the concept that we're all in this together, all part of mankind?"

Jelačić just looked at Banks, incomprehension written on his features.

"Why don't you answer my questions?" Banks went on. "You saw the girl, you've admitted as much. You must have seen her quite often when you were working outside."

"I work inside and out. Clean church. Cut grass . . ."

"Right. So you liked to watch the St. Mary's girls—we know you did—and you must have noticed Deborah. She was very striking and she complained about your making lewd gestures towards her."

"I never—"

"Ive, spare me the bullshit, please. I've heard enough of it to last a lifetime. Nobody's going to arrest you or deport you for this. Bloody hell, they might even give you a medal if you tell us anything that leads to the killer."

Jelačić's eyes lit up. "Medal? You mean there is reward?"

"It was a joke, Ive," said Banks. "No, there isn't a reward. We just expect you to do your duty like any other decent, law-abiding citizen."

"I see nothing."

"Did you ever notice anyone hanging around the grave-yard looking suspicious?"

"No."

"Did you ever see Deborah Harrison meet anyone in St. Mary's churchyard?"

He shook his head.

"Did she ever linger around there, as if she was going to meet someone, or was up to something?"

Again, he shook his head, but not before Banks noticed something flicker behind his eyes, some memory, some sign of recognition.

"What is it?" Banks asked.

"What is what? Is nothing."

"You remembered something?"

But it was gone. "No," said Jelačić. "Like I say, I only see her when she walk home sometimes. She never stay, never meet anyone. That is all."

He was lying about something, Banks was certain. But he was equally certain Jelačić was too stubborn to part with whatever he had remembered right now. Banks would have to find more leverage. Sometimes he wished he had the freedom and power of certain other police forces in certain other countries—the freedom and power to torture and beat the truth out of Jelačić, for example—but only sometimes.

There was no point going on. Banks said goodbye and opened the door to leave. Before he had got ten feet away from the flat, he heard the sound on Jelačić's television shoot up loud again.

III

It was late that Wednesday evening when Owen finally got home. After he had picked up his belongings from the prison, he decided he didn't want to spend even one or two hours of such a beautiful day—his first moments of freedom in over six months—trapped in a car with Gordon Wharton. So he begged off, walked into town and just wandered aimlessly for a while, savoring his liberty. Late in the afternoon, he went into a pub on Boar Lane and had a pint of bitter and a roast beef sandwich, which almost made him gag after months of prison food. Then he walked over to the bus station, and by a circuitous route and a surprising number of changes, he managed to get himself back to Eastvale.

When Owen finally put his key in the lock, the door swung open by itself. He stood in the silence for a moment but could hear nothing. That seemed wrong. He knew there should have been a familiar sound, even if he couldn't, right now, remember what it was. His house had never been in such complete silence. No place ever is. And there was an odd smell. Dust he had expected, after so long away, perhaps mildew, too. He couldn't expect Ivor or Siobhan next door to do his cleaning for him. But this was something else. He stayed by the door listening for a while, then went into the living-room.

It looked like the aftermath of a jumble sale. Someone had pulled the books from the shelves, then ripped out pages and tossed them on the floor. Some of the torn pages had curled up, as if they had been wet and had dried out. Compact disc cases lay strewn, shattered and cracked, along with them. The discs themselves were mostly at the other side of the room, where marks on the wall showed that they had probably been flipped like Frisbees. The TV screen had been smashed. Scrawled on the wall beside the door, in giant, spidery red letters, were the words "JAILS TOO GOOD FOR FILTHY FUCKING PERVERTS LIKE YOU!"

Owen sagged against the wall and let his bag drop to the floor. Just for a moment, he longed for the stark simplicity of his prison cell again, the intractable order of prison life. This was too much. He didn't feel he could cope.

Taking a deep breath, he stepped over the debris and went into the study. His photos and negs lay ripped and snipped up all over the carpet. None of them looked salvageable, not even the inoffensive landscapes. His cameras lay beside them, lenses cracked in spider-web patterns. His art books had also been taken from their shelves and pages of reproductions ripped out by the handful: Gauguin, Cézanne, Renoir, Titian, Van Gogh, Vermeer, Monet, Caravaggio, Rubens, everything. That was bad enough—all or any of that was bad enough—but the thing he hadn't dared look at until last, the thing he had sensed as soon as he entered but hadn't quite grasped, was the worst of all.

The aquarium stood in darkness and silence, lights, pumps and filters switched off. The fish floated on the water's surface—danios, guppies, angelfish, jewelfish, zebrafish—their once-bright colors faded in death. It looked as if the intruder had simply switched off their life-support and left them to die. For Owen, this was the last straw. Misguided vindictiveness against himself he could understand, but such cruelty directed against the harmless, helpless fish was beyond his ken.

Owen leaned against the tank and sobbed until he couldn't get his breath, then he ran to the bathroom and rinsed his face in cold water. After that, he stood gripping the cool sides of the sink until he stopped shaking. In his bedroom, most of his clothes had been ripped or cut up with scissors and scattered over his bed.

In the kitchen, the contents of the fridge and cupboards had been dumped on the lino and smeared in the manner of a Jackson Pollock canvas. The resultant gooey mess of old marmalade, eggs, baked beans, instant coffee, sour milk, cheese slices, sugar, tea bags, butter, rice, treacle, corn flakes and a whole rack of herbs and spices looked like a special effect from a horror film and smelled worse than the yeast factory he had once worked in as a student. Right in the middle, on top of it all, sat what looked like a curled, dried turd.

He knew he should call the police, if only for insurance purposes, but the last people on earth he felt like dealing with right now were the bloody police.

And he couldn't face cleaning up.

Instead, he decided to give up on his first day of freedom. It was only about nine o'clock, just after dark, but Owen swept the torn and snipped-up clothes from his bed, burrowed under the sheets and pulled the covers over his head.

Chapter 14

I

*L*ike Canute holding back the tide, or the Greeks fighting off the Trojans, Banks could only postpone the inevitable, not avoid it altogether. In fact, the inevitable was waiting for him at eight o'clock on Thursday morning when he got to his office—coffee in hand, listening to Barber's setting of "Dover Beach" on his Walkman—in the strutting, fretting form of Chief Constable Jeremiah Riddle.

"Banks, take those bloody things out of your ears. And where the hell do you think you were yesterday?"

Banks told him about talking to Batorac and Jelačić while he was in Leeds, but omitted Pamela's chamber music concert and his quick visit to the Classical Record Shop.

Riddle's presence called for a cigarette, he thought. He was trying to cut out the early morning smokes, but under the circumstances, lighting up now might achieve the double purpose of both soothing his nerves and aggravating Riddle into a cardiac arrest. He lit up. Riddle coughed and waved his hand about, but he wasn't about to be distracted, or to die.

"What have you got to say about that fiasco in court yesterday?" the chief constable asked.

Banks shrugged. "There's nothing much *to* say, sir," he replied. "The jury found Pierce not guilty."

"I know that. Bloody idiots."

"That may well be, sir," said Banks, "but there's still nothing we can do about it. I thought we had a strong case. I'm certain the Crown will appeal. I'll be talking to Stafford Oakes about it when the fuss dies down."

"Hmph. We're going to look like real idiots over this one, Banks, as if we haven't got enough problems already." Riddle ran his hand over his red, shiny head. "Anyway, I want you to know that I've asked Detective Superintendent Gristhorpe to have a look over the case files. Maybe he can bring a fresh viewpoint. Either you get more evidence on Pierce or, if he really didn't do it, you damn well find out who did. I've decided I'm going to give you a week to redeem yourself on this before we hand it over to a team of independent investigators. I don't want to do that, I know how bad it looks, an admission of failure, but we've no bloody choice if we don't get results fast. I need hardly remind you of the impact a negative result might have on your future career, need I?"

"No, sir."

"And go easy on the Harrisons. They're bound to be upset by Pierce getting off, after everything they've been through. Tread softly. Understand?"

"I'll tread softly, sir."

Stupid pillock, Banks cursed after Riddle had left the office. A whole bloody week. And how, he wondered, could he do his job with one hand tied behind his back, and tied because of bloody privilege, class and wealth, not by compassion for a bereaved family? Again, he had the feeling he would soon be walking on very thin ice indeed if he were to get to the bottom of things.

He walked over to the window, pulled up the venetian blind and opened the sash a couple of inches. It was too early for tourists, but the market square was busy with Eastvalers starting their day, heels clicking on the cobbles as bank cashiers, dentists and estate agents went to work in the warren of offices around the town center. The shops were opening and the smell of fresh-baked bread spilled in with sunlight.

Looking to his right, Banks could see south along Market Street, with its teashops, boutiques, and specialty shops, and out front was the square itself, with the NatWest bank, an estate agent, the El Toro coffee bar and Joplin's newsagent's at the opposite side. Over the shops were solicitors' offices, dentists' and doctors' surgeries.

With a sigh, Banks walked over to his filing cabinet, where he kept his own records of the salient points of the Harrison case. The tons of paperwork and electromagnetic traces that a murder case generated couldn't possibly be stored in one detective's office, but most detectives had their own ways of summarizing and keeping track of the cases they worked on. Banks was no exception.

His filing cabinet contained his own notes on all the major cases he had been involved with since coming to Eastvale, plus a few he had brought with him from the Met. The notes might not mean much to anyone else, but with the use of his keen memory, Banks was able to fill in all the gaps his shorthand left out. His own notes also contained the hunches and accounts of off-the-record conversations that didn't make their way into the official files and statements.

It was time, he thought, to clear his mind of Owen Pierce for the moment and go back to basics. Two possibilities remained: either Deborah Harrison had been murdered by someone she knew, or a stranger other than Owen Pierce had killed her. Putting the second possibility aside, Banks picked up the names and strands of the first. Before the Pierce business, he had believed that Deborah might have arranged to meet someone on her way home from the chess club. He would spend the morning reading his notes and thinking, he decided, then after lunch he would go back to where it all started: St. Mary's graveyard.

II

"Siobhan would bloody well kill me if she knew I was here with you now," Ivor said. "You don't understand what it's been like, mate. She's still convinced you did it."

They were standing at the bar of the Queen's Arms on Thursday lunch-time, after Owen had spent the entire morning cleaning up his house.

"That's ridiculous," said Owen. "I know she never really liked me, but I thought she had more sense than that. Is that why you didn't report the break-in?"

"I told you, it only happened the other day. You don't know what it's been like for us."

"Tell me."

Ivor sighed and took a swig from his pint. "You should have seen some of the things you got through your letter-box, for a start."

"What things?"

"Shit, hate-letters, used johnnies, death threats, something that looked like a lump of kidney or liver. I had to go in and clean it all up, didn't I?"

"I'm sorry. Did you report it to the police?"

"Of course I did. They sent a man round, but he didn't do anything. What can you expect?"

"The police thought I was guilty. They still do." Along with the rest of the world, he thought.

"Still," Ivor said, "you weren't living next door. You didn't have to put up with it all."

"Right. I was safely locked up in prison, all nice and comfortable in my little cell. Fucking luxury."

"You don't have to be so sarcastic, Owen. I'm just trying to explain what it was like on the outside, so you can understand people's attitudes."

"Like Siobhan's?"

"Yes."

"And yours?"

Ivor shrugged.

"What exactly is your attitude?" Owen asked.

"What's it matter? You're out now."

"Not just out, Ivor, but not guilty. Remember?"

"Well," he mumbled, "you know what people say."

"No, I don't. Tell me what people say."

"You know, guilty people get off all the time because the system's biased in their favor. We bend over backward to help criminals and don't give a damn for their victims."

"I'm the victim here, Ivor." Owen thrust his thumb at his own chest. "Me. I even found a letter from the college waiting for me. That bastard Kemp has fired me, and he did it *before* the jury even went out."

Ivor looked away. "Yeah, well. I'm just saying what people think, in general, that's all."

"And what do *you* think, Ivor?"

"Look, I really don't want to get into this. All I'm saying, Owen, is that shit sticks."

"Meaning?"

"Oh, come on! For Christ's sake, you're supposed to be the English teacher. Meaning exactly what it says. All those rumors that went around during the trial, the stuff they couldn't bring in as evidence? Do you think nobody knew about it? Hell, I found out from one of the students in the local library."

Owen felt a shiver run up his spine. "Found out about what?"

"Everything. Your sex life, your photographic pursuits, your taste for dirty books and magazines, the porn video, how you screwed your students."

Owen toyed with a damp beer-mat. "You already knew that Michelle had been one of my students, I don't think even you would call *Lady Chatterly's Lover* a dirty book these days, and, don't forget, you watched part of one of those videos with me. I'm no worse than anyone else."

"Oh, grow up. You may not be, but the whole country doesn't know everything about anyone else, does it? You know how rumors get exaggerated. As far as they're concerned, you're the one who beats up women when they won't let you fuck them. You're the one who spends his days ogling innocent young schoolgirls and your nights dreaming about defiling and strangling virgins while you're watching video nasties."

Owen felt himself flush. "They're all bloody hypocrites."

"Maybe so, but that doesn't help you, does it?"

"And what does help me?"

"I don't know. I was thinking, maybe you should go away somewhere . . . ?"

"Run away? That's great advice. Thanks a lot, mate."

Owen ordered a couple more pints. At least the barmaid didn't seem to have recognized him. She actually *smiled* as she put down the drinks. A woman smiling, something he hadn't seen in ages, apart from Shirley Castle in her moment of victory. Either she didn't watch telly or read the papers, or prison had changed his appearance enough to fool some people. Not everyone, of course, but some people.

"Look," he went on, "get this into your thick skull. I haven't done anything. I never beat up anyone, and I certainly never raped and murdered anyone. I've been a victim of the system. They owe me something. It's doubtful they'll pay, but they owe me. In the meantime, I've lost a few months out of my life and my reputation's taken a bit of a bashing. I've got to put things in order again, and I'm damned if I'm going to start by running away. How do you think that'll look?"

Ivor paused and scratched his beard before answering. "It's not a bad idea, you know. It's not really like running away. New life somewhere else. Fresh start. You could even go live and teach English on the continent somewhere. France maybe. Your French is pretty good, as I remember. Or Japan."

Owen sniffed. "I can't believe what I'm hearing. You think that's the solution to my problems? Go live in obscurity in a foreign country? A sort of self-imposed exile. I'm telling you for the last time, Ivor, *I haven't done anything.*"

Ivor paused a little before saying, "You might find it more difficult than you think—putting things in order."

"What do you mean?"

"Nothing specific. I'm just pointing out that Siobhan's attitude isn't unique. There's probably a few others feel the same way. Locally, like. Feelings can get pretty strong."

"Are you telling me I'm in danger? A lynch mob or something?"

"All I'm saying is that when people get frightened they lash out."

"And what do you feel, Ivor? You never really answered my original question, you know. You're my neighbor. You're also supposed to be my friend. Do you think I'm a pervert?"

"What can I say? How do I know? I watched part of that video with you, like you said, didn't I? I don't think doing that turned me into a pervert. Mind you, I can't say it did a lot for me, but I watched it. More of a laugh than anything, if—"

"Fuck off, Ivor."

"What? Look—"

"Just fuck off and leave me alone."

Ivor banged his pint down on the bar; the barmaid glanced over anxiously. "All right, if that's the way you want it, mate. Just don't expect any more help from me."

Owen snorted. "Believe me, Ivor, you've earned my undying gratitude for what you've done for me already. Now just fuck off."

Ivor stormed out, red-faced above his beard, and the barmaid gave Owen an odd look, perhaps of recognition, of disapproval. Then the landlord, Cyril, he of the Popeye forearms, appeared from the back.

"What's all the noise about?" he said. He seemed to recognize Owen and started walking towards him.

"Well, you can fuck off, too!" Owen slammed his glass down on the bar so hard it broke and beer swilled over the counter.

"Here!" yelled Cyril, making for the hinged flap. But Owen shot out of the door and down the street, the base of his thumb stinging and bleeding from where a sliver of glass had pierced it.

He hurried along North Market Street, head down and hands thrust deep in his pockets, fists clenched. Ivor. That slimy, backpedaling little turd. And Michelle? Just what was she trying to do to him?

But Perhaps Ivor was right about moving. The thought wasn't quite as upsetting as it might have been a year or so earlier; somehow, the mess he had found on his release from prison had soured the house for him anyway. There were also, he realized, still too many memories of Michelle there. And moving would be a project, something to do, start looking for a new place, perhaps somewhere a little cheaper in a different part of the country. Not abroad, but in Devon, maybe, or Cornwall. He had always liked the south-west.

As he walked down the street, head bowed, Owen felt like an outsider, as if the rest of the world were swimming happily together in a huge tank and he was knocking on the glass unable to find a way in. One or two people gave him strange looks as he passed, and he realized he must have been mumbling to himself. Or maybe they recognized him. *Shit sticks,* Ivor had said. People would see him the way the rumors had depicted him, and would perhaps move aside and whisper to one another, "Here comes the Eastvale Strangler. You know, the one that got off."

When he finally looked up to see where he was, he saw he was in St. Mary's. Despite all his resolutions, he had walked there, as if by instinct.

He stood at the church gate, uncertain what to do, then on an impulse he decided to go in. It was a beautiful day, and the few hawthorn trees scattered among the yews bore white, yellow or pink blossoms. Wildflowers pushed their way through the grass around some of the plots. Thriving on decomposing remains, Owen thought fancifully, before he noticed that most of the graves were from the eighteenth and nineteenth centuries. There were some recent ones, but not many.

The graveyard was peaceful; the muffled sounds of traffic on North Market Street and Kendal Road formed only a distant backdrop to the birdsongs.

Owen followed the tarmac path where it curved past the church and arrived at the Kendal Road exit. There, he walked up to the bridge and stared down at the swirling water, the color of a pint of bitter, from the peat it picked up on its way through the dale. Ahead, facing south, he could see the formal gardens, the riverside willows and the castle high on its hill, dominating the town. It seemed so long ago he had stood here that foggy November night. No, he would not think about that again.

He took the river path home, and as he passed by the vicarage, he saw, over the garden gate, a woman hanging up washing on the line and stopped to watch her.

The plain white T-shirt she was wearing stretched taut against her heavy round breasts as she reached to peg up a sheet. Owen fancied he could see the dark nipples harden at the wind's caress.

Then she looked his way. He recognized her; he had seen her in court. She was the woman who had found the body, the one whose husband had been accused of molesting a church worker.

For a moment, she seemed about to smile and say hello, then she frowned, her jaw dropped, and she backed away inside the house, shutting the door behind her. Owen could hear the sound of a chain being fastened. She hadn't hung the sheet properly on the washing-line, and at the first light gust of wind it filled like a sail then broke free and fluttered onto the flower-bed like a shroud.

III

Banks saw the curtain in the bay window twitch just after he rang the vicarage bell, and a few moments later a nervous and jumpy looking Rebecca Charters answered the door. She looked relieved to see him and ushered him down the hall into the living-room.

It was a lot more cozy than on his previous visits, he noticed immediately, and it felt much more like a family home than a temporary encampment. The whole place had been redecorated: new wallpaper, cream with rose patterns; a new three-piece suite in a matching floral design; and three vases of flowers placed around the room. Ezekiel, the mound of brown-and-white fur, was in his usual place by the empty fireplace.

"How about some tea?" Rebecca asked. "Freshly brewed. Well, ten minutes ago."

"That'll be fine," said Banks. "No milk or sugar, thanks."

Rebecca went into the kitchen and returned seconds later with two mugs of tea. Today, she wore her hair tied back, fixed in place by a tooled-leather slide and a broad wooden pin. The style made her olive-complexioned face seem to bulge forward a little, emphasizing the slightly long nose, weak chin and curved brow, like a photograph through a fish-eye lens, but she still looked attractive, especially the dark eyes and full lips.

"I noticed you were in court for the verdict," Banks began.

Rebecca cradled her mug in her hands. "Yes," she said. "I can hardly believe it. He was here earlier. That was why I was a bit nervous when you rang."

"Owen Pierce was here? Why?"

"Not actually *here,* but he walked past on the river path. I was in the garden. I saw him."

"It's a free country, I suppose," Banks said. "And he's a free man."

"But isn't he dangerous? I mean, people still think he did it, even if he did get off."

"They're free to believe what they want. I don't think you have anything to worry about, though."

"Easy for you to say."

"Perhaps. Keep your doors and windows locked if it makes you feel better."

"I'm sorry," Rebecca said. "I don't mean to be sharp. I . . ."

"It's all right," said Banks. "You're worried. You think there's a killer been set free and he's got his eyes on you. The quicker we find out whether he did it or not, the sooner you'll feel safe again."

"Do you think he did it?"

Banks scratched the little scar beside his right eye. "Right now, I don't know," he admitted. "There were times when I did, certainly, but the more I look at some of the things that struck me as odd before we latched onto Pierce, the more I start to wonder. The courts set innocent people free as well as guilty ones, sometimes, and if anyone knows the truth, he's a lucky man."

"What brought you back here?"

"I'm not really sure, except that this is where it all started."

"Yes," said Rebecca. "I remember." She gave a small shudder and fingered the neck of her dress. "And I'd like to apologize."

"For what?"

"For the last time we met. In the Queen's Arms. I seem to remember I was very rude to you. I seem to be making a habit of it."

"Don't worry," Banks said. "You get used to it in my job."

"But you shouldn't have to. I mean, I shouldn't have be-haved the way I did." She put her mug down on the table. "I'm not that kind of person. Rude . . . I. . . . Look, I don't know why I'm telling you this, except that your coming here again brings it all back."

"Brings what back? Finding the body?"

"That, yes, certainly. But it was a terrible time for me all round. The charges against Daniel, all the turmoil they caused." She took a deep breath. "You see, Chief Inspector, you didn't know the half of it. Of course you didn't, it wasn't relevant, not to your inquiries, but I lost a baby about three months before that business with Jelačić, and the doctor said it would be dangerous for me to try for another. Daniel and I hadn't talked about it as much as we should, and we had started drifting apart. We had just made some tentative inquiries about adoption when Jelačić brought the charges. Of course, everything fell through. It was worse than it was before. I'm afraid I withdrew. I blamed Daniel. There was even a time when I thought he was guilty. Since I lost the baby, we hadn't been . . . well, you know . . . and I thought he'd lost interest in me. It was easier to explain that by assuming he was really interested in men. What can I say? I started to drink too much. Then there was Patrick." She laughed nervously. "I don't know why I'm telling you all this. Except that you witnessed the final scene."

Banks smiled. "You'd be surprised the things people tell us, Mrs. Charters. Anyway, I hope life has improved since then."

She beamed. "Yes. Yes, it has. Daniel and I are stronger than we've ever been. There are still . . . well, a few problems . . . but at least we're working together now."

"How's the Jelačić problem progressing?"

"It drags on. We've not heard anything for over a month now, but I believe he's got some human-rights lawyer working on it."

"And the drink?"

"Six months without."

"Patrick Metcalfe?"

"Not since that time you were here, when he caused all that fuss."

"Has he pestered you at all since then?"

She smiled. "No. I think he realized pretty quickly how carried away with himself he was getting. And I think your interest in him helped keep him at bay, too. I should thank you for that. You don't still suspect him, do you?"

"He's not off the hook yet," Banks said. "Anyway, that's

not why I came. Actually, I was hoping for another look at the area where the body was found."

"Surely you don't have to ask my permission to do that?"

"No, but it's partly a matter of courtesy. And you know the area better than I do. Will you come with me?"

"Certainly."

To retrace Deborah's steps, they walked first along the riverside path from the vicarage towards the Kendal Road bridge, where worn stone steps led up to the pavement. It was another beautiful day, and over the road in St. Mary's Park, lovers lay entwined, students sat reading in the shade of the trees, and children played with balls and Frisbees.

"This was where she would enter," said Rebecca, holding the wooden gate open for Banks. It was a lych-gate, with a small wooden roof, where the coffin would await the arrival of the clergyman in days gone by. "Seventeenth century," Rebecca said. "Isn't it superb?"

Banks agreed that it was.

"This is the main path we're on now," Rebecca explained.

It was about a yard and a half wide and had a pitted tarmac surface. Ahead, it curved around slightly in front of the church, separated from the doors only by a swath of grass, across which led a narrow flagstone path.

"It leads to North Market Street," Rebecca said, "near the zebra crossing where Deborah would cross to go home. And this path," she said, taking Banks by the elbow and diverting him to the right, where the entrance to the path was almost obscured by shrubbery, "is the path that leads to the Inchcliffe Mausoleum."

It was the gravel path Banks remembered from last November. After a couple of yards, the shrubbery gave way to yews and lichen-stained graves. Warm sunlight filtered through the greenery and flying insects buzzed around the dandelions and forget-me-nots.

Some of the graves were above-ground tombs with heavy lids and flowery religious epitaphs. By far the most impressive and baroque was the Inchcliffe Mausoleum, to the right.

"Now," said Banks, "we were assuming that Deborah reached the junction between the main path and this one when someone either grabbed her and dragged her up here or persuaded her to go with him of her own free will."

"But why couldn't she have come this way herself?" Rebecca asked.

"Why should she? It's out of her way."

"She had done before. I noticed her do it once or twice."

Banks raised his eyebrows. "You never mentioned this before."

Rebecca shrugged. "You never asked. And it didn't seem relevant."

"But didn't it strike you as odd?"

"No. I'm sorry. It wasn't something I was paying a lot of attention to. I suppose I assumed that she liked graveyards, as I do. And this is where the most interesting old tombs are, and the Inchcliffe Mausoleum, of course." She blushed. "Maybe she went to talk to the angel, like I did."

"When did she start using the path?"

"I've no idea. I don't remember *noticing* her go that way before last September, when school started up, but that doesn't mean she never did."

"Did you ever see anyone else with her? Or anyone going along the path before or after her?"

"No. You did ask me about that before, and I would have told you if I'd seen her meeting anyone. I would have noticed something like that. Do you think it's important that she took this path?"

Banks paused. "From the start," he explained, "I'd been working on the theory that if Owen Pierce or someone else hadn't followed Deborah into the graveyard, dragged her off the main path and killed her, then she might have been meeting the person who did. Now you're telling me you've seen her take this path before, I'm wondering if this is where she arranged the meeting. By the mausoleum. Her friend Megan Preece said Deborah had a morbid streak, that she liked spooky things. A rendezvous in the depths of a foggy graveyard beside an old mausoleum might have appealed to her."

"To meet someone she knew?"

"Yes. A lover, perhaps. Or someone else. We know that Deborah had a secret. It did cross my mind that she might have arranged to meet the person involved to discuss it, what to do about it."

"But what could she have possibly known that was so important?"

"If we knew that, then we'd probably know who the killer is."

"And do you still believe that she was meeting someone?"

"I think it's a strong possibility. She didn't tell Megan, but perhaps she wanted to be really secretive. Ive Jelačić told me he never saw her meeting anyone, but he's a pathological liar. On the other hand, you just told me yourself that you never saw anyone else around."

"It doesn't mean that there couldn't have been someone," Rebecca said. "The woods are quite deep here. And it was a foggy night. I just wish I could be of more help."

Banks stood and looked around. Rebecca was right. You could just about see the church through the trees to the south, but to the north, between the Inchcliffe Mausoleum and Kendal Road, it was a different matter. There, the yews were thicker, the undergrowth denser. It would be an ideal place for a secret meeting. And if he had learned anything from returning to the scene, it was that Deborah might have taken the gravel path of her accord, and that she had done so before.

He looked up at the Inchcliffe Mausoleum. It could have been the angle he was viewing it from, or perhaps a trick of the light, but he could have sworn the marble angel with the chipped wings was smiling.

Chapter 15

I

"Let's assume Pierce didn't do it, just for the moment," said Banks. "That'll make things easier."

It was the first Friday in June, and the rays of late morning sunlight flooded the market square. Banks sat in Gristhorpe's office trying to get a fresh perspective on the Deborah Harrison murder.

Gristhorpe, a bulky man with a pock-marked face and bushy eyebrows, sat sideways at his large teak desk, one leg stretched out and propped up on a footstool. He insisted that the broken leg had healed perfectly, but he still got the odd twinge now and then. Given that it was same leg he had also been shot in not so long ago, that wasn't surprising, Banks thought.

Banks took a sip of coffee. "On the generous side, I'd say we've got maybe five or six suspects. If Deborah didn't have a lover we don't know about—and I don't think she did—then the key to it all might lie in the secret she had. And if Deborah knew something about someone, she might easily have misjudged the importance of what she knew, underestimated the desperation of that person. Adults can have some pretty nasty secrets. The Pierce trial redirected all our time and energy towards proving that the killer *didn't* know her, that she was a random victim, or became a victim because she had the misfortune of resembling Pierce's ex-girlfriend Michelle Chappel."

"What's happening with that now?"

"I talked to Stafford Oakes about an hour ago," Banks said, "and he's ninety-nine per cent certain the Crown will appeal the verdict on the basis of the similar fact evidence being declared inadmissible. If they get a judge who allows it in, another trial could be disastrous for Pierce, whether he did it or not."

Gristhorpe scratched his chin. "As you know, Alan," he said, "I've been able to keep an open mind on this because I wasn't part of the original investigation. I'd just like to say in the first place that I think you did good detective work. You shouldn't flagellate yourself over the result. It may still turn out that Pierce didn't do it. But I agree we should put that aside for a moment. From what I've read so far, Barry Stott seemed particularly sold on Pierce. Any idea why?"

"It was *his* lead," Banks said. "Or so he thought. Actually, if it hadn't been for Jim Hatchley stopping for a pint in the Nag's Head, he might never have turned it up. But Barry's ambitious. And tenacious. And let's not forget, Jimmy Riddle was dead set on Pierce, too."

"He's a friend of the family," Gristhorpe said. "I should imagine he just wanted an early conclusion, no matter who went down for it."

Banks nodded.

"Now," Gristhorpe went on, "the two things we have to ask ourselves are what possible secret Deborah Harrison could have learned that was important enough to kill for, and who, given the opportunity, could have killed her because of it."

Banks told him about his visit to Rebecca Charters and what he had learned about Deborah's occasional detours from the main path.

"You think she had arranged to meet her killer?" Gristhorpe asked.

"Rebecca never actually saw her meet anyone, but it's one possibility."

"Blackmail?"

"Perhaps. Though I'm not sure from what I know of Deborah that she was the type to do that. I suppose it *is* possible. After all, her satchel was open when we found her, and that has always bothered me. Perhaps she had some sort of hard evidence and the killer took it. On the other hand, maybe she just wanted to let whoever it was know that she knew the secret, or how she had found out. Perhaps she just wanted to flaunt her knowledge a little. Her friends say she could be a bit of a show-off. Anyway, let's say she didn't know the power or the value of what she was playing with."

"Which takes us to my questions: why and who?"

"Yes." Banks counted them on his fingers, one by one. "For a start, there's John Spinks. He was Deborah's boyfriend for part of the summer, and he's a nasty piece of work. They parted on very bad terms and I think he's the type to bear a grudge. He also has an alibi that doesn't hold much water. Ive Jelačić has a solid alibi, I'd say, in Vjeko Batorac, but I'm still certain he's involved, he knows something."

"Any idea what?"

"I'd guess he might have seen Deborah meeting someone."

"Why not tell us who, then?"

"That's not Jelačić's style. If you ask me, I'd say he's trying to work out what might be in it for him first. For crying out loud, he even asked me if there was a reward."

"What do we do, beat it out of him?"

"Believe me, that thought's crossed my mind. But no. We'll get him one way or another, don't worry about that. I'm not finished with Mr. Jelačić yet."

"Who else have we got? What about that schoolteacher?"

"Patrick Metcalfe? Another possibility. Though I doubt very much that he's got the bottle, we have to consider him.

He was Deborah's history teacher and he was having an affair with Rebecca Charters, the vicar's wife. One might reasonably assume that's a poor career move for a male teacher at an Anglican girls' school. If Deborah knew about the affair—and she could easily have seen Metcalfe entering or leaving the vicarage on occasion—then it could have cost Metcalfe not only his job, but his entire teaching career."

"And as I recall from the statement," Gristhorpe said, "he says he stayed home alone in his flat after Daniel Charters left."

Banks nodded. "And we've no way of confirming or denying that unless someone saw him, which no-one has admitted to so far."

"What about the vicar?"

"I've been wondering about him, too," Banks said. "In general I've been pretty sympathetic towards him, but looking at things objectively, he could be our man. He certainly has no alibi, and he's both tall and strong enough."

"Motive?"

"We know that Ive Jelačić accused him of abusing his position by making homosexual advances. Given Jelačić's character, this is probably pure fabrication—Vjeko Batorac certainly thinks it is—but let's say it's true, or it approximates the truth. And let's say Deborah saw something that could confirm it, either involving Charters and Jelačić or Charters and someone else. If it got out, he also stood to lose everything. That might give him a powerful enough motive."

"Or his wife?" Gristhorpe suggested.

"Yes. It *could* have been a woman," Banks agreed. "After all, there was no evidence of rape, and the body could have been arranged to make it look like a sex murder. Rebecca Charters is probably tall and strong enough."

"And she could have had either of two motives," Gristhorpe added. "To protect the knowledge of her affair with Metcalfe, or to protect her husband from certain dismissal." He shook his head. "It's a real *Peyton Place* we've unearthed here, Alan. Who'd think such goings on occurred in a nice little Yorkshire town like Eastvale?"

Banks smiled. " 'It is my belief, Watson, founded upon my experience, that the lowest and vilest alleys in London do not present a more dreadful record of sin than does the smiling and beautiful countryside.' "

Gristhorpe smiled back. "And what about Jimmy Riddle's mates?" he said.

"Certainly not out of the question. I was beginning to think that Michael Clayton might have been having an affair with Sylvie Harrison, unlikely as it sounds. Sir Geoffrey and Michael Clayton have been close friends since university. If Clayton *were* having an affair with his wife, and if Deborah knew about that, it could have had a devastating effect. Think of how much money and prestige were at stake there."

"As I understand it, none of them have alibis either."

"That's right. And they all knew Deborah went to the chess club on a Monday, and what time she usually came home. *And* by what route. But even if we accept the horrible possibility that she was *capable* of such a crime, Sylvie Harrison is neither tall nor strong enough to have killed her daughter. Rebecca Charters is the only woman in this case who could remotely have done it."

"Clayton, then?"

"Possible. Certainly he's the more likely of the two. Though, again, he was the child's *godfather.*"

"Let's also not forget," Gristhorpe added, "that HarClay Industries had a lot of MoD contracts. They do a lot of hush-hush work. If Deborah found out about any hanky-panky going on there, contracts with foreign governments and the like . . ."

"Or even something our own government didn't want the general public to know?"

"I wouldn't put it past them," Gristhorpe agreed. "According to your notes, at the time of his daughter's murder, Sir Geoffrey Harrison was in a private meeting with a man from the government called Oliver Jackson. I happen to know Oliver Jackson, and he's not exactly from the government, he's Special Branch."

"Aren't we getting a bit far-fetched here?" Banks said. "Maybe it's just someone else with the same name?"

Gristhorpe shook his head. "I checked with the York CID. It was the same Oliver Jackson all right. They knew he was in town, but they weren't told why. It's just another aspect to consider. Any other angles?"

Banks sighed. "Not that I can think of," he said. "Unless Deborah stumbled on something illegal going on in the school—something to do with sex or drugs, perhaps—but we couldn't dig anything up there."

"It's still plenty to be going on with for the moment."

Banks stood up and walked to the door, already reaching in his pocket for his Silk Cuts.

"By the way," Gristhorpe asked, "how is DI Stott doing?"

Banks paused at door. "He's been walking around looking like death warmed up ever since Pierce got off. I'm getting a bit worried about him."

"Maybe he'll be better after a weekend's rest?"

"Maybe."

As he walked back to his own office, Banks heard raised voices down the corridor and went to see what was happening. There, at the bottom of the staircase, stood John Spinks and DC Susan Gay.

II

"The problem is not with your teaching ability, Owen. You have demonstrated that to us quite clearly over the years."

"Then I don't understand," Owen said. "Why can't I have my job back?" He was sitting in the chairman's book-lined office. Peter Kemp, with his rolled-up shirtsleeves, his freckles and ginger hair like tufts on a coconut sat behind the untidy desk. "Kemp the Unkempt," the staff members had nicknamed him. To one side, a computer hummed, white cursor blinking in anticipation on an empty blue screen.

Kemp leaned back in his chair and linked his hands behind his head. Owen could see a dark patch of sweat under each arm. "Technically, Owen," Kemp said, "you can't demand back a job you never had. Remember, you were employed purely on a term-to-term basis, no guarantees. We simply can't use you next term."

As he spoke, Kemp looked at Owen down his nose, under the tortoiseshell rims of his glasses, as an entomologist might regard an especially interesting but ugly new bug. The office smelled of Polo mints and fresh paint. Owen longed to let in some air, but he knew from experience that none of the windows opened.

"I was depending on you," Owen said. "You've always renewed my contract before."

Kemp sat forward and rested his hairy forearms on the desk. "Ah, yes. But this time you left us in a bit of a mess, didn't you? We had to bring in someone to finish your classes. She did a good job, a very good job, under the circumstances. We can't very well chuck her out without so much as a by-your-leave, can we?"

"I don't see why not. You seem to be doing it to me, and at least I've got seniority. Besides, it was hardly my fault I got arrested."

Kemp sniggered. "Well, it *certainly* wasn't mine. But that's irrelevant. There's no such thing as seniority in temporary appointments, Owen. You know that. I'm sorry, but my hands are tied." And he held them together, linking his fingers as if to demonstrate.

"What about next January? I can just about get by until then."

Kemp pursed his lips and shook his head. "I can't see any vacancies opening up. Budgets are tight these days. Very tight."

"Look," Owen said, sitting forward. "I'm getting fed up with this. Ever since I've been in your office—and I had to wait long enough before I got to see you, by the way—I've heard nothing but flannel. You know damn well that you

could find courses for me if you wanted to, but you won't.
If it's nothing to do with my teaching abilities, then maybe
you'd better tell me what really is the problem." Owen had
a good idea what he would hear—he had read the letter, after
all—but he wanted to put Kemp through the embarrassment
of having to say it.

"I've told you—"

"You've told me bugger-all. Is it the trial? Is that it?"

"Well, you could hardly imagine something like that
would endear you to the board, could you? But we all understand that you were mistakenly accused, and we deeply
regret any hardship you suffered."

Owen laughed. "Mistakenly accused? I like that. That's a
nice way of putting it."

Kemp pursed his lips. "Owen, we know how you suffered,
believe me."

"Do you?" Owen felt himself redden with anger. He
gripped the sides of the chair. "Do you also believe in my innocence?"

"One must put faith in the justice system, Owen, abide by
the verdict of the jury."

"So you *do* believe they were right?"

"The court found you not guilty."

"That's not the same thing."

"But what else are we to base our judgments on?"

"What else? On your knowledge of the person, on character. On *trust,* damn it. After all, I've worked here for eight
years."

Kemp shrugged. "But I can hardly say I *know* you, can I?
Ours has always been a professional relationship, a work relationship, if you like."

"And my work has always been of the highest quality. So
what about my job, then? If you believe I've done nothing
wrong and you have faith in my teaching ability, why don't
I get my job back?"

"You're making this very difficult for me, Owen."

Owen thumped the desk. "Oh, am I? I'm really sorry

about that. Maybe it just hasn't occurred to you how fucking difficult this is for *me*."

Kemp backed away slowly on his wheeled office-chair. "Owen, you're not helping yourself at all by behaving in this manner."

"Don't give me that. You've already made it clear what my position is. I want you to admit why. And please don't tell me how bloody *difficult* it is for you."

Kemp stopped edging back and leaned forward on the desk, making a steeple of his fingers. "All right," he said. "If that's the way you want it. The college has expressed its unwillingness to employ an instructor who has a reputation for bedding his female students and photographing them in the nude. It's bad for our image. It'll make parents keep their daughters away. And seeing as we depend on the students for our livelihood, and a good percentage of them are females of an impressionable age, it was felt that your presence would be detrimental to our survival. And besides that, the college also takes a dim view of its lecturers giving marks for sexual favors rather than for academic excellence." He took a deep breath. "There, Owen, does that suit you better?"

Owen grinned at him. "It'll do. It certainly beats the bullshit you were giving out earlier. But none of what you say has been proven. It's all hearsay."

Kemp looked at the blinking cursor. "You know how rumors spread, what damage they can do. And people here were aware of your . . . er . . . relationship with Ms. Chappel. Even at the time."

"You did nothing then. Why now?"

"Circumstances have changed."

"So I lost my job because circumstances have changed?"

"No smoke without fire."

"You smug bastard."

"Goodbye, Owen." Kemp stood up. He didn't hold out his hand.

Michelle, again. Owen felt like picking up the computer

monitor and hurling it through the window, then punching
Kemp on the nose. But he restrained himself. His teaching
career was over here, perhaps everywhere. People would
know about him wherever he applied. The academic community is small enough; word gets around quickly.

Instead of hitting Kemp, Owen contented himself with
slamming the door. Striding down the corridor, he almost
bumped into Chris Lorimer.

"Owen." Chris had a pile of essays under his arm and
seemed to be struggling to hold onto them. "I . . . it's . . ."

"Kemp won't take me back."

"Hmm . . . well. I suppose you can understand his position."
Lorimer shifted from one foot to the other as if he desperately
wanted to go to the toilet.

"Can you? Look, Chris, it's noon, the sun's over the yard-
arm, as they used to say, and I'm a bit cheesed off. It's been
a bad day, so far. How about a pint and a spot of lunch over
the road? My treat."

Lorimer contorted to glance at his watch. "I'd like to,
Owen, I really would, but I have to dash." And he really was
dashing as he spoke, edging away down the corridor as if
Owen had some infectious disease. "Maybe some other
time, perhaps?" he called over his shoulder, before disappearing round a corner.

Sure, Owen thought, some other time. Fuck you, too,
Chris Lorimer. You and the horse you rode in on.

III

"Well, well, well," said Banks, standing at the top of the
stairs overlooking the open-plan ground floor. "Speak of the
devil. Just the fellow I've been wanting to see. I've been
looking over your file. And guess who's turned eighteen
since we last met?"

Spinks looked at him. "Uh?"

"No more youth court." Banks glanced towards Susan and raised an eyebrow.

"Taking and driving away, sir," she said. "Under the influence."

"Influence of what, I wonder?" said Banks. "And so early in the day."

Spinks struggled, but Susan managed to hold onto him. "Not to mention crashing it through the window of Henry's fish and chip shop on Elmet Street," she said through gritted teeth.

Banks smiled and opened the door of the nearest interview room. "Be my guest," he said to Spinks, stretching an arm out through the open door. "Take a pew."

"I need a doctor," Spinks moaned. "The fucking steering was fucked. I hurt my head. I got whiplash. I could've been killed."

"Shut up and sit down," Banks said with enough authority that Spinks paused and obeyed. "I suppose you'll be suing the owner next?"

Spinks licked his lips. "Maybe I will."

There was a small cut just above his right eye. It was nothing serious, but Banks knew that if they didn't get him medical attention they'd be breaking a PACE directive and Spinks would probably succeed in getting his case dismissed.

"See if you can get Dr. Burns, will you, Susan?" Banks asked, indicating by a private gesture that she should take her time.

Susan nodded, straightened her dress and left.

"What are you on?" Banks asked.

Spinks looked away. "I don't know what you mean."

Banks grabbed Spinks's chin with one hand and held his head up, staring at the pinpoint pupils. "Crack, is it, John? Or solvent? Maybe heroin?"

"I don't do drugs."

"Like hell you don't. You know taking and driving away is an arrestable offense, don't you, John?"

Spinks said nothing.

"Do you know what that means?"

Spinks gave a lopsided grin. A little drool had formed at the side of his mouth. "It means you can arrest me for it." He giggled.

"Good," said Banks, patting his shoulder gently. "Very good, John. Now, you might not know this, but to put it nice and simply that also means we can detain you for up to twenty-four hours, longer if the superintendent authorizes it. Which he will. But wait a minute. Do you know what day it is, John?"

"What do you mean? Course I know. It's Friday."

"That's right." Banks looked at his watch. "Pity for you, John. See, a day like this, the magistrates will all be on the golf course by now. And they don't sit on Saturday or Sunday, so you'll have to stay with us until Monday morning."

"So what?"

"Your arrest also gives us powers of search, John. We don't need a warrant. That means there'll be coppers all over your mum's place, if there aren't already. Bound to turn up something. Your mum will love you for that, won't she?"

"She doesn't give a fuck."

Banks turned the free chair around and sat with his arms resting on the back. "Anyway," he said, "I'm not interested in petty stuff like car theft and drug abuse. You don't think a detective chief inspector concerns himself with run-of-the-mill stuff like that, do you?"

Spinks sniffed. "Can't say I care one way or another."

"No. Course not. I don't suppose you do. Well, I'm not doing this by the book, John. I want you to know that. Like I said, I'm not really interested in some gormless pill-popping pillock who steals a car and can't even drive it straight."

Spinks bristled. "I can fucking drive! I told you, the steering was fucked. Fucking owner ought to be locked up."

"Know what they say about a poor workman, John? He always blames his tools."

"Fuck off."

"Look, I'm getting sick and tired of your severely limited vocabulary. Know what I think we ought to do with people like you instead of community service or jail? I think we ought to have compulsory education for gobshites like you who spent so much time blitzed on model airplane glue that they never set foot in school more than a couple of weeks a year. Know what I'd do? I'd make you read the dictionary, for a start. At least ten new words a day. And spelling tests. Every morning, first thing after slopping out. A dozen lashes for every word you get wrong. Literature, too. Lots of it. Austen, Hardy, Dickens, Trollope, George Eliot. Long books. Poetry, as well—Wordsworth, Shelley, Dryden, Milton. And Shakespeare, John. Tons and tons of Shakespeare. Memorizing poems and long, lovely speeches. Analyzing the imagery in *Macbeth* and *Othello*. Sound like fun?"

"I'd rather be in fucking jail."

Banks sighed. "You will be, John. You will be. It's just a fantasy of mine. Now I'd like you to travel back in time through that addled, worm-eaten brain of yours. I'd like you, if you can negotiate through that lump of Swiss cheese you call a mind, to go back to last summer. Specifically, to last August. Can you do that?"

Spinks frowned. "Is this about that bird what got snuffed?"

"Yes," said Banks. "This, as you so eloquently put it, is 'about that bird what got snuffed.' Remember her name, John? Deborah Harrison."

"That's right. Yeah, Debbie."

"Good. Now something happened, didn't it? Something nasty?"

"Don't know what you mean."

"Her mother and her godfather warned you off, didn't they?"

"Oh, right. Stuck-up motherfuckers. Look, what's this got to do with—"

"I told you, John. I'm not doing this by the book. This is unofficial, off the record. Okay?"

Spinks nodded, a look of suspicion forming in his glazed eyes.

"One day you went around to ask Lady Sylvie Harrison to give you money to leave her daughter alone. Right?"

"So? There's no law against it. They'd got plenty. I didn't see why I shouldn't get some compensation. Bird wasn't much of a fuck, really. More like a sack of potatoes. But—"

Banks gripped the back of the chair so hard his knuckles turned white. "Spare me your erotic memoirs, John," he said. "They might make me do something I'll regret. You might not realize it, but I'm exercising great restraint as it is."

Spinks laughed. A little more drool dripped down his chin. Banks felt so much like clocking him one that he had to look away. "Who was in the house that day?"

"What?"

"You heard. Who else was there as well as you?"

"Oh. Didn't I already tell you that? I seem to remember—"

"Humor me. Tell me again."

"Right. There was Debbie's mother, the blonde bitch. And that stuck-up prick Clayton. Fucking snobs."

"And Deborah wasn't there?"

"I already told you. No." Spinks's head started to roll from side to side. The drugs, whatever they were, wearing off. Either that or he had sustained more than superficial damage in the car crash. Just as well they had sent for Dr. Burns.

"When you went to the house and found Michael Clayton there," Banks asked, "did you get the feeling that there was anything going on?"

Spinks closed his eyes. His head stopped lolling. "Don't know what you mean."

"Did you interrupt anything?"

"Interrupt?"

"Stop behaving like a parrot. Did you get the feeling there was anything going on between them?"

Spinks frowned and wiped the drool from his mouth with the back of his hand. His eyes opened again and seemed to keep shifting in and out of focus. "Going on?" he repeated. "You mean was he fucking her? You mean do I think Clayton was fucking the wicked witch?" He laughed out loud.

Banks waited patiently until he had stopped. "Well," he said. "Do you?"

"You've got a dirty mind. Do you know that?"

"Do you?"

Spinks shrugged. "Could've been, for all I know."

"But you didn't notice anything special about them, the way they behaved towards one another?"

"No."

"Were they both fully dressed?"

"Course they were."

"Did they look disheveled at all?"

"Come again. Dish what?"

"See what I mean about the need for compulsory education? It means messed up, ruffled, untidy."

"Oh. No. I don't think so. Can't really remember, though."

"Did Deborah ever say anything about them?"

He shook his head, stopped abruptly and opened his mouth as if to say something, then carried on shaking it. "No."

Banks leaned forward on the chair back. The two front legs raised off the floor. "What were you going to tell me, John?"

"Nothing. She never said nothing." He coughed and a mouthful of yellow vomit dribbled down his chin onto his T-shirt. The smell was terrible: booze, cheese-and-onion crisps and tacos. Banks stood up and stepped back.

At that moment, there was a knock on the door and Susan Gay came in, followed by Dr. Burns, the police surgeon, whose surgery was just across the market square.

"Sorry, sir," Susan said, "but the doctor's here."

"Right," said Banks, shaking hands with Burns. "He's all

yours. I've had enough. Take good care of him, Nick. I might want to talk to him again."

And as he walked back to his own office, he had the strange feeling that not only had Spinks been holding back, hiding something, but that he, himself, hadn't even been asking the right questions. Something was eluding him, and he knew from experience that it would drive him around the bend until he thought of it.

Chapter 16

I

*B*anks took a deep breath outside Michael Clayton's house on Saturday morning, then he got out of his car and walked up the garden path. If Chief Constable Riddle found out about this, Banks's life probably wouldn't be worth living.

Clayton's house wasn't quite as large as the Harrisons', but it was an impressive enough construction, solidly built of redbrick and sandstone, detached and surrounded by an unkempt garden. The lawn looked as if it hadn't been trimmed yet this year, and weeds choked the flower-beds.

After he rang the doorbell the first time, Banks heard nothing but silence and began to suspect that Clayton was out. He tried again. About thirty seconds later, just as he was about to head off down the path, the door opened and Clayton stuck his head out.

"Yes, what is it?" he asked crossly. "Oh, it's you, Chief Inspector." He moved aside and opened the door fully. "You'd better come in. Sorry about the mess."

Banks followed him through a door from the hallway into a room full of computer equipment. At least three computers, state-of-the-art, by the look of them, sat on their desks, two of them displaying similar graphic images. These were incomprehensible to Banks, and looked like a cross between circuit diagrams and the molecular structures he remembered from school chemistry. They were all multi-colored, and some of the nodes and pathways between them flashed, different on each screen. The third VDU showed a deck of cards set out in what Banks recognized as the solitaire "pyramid" fashion.

"I always have a game going when I'm working," Clayton said, smiling. "It helps me concentrate. Don't ask me why."

The floor was a mass of snaking cables and Banks trod carefully not to trip over any of them.

He could almost feel the room vibrating with the electrical hum running through them.

Clayton cleared a stack of computer magazines from a hard-backed chair. Banks almost asked him what the diagrams on the screens were, but he knew that either Clayton wouldn't tell him or he wouldn't understand anyway. Best not start off looking like an ignoramus.

Sheets of paper hissed as they slid out of a laser printer. One of the computers started to emit a loud, pulsating beep. Clayton excused himself while he went over and hit a few keys.

"Diagnostic programs," he said when he got back.

Well, that was clear enough, Banks thought. Even he knew what diagnostic programs were. Though what they were supposed to diagnose was another matter entirely.

"Computers," Clayton went on. "They've changed the world, Chief Inspector. Nothing is the same as when you and I were children. And they're still changing it. Believe me, in the not-too-distant future, nothing will be the same as it is now. But I don't suppose you came here to talk technology with me, did you? Are you coming to apologize?"

"What for?"

"For letting the bastard who killed Deborah slip through the cracks. I was there, you know, in court with Geoff and Sylvie. They're devastated. And I've hardly been able to concentrate on my work since then. How could you let it happen?"

Banks shrugged. "I've seen it happen more often than you have. We're not living in a perfect world."

"You can say that again. I don't know what the procedure is now, but if I can help in any way . . ." Clayton scratched his smooth chin. "Look, I've heard one or two disturbing rumors about this Pierce fellow beating up young girls and raping them. Is that true?"

"I can't comment on that," said Banks.

"But there *is* some evidence that wasn't admissible, isn't there? Something that might have got him convicted if it had been heard in the trial?"

"The judge rules on matters of law," Banks said. "So there might be a strong basis for the appeal. That's really all I can tell you at the moment."

Clayton paused and glanced quickly around at the computer screens. "Well, Chief Inspector, thank you for bringing me up to date. Can I help in any way?"

Banks leaned forward. "As a matter of fact, there is something. One of the results of the court's decision is that we have decided to reopen the case and examine some of the other angles again."

Clayton frowned. "I don't understand. Did you get the right man or didn't you?"

"The jury thinks we didn't."

"But what about *you*. You know more about him than you're ever allowed to tell the jury. What do *you* think?"

Banks was getting sick of that question. Now he knew what defense barristers felt when people kept asking them how they could possibly defend people they knew must be guilty. "I didn't see him do it," he said, "so there's always room for doubt."

Clayton snorted. "So just because the justice system fouls up yet again, you're going to run around reopening old wounds."

"I hoped you might look at it as co-operation," Banks said.

"About what?"

"John Spinks, for a start."

"That moron who caused all the trouble last summer?"

"That's the one."

"Sylvie told you about him?"

"Yes. And I talked to him again yesterday."

"You surely don't think *he* could have done it?"

"It's possible," Banks said.

"He doesn't have either the guts or the brains."

"Since when did it take brains to murder someone? Outside a detective novel, that is."

"It takes brains to do it and get away with it."

"Brains or luck."

Clayton shrugged. "No point in arguing. Look at it that way and anything's possible. He was certainly angry at her about what happened. I imagine anger is a familiar enough part of his limited emotional range. I suppose he could have laid in wait for her and lost his temper."

"Did he know she attended the chess club?"

"How should I know?"

"Somehow, I doubt it," said Banks. "Not if he hadn't been seeing her *after* term started. Anyway, that's beside the point. As you say, he would know the route she took and he could have simply lain in wait in the foggy graveyard ever since school came out. Now, as I understand it, Spinks came to Sir Geoffrey's house to extort money from Lady Sylvie Harrison, is that right?"

"Yes."

"And you hit him."

"No more than a little cuff. You're not going to arrest me for assault and battery are you?"

Banks smiled. "No. Believe me, sir, I've felt like doing the same thing myself on more than one occasion."

"Then you understand my feelings about him."

"Entirely. You hit him, and later you paid him off?"

"Yes. It seemed the easiest way."

"How much did you give him?"

"A hundred pounds."

"That was all?"

"Yes."

"He didn't come back for more?"

"No."

"Why?"

Clayton leaned forward and rested his hands on his knees. "Because I told him that if he did, I would certainly inform Sir Geoffrey, who would at the very least have him horse-whipped, no matter what vile threats he made." Clayton frowned and sat back. "You say you talked to Spinks again? Why? Was this in connection with reopening the case?"

"Not really. No, it was coincidence. He stole a car and crashed it."

"Pity he didn't break his neck. Serves the little bastard right."

"I suppose so," Banks said. He paused, feeling his heartbeat speed up. "What were you doing here when Spinks came?"

"What do you mean?"

"I got the impression that you're here an awful lot. Especially when Sir Geoffrey is out and his wife is at home."

Clayton's mouth dropped open and he started shaking his head very slowly. "My God, you've got a mind like a sewer," he said. "I don't believe it. On the basis of that you're suggesting . . ." He put his fingertips to his temple. "Let me get this clear . . . Your theory is that Sylvie and I were having a torrid affair and Deborah found out and threatened to tell her father. Instead of allowing that to happen, I waited for Deborah, my own goddaughter, in the graveyard after her school chess club one day and strangled her. Is that your theory?"

"I hadn't thought it out that far," Banks said. "I was just trying to get the lie of the land, that's all. But I must admit you've got a way of reducing things to their essentials. Thank you for putting it so succinctly."

Clayton stood up. His face was red. "This is insane, Banks. You're clutching at straws. I think you'd better leave now."

"I was just on my way. But I do have one more question."

Clayton gritted his teeth. "Very well."

"About the kind of work HarClay Industries does. Some of it is highly secret, isn't it, MoD stuff?"

"Yes. So?"

"Is there any chance that Deborah might have stumbled across something she shouldn't have, say in her father's papers?"

Clayton shook his head. "First you practically accuse me of murder, then you bring up all this James Bond stuff. No, Chief Inspector, Deborah *couldn't* have stumbled across any government secrets that got her killed. I think you already had the killer and you let him get off. Now you're casting about wildly for some sort of scapegoat."

Banks stood up to leave. "Maybe," he admitted.

"And for your information," Clayton went on, "I've known Geoff and Sylvie for years. I was there when they met. I was at university with Geoff. I have never had, nor am I having now, any other sort of relationship with Sylvie Harrison than that of a close friend. Am I making myself clear?"

Banks turned and met his gaze. "Perfectly."

"And just for this one time I'm willing to forget that this meeting ever took place. But if you ever dare come here again with your—"

Banks held his hand up. "I get the message, sir. If I ask any more questions, you'll go tell the chief constable. Fair enough."

When Banks got outside and back into his car, his hands were shaking as he lit his first cigarette of the day.

II

Rebecca Charters hadn't known what to do at first when Owen Pierce surprised her in the garden on Thursday. She had been scared, as she told Chief Inspector Banks, and her instinct had been to run inside, bolt the door and put the chain on. He hadn't tried anything after that, even though he must have known she was alone in the house, but she had looked through the window and watched him stand by the garden gate for a moment before walking off. Her heart had beat fast.

After Banks had left, she rationalized her fear away. Pierce hadn't *done* anything, after all, or even said or threatened anything. Perhaps she was overreacting. Pierce might not be guilty of anything. Certainly Inspector Banks had his doubts, and his idea of Deborah having *arranged* to meet the person who ultimately turned out to be her murderer made sense.

But when Owen Pierce came and knocked at her door on Saturday afternoon, while Daniel was out visiting the terminally ill patients in Eastvale General Infirmary, she felt afraid all over again.

Because it was a warm day and she liked the way the scents of the flowers drifted into the living-room, Rebecca had opened the bay window. Before moving to shut it and lock it, she shouted, "Go away or I'll call the police."

"Please," he said. "Please listen to me. I'm not going to hurt you. I've never hurt anyone. I just want to talk to you."

She left the window open but put her hands on top of the frame, ready to slam it down if he made any suspicious moves. "What about?" she asked.

"Just talk, that's all. Please. I need someone to talk to."

There was something in his tone that touched Rebecca, but not enough to open the door to him.

"Why me?" she asked. "You don't even know me."

"But I know *about* you. I know what you've been through. You're the vicar's wife. I've read about the accusations and everything. I just felt . . . I'm not trying to say I'm especially religious or anything. I don't want to lie to you about that. Please, will you just let me come in and talk? Will someone just treat me like a human being. Please."

Rebecca could see tears in his eyes. She still didn't know why he had come. She couldn't let him in, nor did she feel she could turn him away. After all, she was a Christian, *and* a minister's wife.

"Stay there," she said. "I'll come out." She would feel safe outside in the garden, with the constant flow of people on the river path.

Why was she doing it? she asked herself as she went outside. She knew part of the answer. Not too long ago, she had allowed herself to doubt Daniel, her own husband. Instead of offering him her unqualified support and devotion, she had turned to liquor and carnality to escape her obligations. More than that. It wasn't just her obligations she was running away from, but the horrible realization that she *had* doubted Daniel, she *had* believed him guilty. And now, here was this pathetic man, found not guilty by a jury and presumed guilty by the rest of the world. Call it pity, compassion, Christian charity or mere folly, but she *couldn't* turn him away.

Daniel had put out a couple of folding chairs in the garden. When the weather was nice, he liked to sit and watch the river as he composed his sermon. There was also a beautiful view of St. Mary's Hill, the fine old houses above the gentle slope of grass and trees. Here I am, Rebecca thought, sitting in the garden with a possible murderer on a warm June afternoon.

"I still don't understand why you're here," she said.

"I told you. I want—I *need*—a friend. Or friends. Everywhere I go people turn their backs. I'm lonely and I'm scared. I heard somewhere about what your husband's been going through. But you have obviously stood by him however hard it's been. I've got nobody."

Rebecca almost laughed out loud at the irony of it. Instead she said, "Yes. It has been hard. But the court found you innocent. You're free now."

Owen sniffed. "Not innocent. Just *not guilty* as charged. It's a different thing. Anyway, it doesn't matter. I'm not really free. Everyone believes I'm guilty."

"Are you?"

"Will you believe me if I promise to answer truthfully?"

Rebecca felt her heart speed up. It was such a simple question, but it seemed to her that so much depended on it. Not just Owen Pierce, here and now, but her whole moral reality, her sense of trust and, even, her faith itself. She became aware of Pierce looking at her and realized that she had probably been holding her breath. Finally, she let it out and took the leap.

"Yes," she said. "I'll believe you."

Pierce looked her in the eye. "No," he said. "No, I didn't do it."

Somehow, Rebecca felt great relief. "What can we do for you?" she asked.

Almost as if he didn't believe his good fortune, Pierce remained speechless for a while. His eyes filled with tears and Rebecca felt, for a moment, like taking his hand. But she didn't.

Finally, in a cracking voice, he said, "I need help. I have to put my life back together again and I can't do it alone." As he spoke, he regained his composure and wiped the tears away briskly. "It may seem cold, calculated," he said, "but it isn't. When I found out who you were, I remembered you from court and I was drawn to you because I thought you'd understand, you know, about being thought guilty when you're innocent, about all the hypocrisy they talk about truth and justice. I'm sure your husband didn't do what he's been accused of. No more than I did."

"But I thought you would be angry with us. My husband gave evidence against you."

Owen shook his head. "All he did was tell the truth. It didn't make any difference to the case. It *was* me on the bridge. I never denied that. And it must have been terrible for you finding the body. No, I hold nothing against you or your husband. Look, I have no friends, Mrs. Charters. Everyone's deserted me. I have no close family. Even strangers treat me like some sort of monster if they recognize me. I need support, public support. I need it to be seen that decent, intelligent people don't think I'm a monster. I need you on my side. You and your husband."

"You might have come to the wrong place," Rebecca said. "You wouldn't want to join a losing cause. Remember, my husband is still under suspicion."

"Yes, but he has carried on in the face of it all. And I know you believe in him. You've stuck by him. So have a lot of other members of the congregation, I'm sure. Don't you see, Mrs. Charters, we're both victims, your husband and I?"

Rebecca thought for a moment, remembering the hypocrisy of some parishioners. "All right, then," she said. "I can't guarantee anything, but I'll talk to my husband."

"Thank you," breathed Owen.

"But will you do one thing for me?"

"Of course."

"Will you come to church tomorrow morning? I'm not trying to convert you or anything, but it would be good if you could be *seen* there. The people who still come to St. Mary's have, for the most part, stuck up for Daniel and believed in his innocence, as you say. If we take you into the congregation, they might do the same for you. I know it might sound hypocritical, the way people judge by appearances, but they do, you know, and perhaps if . . . Why are you laughing?"

"I'm sorry, Mrs. Charters, I really am. I just can't help it. Of course I'll come to church. Believe me, it seems a very small price to pay."

III

It was just after two o'clock in the morning and Banks kept waking up from disturbing dreams. He and Sandra had been out to a folk night in the Dog and Gun, in Helmthorpe, with some old friends, Harriet Slade and her husband, David. The star of the evening was Penny Cartwright, a local singer who had given up fame and fortune to settle back in Helmthorpe a few years ago. Banks had first met her while investigating the murder of Harold Steadman, a local historian, and he had seen her once or twice in the intervening years. They chatted amicably enough when they met, but there was always a tension between them, and Banks was glad when the chit-chat was over.

Her singing was something to be relished, though. Alto, husky on the low notes but pure and clear in the higher range, her voice also carried the controlled emotion of a survivor. She sang a mix of traditional and contemporary—from Anon to Zimmerman—and her version of the latter's "I Dreamed I Saw St. Augustine" had made Banks's spine tingle and his eyes prickle with tears.

But now, after a little too much port and Stilton back at Harriet and David's, Banks was suffering the consequences. He had often thought that the blue bits in Stilton, being mold, had mild hallucinogenic properties and actually gave rise to restless dreams. It didn't matter that he hadn't yet found a scientist to agree with him; he was sure of it. Because every time he ate Stilton, it happened.

These weren't satisfying dreams, the kind you need to make you feel you've had a good night's sleep, but abrupt and disturbing transformations just below the threshold of consciousness: computer games turned into reality; cars crashed through monitor screens; and the ghost of a young woman walked through a foggy graveyard. In one, he had terminal cancer and couldn't remember what his children looked like. All the while, voices whispered about demon lovers, and crows picked bodies clean to the bone.

Thus Banks was not altogether upset when the phone rang. Puzzled, but relieved in a way to be rescued from the pit of dreams. At the same time, apprehension gripped his chest when he turned over and picked up the receiver. Sandra stirred beside him and he tried to keep his voice down.

"Sir?"

"Yes," Banks mumbled. It was a woman's voice.

"This is DC Gay, sir. I'm calling from the station."

"What are you doing there? What's happened?"

"I'm sorry to bother you, sir, but it looks like there's been another one."

"Another what?"

"Another girl disappeared, sir. Name's Ellen Gilchrist. She went to a school dance at Eastvale Comprehensive tonight and never arrived home. Her mum and dad are climbing up the walls."

Banks sat up and swung his legs from under the covers. Sandra turned over. "Where are they?" he asked.

"They're here, sir, at the station. I couldn't keep them away. I said we're doing all we can, but . . ."

"Have you called her friends, boyfriends?"

"Yes, sir. That's all been done. Everyone her mum and dad and her friends from the dance could think of. We've woken up half the town already. As far as I can gather, she left the dance alone just after eleven o'clock. Had a headache. Her parents only live on the Leaview Estate, so it's not more than a quarter of a mile down King Street. They got worried when she hadn't turned up by midnight, her curfew. Called us at twelve-thirty. Sir?"

"Yes?"

"They said normally they'd have given her till one, more likely, then give her a good talking to and pack her off to bed. But they said they'd heard about that killer who got off. Owen Pierce. That's why they called us so soon."

Sitting on the edge of the bed, Banks rubbed his eyes, trying once and for all to rid himself of the Stilton dreams. He sighed. From one nightmare to another. "All right," he said. "Get someone to put on a strong pot of coffee, will you, Susan? I'll be right over."

Chapter 17

I

An early rambler from Middlesborough set off from a bed and breakfast in Skield and found the girl's body tucked away in a fold of Witch Fell, above the village, at eight o'clock on Sunday morning. An hour later, the detectives from Eastvale and the Scene-of-Crime Officers began to dribble in, closely followed by Dr. Glendenning, who was out of breath by the time he had climbed up to where the body was.

Banks stood at the edge of the terrace, which he suspected was a lynchet, an ancient Anglian plowing strip leveled on a hillside. Such lyncheted hills went up in a series of steps, of which this was the first. The strip was about ten yards wide and dipped a little in the middle.

The girl's body lay spread-eagled in the central depression, as if cupped in the petals of a flower. The little meadow was full of buttercups and daisies; flies and more delicate winged insects buzzed in the air, some pausing to light on the girl's pale, unyielding skin for a moment.

Several buttercups and daisies had been twined in her long blonde hair, which lay spread out on the bright green grass around her head like the halo in a Russian icon. Her blouse had been torn open and her bra pulled up, revealing small, pale breasts, and her short skirt was up around her thighs, her discarded panties on the grass beside her. As Banks got closer, he noticed the discoloration around her neck, and the open shoulder-bag by her arm, some of its contents spilled on the grass: lipstick, a purse, compact, nail-file, chewing gum, perfume, keys, address book, earrings, hairbrush.

The similarities to the Deborah Harrison scene were too close to be ignored. And Banks had just convinced himself that Deborah had been murdered by someone she knew for some sort of logical reason. Now it looked as if they were dealing with a sexual psychopath—one who had murdered two young girls in the area.

Banks stood back as Peter Darby took photographs and then watched Dr. Glendenning perform the on-scene examination. By then, Superintendent Gristhorpe had arrived and Jimmy Riddle was rumored to be pacing at the bottom of the hill trying to decide whether to attempt the short climb or wait until the others came down to him.

Banks sniffed the air. It was another fine morning. A couple of sheep stood facing the drystone wall as if just wishing it would all go away. Well, it wouldn't, Banks knew. No more than the tightness in his gut, which felt like a clenched fist, would go away before tomorrow.

"Well?" he asked, after the doctor had finished his examination.

"As we're not in court, laddie," said Glendenning, with a crooked grin, "I can tell you that she probably died between ten o'clock last night and one or two o'clock in the morning."

"Do you think she was killed here?"

"Looks like it from the lividity on her back and thighs."

"So he brought her here alive all the way from Eastvale?"

Banks made a mental calculation. The girl, Ellen Gilchrist, had disappeared on her way home shortly after eleven o'clock last night. By car, it was about thirty miles from Eastvale to Skield, but some of that journey was on bad moorland roads where you couldn't drive very fast, especially at night. For one thing, the sheep were inclined to wander, and as anyone it has happened to will tell you, running into a sheep on a dark road is a very nasty experience indeed. Especially for the sheep.

It would probably have taken the killer an hour, Banks estimated, particularly if he took an indirect route to avoid being seen. Why bother? Why not just dump her in Eastvale somewhere? Was location important to him, part of his profile? Did he hope the body would remain undiscovered for longer here? Not much hope of that, Banks thought. Skield and Witch Fell were popular spots for ramblers, especially with the good weather.

"There's a nasty gash behind her left ear," Glendenning said, "which means she was probably unconscious when he brought her here, before he strangled her. It looks like it could have been caused by a hammer or some such heavy object. Cause of death, off the record, of course, is ligature strangulation, just like the last one. Shoulder-bag strap this time, instead of a satchel."

"And the bag's open, also like last time," Banks mused.

"Aye," said Glendenning. "Well, you can have the body sent to the mortuary now." And he walked off.

Banks tried to run the scenario in his mind as if it were a film: girl leaves friends at end of School Lane, walks onto King Street, busy during tourist hours but quiet at night, apart from the odd pub or two. Some street-lamps, but not an especially well-lit area. Most kids are still at the dance, but Ellen's going home ahead of her curfew because she has a headache, or so her friend said. She walks alone down the hill towards the Leaview Estate, not more than ten minutes at the most. Car pulls up. Or is it already waiting down the road, lights turned off, knowing there's a school dance, hoping someone will be careless enough to walk home alone?

He's standing by the car, looking harmless enough. He can't believe his luck. Another blonde, just like Deborah Harrison, and about the same age. Or did he know who he wanted? Had he been watching her? Did he *know* her?

As she passes, he grabs her and drags her into the passenger seat before she knows what's happening. She tries to scream, perhaps, but he puts his hand over her mouth to muffle her. He knocks her out. Now she's in the passenger seat, unconscious, bleeding behind her ear. He straps her in with the safety belt and sets off. Maybe someone saw the car, someone else leaving the dance? He has to get her to an isolated spot before he's seen.

All the way to Skield, he savors what he's going to do to her. The anticipation is almost as thrilling as the act itself, maybe even more so. He anticipates it, and later he relives it, replays it over and over in his mind.

He parks off the road, out of the way, car hidden behind a clump of trees, perhaps, and drags her up the hillside. It's not very far or very steep, the first lynchet, but he's sweating with the effort, and maybe she's coming round now, trying to struggle, beginning to realize that something terrible is about to happen to her. They get to the lynchet, and he lays her down on the grass and does . . . whatever he does.

"Alan?"

"What? Oh, sorry, sir. Lost in thought."

Superintendent Gristhorpe and DC Gay had come to stand beside him as uniformed officers searched the area.

"We'd better get back to the station and get things moving," said Gristhorpe. "We can start by questioning all the friends who were at the dance with her again, and then do a house-to-house along King Street, check out the pubs, too. I'll get someone to ask around Skield as well. You never know. Someone might have been suffering from insomnia."

"Sir?"

Both Banks and Gristhorpe looked around to see PC Weaver, one of the searchers, approach with something hooked over the end of a pencil. When he got closer, Banks could see that it was one of those transparent plastic containers that 35mm films come in. Living with Sandra, he had seen plenty of those.

"Found this in the grass near the body, sir," he said.

"Near the shoulder-bag?" Gristhorpe asked.

"No, sir, that's why I thought it was odd. It was on the other side of her, a couple of yards away. Do you think it could be the killer's?"

"It could be anyone's, lad," Gristhorpe said. "A tourist's, maybe. But we'd better check it for prints as quickly as we can." He turned to Banks. "Maybe we've got one who likes to photograph his victims?"

"Possible," Banks agreed. "And we already know one keen amateur photographer, don't we? I'll get Vic Manson on it right away. He should be able to do a comparison before the morning's over."

Just at that moment, a red bald head, shiny with perspiration, appeared over the rim of the meadow. "What's going on?" grunted Chief Constable Riddle.

"Oh, we've just finished here, sir," said Banks, smiling cheekily as he walked past Riddle and headed down the slope.

II

The church was hot and smelled like dust burning on the element of an electric fire. Owen remembered hearing somewhere that most household dust was just dead skin. Which meant the church smelled like dead bits of people burning. Hell? All flesh is grass. The heaps of dead, dry grass burning in allotments, or autumn stubble burning in the country fields, vast, rolling carpets of fire spread out in the distance, palls of smoke hanging and twisting in the still twilight air.

Owen took off his jacket and loosened his tie. He had never been comfortable in churches. His parents were both dyed-in-the-wool atheists, and the only times he had really been in church were for weddings and funerals. So he always wore a suit and tie.

Of course, it was all right when you were a tourist checking out the Saxon fonts and Gothic arches, but a different

story altogether when there was a vicar up front prattling on
about loving thy neighbor. Owen had always distrusted
overly churchy types before, feeling that the church offered
a public aura of respectability to many who pursued their
perversions in private. But the vicar in this case was Daniel
Charters, now one of the few allies Owen had in the entire
world.

Today it was the hoary old chestnut about how you get
nothing but bad news in the papers and how that can make
you cynical about the world, but really there are wonders
and miracles going on all around you all the time.

That morning, Owen could certainly relate to the first part
of the sermon, if not the uplifting bit. Just before he had set
off for church, he had screwed up the *News of the World* in
a ball and tossed it across the room.

Judging by the looks he got when he walked into St.
Mary's, and by the way so many members of the congregation leaned towards one another and whispered behind
cupped hands, even the upmarket clientele of St. Mary's had
had a butcher's at the *News of the World* over their cappuccino and croissants.

And there it was, blazoned across the front page in thick
black letters: **THE STORY THEY COULDN'T TELL IN
COURT.** Obviously Michelle's journalist friend had probed
her thoroughly. There was a reference to Owen's *liking to
take photographs,* phrased in such a way that it sounded
downright sinister, and a mention of his love of *kinky positions.* He also, it appeared, liked his sex rough and, as far as
partners were concerned, the younger the better. Michelle
came out of it sounding more like a victim than a willing
lover. Which, Owen supposed, was the intention.

There was also an old, slightly blurred, photograph of the
two of them and a scrap of a letter Owen had written
Michelle once when he was away at a conference. The letter
was a perfectly innocuous can't-wait-to-see-you-again sort
of thing, but in this context, of course, it took on a far more
disturbing aspect.

He recalled the day the photograph was taken. Shortly after Michelle had moved in with him, they had taken a holiday in Dorset, visiting various sites associated with Thomas Hardy's novels. In the small graveyard at Stinsford, where Hardy's heart was buried, they had asked an American tourist to take a photograph of them with Owen's camera. It turned out a little blurred because the tourist hadn't quite mastered the art of manual focusing.

Somehow, seeing the photograph and handwriting reproduced in a Sunday tabloid angered Owen even more than the innuendos in the article. Michelle had obviously handed them over to the reporter. It was a violation, a deeper betrayal even than what she said about him. He was quickly beginning to wish that he *had* killed Michelle.

The whole article screamed out his guilt, of course, protested a miscarriage of justice, though the writer never said as much, not in so many words. Mostly, he just posed questions. Owen wondered if he should consider suing for libel. They were clever, though, these newspaper editors; they vetted everything before they printed it; they could afford a team of lawyers and they had the money put aside to finance large law suits. Still, it was worth considering.

The pew in front of Owen creaked and brought him back to the present. He realized he was sweating, *really* sweating, and beginning to feel dizzy and nauseated, too. Churches weren't supposed to be this hot. He hoped it wouldn't go on much longer; he especially hoped that Daniel wouldn't say anything about him.

They sang a hymn he remembered hearing once at a wedding, then there were more readings, prayers. It seemed to be going on forever. Owen wanted to go to the toilet now, too, and he shifted uncomfortably in his seat.

One of the readers mentioned seeing something "as in a mirror, dimly" and it took Owen a moment or two to realize this was the approved modern version of "through a glass darkly," which he thought pretty much described his life. How could they, the English teacher in him wondered, utterly destroy one of the most resonant lines in the Bible, even if people did have trouble understanding what it meant. Since when had religion been about clear, literal, logical meaning anyway?

Finally, it was over. People relaxed, stood, chatted, ambled towards the doors. Many of them glanced at him as they passed. One or two managed brief, flickering smiles. Some pointedly turned away, and others whispered to one another.

Owen waited until most of them had gone. It had cooled down a little now, with the doors open and most people gone home. He still needed to go to the toilet, but not so urgently; he could wait now until he got to the vicarage. That was the plan: tea at the vicarage. He could hardly believe it.

When there were only one or two stragglers left, Owen got up and walked to the door. Daniel and Rebecca stood there chatting with a parishioner. Rebecca put her hand on his arm to stop him going immediately outside, and smiled. Daniel shook his hand and introduced him to the old woman. She looked down at her sensible shoes, muttered some greeting or other, and scurried off. This would obviously take time.

"Well," said Daniel, taking out a handkerchief and wiping his moist brow. "I suppose we should be grateful Sir Geoffrey and his wife weren't here."

Owen hadn't even thought of that. If he had considered the mere possibility of bumping into Deborah Harrison's parents, he wouldn't have gone near the place.

Daniel obviously saw the alarm in Owen's expression because he reached out and touched his shoulder. "I'm sorry," he said. "It was insensitive of me to say that. It's just that they used to attend. Anyway, come on, let's go."

Owen walked outside with Daniel and Rebecca, pleased to be in the breeze again and glad to know he wasn't entirely alone against the world. Then he saw four policemen hurrying down the tarmac path from the North Market Street gate. He told himself to run, but like Daniel and Rebecca, he simply froze to the spot.

III

"So, we meet again, Owen," said Banks later that Sunday in an interview room at Eastvale Divisional Headquarters. "Nice of you to assist us with our inquiries."

Pierce shrugged. "I don't think I have a lot of choice. Just for the record, I'm innocent this time, too. But I don't suppose that matters to you, does it? You won't believe me if it's not what you want to hear. You didn't last time."

Very little light filtered through the barred, grimy window and the bare bulb hanging from the ceiling was only thirty watts. There were three people in the room: Banks, Susan Gay and Owen Pierce.

One of the public-spirited parishioners at St. Mary's had heard about the Ellen Gilchrist murder on the news driving home after the morning service, and he had wasted no time in using his car-phone to inform the police that the man they wanted had been at St. Mary's Church that very morning, and might still be there if they hurried. They did. And he was.

In the distance, Banks could hear the mob chanting and shouting slogans outside the station. They were after Pierce's blood. Word had leaked out that he had been taken in for questioning over the Ellen Gilchrist murder, and the public were very quick when it came to adding two and two and coming up with whatever number they wanted.

People had started arriving shortly after the police delivered Pierce to the station, and the crowd had been growing ever since. Growing uglier, too. Banks feared he now had a lynch mob, and if Pierce took one step outside he'd be ripped to pieces. They would have to keep him in, if for no other reason than his own safety.

Already a few spots of blood dotted the front of his white shirt, a result of his "resisting arrest," according to the officers present; there was also a bruise forming just below his right eye.

Banks started the tape recorders, issued the caution and gave the details of the interview time and those present.

"They hit me, you know," Pierce said, as soon as the tape was running. "The policemen who brought me here. As soon as they got me alone in the car they hit me. You can see the blood on my shirt."

"Do you want to press charges?"

"No. What good would it do? I just want you to know, that's all. I just want it on record."

"All right. Last night, Owen, about eleven o'clock, where were you?"

"At home watching television."

"What were you watching?"

"An old film on BBC."

"What film?"

"Educating Rita."

"What time did it start?"

"About half past ten."

"Until?"

"I don't know. I was tired. I fell asleep before the end."

"Do you usually do that? Start watching something and leave before the end?"

"If I'm tired. As a matter of fact I fell asleep on the sofa, in front of the television. When I woke up there was nothing on the screen but snow."

"You didn't check the time?"

"No. Why should I? I wasn't going anywhere. It must have been after two, though. The BBC usually closes down then."

His voice was flat, Banks noticed, responses automatic, almost as if he didn't care what happened. But still the light burned deep in his eyes. Innocence? Or madness?

"You see, Owen," Banks went on steadily, "there was another young girl killed last night. A seventeen-year-old schoolgirl from Eastvale Comprehensive. It's almost certain she was killed by the same person who killed Deborah Harrison—same method, same ritual elements—and we think you are that person."

"Ridiculous. I was watching television."

"Alone?"

"I'm always alone these days. You've seen to that."

"So, can you see our problem, Owen? You were home, alone, watching an old film on television. Anyone could say that."

"But I'm not just anyone, am I?"

"How's the photography going, Owen?"

"What?"

"You're a keen photographer, aren't you? I was just asking how it was going."

"It isn't. My house was broken into while I was on trial and the bastard who broke in killed my fish and smashed my cameras."

Banks paused. "I'm sorry to hear that."

"I'll bet you are."

Banks took out the plastic film container and held it up for Owen to see. "Know what that is?"

"Of course I do."

"Is it yours?"

"How would I know. There are millions of them around."

"Thing is, Owen, we found this close to the body, and we found your fingerprints on it."

Owen seemed to turn rigid, as if all his muscles tightened at once. The blood drained from his face. "What?"

"We found your fingerprints on it, Owen. Can you explain to us how they got there."

"I . . . I . . ." he started shaking his head slowly from side to side. "It must be mine."

"Speak up, Owen. What did you say?"

"It must be mine."

"Any idea how it got out in the country near Skield?"

"Skield?"

"That's right."

He shook his head. "I went up there the other day for a walk."

"We know," said Susan Gay, speaking up for the first time. "We asked around the pub and the village, and several people told us they saw you in the area on Friday. They recognized you."

"Not surprising. Didn't you know, I'm notorious?"

"What were you doing, Owen?" Banks asked. "Reconnoitring? Checking out the location? Do you do a lot of advance preparation? Is that part of the fun?"

"I don't know what you're talking about. I admit I was there. I went for a walk. But that's the only time I've been."

"Is it, Owen? I'm trying to believe you, honest I am. I want to believe you. Ever since you got off, I've been telling people that maybe you didn't do it, maybe the jury was right. But this looks bad. You've disappointed me."

"Well, excuse me."

Banks shifted position. These hard chairs made his back ache. "What is this thing you have for rummaging around in girls' handbags or satchels?"

"I don't know what you mean."

"Do you like to take souvenirs?"

"Of what?"

"Something to focus on, help you replay what you did?"

"What did I do?"

"What did you do, Owen? You tell me how you get your thrills."

Pierce said nothing. He seemed to shrink in his chair, his mouth clamped shut.

"You can tell me, Owen," Banks went on. "I want to know. I want to understand. But you have to help me. Do you masturbate afterwards, reliving what you've done? Or can't you contain yourself? Do you come in your trousers while you're strangling them? Help me, Owen. I want to know."

Still Pierce kept quiet. Banks shifted again. The chair creaked.

"Why am I here?" Pierce asked.

"You know that."

"It's because you think I did it before, isn't it?"

"Did you, Owen?"

"I got off."

"Yes, you did."

"So I'd be a fool to admit it, wouldn't I? Even if I *had* done it."

"Did you do it? Did you kill Deborah Harrison?"

"No."

"Did you kill Ellen Gilchrist?"

"No."

Banks sighed. "You're not making it easy for us, Owen."

"I'm telling you the truth."

"I don't think so."

"I am."

"Owen, you're lying to us. You picked up Ellen Gilchrist on King Street last night. First you knocked her unconscious, then you drove her to Skield, where you dragged her a short distance up Witch Fell and strangled her with the strap of her handbag. Why won't you tell me about it?"

Pierce seemed agitated by the description of his crime, Banks noticed. Guilty conscience?

"What was it like, Owen?" he pressed on. "Did she resist or did she just passively accept her fate. Know what I think? I think you're a coward, Owen? First you strangled her from behind, so you didn't have to look her in the eye. Then you lay her down on the grass and tore her clothes away. You imagined she was Michelle Chappel, didn't you, and you were getting your own back, giving her what for. She didn't have a chance. She was beyond resistance. But even then you couldn't get it up, could you? You're a coward, Owen. A coward and a pervert."

"No!" The suddenness with which Pierce shot forward and slammed his fist into the desk startled Banks. He saw Susan Gay stand and make towards the door for help, but waved her down.

"Tell me, Owen," he said. "Tell me how it happened."

Pierce flopped back in his chair again, as if the energy of his outburst had depleted his reserves. "I want my lawyer," he said tiredly. "I want Wharton. I'm not saying another word. You people are destroying me. Get me Wharton. And either arrest me or I'm leaving right now."

Banks turned to Susan and raised his eyebrows, then sighed. "Very well, Owen," he said. "If that's the way you want it."

Chapter 18

I

*B*y late Sunday evening, it was clear that the crowd wasn't going to storm the Bastille of Eastvale Divisional HQ, and by early Monday morning, there were only a few diehards left.

Banks turned his Walkman up loud as he passed the reporters by the front doors; Maria Callas drowned out all their questions. He said hello to Sergeant Rowe at the front desk, grabbed a coffee and headed upstairs. When he got to the CID offices, he took the earphones out and walked on tiptoe, listening for that snorting-bull sound that usually indicated the presence of Chief Constable Riddle.

Silence—except for Susan Gay's voice on the telephone, muffled behind her closed door.

Dr. Glendenning's post-mortem report on Ellen Gilchrist was waiting in Banks's pigeon hole, along with a preliminary report from the forensic lab, who had put a rush on this one.

In the office, Banks closed his door and pulled up the venetian blinds on yet another fine day. Much more of this and life would start to get boring, he reflected. Still, there was a bit of cloud gathering to the south, and the weather forecast threatened rain, even the possibility of a thunderstorm.

He opened the window a couple of inches and watched the shopkeepers open their doors and roll down their awnings against the sunshine. Then he stretched until he felt something crack pleasantly in his back, and sat down to study the report. He tuned the portable radio he kept in his office to Radio 4 and listened to "Today" as he read.

Glendenning had narrowed the time of death to between eleven and one, confirmed that the victim had been killed in the place where she was found, and matched the strap of her shoulder-bag to the weal in her throat.

The wound behind her ear was round and smooth, he also confirmed, about an inch in diameter, and most likely delivered by a metal hammer-head.

This time, unfortunately, there was no scratched tissue beneath her fingernails. In fact, her fingernails were so badly chewed they had been treated with some vile-tasting chemical to discourage her from biting them.

According to the lab, though there was no blood other than the deceased's at the scene, there were several hairs on her clothing that didn't come from her body. That was understandable, given that she had been at a crowded dance. What was damning, though, was that four of the hairs matched those found on Deborah Harrison's school blazer—the ones that had already also been tested against the sample Owen Pierce had given almost eight months ago.

Hairs could be dodgy evidence, as Pierce's trial had shown. Banks read through a fair bit of jargon about melanin and fragmented medullas, then considered the neutron activation analysis printout specifying the concentration of various elements in the hair, such as antimony, bromine, lanthanum, strontium and zinc.

The lab would need another sample of the suspect's hair, the report said, because the ratios of these elements could have changed slightly since the last sample was taken, but even at this point, it was 4500 to one *against* the hair originating from anyone but Pierce.

Unfortunately, none of the hairs had follicular tissue adhering to their roots; in fact, there were no roots, so it was impossible to identify blood factors or carry out DNA analysis.

As in the Deborah Harrison murder, the swabs showed no signs of semen in the mouth, vagina or anus, and there was no other evidence of sexual activity.

But the hairs and the fingerprints Vic Manson had identified on the plastic film container would probably secure a conviction, Banks guessed. Pierce wasn't going to slip through the cracks this time.

In a way, Banks felt sad. He had almost convinced himself that Pierce had been an innocent victim of the system and that Deborah's killer was closer to home; now it looked as if he were wrong again.

He tuned in to Radio 3—where "Composer of the Week" featured Gerald Finzi—and started making notes for the meeting he would soon be having with Stafford Oakes.

Things started to get noisy at around eleven-thirty, with Pierce on his way to court for his remand hearing, the phone ringing off the hook and reporters pressing their faces at every window in the building. Banks decided it was time to sneak out by the side exit and take an early lunch.

He opened the door and popped his head out to scan the corridor. Plenty of activity, but nobody was really paying him much attention. Instead of going the regular way, down to the front door, he tiptoed towards the fire exit, which came out on a narrow street opposite the Golden Grill, called Skinner's Yard.

He had hardly got to the end of the corridor, when he heard someone call out behind him. His heart lurched.

"Chief Inspector?"

Thank God it wasn't Jimmy Riddle. He turned. It was DI Barry Stott, and he was looking troubled. "Barry. What is it? What can I do for you?"

"Can I have a word? In private."

Banks glanced around to see if anyone else was watching them. No. The coast was clear. "Of course," he said, putting his hand on Stott's shoulder and guiding him towards the fire door. "Let's go for a drink, shall we, and get away from the mêlée."

II

It was a long time since Rebecca had been to talk to the angel, but that Monday she felt the need again. And this time she wasn't drunk.

As she turned off the tarmac path onto the gravel, she wondered how she could have been so wrong about Owen Pierce. She remembered how scared she was when she first saw him after his release, then how like a little boy lost he had been when he came to talk to her. When she had asked him the all-important question and he had said he would answer truthfully, she had believed him. Now it looked as if he had lied to her. How could she be sure of anything any more? Of anyone? Even Daniel?

The air around the Inchcliffe Mausoleum was warm and still, the only sounds the drone of insects and the occasional car along Kendal Road or North Market Street. The angel continued to gaze heaven-ward. Rebecca wished she knew what he could see there.

Sober, this time, and feeling a little self-conscious, she couldn't quite bring herself to speak out loud. But her thoughts flowed and shaped themselves as she stood there feeling silly. She wondered what the policeman, Chief Inspector Banks, would think of her.

The police had claimed that Owen Pierce had killed *another* girl. That meant they also believed he had killed Deborah Harrison. There could be no way out for him now, Rebecca thought, not with public feeling as strong as it was against him.

But he had visited her at the vicarage only that Saturday afternoon, full of talk about his innocence, the need for support and understanding. She couldn't get over that, how *convinced* she had been. Was that the behavior of someone who was intending to go out later that night, pick up a teenage girl and murder her? Rebecca didn't think so. But what did she know? Experts had done studies on these kinds of people—serial murderers, they called them—though she didn't know if having killed only two people qualified Owen for that designation.

She had, however, seen enough television programs about psychopaths to know that some could *appear* perfectly charming, live quite normal lives outside their need to kill. Ted Bundy, for example, had been a handsome and intelligent man who had killed God knew how many young women in America. Watch out for the nice, friendly, polite boy next door, the message seemed to be, not the raggedy man with the cruel eyes muttering to himself in a corner.

A fly settled on her bare forearm and she stared at its shiny blue and green carapace for a moment before brushing it off. Then she looked up at the angel again. If only he could make things clear for her.

Perhaps the police had arrested Owen only because they still believed he had killed Deborah Harrison. Maybe they had no real evidence that he had killed the other girl. She didn't know why she should care so much. After all, Owen was still practically a stranger to her—and for a long time she had *believed* him to be a killer. Why should she be so upset when it turned out that he really was? She still couldn't help feeling that he had let her down somehow, silly as the idea was.

"Why?" she asked, surprised to find herself speaking out loud at last, face turned up to look at the angel. "Can you tell me why I care?"

But she got no answer.

She already knew part of the answer. Talking to Owen, taking him under her wing, had been a test for her. In a way, his presence had challenged her faith, her Christian feelings. For when it came to Christianity, Rebecca was a humanist, not one of these cold-fish theologians like some of the ministers she had met. Perhaps a better existence did await us in heaven, but to Rebecca, Christianity was useless if it forgot people and the here and now. Faith and belief, she felt, were no use without charity, love and compassion; religion was nothing if it focused entirely on the afterlife. Daniel had agreed. That was why they had done so well together. Up to last year.

"Why am I telling you this?" she asked the angel. "What do you know of life on earth? What is it I want from you? Can you tell me?"

Still the angel gazed fixedly heaven-ward. His expression looked stern to Rebecca, but she put that down to a trick of the light.

"Am I to be a cynic now?" she asked. "After I put so much faith in Owen and he turns out to be a killer after all?"

Again, she didn't hear any answer, but she did hear a movement coming from deeper in the woods. The area behind the Inchcliffe Mausoleum was the most overgrown in the entire graveyard, all the way back to the wall at Kendal Road. The oldest yews grew there, and the wild shrubbery was so dense in places you couldn't even walk through it easily. If there were any graves, nobody had visited them for a long time.

It must have been a small animal of some kind, Rebecca decided. Then she remembered that she had told the police and the court that the cry she heard that November evening could have come from an animal. When she really thought about it, she knew it never could have. She had simply refused to acknowledge, either to herself or to anyone else that the scream she heard was the last cry for help of a girl about to be murdered. This sound, too, was too loud to be a dog, a cat or a bird. And there were no horses or sheep in the graveyard.

She took a step towards the back of the mausoleum, aware as she did so that this was where Deborah's body had been found. "Is anybody there?" she called out.

No answer.

Then she heard another rustling sound, this time closer to the North Market Street wall.

Rebecca turned and wandered thigh-deep into the tangled undergrowth. She felt nettles sting her legs as she walked. "Is anyone there?" she called again.

Still no answer.

She paused and listened for a moment. All she could hear was her heart beating.

Suddenly to her left, through the trees, she saw a dark figure break into a run. It looked like a man dressed in brown and green, but she couldn't be certain because of the way the colors blended in with the background. Whoever it was, he couldn't get over the high wall before she caught up with him. His only alternative was to head along the wall to the North Market Street gate. If she hurried, perhaps she could catch a glimpse of him before he got away.

She turned back towards the back of the Inchcliffe Mausoleum and the gravel path. He was to her right now. She could hear him running towards the gate.

Before she could get out of the wooded area, something snagged at her ankle and she tripped, scratching her knees and hands on thorns. It only delayed her a few seconds, but when she got to her feet and ran past the mausoleum along the gravel path into the open area, all she saw was the wooden gate slam shut. She stood there and cursed whoever it was. When she looked down, she saw she had blood on her hands.

III

Avoiding the Queen's Arms, which everyone knew was the Eastvale CID local, Banks spirited Stott along Skinner's Yard, down to the Duck and Drake on one of the winding alleys off King Street. The cobbled streets were chock-a-block with antique shops, antiquarian booksellers and food specialists, all with mullioned windows and creaky wooden floors.

The Duck and Drake was a small, black-fronted Sam Smith's house with etched, smoked-glass windows and a couple of tatty hanging baskets over the door. Inside, the entrance to the snug was so low that Banks felt as if he were crawling under a particularly tight overhang in Ingleborough Cave.

The snug was also tiny, with dark wood beams and white-washed walls hung with hunting prints and brass ornaments. They were the only two people in the place. The bench creaked as Banks sat down opposite Stott with his pint of Old Brewery Bitter and his ham and cheese sandwich. Stott hadn't wanted anything at all, not even a glass of water.

"What is it, Barry?" Banks asked, chomping on his sandwich. "Off your food? You look bloody awful."

"Thanks."

"Don't mention it."

Stott was pale, with dark bags under his eyes and a two-day stubble around his chin and cheeks. His eyes themselves, behind the glasses, were dull, distant and haunted. Banks had never seen him like this before. Normally, you could depend on Barry Stott to look bright-eyed and alert at all times. Not to mention well groomed. But his suit was creased, as if he had slept in it, his tie was not properly fastened, and his hair was uncombed. He looked so miserable that even his ears seemed to droop.

"You ill?"

"As a matter, of fact," said Stott, "I *haven't* been sleeping well. Not well at all."

"Something on your mind?"

"Yes."

Banks finished his sandwich, took a sip of beer and lit a cigarette. "Out with it, then."

Stott just pursed his lips and frowned in concentration.

"Barry, are you sure it's something you want to talk to me about?"

"I *have* to," Stott replied. "By all rights, I should go to the super, or even the CC. God knows, it's bound to get that far eventually, but I wanted to tell you first. I don't know why. Respect, perhaps. It's just so difficult. I've been up wrestling with it all night, and I can't see any other way out."

Banks sat back. He had never seen Barry Stott so upset, so *consumed* by anything before, except that day when Pierce was found not guilty. Stott was a private person, and Banks wasn't sure how to handle him on a personal level, outside the job.

Was this a private, intimate matter, perhaps? Was Stott going to admit he was homosexual? Not that it mattered. Banks knew for a fact that two of the uniformed officers at Eastvale were gay. So did everyone else. They came in for a bit of baiting now and then from the more macho among their colleagues, who weren't entirely sure of their own sexuality, and for a certain amount of righteous moral disapproval from the one or two Christian fundamentalists in uniform. But Barry Stott? Banks realized he didn't even know whether Stott was married, divorced or single.

"Is this off the record, Barry?" Banks asked. "I mean, is it something personal?"

"Partly. But not really." He shook his head. "I can't understand it myself. I was so sure. So damn *certain.*" He banged the table. Banks's beer-glass jumped. "Sorry."

"I think you'd better just tell me."

Stott paused. He took a handkerchief from his pocket and cleaned the lenses of his glasses. In the background Banks could hear the radio playing Jim Reeves singing "Welcome to My World."

Finally, Stott put his glasses back on, nodded and took a deep breath. "All right," he said. "I suppose the most important thing is that Owen Pierce is innocent, at least of Ellen Gilchrist's murder. We have to let him go."

Banks's jaw dropped. "What are you talking about, Barry?"

"I was *there,*" Stott said. "I *know.*"

Christ, what was this? A murder confession? Banks held his hand up. "Hold on, Barry. Take it easy. Go slowly. And be very careful what you say." He almost felt as if he were giving Stott a formal caution. "Where were you? King Street? Skield?"

Stott shook his head and licked his lips. "No. Not either of those places. I was outside Owen Pierce's house."

"Doing what?"

"Watching him. I've been doing it ever since he got off."

"So that's why you're looking so washed out?"

Stott rubbed his hand over his stubble. "Haven't had any sleep in a week. Soon as I finish at the station, I grab a sandwich, then head for his street and park. If he goes out, I follow him."

"All night?"

"Most of it. At least till it looks like he's settled. Sometimes as late as three or four in the morning. He doesn't go out much. Most nights he gets drunk and passes out in front of the telly."

"And he hasn't spotted you?"

"I don't know. I haven't taken any great pains to hide myself, but he hasn't said anything."

"But *why,* Barry?"

Stott smoothed down his hair with his hand, then shrugged. "I don't know. I got obsessed, I suppose. I just couldn't stop myself. I was so *sure* of his guilt, so certain he'd beaten the system. . . . And I knew he'd do it again. It was that kind of crime. I could feel it. I wanted to make sure he didn't kill another girl. I thought if I watched him, kept an eye on him, then either I'd catch him, stop him or, if he knew I was onto him, he wouldn't be able to do it again and the tension would get unbearable. Then maybe he'd confess or something. I wasn't thinking clearly."

Banks stubbed out his cigarette. "But why, Barry? You're a good copper. Brainy, diligent, logical. You passed all your exams. You've got a bloody university degree, for Christ's sake. You're on accelerated promotion. You ought to know better."

Stott shrugged. "I know. I know. I can't explain it. Something just . . . went in me. Like I said, I thought if I watched him long enough I'd catch him one way or another."

Banks shook his head. "Okay. Let's get this straight. You were parked outside Owen Pierce's house on Saturday night?"

"Yes."

"What time?"

"From about five o'clock on."

"Until?"

"About two-thirty in the morning, when he turned the lights off. He didn't go out at all except to buy a bottle of something at the off-license around nine o'clock."

"You're absolutely certain?"

"Positive. The curtains weren't quite closed. I could see him clearly whenever he got up. He was watching telly in the front room, but every now and then he'd get up to go to the toilet, or pour a drink, whatever."

"And you're certain he was there all the time? He didn't sneak out the back and come back?"

Stott shook his head. "He was there, sir. Between the crucial times. Definitely. I saw him get up and cross the room twice between eleven o'clock and midnight."

"Are you sure it couldn't have been anyone else?"

"Certain. Besides, his car was parked in front of the house the whole time."

That didn't mean much. Pierce could have stolen a car to commit the crime, and then returned it, rather than risk using his own and having his license number taken down. When that thought had passed through his mind, Banks had experienced another irritating sense of *déjà vu*. He had felt the same thing the other day while going over the case files. It couldn't really be *déjà vu*, because it wasn't something he had already experienced, but it came with the same sort of frisson.

"What happened then?" he asked.

"He must have fallen asleep in front of the telly, as usual. I could see the light from the screen. It changed to snow at one fifty-five, when the programs ended, but Pierce didn't move again until two-thirty. Then he drew the curtains fully, turned out the lights and went upstairs to bed. That's all."

"That's *all*. Jesus Christ, Barry, do you have any idea what you've done?"

"Of course I have. But I had to speak out. I've been struggling with my conscience all night. I could have spoken up yesterday and saved Pierce another night in jail, but I didn't. I didn't dare. That's my cross to bear. I was worried about the consequences to my career, partly, I'll admit that, but I was also trying to convince myself that I *could* have been wrong, that he *could* have done it. But there's no way. He's innocent, just like he says."

Banks shook his head. "I don't see how we can cover this up, Barry. I'm not sure what's going to happen."

Stott sat bolt upright. "I don't want you to cover it up. As I said, I grappled with my conscience all night. I prayed for an answer, an easy way out. There isn't one. I'll speak up for Pierce. I'm his alibi. I've abused my position." He reached in his inside pocket and brought out a white, business-size envelope, which he placed on the table in front of Banks. "This is my resignation."

IV

Owen was confused. The Magistrates' Court had bound him over without bail, as he had expected, but instead of being en route to Armley Jail, he was back in the cell at Eastvale. And nobody would tell him anything. Wharton had received a message from one of the uniformed policemen just as they returned to the van after the court session, and he seemed to have been running around like a blue-arsed fly ever since. Something was going on, and as far as Owen was concerned, it could only be bad.

He ate a lunch of greasy fish and chips, ironically

wrapped in Sunday's *News of the World*, washed it down with a mug of strong sweet tea, and paced his cell until, shortly after one o'clock, Wharton appeared in the doorway, waistcoat buttons straining over his belly, a scarlet crescent grin splitting his bluish jowls.

"You're free to go," he announced, thumbs hooked in his waistcoat pockets.

Owen flopped on the bed. "Don't joke," he said. "What do you want?"

"I told you." Wharton came close to what looked like dancing a little jig like Scrooge on Christmas morning. "You're free. Free. Free to go."

Had he gone mad? Owen wondered. Had this new arrest been the straw that broke the camel's back? By all rights, it should be *Owen* going mad, not his solicitor, but there was no accounting for events these days. "Please," Owen said putting his fists to his temples in an attempt to stop the clamor rising inside his head. "Please stop tormenting me."

"He's right, Owen," said a new voice from behind Wharton in the doorway.

Owen looked up through the tears in his eyes and saw Detective Chief Inspector Banks leaning against the jamb, tie loose, hands in his pockets. So it wasn't a dream; it wasn't a lie? Owen hardly dared believe. He didn't know how he felt now. Choked, certainly, his head spinning, a whooshing sound in his ears. Mostly, he was still confused. That and tearful. He felt very tearful. "You *believe* me?" he asked Banks.

Banks nodded. "Yes. I believe you."

"Thank God." Owen let his head fall in his hands and gave in to the tears. He cried loud and long, wet and shamelessly, and it wasn't until he had finished and started to wipe his nose and eyes with a tissue that he noticed the two men had left him alone, but that the cell door was still open.

Gingerly, he walked towards it and poked his head out, afraid that it would slam on him. Nothing happened. He walked along the tiled corridor towards the other locked

door that led, he knew, upstairs, then out to the world beyond, worried that it wouldn't be opened for him. But it was.

Banks and Wharton stood outside, in the custody suite,
and Owen now feared he would be rearrested for something
else, still anxious that it was all some sort of ruse.

When Banks approached him, he backed away in apprehension.

"No," said Banks, holding his hands out, palms open. "I
meant it, Owen. No tricks. It's over. You're a free man.
You're completely exonerated. But I'd really appreciate it if
you would come to my·office with me for a chat. You might
be able help us find out who really did commit these murders."

"*Murders?* You believe I'm innocent of both?"

"They're too similar, Owen. Had to be the same person.
And that person couldn't have been you. Please, come with
me, will you? I'll explain."

As Owen preceded Banks up the stairs, he felt as if he
were walking in a dream and half-expected his feet to disappear right through the steps. On the open-plan ground
floor, everyone fell silent as he passed, watching him, and he
felt as if he were floating, weightless in space. His vision
blurred and his head started to spin, as if he had had too
much to drink, but before he stumbled and fell, he felt
Banks's strong hand grasp his elbow and direct him towards
the stairs.

"It's all right, Owen," Banks said. "We'll have some
strong coffee and a chat. You've nothing to worry about
now."

Instead of taking him into a dim, smelly interview room,
as Owen had been half-expecting, Banks led him into what
must be his own office. It was hardly palatial, but it had a
metal desk, some matching filing cabinets and two comfortable chairs.

On the wall was a *Dalesman* calendar set at June and
showing a photograph of a couple of ramblers with heavy
rucksacks on their backs approaching Gordale Scar, near

Malham. Oddly, Owen found himself thinking he could have done a better job of the photograph himself. The venetian blinds were up, and before he sat down Owen glimpsed the cobbled market square, full of parked cars. Freedom. He sat down. God, he felt tired.

"What happened?" he asked.

"You were under surveillance," said Banks.

"What? So there was . . . I mean, it was *you*?"

"Not me, exactly, but someone. Did you know there was someone watching you?"

"I had a funny feeling once or twice. But no, I can't honestly say I knew." Owen started to laugh.

"What is it?" Banks asked.

Owen wiped his arm over his eyes. "Oh, nothing. Just the irony of it, that's all. I was under surveillance because you thought I'd commit a crime, but as it turns out the surveillance gives me an alibi. Don't you think that's funny?"

Banks smiled. "Ironic, yes. But a young girl did get killed, Owen. Horribly. Just like Deborah Harrison."

"I know. I wasn't laughing at that. And I didn't have anything to do with it. I don't know how I can help you."

"I think you do. I don't believe you haven't considered the problem over the past couple of days."

"What problem?"

Banks sat forward and rested his palms on the blotter. "You want me to spell it out? Okay. The reason we arrested you, Owen, was partly because you had been accused of a very similar crime before, and partly because we found strong physical evidence against you at the scene. It still looks very much as if the same person killed both of those girls, and we found evidence against you at both scenes."

"The fingerprints and the hairs? Yes. And you're right: I *have* been thinking about how they could have got there."

"Any ideas?"

Owen shook his head. "I *did* go up Skield way, and I probably walked past the spot where . . . you know. I suppose I could have dropped such a film container, but I don't think I had one with me. I told you about my camera. I didn't have it with me. As for the hairs, I suppose I must have shed a few during my walk, but I can't explain how they got on the victim's clothes. Unless . . ."

"Yes?"

The coffee arrived. Banks poured. Owen blew into his cup first, then took a sip. "This is good. Thank you. Unless," he went on, "and I know this sounds crazy, paranoid even, but I can't see how any of it could have happened unless someone, the real killer, had decided to capitalize on my bad reputation, blame it on me, the way he knew everyone else would. It doesn't make sense unless someone tried to *frame* me for Ellen Gilchrist's murder."

Banks started tapping a pencil against his blotter. "Go on," he said.

"Well, if you accept that premise, then whoever it was must have broken into my house while I was in jail and wrecked the place to cover up his true intentions. Or he could have walked in easily *after* the place had been done over. The front door was unlocked when I got back. The lock was broken, in fact. This person must have thought there was a good chance I'd get off, and he wanted some insurance in case that happened and suspicion turned back on him. He must have found the empty film container in the waste-paper bin and guessed it would have my fingerprints on it. I mean, if it were empty, and I'd opened it. . . . Then he must have picked up some hairs from the pillow in the bedroom. That would have been easy enough to do."

Banks nodded. "Why not choose something more *obvious* to link you to the crime?"

"Failing my blood, which he couldn't get hold of, I can't think of anything more obvious than my hair and fingerprints, can you?"

Banks smiled. "I meant something with your name on, perhaps. So there could be no mistake. After all, the prints on the film container might have been blurred. He couldn't be *certain* they'd lead us to you."

"But if you think about it," Owen said, looking pointedly at Banks, "he didn't need very much, did he? You all believed I'd murdered Deborah Harrison, so it was easy to convince you I'd also killed Ellen Gilchrist. There was no point risking anything more obvious, like something with my name or photograph on it, because that would only draw suspicion. No, all he needed were my prints and hair. He knew my reputation would do the rest. Even without the prints he could have been fairly certain you'd pick on me. I'll bet the minute you saw the film container you thought of me because you knew I was an amateur photographer."

"That still leaves us one important question to answer," Banks said. "Who? Of course, it might be that the murderer was simply using you as a convenient scapegoat—that it was nothing personal—but it *could* have been someone who really wanted you to suffer. Have you any idea who would want to do that to you?"

"I've racked my brains about it. But no. The only person who hates me that much is Michelle. *Could* it have been a woman?"

"I don't think Michelle is tall enough," Banks said. "But, yes, it *could* have been a woman."

Owen shook his head. "I'm sorry. I wish I could help. Like you said, it was probably nothing personal. I mean, whoever did it just wanted *someone else* to blame. It didn't matter who."

"You're probably right. But if you think of anyone . . ."

"Of course. One of the neighbors might have seen someone, you know. They wouldn't speak out before because they all thought I was guilty and deserved having my house wrecked, but now . . . ? I don't know. It's worth asking them, anyway. You might start with that prick Ivor and his wife, Siobhan, next door."

"We'll do that," said Banks, standing up to indicate the interview was at an end.

Owen finished his coffee, stood awkwardly and moved towards the door. He could still hardly believe that freedom was just a few steps away again.

"What now?" Banks asked him.

He shrugged. "I don't know. I've got a lot to think about. Maybe I'll go away for a while, just get lost, like everyone suggested I should do in the first place."

Banks shook his head. "No need to run away," he said. "We know you didn't do it now. The press will fall all over themselves to support your cause, and they'll crucify us for getting the wrong man. Police incompetence."

Owen forced a smile. "Maybe. Eventually. And I can't say I'll be sorry. You deserve it. I remember what you've put me through. I remember all the terrible things you accused me of only yesterday. Perversion. Cowardice. Not to mention murder. But I can't see me getting my job or my friends back, can you? And I imagine there'll be a lot of people around these parts slow to change their minds, no matter what. Shit sticks, Chief Inspector. That's one thing I've learned from all this."

Banks nodded. "Perhaps. For a while."

Owen paused at the door. "Look," he said, "I don't expect an apology or anything, but could you just tell me again that you believe I'm innocent? Not just not guilty but *innocent*. Will you *say* it. I need to hear it."

"You're innocent, Owen. It's true. You're free to go."

"Thank you." Owen turned and started to pull the door shut behind him.

"Owen?" Banks called after him.

Owen felt a little shiver of panic. He turned. "Yes?"

"I *am* sorry. Good luck to you."

Owen nodded, shut the door and left the building as fast as he could.

Chapter 19

I

*I*t wasn't until late Tuesday afternoon that a number of things clicked into place for Banks, and what had been eluding him, niggling him for days, suddenly became clear.

So far, there were no leads on the Ellen Gilchrist murder. Several cars had been spotted on King Street that night—big, small, light, dark, Japanese, French—but no-one had any reason to take down license numbers or detailed descriptions. If the killer had used his own car, Banks reflected, then he may have parked out of sight, just around the corner on one of the sidestreets.

A couple of tourists unable to sleep on a lumpy mattress at a Gratly B & B said they heard a car pass shortly after eleven-thirty, which would have been about the right time, but they hadn't seen anything. So far, no-one in Skield had been disturbed by Saturday night's events, but that didn't surprise Banks. If the killer were clever, which he apparently was, then he would have parked off the road, well out of the hamlet itself.

Under Superintendent Gristhorpe's co-ordination, Susan Gay and Jim Hatchley were still out checking the victim's friends and acquaintances to see if she could have been killed by someone who knew her, or if anyone knew more than he or she was telling. The more he thought about it, though, the more Banks was convinced that the solution to Ellen Gilchrist's murder lay in Deborah Harrison's.

Also, when Banks arrived at the office that morning, he found a telephone message in his pigeon-hole from Rebecca Charters, dated the previous afternoon, asking him to phone her. When he rang Rebecca, she told him about surprising someone in St. Mary's graveyard the previous afternoon. No, she hadn't seen who it was, couldn't even give a description. She laughed at her fears now, apologized for bothering him and said she'd been a bit jumpy lately. Yesterday, she hadn't hesitated to call, but now she had had time to think about it. Probably just a kid, she decided. Banks wasn't too sure, but he put it on the back burner for the moment.

Since Stott's revelation, after the inevitable bollocking from Jimmy Riddle and a reminder that he was close to the end of his allotted week, Banks and Superintendent Gristhorpe had also been engaged in damage control.

So far, they had managed to keep Stott's illegal surveillance from the press. And Owen Pierce certainly wasn't interested in blowing the whistle. As far as the media were concerned, Pierce had an unimpeachable alibi. All that had happened was that another innocent person had spent a night in the cells because of police incompetence. Nothing new about that. Eastvale CID came out of it looking only like prize berks, not like a combination of the Gestapo and the KGB.

As for Barry Stott, he hadn't resigned, but he had taken some of the leave due to him. God knew where he was. Wrestling with his conscience somewhere, Banks guessed. As far as Banks was concerned, though, Stott was overreacting. So, he had let himself get a bit obsessed with Pierce's guilt. So what? Things like that happened sometimes, and they rarely had dire consequences. After all, Stott had only *watched* Pierce; he hadn't beat him up or assassinated him.

Despite the hours of work a murder inquiry consumed, routine work still went on at Eastvale Divisional HQ, and routine papers still found their way to Banks's desk. On that

Tuesday afternoon, when he was distracted by thoughts of
Ellen Gilchrist, Deborah Harrison, Barry Stott and Owen
Pierce, a proposal requiring every patrol car be fitted with a
dashboard computer passed over his desk for perusal after a
report on the increase of car theft in North Yorkshire.

Because Banks wasn't thinking about it, because the
words simply floated into that chaotic, intuitive and creative
part of his mind rather than engaging his sense of reason and
logic, he was struck with that rare feeling of epiphany as a
missing piece fell into place. It felt like the simultaneous
telescoping and expansion of a chain of unrelated words into
one inevitable conclusion: each element rolled firmly into
place like the balls with the winning lottery numbers: Car.
Computer. Theft. *Spinks.*

It wasn't really intuition, but a perfectly logical process,
taking a number of facts and relating them in a way that
made sense. It only felt like a sudden revelation.

On Friday, when Banks had questioned John Spinks about
Michael Clayton and Sylvie Harrison, it had been staring
him in the face. But he hadn't seen it. On Saturday, after his
talk with Clayton, he had felt close to something. But he
hadn't known what. Now he did. He still had some dates to
check, but as he pushed the proposal aside, he was certain
that John Spinks had stolen Michael Clayton's car and computer in August of last year. Whether that actually meant
anything remained to be seen.

Excited by the theory, Banks checked the dates and
dashed into Gristhorpe's office, where he found the superintendent immersed in the statement of Ellen Gilchrist's best
friend. Gristhorpe stretched and rubbed his bushy eyebrows
with his fingertips when Banks entered. After he'd done,
they looked like birds' nests.

"Alan. What can I do for you?"

Banks explained about his chain of reasoning. Gristhorpe
nodded here and there, and when Banks had finished, put his
forefinger to his lips and furrowed his brow.

"So Lady Sylvie Harrison and Michael Clayton found

Spinks and Deborah drinking wine in the back garden on August 17, right?" he said.

Banks nodded.

"And Clayton reported his car stolen on August 20. I remember it because when he came to inquire about our progress, he thought he was so important he had to see the top man on the totem pole. About a bloody stolen car. I ask you."

"I'm surprised he didn't go directly to Jimmy Riddle."

"Oh, he did. First off. But Riddle's in Northallerton and that was too far for Clayton to go every day. So Riddle told him to keep checking with me. I put Barry and Susan on it. Clayton was like a cat on a hot tin roof. Not over the car, though."

"The computer?"

"Got it in one."

"Yes. That's what Susan said," Banks mused. "When Clayton recognized her that time we went to talk to the Harrisons. I should have realized at the time."

Gristhorpe smiled indulgently. "I think you can be forgiven that, Alan," he said. "Wasn't it about the same time the lead on Pierce came up?"

"Yes. But—"

"Anyway, let's assume that Spinks stole Clayton's car on August 20," Gristhorpe went on. "He did some damage, but not much. It was the missing notebook computer that really had Clayton dancing on hot coals. We know it was a very expensive one, with all the bells and whistles, but Clayton's a rich man. He could afford a new one easily. It was what was *on* the computer that he was worried about. As I recollect, it turned up on the market a couple of weeks later, no worse for wear."

"From what I've seen," Banks went on, "Spinks would have about as much chance of operating Clayton's computer as an orangutan. But the point is that he was still seeing Deborah at that time. There's a chance she knew what he'd done. She wouldn't necessarily tell Clayton or her parents what happened, not when she was right in the middle of being rebellious, slumming it. And Deborah was bright, good at sciences. That computer would have probably been child's play to her."

"So what if she found out something from it?" Gristhorpe suggested. "Something important."

"Maybe it wasn't that Clayton was having an affair with Lady Harrison, after all," Banks said. "That's what I thought earlier. But maybe they were involved in some scam. Perhaps Clayton had been cheating Sir Geoffrey or something."

"You don't even need to go that far," Gristhorpe said. "Remember, HarClay Industries is big in the defense business. Big enough that Sir Geoffrey met in private with Oliver Jackson, of Special Branch, on the day his daughter was murdered."

"And you think there's a connection?"

"I'm saying there *could* be. Micro-electronics, computers, microchips, weapons circuits, that sort of thing. They're not only big money, but they have a strong political dimension, too. If Deborah came across something she shouldn't have seen. . . . If Clayton was working for someone he shouldn't have been . . . selling weapons systems to enemy governments, for example. . . ."

"Then either Clayton or his bosses could have had Deborah killed if she threatened to blow the whistle?"

"Yes."

"And whoever killed Ellen Gilchrist simply chose a random victim to implicate Pierce?"

Gristhorpe shrugged. "Nothing simpler. Not to people like that."

"But they didn't bargain on Barry Stott's ego."

" 'The best laid plans . . .' "

"Why wait so long?" Banks asked. "That's what I don't understand. Deborah cracked the computer around August 20—if indeed that's what happened—and she wasn't killed until November 6. That's nearly three months."

Gristhorpe scratched his stubbly chin. "You've got me

there," he said. "But there could be an explanation. Maybe it took her that long to fathom out what she'd got. Or maybe it took Clayton that long to figure out someone had been tampering. You know how quickly things change, Alan. Maybe the information she got didn't actually *mean* anything until three months later, when other things happened."

Banks nodded. "It's possible. But I'm not sure even Deborah was bright enough to understand Clayton's electronic schematics. I know I'm not. I saw some of them the other day and they left me dizzy."

"Well, you know what a Luddite I am when it comes to computers," Gristhorpe said. "But it could have been something obvious to her. She didn't have to understand it fully, just recognize a reference, a name or something. Perhaps someone else she knew was involved?"

"Okay," said Banks. "But we're letting our imaginations run away with us. Would Clayton even be likely to enter such important information in his notebook? Anyway, I've got a simple suggestion: why don't we bring Spinks in? See if we can't get the truth out of him?"

"Good idea," said Gristhorpe.

"And this time," Banks added, "I think we might even have something to bargain with."

II

Where was he? Swiss Cottage, that was it. London. The cash register rang and the swell of small-talk and laughter rolled up and down. He thought he could hear the distant rumble of thunder from outside, feel the tension before the storm, that electrical smell in the air, like burning dust in church.

After the police set him free he had gone back home, pushed through the throng of reporters, then got in his car and driven off, leaving everything behind. He hadn't known where he was heading, at least not consciously. Mostly, he was still in a daze over what had happened: not only his release, but the fact that someone must have deliberately set out to frame him.

And, as he told the police, the only person who hated him that much was Michelle.

They didn't seem to suspect her—they were sure it was a man, for a start—but Owen knew her better. He wouldn't put it past her. If she hadn't done it herself she might have enlisted someone, used her sex to manipulate some poor, sick bastard, the way she did so well.

So with these thoughts half-formed, one moment seeming utterly fantastic and absurd and the next feeling so real they had to be true, he had found himself heading for London, and now he was drinking in Swiss Cottage, trying to pluck up courage to go and challenge Michelle directly.

He was interested to find out what she would have to say if he turned up on her doorstep. Even if she hadn't engineered the murders to discredit him, she had slandered him in the newspapers. He knew that *for a fact*. Oh, yes. He was looking forward to hearing what she had to say for herself.

"Are you all right, mate?"

"Pardon?" It was the man next to him. He had turned his head in Owen's direction.

"I said are you all right?"

"Yes, yes . . . fine." Owen realized he must have been muttering to himself. The man gave him a suspicious look and turned away.

Time to go. It was nine o'clock. What day of the week? Tuesday? Wednesday? Did it really matter? There was a good chance she'd be in. People who work nine-to-five usually stay in on weeknights, or at least get home early.

He found the telephone and the well-thumbed directory hanging beside it. Some of the pages had been torn out or defaced with felt-tipped pens, but not the one that counted. He slid his finger down until he came to her name: Chappel. No first name, just the initials, M.E. Michelle Elizabeth. There was her number.

Owen's chest tightened as he searched his pockets for a

coin. He felt dizzy and had to lean against the wall a moment before dialing. Two men passed on their way out and gave him funny looks. When they had gone, he took four deep breaths to steady himself, picked up the phone, put the coin in and dialed. He let it ring once, twice, three times, four, and on the fifth ring a woman's voice said, rather testily, "Yes, who is it?"

It was *her* voice. No doubt about it. Owen would recognize that reedy quality with its little-girlish hint of a lisp anywhere.

He held the phone away and heard her repeat the question more loudly—"Look, who is it?"

After he still said nothing, she said, "Pervert," and hung up on him.

Owen looked at the receiver for a moment, then he smiled and walked out into the gathering storm.

III

John Spinks didn't seem particularly surprised to find himself back at Eastvale nick shortly after dark that evening. As predicted, he had been at the Swainsdale Center bragging to his mates about how he spent the weekend in jail and gone up before the magistrate. The arrival of two large uniformed officers only added more credibility to his tales, and he got quite a laugh, the officers told Banks, when he stuck out his hands for the cuffs, just like he'd seen people do on television.

He did look surprised, however, to find himself in Banks's office rather than a smelly interview room. And he looked even more surprised when Banks offered unlimited coffee, cigarettes and biscuits.

Gristhorpe and Banks had decided to tackle him together, to attempt a good-cop bad-cop approach. Spinks already knew Banks, but the superintendent was an unknown quantity, and though his baby blue eyes had instilled fear into more villains than a set of thumbscrews, Gristhorpe could appear the very model of benevolence. He also outranked Banks, which was another card to play. They had Stafford Oakes waiting in Gristhorpe's own office, should their plan be successful.

"Right, John," said Banks, "I won't beat about the bush. You're in trouble, a lot of trouble."

Spinks sniffed as if trouble were his business. "Yeah, right."

"Not only have we got you on taking and driving away," Banks went on, "but when our men searched your house, they found sufficient quantities of crack cocaine, Ecstasy and LSD for us to bring some serious drug-dealing charges against you."

"I told you, that stuff wasn't mine."

"Whose was it, then?"

"I don't know her name. Just some slag spent the night there. She must've forgotten it."

"You expect me to believe that someone would leave a fortune in drugs behind? In *your* bedroom? Come off it, John, that stuff's yours until someone else claims it, and it'll be a cold day in hell before that happens."

Spinks bit on his lower lip. He was starting to look less like a Hollywood dream-boy and more like a frightened teenager. A lock of hair slid over his eye; he started chewing his fingernails. Bravado could only take someone so far, Banks thought, but he knew it would be a mistake to act as if he were shooting fish in a barrel. Stupidity, along with stubbornness, can be valuable resources when all the big guns are turned on you. And they had served Spinks well for eighteen years.

"Got anything to say?" Banks asked.

Spinks shrugged. "I told you. It's not mine. You can't prove it is."

"We can prove whatever we want," Banks said. "A judge or a jury has only to take one look at you to throw away the key."

"My brief says—"

"These legal-aid briefs are about as useful as a sieve in a flood, John. You ought to know that. Overworked and underpaid."

"Yeah, well, my brief says you can't pin it on me. The drugs."

Banks raised his eyebrows. "She did? That's really bad news, John," he said, shaking his head. "I thought things were pretty bad, but I didn't realize that lawyers were setting up in practice before they even finished their degrees these days."

"Ha fucking ha."

The other chair creaked as Gristhorpe leaned forward. "My chief inspector might be acting a little harshly towards you, son," he said. "See, it's personal with him. He lost a son to drugs."

Spinks squinted at Banks. "Tracy never said nothing about that."

"She doesn't like to talk about it," said Banks quickly. They had decided to improvise according to responses and circumstances, but Gristhorpe had thrown him a spinner here. He smiled to himself. Why not? Play the game. As far as he knew, Brian was alive and well and still studying architecture in Portsmouth, but there was no reason for Spinks to know that.

"Like everyone his age," Banks went on, "he thought he was immortal, indestructible. He thought it couldn't happen to him. Anyone else, sure. But not him." He leaned forward and clasped his hands. "Now, I don't give a tinker's whether you smoke so much crack your brains blow out of your arsehole, but I *do* care very much that you're selling to others, especially to a crowd that at one time included my daughter. Do we understand one another?"

Spinks shifted in his chair. "What's this all about? What you after? A confession? I'm not saying anything. My brief—"

"Fuck your brief," said Banks, thumping the rickety metal
desk. "And fuck *you*! Do you understand what I'm saying?"

Spinks looked rattled. Gristhorpe cut in again and said to
Banks, "I don't think it's really appropriate to talk that way
to Mr. Spinks, Chief Inspector," he said. "I'm sure he understands you perfectly well."

"Sorry, sir," said Banks, wiping his brow with the back of
his hand. "Got a bit carried away." He fumbled for a cigarette and lit it.

"You his boss?" Spinks asked, turning, wide-eyed, to look
at Gristhorpe. "He called you 'sir.' "

"I thought I'd already made that clear," Gristhorpe said,
then he winked. "Don't worry, son. I won't let him off his
leash."

He looked back at Banks, who had removed his jacket and
was loosening his tie. "He ought to be locked up, that one,"
Spinks went on, emboldened. "And his mate. The fat one.
Hit me once, he did. Bounced my nose off a fucking table."

"Aye, well, people get carried away sometimes," said
Gristhorpe. "Stress of the job. The thing is, though, that he's
right in a way. You *are* in a lot of trouble. Right now, we're
about the only friends you've got."

"Friends?"

"Yes," said Banks, catching his attention again. "Believe
it or not, John, I'm going to do you the biggest favor anyone's ever done you in your life."

Spinks narrowed his eyes. "Oh yeah? Why should I believe you?"

"You should. In years to come you might even thank me
for it. You're eighteen now, John, there's no getting around
that. With the kind of charges you're looking at, you'll go to
jail, no doubt about it. Hard time. Now I know you're a big
boy, a tough guy and all the rest, but think about it. *Think*.
It's not only a matter of getting buggered morning, afternoon and evening, of giving blow-jobs at knife-point, maybe
catching AIDS, but it's a life of total deprivation, John. The

food's lousy, the plumbing stinks and there's no-one to complain to. And when you get out—if you get out—however many years later, you'll have lost a good part of your youth. All you'll know is prison life. And you know what, John? You'll be back in there like a flash. It's called *recidivism.* Look it up, John. Call it a sort of death wish, but someone like you gets institutionalized and he can't survive on the outside. He gets to need jail. And as for the blow-jobs and the buggery . . ." Banks shrugged. "Well, I'm sure you'd even get to like that after a while."

Banks's monologue produced no discernible effect on Spinks, as he had suspected it wouldn't. It was intended only to soften him to the point of accepting a deal. Banks knew that Spinks was already doomed to exactly the kind of existence he had just laid out for him, but that he couldn't, wouldn't, recognize the fact, and wasn't capable of making the changes necessary to avoid it.

No. What they were about to offer was simple, temporary relief, the chance for Spinks to walk free and keep on doing exactly what he was doing until the next time he got caught, if he didn't kill himself or someone else first. A sprat to catch a mackerel. Very sad, but very true.

"So what is this big favor you're going to do me?"

"First," said Banks, "you're going to tell us the truth about what happened last August. You're going to tell us how you stole Michael Clayton's car and his computer and *exactly* what happened after that."

Spinks paled a little but stood his ground. "Why would I want to do something like that?"

"To avoid jail."

"You mean confess to one crime and get off on another one?"

"Something like that."

"Christ, you're worse than the bloody criminals, you lot are." He turned to Gristhorpe. "Can he do that?" he asked. "Has he got the authority?"

"I have," said Gristhorpe softly. "I'm a superintendent, remember?"

"Don't we need a lawyer or something?"

"What's wrong, John?" said Banks. "Don't trust us?"

"I don't trust *you*. Anyway, why talk to the monkey when the organ-grinder's here?"

Banks smiled. It was working. And he hadn't denied stealing Clayton's car yet.

"There's a Crown attorney in the building," said Gristhorpe, "and he can deal with the particulars about the charges and likely sentences, if you want to talk to him."

Spinks squinted. "Maybe I'll do that. What's the deal?"

"You tell us what we want to know," said Gristhorpe, "and we'll see you stay out of jail. Dealing becomes simple possession."

"That's not enough. I want all charges dropped."

Gristhorpe shook his head. "Sorry, son. We can't do that. You see, the paperwork's already in the system."

"You can lose it."

"Maybe the odd sheet or two," said Gristhorpe. "But not all of it. The lawyer will explain it."

Spinks sat silently, brow furrowed in thought.

Banks stood up. "I've had enough of this," he said to Gristhorpe. "I told you it was no use. His brain's so addled he doesn't even recognize a piece of good fortune when he trips over it. Besides, it makes me puke sitting with a drug-dealing moron like him. Let him go to jail. He belongs there. Let him catch AIDS. See if I care." And he headed towards the door.

"Wait, just a minute," said Spinks, holding his hand up. "Hold your horses. I haven't said anything yet."

"That's the problem," said Gristhorpe. "You'd better make your mind up quickly, sonny. You don't get chances like this every day. We can probably get it down to probation, maybe a bit of community service, but you can't just walk away from it."

Spinks glared at Banks, who stood scowling with his hand on the doorknob, then looked back at Gristhorpe, all benevolence and forgiveness. Then he put his feet on Banks's desk. "All right," he said. "All right. You've got a deal. Get the brief in."

IV

Large raindrops blotched the pavement when Owen left the pub. Lightning flickered in the north and the thunder grumbled like God's empty stomach. The drinkers out on the muggy street hurried inside before the deluge arrived.

Owen felt light-headed after all the drinks, and he knew he wasn't thinking clearly. Booze had made him just brave and foolhardy enough to face Michelle.

He walked along the main road past pubs and shops open late, head bowed, jacket collar turned up in a futile attempt to keep dry. Shop-lights and street-lights smeared the pavement and gutter. Hair that had been damp with sweat before was now plastered to his skull by rain.

He had forgotten exactly where he parked his car, but it didn't matter. Michelle's place couldn't be far.

He stopped a young couple coming out of a pub and asked them where her street was. They gave him directions as they fiddled with their umbrella. As he suspected, it was only a couple of hundred yards up the road, then left, short right and left again. He thanked them and walked on, aware of them standing watching him from behind.

Now he knew he was going to see her, his mind shot off in all directions. She wouldn't want to let him in, of course, not after what she had tried to do to him, not after what she had said about him.

Did he feel reckless enough to break in? Maybe. He didn't know. Given the address, her flat would probably be in one of those three- or four-story London houses. Perhaps if he waited outside for her to go out, approached her in the street . . . She might have to go to the shop or go out to meet someone. But it was a bit late in the evening for that. Maybe if he waited until one of the other tenants went in, he could get to the door before it locked and at least gain entry to the building.

A white sports car honked as he crossed a sidestreet against a red light. He flicked the driver the V sign, then caught his foot on the curb and stumbled, bumping into an elderly man walking his dog in the rain. The man gave him a dirty look, adjusted his spectacles and walked on.

He turned left where the couple had told him to and found himself the only pedestrian in quiet backstreets. The houses were all about three stories high, divided into flats, with a buzzer and intercom by the front door. It wouldn't be easy.

Many rooms were lit, some without curtains, and as he walked he looked in the windows and saw fragments of blue wall, the top corner of a bookshelf, a framed Dali print, an ornate chandelier, flickering television pictures, two people talking, a cat sitting on the window-sill watching the rain— a panorama of life.

The walk had taken some of the steam out of Owen, but he still wanted to see Michelle face to face, if only to watch her squirm as he accused her of her crimes.

He climbed the steps and looked at the list by the door. M.E. Chappel, Flat 4. Would that be on the first or second floor? He didn't know. He crossed the street and looked up. Both second-floor windows were in darkness, as were those on the ground floor. On the first floor, bluish light filtered through the curtains of one, and the other was open to reveal a William Morris wallpaper design. That wasn't Michelle at all. The blue room was more like her.

He stood in the shadows wondering what to do. Rain drummed down, an oily sheen on the street. He didn't feel as brave now as he had on leaving the pub. The booze had worn off, and he had a headache. He needed another drink, but it was close to eleven; the pubs would be closing. Besides, Michelle would probably be going to bed soon. Now he was here, he couldn't wait until tomorrow.

A man and a woman huddled together under an umbrella approached the house, turned up the path and climbed the

steps. The way they walked, Owen guessed they were a little tipsy. Probably unemployed and didn't have to go to
work in the morning. He shrank back into the shadows. The
man said something, and the woman laughed. She shook out
her umbrella over the steps. It wasn't Michelle.

When she turned back to the door, Owen hurried across
the street behind them. It was a hell of a long shot, but it
might just work. They had their backs turned, the street
wasn't well lit, and they couldn't hear him because of the
rain and the rumbles of thunder. Adrenalin pumped him up
and seemed to rekindle some of the earlier bravado. He was
close now. It all depended on how slowly the door closed on
its spring behind them.

As soon as they were both inside and the man let go of the
door, Owen dashed on tiptoe up the steps and put his hand
out. He stopped the door just before it had completely
swung back and relatched.

He looked around at the houses across the street. As far as
he could make out, nobody was watching him. He heard another door open and close inside the building, and the lights
went on in one of the ground floor flats.

Softly, Owen pushed the front door open and slipped inside.

V

Stafford Oakes quickly assured Spinks that the charges
against him could be reduced to a manageable level—the
drugs, especially. Add that he had no prior record, that he
had been upset over a missed job opportunity and any number of other mitigating circumstances that affected his
stress-level when he stole and crashed the car, and he'd
probably get a few months community service. Lucky community.

"So," Banks asked him when Oakes had left. "Why don't

you tell us about it? Then we'll get the Crown to put the lesser charges in writing. More coffee? Cigarette?"

Spinks shrugged. "Why not."

Banks poured from the carafe he had had sent up. "Off the record," he asked, "did you steal Michael Clayton's car on August 20 last year?"

Spinks snapped the filter off the cigarette and lit it. "I don't remember the exact date, but it was around then. And I didn't *steal* it. Just borrowed it for a quick spin, that's all."

"Why?"

"What do you mean, why? Because he treated me like shit, that's why. Fucking snob. Like I wasn't good enough to wipe his precious goddaughter's nose with."

"This was just after he and Lady Harrison found you and Deborah drinking wine in the back garden?"

"Yeah. We weren't doing no harm. Just having a barbie and a drop or two of the old vino. He acted like it was too good for the likes of me. It was only a fucking bottle of wine, for Christ's sake. He'd no call to be so rude to me, calling me an idle lout and a thickie and all that. It's not my fault I can't get a job, is it?"

"And you did some damage to the car, for revenge?"

"No. It was an accident. I was still learning, wasn't I? That car's got a very sensitive accelerator."

From what Banks had heard of Spinks's driving history so far, it might be a good idea if the court could somehow prevent him from ever getting a license. Not that it seemed to have stopped him so far.

"Did you also take a notebook computer out of the car?"

"It was in the back seat under a coat."

"Did you take it?"

Spinks looked at Gristhorpe. "It's all right, sonny," the superintendent said, "you can answer any question Chief Inspector Banks asks you with complete impunity."

"Uh? Come again."

"No blame attached. It's all off the record. None of it is

being recorded or written down. Remember what the solicitor told you. Relax. Feel free."

Spinks drank some coffee. "Yes," he said. "I thought it might be worth something."

"And was it?"

He shrugged. "Piss all. Bloke on the market offered me seventy-five measly quid."

And the market vendor was reselling it for a hundred and fifty, Banks remembered. A hundred and fifty quid for a six-thousand-pound computer. "So you sold it to him?"

"That's right."

"Before you sold it, did you use it at all?"

"Me? No. Don't know how to work those things, do I?"

"What about Deborah?"

"What about her?"

"She was a bright girl. Studied computers at school. She'd know how to get it going."

"Yeah, well . . ."

"You *were* still seeing Deborah at that time, weren't you?"

"Yeah."

"And did she ever visit your house?"

"Yeah. Once or twice. Turned her nose up, though. Said it smelled and it was dirty." He laughed. "Wouldn't use the toilet, no matter how much she wanted to go."

"Right," said Banks. "Now what I'd like to know, John, is did Deborah have a go with the computer?"

"Yeah, well, she did, as a matter of fact." He turned to Gristhorpe, as if for confirmation that he could continue with impunity. Gristhorpe nodded like a priest. Spinks went on, "Yeah. Deb, she was with me, like, when I . . . you know . . . went for a ride."

"Deborah was with you when you stole Michael Clayton's car?"

"Yeah, that's what I said. Only don't use that word 'stole.' I don't like it. See, it was even more in the family with her being there wasn't it? Just like borrowing the family car, really."

"Did you ever tell him it was the two of you who'd 'borrowed' his car?"

"Course not. You think I'm stupid or something?"

"Go on."

"Anyway, she didn't like the idea at first. No bottle, hadn't Deb. But soon as I got us inside, quiet as could be, like, and got that Swedish engine purring, she took to it like a duck to water, didn't she? It was Deb noticed the computer. Said she was surprised Clayton let it out of his sight given as how he was the kind of bloke couldn't even jot down a dental appointment without putting it on his computer. I said let's just leave it. But she said no, she wanted to have a go on it."

"So what did you do?"

"After we'd finished with the car we went back to my house. My mum was out, as usual, and I was feeling a bit randy by then, after a nice fast drive. I fancied a bit of the other, but she went all funny, like she did sometimes, and after a while I didn't even want it any more. She had a way like that, you know. She could be really off-putting, really cold."

"The computer, John?"

"Yeah, well once Deb got it going I couldn't drag her away from it."

"What about the password?"

"Whatever it was, if there was one, it didn't take her very long. I will say this, though, she seemed a bit surprised at how easy it was."

"The password?"

"Whatever it took to get the bloody thing going."

"What did she say?"

" 'Well, bugger me!' Not exactly those words, mind you, but that was the feeling. She didn't like to swear didn't Deb. More like gosh or golly or something."

"And then?"

Spinks shrugged. "Then she just played around with it for a while. I got bored and went upstairs for a lie-down."

"Was she still playing with it when you went back down?"

"Just finishing. It looked like she was taking something out of it. One of those little square things, what do you call them?"

"A diskette?"

"That's right."

"Where did she get it from?"

"I don't know. The computer was in a carrying case and there were a whole bunch of them there, in little pockets, like. I suppose that's where she got it from."

"What did she do with it?"

"Put it in her pocket."

"Any idea what was on it?"

"No. I asked her what she was up to but she told me to mind my own business."

"Did she do anything else with computer?"

"Yeah. She tapped a few keys, watched the screen for a while, smiled to herself, funny like, then turned it off."

"And then?"

"She told me I could sell it if I wanted and keep the money." He looked towards Gristhorpe. "I mean, she practically gave it to me, right? And it was in the family. Well, he was her godfather, anyway. That has to count, doesn't it."

"It's all right," Gristhorpe assured him. "You're doing fine. Just keep on answering the questions as fully and as honestly as you can."

Spinks nodded.

"Did she tell you at any time what she'd found on the computer?"

"No. I mean, I didn't pester her about it. I could tell she didn't want to say anything. If you ask me she found out he'd been fiddling the books or something."

"What makes you say that?"

"Stands to reason, doesn't it?"

"Did she ever refer to the incident again?"

"No. Well, it wasn't much more than a week or so later when her mother caught us in bed. Then it was cards for me. On your bike, mate."

"Do you know if Michael Clayton ever found out that you took it, or that Deborah used it?"

"I certainly didn't tell him. Maybe Deb did, but neither of them ever said anything to me about it."

"And you got your seventy-five quid?"

"Right."

"Is there anything else?"

"No, that's everything. I've told you everything." He looked at Gristhorpe. "Can I go now?"

"Alan?"

Banks nodded.

"Aye, lad," said Gristhorpe. "Off you go."

"You won't forget our deal, will you?"

Gristhorpe shook his head. Spinks cast a triumphant grin at Banks and left.

"Christ," said Banks. "I need a drink to get the taste of shit out of my mouth after that."

Gristhorpe laughed. "Worth it, though, wasn't it. Come on, I'll buy. We've got a bit of thinking to do before we decide on our next move."

But they hadn't got further than the Starrs when Banks heard his telephone ring. He looked at his watch. Almost ten-thirty.

"I'd better take it," he said. "Why don't you go ahead. I'll meet you over there."

"I'll wait," said Gristhorpe. "It might be important." They went into the office and Banks picked up the phone.

"Chief Inspector Banks?"

"Yes."

"It's Vjeko. Vjeko Batorac." The voice sounded a little muffled and hoarse.

"Vjeko. What is it? Is something wrong?"

"I thought I should tell you that Ive Jelačić was just here. We fought. He hit me."

"What happened, Vjeko? Start from the beginning."

Vjeko took a deep breath. "Ive came here about a half an hour ago and he was a carrying a book of some kind. A notebook, I thought. It was a diary, bound in good leather, written in English. He said he thought it would make him rich. He couldn't read English so he brought it to me to tell him what it said. He said he would give me money." Vjeko paused. "That girl, the one who was killed, her name was Deborah Harrison, wasn't it?"

"Yes." Banks felt his grip tighten on the receiver. "Go on, Vjeko."

"It was *her* diary. I asked him where he got it, but he wouldn't tell me. He wanted me to translate for him."

"Did you?"

"I looked at it. Then I told him it was nothing important, not worth anything, and he should leave it with me. I'd throw it away."

"What happened then?"

"He became suspicious. He thought I'd found out something and wanted to cheat him out of his money. I think he was hoping to find someone he could blackmail. He said he'd take it to Mile. Mile can read some English, too. I said it was worthless and there was no point. He tried to snatch it from my hand. I held on and we struggled. He is stronger than me, Chief Inspector. He hit me. Dragica was screaming and little Jelena started crying. It was terrible."

"What happened?"

"Ive ran away with the diary."

"You said you read it?"

"Some of it."

"What did it say?"

"If I am right, Chief Inspector, that girl was in terrible trouble. I think you should send someone to get it right away before Ive does something crazy with it."

"Thanks, Vjeko," Banks said, already reaching out to cut the call off. "Stay where you are. I'm calling West Yorkshire CID right now. Jelačić was heading for Mile Pavelič's house, you said?"

VI

Owen walked up the carpeted stairs in the dark to the first-floor landing. There, he found a timer-switch on the wall and turned the light on. He knocked on the door of Flat 4, noticing it didn't have a peep-hole, and held his breath. The odds were that, if she had friends in the building, especially friends who were in the habit of dropping by to borrow a carton of milk or to have a chat, she would open it. After all, nobody had buzzed her, and not just anyone could walk in from the street.

He heard the floor creak behind the door and saw the knob begin to turn. What if it was on a chain? What if she were living with someone? His heart beat fast. Slowly the door opened.

"Yes?" Michelle said.

No chain.

Owen pushed. Michelle fell back into the room and the door swung fully open. He shut it behind him and leaned back on it. Michelle had stumbled into her sofa. She was wearing a dark-blue robe, silky in texture, and it had come open at the front. Quickly, she wrapped it around herself and looked at him.

"You. What the hell do you want?" There was more anger than fear in her voice.

"That's a good question, that is, after what you've done to me."

"You've been drinking. You're drunk."

"So what?"

"I'm going to call the police."

Michelle lunged for the telephone but Owen got there first and knocked it off its stand. This wasn't going the way he had hoped. He had just wanted to talk, find out why she had it in for him, but she was making it difficult.

They faced each other like hunter and prey for a few seconds, completely still, breathing hard, muscles tense, then she ran for the door. Owen got there first and pushed her away. This time she tipped backwards over the arm of the sofa. Owen walked towards her. Her robe had risen up high over her thighs and split open at her loins to show the triangle of curly golden hair. Owen stopped in his tracks. Michelle gave him a cool, scornful look, covered herself up and sat down.

"Well, then," she said, pushing her hair back behind her ears. "So you're here. I must admit I'm a bit surprised, but maybe I shouldn't be." She reached for a cigarette and lit it with a heavy table-lighter, blowing the smoke out through her nose. He remembered the mingled taste of tobacco and toothpaste on her mouth in bed after lovemaking. "Why don't you sit down?" she said.

"Aren't you frightened?"

Michelle laughed and put her little pink tongue between her teeth. "Should I be?"

Her blue eyes looked cool, in control. Her long, smooth neck rose out of the gown, elegant and graceful. Even at twenty-four she still looked like a teenager. It was partly the flawless, marble complexion, the delicately chiseled nose and lips whose fine lines any sculptor would be proud of.

But it was mostly in her character, Owen realized, not her looks. She *was* the cruel teenager who called others names, the leader of the gang who suggested new cruelties, new kicks, with not a care in the world for the feelings of the ones she bullied and taunted.

"If you really believe I murdered those women, then you should be scared," he said. "They looked like you, you know."

"You were killing me by proxy. Is that what you're saying?"

"Can you give me one good reason why I shouldn't? You're not afraid because you know I didn't do it. Am I right?"

"Well," Michelle said, "I really found it hard to believe you had the guts, I'll admit. But then I was mistaken enough to think it takes guts to strangle a woman."

"And you found out different?"

She frowned. "What do you mean?"

"You did it, didn't you, Michelle? I'm not sure about the first one, about Deborah Harrison, but you did the second, didn't you? You killed her to frame me. Or you got someone to do it."

Michelle laughed and glanced towards the door again. "You're mad," she said. "Paranoid. If you think I'd do something like that, go to all that trouble, you're insane." She stood up and walked over to the cocktail cabinet. Her legs swished against the robe. Owen stayed close to her. "I'd offer you a drink," she said, "but I think you've had too much already."

"Why did you do it, Michelle? For God's sake why?"

She raised her eyebrows. "Why did I do what?"

"You know what I mean. Kill that girl to implicate me. You broke into my house, stole the film container with my fingerprints on it and took hairs from my pillow. Then you messed the place up to make it look like a hate-crime."

Michelle shook her head "You're crazy." She poured neat Scotch into a crystal glass. Owen could see her hand was shaking.

"And what you said to the police about us," he pressed on. "That stuff in the newspapers. Why did you tell those lies about me?"

"They paid well." She laughed. "Not the police, the newspapers. And I didn't kill anyone. Don't be an idiot, Owen. I couldn't do anything like that. Besides, I didn't tell any lies."

"You *know* it didn't happen like that."

"It's all versions, Owen. That's how it happened from my perspective. I'm willing to admit yours might be different. I'm sorry. I know I shouldn't sound so ungrateful. You did help me through college. You helped me financially, you gave me somewhere to live, and you certainly helped with my marks. It was fun for a while. . . . But you'd no right to start spying on me, following me everywhere I went. You didn't own me. And you had no right to throw me out in the

street like that. Nobody ever treats me like that." Her eyes
blazed like ice.

"Fun . . . for a while? Michelle, I was in love with you.
We were going to . . . I can't believe you'd say that, make it
all sound so meaningless. Why do you hate me so much?"

She shrugged. "I don't hate you. I just don't give a damn
about you one way or another."

"You bitch."

Owen stepped towards her. She stood her ground by the
cabinet and sipped her drink. Then she jerked her head back
to toss her hair over her shoulders again. It was a gesture he
remembered. She looked at him down her nose, lips curled
in a sneer of contempt.

"Oh, come on, Owen," she said, twisting the belt of her
robe around one finger. "You can do better than that. Or
can't you? Do you have to murder schoolgirls these days to
get your rocks off?" The smile tormented him: a little
crooked, icy in the eyes and wholly malevolent. "I'm glad
you've found something that turns you on at last. What are
you going to do, Owen? Kill me, too? Do you know what?
I don't think you can do it. That's why you have to do it to
the schoolgirls and pretend it's me. Isn't that true, Owen?"

Owen snatched the tumbler from her hand and tossed it
back in one.

"More Dutch courage? Is that what you need? I still don't
believe—"

He didn't know how it happened. One moment he was
looking at his own reflection in her pupils, and the next he
had his hands around her throat. He shoved her back against
the cabinet, knocking bottles and glasses over. She clawed at
his eyes, but her arms weren't long enough. She scratched
and pulled at his wrists, making gurgling sounds deep in her
throat, back bent over the cabinet, feet off the ground, kicking him.

He was throttling her for everything she'd ever done to
him: for being a faithless whore and spreading her legs for
anyone who took her out for an expensive dinner; for telling

the whole country he was a sick pervert who would be in jail if there were any real sting in the justice system; for framing him.

And he was strangling her for everything else, too: his arrest; the humiliation and indignity of jail; the loss of his friends, his job. The whole edifice that had been his life exploded in a red cloud and his veins swelled with rage. For all that, and for treating him like a fool, like someone she could keep on a string and order around. Someone she didn't even believe had the courage to kill her.

He pressed his fingers deep into her throat. One of her wild kicks found his groin. He flinched in pain but held on, shoving her hard up against the wall. She was sitting on the top of the cabinet among the broken crystal and spilled liquor, her legs wrapped around him in a parody of the sex act. He could smell gin and whisky. The robe under her thighs was sodden with blood and booze, as if she had wet herself.

Michelle continued to flail around, knocking over more bottles, making rasping sounds. Once she pushed forward far enough that her nails raked his cheek, just missing his eyes.

But just as suddenly as it had started, it was over. Owen loosened his grip on her throat and she slid off the cabinet onto the floor, leaning back against it, not moving.

Someone hammered on the door and yelled, "Michelle! Are you all right?"

Owen stood for a moment trying to catch his breath and grasp the enormity of what he had done, then he opened the door and rushed past the puzzled neighbor back down to the street.

VII

"I think Deborah Harrison lied to her mother about losing her diary," Banks said to Gristhorpe as they waited for Ken

Blackstone's call. It was well after closing-time. No hope of a pint now. "I think she kept it hidden."

"So it would seem," Gristhorpe agreed. "The question is, how did it get into Jelačić's hands? We already know he couldn't have been in Eastvale the evening she was killed. Even if the diary had been in her satchel, Jelačić couldn't have taken it."

"I think I know the answer to that," Banks said. "Rebecca Charters surprised someone in the graveyard yesterday, in the wooded area behind the Inchcliffe Mausoleum. I thought nothing of it at the time—she didn't get a good look at whoever it was—but now it seems too much of a coincidence. I'll bet you a pound to a penny it was Jelačić."

"It was hidden there?"

Banks nodded. "And he knew where. He'd seen her hide it. When Pierce was released, and I went to question Jelačić again last week, he must have remembered it and thought there might be some profit in getting hold of it. It's ironic, really. That open satchel always bothered me. When I first saw it, I thought the killer might have taken something incriminating and most likely got rid of it. But Lady Harrison told me Deborah had lost her diary. I saw no reason why either of them would lie about that."

"Unless there were secrets in it that Deborah didn't want anyone to stumble across?"

"Or Lady Harrison. If you think about it, either of them could have lied. Sir Geoffrey had already told me that Deborah *did have* a diary, so his wife could hardly deny its existence."

"But she *could* say Deborah had told her she lost it, and we'd have no way of checking."

"Yes. And we probably wouldn't even bother looking for it. Which we didn't."

"Didn't the SOCOs search the graveyard the day after Deborah's murder?"

"They did a ground search. We weren't looking for a murder weapon, just Deborah's knickers and anything the killer might have dropped in the graveyard. All we found were a few empty fag packets and some butts. Most of those were down to Jelačić, who we knew had worked in the graveyard anyway. We put the rest down to St. Mary's girls sneaking out for a smoke. Besides, it's only in books that murderers stand around smoking in the fog while they wait for their victims. Especially since now everyone knows we've a good chance of getting DNA from saliva."

"What about the Inchcliffe Mausoleum? Deborah could have gained access to that, couldn't she?"

"Yes. But we searched that, too, after we found the empty bottles. At least—"

The phone rang. Banks grabbed the receiver.

"Alan, it's Ken Blackstone. Sorry it took so long."

"Any luck?"

"We've got him."

"Great. Did he give you any trouble?"

"He picked up a bruise or two in the struggle. Turns out he'd just left Pavelić's house when our lads arrived. They followed him across the waste ground. He saw them coming and made a bolt for it, right across York Road and down into Richmond Hill. When they finally caught up with him he didn't have the diary."

Banks's spirits dropped. "Didn't have it? But, Ken—"

"Hold your horses, mate. Seems he dumped it when he realized he was being chased. Didn't want to be caught with any incriminating evidence on him. Anyway, our lads went back over the route he'd taken and we found it in a rubbish bin on York Road."

Banks breathed a sigh of relief.

"What do you want us to do with him?" Blackstone asked. "It's midnight now. It'll be going on for two in the morning by the time we get him to Eastvale."

"You can sit on him overnight," Banks said. "Nobody in this case is going anywhere in a hurry. Have him brought up in the morning. But, Ken—"

"Yes, it is Deborah Harrison's diary."

"Have you read it?"
"Enough."
"And?"
"If it means what I think it does, Alan, it's dynamite."
"Tell me about it."
And Blackstone told him.

Chapter 20

I

At ten o'clock the next morning, with Jelačić cooling his heels in a cell downstairs, Banks sat at his desk, coffee in hand, lit a cigarette and opened Deborah Harrison's diary. Ken Blackstone had given him the gist of it over the phone the previous evening—and he had not slept well in consequence—but he wanted to read it for himself before making his next move.

Like the inside of the satchel flap, it was inscribed with her name and address in gradually broadening circles, from "Deborah Catherine Harrison" to "The Universe."

First he checked the section for names, addresses and telephone numbers, but found nothing out of the ordinary, only family and school friends. Then he started to flip the pages.

He soon found that many of her entries were factual, with little attempt at analysis or poetic description. Some days she had left completely blank. And it wasn't until summer, when she had supposedly "lost" it, that the diary got really interesting:

August 5

Yawn. This must be the most boring summer there has ever been in my entire existence. Went shopping today in the Swainsdale Center, just for something to do. What a grim place. Absolutely no decent shoes there at all and full of local yokels and horrible scruffy women dragging around even more horrible dirty children. I must work hard on mummy and persuade her to take me shopping to Paris again soon or I swear I shall just die from the boredom of this terrible provincial town. In the shopping center, I met that common little tart Tiffy Huxtable from dressage. She was with some friends and asked if I'd like to hang around with them. They didn't look very interesting. They were all just sitting around the fountain looking scruffy and stupid, but there was one fit lad there so I said I might drop by one day. Life is so (yawn) boring that I really might do. Oh, how I do so need an adventure.

There were no entries for the next few days, then came this:

August 9
Tiffy's crowd are a bunch of silly, common bores, just as I thought. All they can talk about is television and football and sex and pop music. I mean, really, darling, who gives a damn? I'm sure not one of them has read a book in years. Quite frankly, I'd rather stay at home and watch videos. Tracy Banks seems quite intelligent, but it turns out that she's a policeman's daughter, of all things. One boy looks a bit like that really cool actor from "Neighbors" and wears a great leather jacket. He really does have very nice eyes, too, with long lashes.

After that, things started to move quickly:

August 12
John (Oh, such disappointment! What a terribly common, dull and ordinary name, like "Tracy"!) stole a

car *tonight and took me for a joy-ride.* Me!! *Little miss goody-two-shoes. It was brill! If Daddy knew about it he would have apoplexy. It wasn't much of a car, just a poky little Astra, but he drove it really fast out past Helmthorpe and parked in a field. It was so exciting even though I was a bit frightened we'd get caught by the police. When we parked he was like an octopus! I told him I'm not the kind of girl who does it the first time you go out, even if he did steal a car for me. Lads! I ask you. He asked me what he could do the first time, and I told him we could just kiss. I really didn't mind when he put his tongue in my mouth but I wouldn't let him touch my breasts. I didn't tell him I had never done it before. Though I came close with Pierre at Montclair last year, and if he hadn't been too much in a hurry and had that little accident first we might have done it.*

Then, three days later, she wrote:

August 15
Tonight, in another "borrowed" car, as John calls them, we actually did it for the first time! I made him take a van this time, because it's cramped in a little Astra, and we went in the back. I wasn't going to go all the way at first but things just got out of control. It didn't hurt, like they say it does. I don't know if I like it or not. I did feel excited and sinful and wicked but I don't think I had an orgasm. I don't really know, because I don't know what they feel like, but the earth didn't move or anything like that, and I didn't hear bells ringing, just a funny feeling between my legs and I felt a bit sore after. I wonder if I will ever have multiple orgasms? Charlene Gregory at school told me she can have orgasms just from the vibrations of the engine when she's on a bus, but I don't believe her. And Kirsty McCracken says she can get them from

rubbing against her bicycle saddle while she's riding. Maybe that's true. I sometimes feel a bit funny when I'm horse-riding. Anyway, when he finished, it was really disgusting the way he just tied a knot in the condom and threw it out of the window into the field, and then he didn't even seem to want to talk to me all the way back. Is this what happens when you give in to lads and let them have what they want? That's what Mummy would say, even though she is French and they're supposed to be so sexy and all.

August 17
John came to the house today. Mummy was out and he wanted us to go and do it upstairs but I was too frightened we'd get caught. Anyway, we barbecued some hot dogs on the back patio and I took a bottle of Father's special wine from the cellar and we drank that. Of course, Mother came home! She was very nice about it, really, but I could tell she didn't like John. Uncle Michael was there, too, and I could tell he really hated John on sight. John says nobody ever gives him a chance.

August 20
They all went to Leeds today—Mummy and Daddy and Uncle Michael—to some naff cocktail party or other, so I told John he could come over to the house again. This time I knew they'd be gone a long time so we did it in my bed! How sinful! How wickedly, deliciously sinful! I don't know if I had an orgasm or not, but I certainly tingled a bit, and I didn't feel at all sore. John wants me to do it without a condom, but I told him not to be stupid. I wouldn't even think of it. I don't want to get pregnant with his baby or get some sexual disease. That hurt him, that I thought he would have some disease to pass on to me. He can be so childish at times. Childish and boring.

But it wasn't until a later entry that Banks found out for himself what Ken Blackstone meant when he said the diary might be "dynamite."

August 21

I can hardly believe it, Uncle Michael is in love with me! He says he has loved me since I was twelve, and has even spied on me getting undressed at Montclair. He says I look like Botticelli's Venus! Which is stretching it a bit, if you ask me. I remember seeing it in the Uffizi when Mummy and I went to Florence last year, and I don't look a bit like her. My hair's not as long, for a start, and it's a different color. I never thought Uncle Michael knew literature and art at all. Some of what he wrote sounds very poetic. And it's all about me!! I don't know what I shall do. For the moment, it will be my little secret. He's not really my uncle of course, just my dad's friend, so I suppose it is all right for him to be in love with me, it's not incest. It feels funny, though, because I've known him forever. Oops, I forgot to say how I know. Last night John and me stole Uncle Michael's car because he was so beastly to him last week at the barbecue (now I know why: Uncle Michael must have been jealous!!). Well, Uncle Michael had left his computer in the back seat. We took it to John's house (and thank the lord his horrible smelly mother was out—she really gives me the creeps)—and I couldn't get into all his technical stuff but it only took me about fifteen minutes to get the password to his word-processing directories: it's MONTCLAIR, of course. After that, it was easy. Uncle Michael puts everything on his computer, even his shopping-lists! When I'd finished, I reformatted his hard drive. That'll show him!

Banks put the diary aside and walked to the window. Mid-morning on a hot and humid June day, cobbled market square already full of cars and coaches. He wondered if this summer was going to be as hot as the last one. He hoped not. Naturally, there was no air-conditioning in Eastvale Divisional HQ, or in the whole of Eastvale, as far as he knew. You just had to make do with open windows and fans—not a lot of use when there's no breeze and the air is hot.

The diary wasn't evidence, of course. Deborah Harrison had read some of Michael Clayton's private files and discovered that he was sexually infatuated with her; it didn't mean that he had killed her. But as Banks sat down again and read on, it became increasingly clear that Clayton, in all likelihood, *had* killed Deborah.

The telephone rang. Banks picked it up and Sergeant Rowe told him there was a Detective Sergeant Leaside calling from Swiss Cottage.

Banks frowned; he didn't recognize the name. "Better put him on."

Leaside came on. "It's about a woman called Michelle Chappel," he said. "I understand from the PNC that she was part of a case you've been involved in recently up there?"

Banks gripped the receiver tightly. "Yes. Why? What's happened?"

"She's been assaulted, sir. Quite badly. Lacerations and bruises, attempted strangulation."

"Rape?"

"No, sir. I was wondering . . . We got a description of the suspect from a neighbor . . ." He read the description.

"Yes," Banks said when he'd finished. "Dammit, yes. That sounds like Owen Pierce. All right, thanks Sergeant. We'll keep an eye open for him."

II

Ive Jelačić was surly after his night in the cells. Banks had him brought up to an interview room and left him alone there for almost an hour before he and Superintendent

Gristhorpe went in to ask their questions. They didn't turn the tape recorder on.

"Well, Ive," said Banks, "you're in a lot of trouble now, you know that?"

"What trouble? I do nothing."

"Where did you get that diary?"

"What diary? I never see that before. You policeman put it on me."

Banks sighed and rubbed his forehead. He could see it was going to be one of those days. "Ive," he said patiently, "both Mile Pavelič and Vjeko Batorac have seen you with the diary. You asked them to read it for you. You even hit Vjeko when he tried to hang onto it."

"I remember nothing of this. I do nothing wrong. Vjeko and I, we quarrel. Is not big deal."

"Come on, lad," said Gristhorpe, "help us out here."

"I know nothing."

Gristhorpe gestured for Banks to follow him out of the room. He did so, and they stood silently in the corridor for a few minutes before going back inside. It seemed to work; Jelačić was certainly more nervous than he had been before.

"Where you go?" he asked. "What you do?"

"Listen to me, Ive," said Banks. "I'm only going to say this once, and I'll say it slowly so that you understand every word. If it hadn't been for you, an innocent man might not have spent over six months in jail, suffered the indignity of a trial and incurred the wrath of the populace. In other words, you put Owen Pierce through hell, and even though he's free now, a lot of people still think he really killed the girls."

Jelačić shrugged. "Maybe he did. Maybe court was wrong."

"But more important even than Owen Pierce's suffering is Ellen Gilchrist's life. If it hadn't been for you, Ive Jelačić, that girl might not have had to die."

"I tell you before. In my country, many people die. Nobody ca—"

Banks slammed his fist on the flimsy table. "Shut up! I

don't want to hear any more of your whining self-justification and self-pity, you snivelling little turd. Do you understand me?"

Jelačić's eyes were wide open now. He nodded and glanced over at Gristhorpe for reassurance he wasn't going to be left alone with this madman. Gristhorpe remained expressionless.

"Because of you, an innocent girl was brutally murdered. Now, I might not be able to charge you with murder, as I would like to do, but I'll certainly get something on you that'll put you away for a long, long time. Understand me?"

"I want lawyer."

"Shut up. You'll get a lawyer when we're good and ready to let you. For the moment, listen. Now, I don't think we'll have much trouble getting Daniel and Rebecca Charters to testify that you tried to extort money from them in order to alter the story you told against Daniel Charters. That's extortion, for a start. And we'll also get you for tampering with evidence, wasting police time and charges too numerous to mention. And do you know what will happen, Ive? We'll get you sent back to Croatia is what."

"No! You cannot do that. I am British citizen."

Banks looked at Gristhorpe and the two of them laughed. "Well, maybe that's true," Banks said. "But you do know who Deborah Harrison's father is, don't you? He's *Sir* Geoffrey Harrison. A very powerful and influential man when it comes to government affairs. Even you must know something of the way this country's run, Ive. What would you say for your chances now?"

Jelačić turned pale and started chewing his thumbnail.

"Are you going to co-operate?"

"I know nothing."

Banks leaned forward and rested his elbows on the table. "Ive. I'll say this once more and then it's bye-bye. If you don't tell us what you know and where you found the diary, then I'll personally see to it that you're parachuted right into the middle of the war zone. Clear?"

Jelačić sulked for a moment, then nodded.

"Good. I'm glad we understand one another. And just because you've behaved like a total pillock, there's one more condition."

Jelačić's eyes narrowed.

"You drop all charges against Daniel Charters and make a public apology."

Jelačić bristled at this, but after huffing and puffing for a minute or two, agreed that he had, in fact, misinterpreted the minister's gesture.

Banks stood up and took Jelačić's arm. "Right, let's go."

They drove him to St. Mary's, and he led them along the tarmac path, onto the gravel one and into the thick woods behind the Inchcliffe Mausoleum. A good way in, he paused in front of a tree and said, "Here."

Banks looked at the tree but could see nothing out of the ordinary, no obvious hiding-place. Then Jelačić reached his hand up and seemed to insert it right into the solid wood itself. It was then that Banks noticed something very odd about the yew trees. Not very tall, but often quite wide in circumference, they were hard, strong and enduring. Some of the older ones must have been thirty feet around and had so many clustered columns they looked like a fluted pillar. The one they stood before had probably been around since the seventeenth century. The columns were actually shoots pushing out from the lower part of the bole, growing upwards and appearing to coalesce with the older wood, making the tree look as if it had several trunks all grafted together. It also, he realized, provided innumerable nooks and crannies to hide things. What Deborah had sought out for a hiding-place, and Jelačić had seen her use, was a knothole in this old yew, angled in such a way that it was invisible when you looked at it straight on.

Banks moved Jelačić aside and reached his hand inside the tree. All he felt was a bed of leaves and strips of bark that had blown in over the years. But then, when he started to dig down and sweep some of this detritus aside, he was sure his fingers brushed something smooth and hard. Quickly, he reached deeper, estimating that Deborah could have easily done the same with her long arms. At last, he grasped the package and drew it out. Gristhorpe and Jelačić stood beside him, watching.

"Looks like you missed the jackpot, Ive," Banks said.

It was a small square object wrapped in black bin-liner, folded over several times for good insulation. When Banks unfolded it, he brought out what he had hoped for: a computer diskette.

III

Back at the station, Banks handed the floppy disk to Susan Gay and asked her if she could get a printout of its contents. He hoped it had survived winter in the knot-hole of the yew. It should have done; it had been wrapped in plastic and buried under old leaves, wood chips and scraps of bark, which would have helped preserve it, and the winter hadn't been very cold.

Ten minutes later, Susan knocked sharply on Banks's office door and marched in brandishing a sheaf of paper. Her hand was shaking, and she looked pale. "I think you'd better have a look at this, sir."

"Let's swap." Banks pushed the diary towards her and picked up the printout.

De-bo-rah. De-bo-rah. *How the syllables of your name trip off my tongue like poetry. When was it I first knew that I loved you? I ask myself, can I pinpoint the exact moment in time and space where that magical transformation took place and I no longer looked at a mere young girl but a shining girl-child upon whose every movement I fed hungrily. When, when did it happen?*

Oh, Deborah, my sweet torturer, why did I ever, ever have to see you pass that moment from childhood to the flush of womanhood? Had you remained a mere child I could never have loved you this way. I could never have entertained such thoughts about your straight and hairless child's body as I do about your woman's body.

I seek you out; yet I fly from you. On the surface, all appears normal, but if people could see and hear inside me the moment you come into a room or sit beside me, they would see my heart pulling at the reins and hear my blood roaring through my veins. That day you won the dressage and walked towards me in your riding-gear, that moist film of sweat glistening on the exquisite curve of your upper lip . . . and you kissed me on the cheek and put your arm around me . . . I felt your small breast press softly against my side and it was all I could do to remain standing let alone furnish the required and conventional praise . . . well done . . . well done . . . wonderful . . . well done, my love, my Deborah.

The first time I saw you naked as a woman you were standing in the old bath-tub at Montclair looking like Botticelli's Birth of Venus. *Remember, my love, there were no locks on the doors at Montclair. One simply knew when private rooms were engaged and refrained from entering. Mistakes were made, of course, but honest mistakes. Besides, it was family. They aren't prudes about such things, the French, Sylvie's people. I hoped only for a brief glimpse of your nakedness as you bathed. I knew I couldn't linger, that I must apologize and dash out as if I had a made a mistake before you even realized I had seen you. So fast, so fleeting a glimpse. And even now I wonder what would have happened had I not witnessed you in your full glory.*

For you were standing up, reaching for the towel, and your loveliness was on display just for me. Steam hung

*in the air and the sunlight that slanted through the
high window cast rainbows all about you. Droplets of
moisture had beaded on your flushed skin; your wet
hair clung to your neck and shoulders, long strands
pasted over the swellings of your new breasts, where
the nipples, pink as opening rosebuds stood erect.
Even that early in womanhood your waist curved in
and swelled out at the narrow hips. Between your legs
a tiny triangle of hair like spun gold lay on the mound
of Venus; the paradise I dream of; drops of water had
caught among the fine, curled hairs, forming tiny
prisms in the sunlight; some just seemed to glitter in
clear light like diamonds. . . .*

*I have other images locked away inside me: the thin
black bra strap against your bare shoulder, the insides
of your thighs when you cross your legs . . .*

And so it went on. Again, it wasn't solid evidence, but it was
all they had. Banks had no choice but to act on it.

IV

Owen gazed out of the train window into the darkness. Rain
streaked the dirty glass and all he could see was reflections
of the lights behind him in the carriage. He wished he could
get another drink, but he was on the local train now, not the
InterCity, and there was no bar service.

As the train rattled through a closed village station on the
last leg of his journey, Owen thought again of how he had
walked the London streets all night in the rain after killing
Michelle, half-hoping the police would pick him up and get
it over with, half-afraid of going back to prison, this time
forever.

He had covered the whole urban landscape, or so it
seemed; the west end, where the bright neons were reflected

in the puddles and the nightclubs were open, occasional drunks and prostitutes shouting or laughing out loud; rain-swept wastelands of demolished houses, where he had to pick his way carefully over the piles of bricks with weeds growing between them; clusters of tower blocks surrounded by burned-out cars, playgrounds with broken swings; and broad tree-lined streets, large houses set well back from the road. He had walked through areas he wouldn't have gone near if he had cared what happened to him, and if he hadn't been mugged or beaten up it wasn't for lack of carelessness.

But nothing had happened. He had seen plenty of dangerous-looking people, some hiding furtively in shop doorways or hanging around in groups smoking crack in the shadows of tower-block stairwells, but no-one had approached him. Police cars had passed him as he walked along Finchley Road or Whitechapel High Street, but none had stopped to ask him who he was. If he hadn't known different, he would have said he was leading a charmed life.

At one point, close to morning, he had stood on a bridge watching the rain pit the river's surface and felt the life of the city around him, restful perhaps, but never quite sleeping, that hum of energy always there, always running through it like the river did. He didn't think it was Westminster Bridge, but still Wordsworth's lines sprung into his mind, words he had read and memorized in prison:

This City now doth, like a garment, wear
The beauty of the morning; silent, bare,
Ships, towers, domes, theaters, and temples lie
Open unto the fields, and to the sky;
All bright and glittering in the smokeless air.

Well, perhaps the air wasn't exactly "smokeless," Owen thought, but one has to make allowances for time.

Owen felt tired and empty. So tired and so empty.

Eastvale Station was in the north-eastern part of the town, on Kendal Road a couple of miles east of North Market

Street. It was only a short taxi-ride to the town center. But Owen didn't want to go to the center, or, tired as he was, home.

He was surprised the police weren't waiting for him at the station, as they probably would be at his house. He didn't want to walk right into their arms, and however empty he felt, however *final* every second of continued freedom seemed, he still didn't want to give it up just yet. Perhaps, he thought, he was like the cancer patient who knows there's no hope but clings onto life through all the pain, hoping for a miracle, hoping that the disease will just go away, that it was all a bad dream. Besides, he wanted another drink.

Whatever his reasons, he found himself walking along Kendal Road. The day had been so hot and humid that the cooler evening air brought a mist that hung in the air like fog. At the bridge, he looked along the tree-lined banks towards town and saw the high three-quarter moon and the floodlit castle on its hill reflected in the water, all blurry in the haze of the summer mist.

Walking on, he came to the crossroads and saw the Nag's Head. Well, he thought, with a smile, it would do as well as anywhere. He had come full circle.

V

By the time Banks and Gristhorpe got Chief Constable Riddle's permission to bring Michael Clayton in for questioning, which wasn't easy, it was already dark. One of the conditions was that Riddle himself be present at the interview.

Banks was pleased to see that Clayton, as expected, was at least mildly intimidated by the sparse and dreary interview room, with its faded institutional-green walls, flyblown window, table and chairs bolted to the floor, and that mingled smell of urine and old cigarette smoke.

Clayton made the expected fuss about being dragged

away from his home, like a common criminal, to the police station, but his confidence had lost a bit of its edge. He was wearing sharp-creased gray trousers and a white short-sleeved shirt; his glasses hung on a chain around his neck.

"Are you charging me with something?" Clayton asked, folding his arms and crossing his legs.

"No," said Gristhorpe. "At least not yet. Chief Inspector Banks has a few questions he wants to ask you, that's all."

Jimmy Riddle sat behind Clayton in the far corner by the window, so the suspect couldn't constantly look to him for comfort and reassurance. Riddle seemed folded in on himself, legs and arms tightly crossed. He had promised not to interfere, but Banks didn't believe it for a moment.

"About what?" Clayton asked.

"About the murder of your goddaughter, Deborah Harrison."

"I thought you'd finished with all that?"

"Not quite."

He looked at his watch. "Well, you'd better tell him to get on with it, then. I've got important work to do."

Banks turned on the tape recorders, made a note of the time and who was present, then gave Clayton the new caution, the same one he had given Owen Pierce eight months ago. Formalities done, he shuffled some papers on the desk in front of him and asked, "Remember when we talked before, Mr. Clayton, and I asked you if you had been having an affair with Sylvie Harrison?"

Clayton looked from Gristhorpe to Banks. "Yes," he said to the latter. "I told you it was absurd then, and it's still absurd now."

"I know."

Clayton swallowed. "What?"

"I said I know it's absurd."

He shook his head. "So you're not still trying to accuse me of that? Then why . . . ?"

"And remember I suggested that Deborah might have gained access to some sensitive business material, or some government secret?"

"Yes. Again, ridiculous."

"You're absolutely right. You weren't having an affair with Sylvie Harrison," Banks said slowly, "and Deborah didn't gain access to any important government secrets. We know that now. I got it all wrong. You were in love with your goddaughter, with Deborah. That's why you killed her."

Clayton paled. "This . . . this is ludicrous." He twisted around in his chair to look at Riddle. "Look, Jerry, I don't know what they're talking about. You're their superior. Can't you do something?"

Riddle, who had read both the diary and the computer journal, shook his head slowly. "Best answer the questions truthfully, Michael. That's best for all of us."

While Clayton was staring open-mouthed at Riddle's betrayal, Superintendent Gristhorpe dropped the printed computer journal on the table in front of him. Clayton first glanced at it, then put his glasses on, picked it up and read a few paragraphs. Then he pushed it aside. "What on earth is that?" he asked Banks.

"The product of a sick mind, I'd say," Banks answered.

"I hope you're not suggesting it has anything to do with me."

Banks leaned forward suddenly, snatched back the pages and slapped them down on the table. "Oh, stop mucking us about. It came from *your* computer. The one John Spinks stole that day he took your car. He's already told us all about that, about how he saw Deborah make a copy of the files onto a diskette. You didn't know about that, did you?"

"I . . . where . . . ?"

"She kept it well hidden. Look, you know it's your journal. Don't deny it."

Even in his shock, Clayton managed a thin smile and rallied his defenses. "Deny it? I most certainly do. And I'm afraid you'll have a hard job proving a wild accusation like that. Your suggestions are outrageous." He glanced back at Riddle. "And Jerry knows it, too. There's absolutely nothing to link that printout with me. It could have been written by anyone."

"I don't think so," said Banks. "Oh, I know that Deborah reformatted your hard drive well beyond anything an 'unerase' or 'undelete' command could bring back to life, but you must admit the contents of the journal, the circumstances, all point to you. Very damning."

"Fiction," said Clayton. "Pure fiction and fantasy. Just some poor lovestruck fool making things up. There's nothing illegal in that. There's no law against fantasies; at least not yet."

"Maybe not," said Banks. "We never checked Deborah's clothing for *your* hairs, you know."

"So?"

"You might not have left any blood or tissue, but I'm willing to bet that if we went over the hair samples again now, we'd find a positive match. That wouldn't be fantasy, would it?"

Clayton shrugged. "So what? It wouldn't surprise me. Deborah was my goddaughter, after all. We spent a lot of time together—as a family. Besides, I was in court for the so-called expert's testimony. Hairs hardly prove a thing scientifically."

"What about Ellen Gilchrist?"

"Never heard of—wait a minute, isn't that the other girl who was killed?"

"Yes. What if we found *your* hairs on her clothing, too, and hers on yours? Was she family, a friend?"

Clayton licked his lips. "I never saw her in my life. Look, I don't know what grounds you've got for assuming this, but—"

Banks dropped a photocopy of Deborah's diary in front of him. "Read this," he said.

Clayton read.

His hands were shaking when he put the diary down. "Fantasy," he said, straining to keep his voice steady. "That's not very much to go on, is it? It could be anyone."

"Come on, Michael," said Banks. "It's all over. Admit it. You know what happened. You've just read her account.

Deborah read your journal and found out you'd been secretly lusting after her since she was twelve. She was both shocked and excited by the idea. But only by the idea. She was flattered, but still too much of a kid to know how serious it all was to you. And she had a bit of a crush on you anyway. So she teased you, made up a bit of romance, flirted a little, the way young girls sometimes do to tease boys they know fancy them. Didn't she, Michael?"

"This is absurd. You're not only insulting me you're also besmirching my goddaughter's memory." He looked around at Riddle again. "Sir Geoff—"

But Banks cut him off. "Besmirching? That's a good word, Michael. I like that. *Besmirching.* Sounds naughty. Very public school. So let's talk about *besmirching.* Eventually, when it became clear you wouldn't leave her alone, Deborah threatened to tell her father. You knew that if Sir Geoffrey found out he would probably kill you. At the very least it would mean the end of your business relationship. That meant a lot to you, didn't it, Michael? The two old Oxford boys, still together after all these years. Sir Geoffrey's friendship meant a lot to you, too, but it didn't stop you lusting after his twelve-year-old daughter, a girl who wasn't even born when the two of you first met."

Clayton glared, the color drained from his face. "You'll regret this," he said, glancing at both Gristhorpe and Riddle. "All of you will, if you don't stop this right now." Banks could almost hear Clayton's teeth grinding together. Gristhorpe said nothing. Riddle polished his buttons with a virgin white handkerchief.

"You waited for Deborah in St. Mary's graveyard," Banks continued calmly. "In the shrubbery that foggy Monday evening when you knew she would be walking home alone from the chess club. You were going to grab her and drag her into the bushes, but when you saw her take the gravel path, you followed her towards the Inchcliffe Mausoleum, where you snatched her satchel and strangled her with the strap. Maybe she knew it was you, and maybe she didn't. Maybe you talked first, tried to persuade her not to say anything, or maybe you didn't. But that's what happened, isn't it, Michael?"

"I'm saying nothing."

"You didn't know she was going to pick up the diary she'd been keeping and hiding ever since summer, did you? Oh, Michael, but if you'd only been patient, given her a few more seconds, she would have led you straight to it and you probably wouldn't be here now. Isn't that how it happened?"

"I won't even dignify your accusation with a response."

"When she told you she'd read your computer journal, Deborah didn't tell you that she'd copied the file about her onto a diskette, did she? But you knew she had a diary at one time. You bought it for her. That's another irony, isn't it, Michael? You knew she'd told Sylvie she lost it, but I wouldn't be at all surprised if you had a good look around her room after you killed her. After all, you had your own key to Sir Geoffrey's house, and he and Lady Harrison were out. Even if they came back and found you there, it wouldn't have surprised them. And you opened Deborah's school satchel, too, didn't you, to see if she kept anything incriminating in there. Just in case. The only place you couldn't really get access to was her school desk, but you reasoned she'd be unlikely to keep anything important or private there."

Clayton put his hands over his ears. "This is ridiculous," he said. "I don't have to listen to this. You'll never be able to prove anything. I want—"

"Now, I'm only guessing," Banks went on, "so stop me if I'm wrong, but I also think, as you murdered Deborah, that you found out you liked it. It stimulated you. Maybe you even had an orgasm as you tightened the strap around her neck. I know you were far too clever to actually rape her because you know about DNA and all that, don't you? But you did mess around with her clothing after you killed her— partly for pure pleasure, I'd guess, and partly to make it look like a genuine sex murder.

"It was the same with Ellen Gilchrist, wasn't it? You'd been over and over it in your mind all week, planning how you'd kill again, anticipating the intimacy of it all, and when you did it, when you felt the strap tightening, pulling her back against you, feeling her soft flesh rubbing against you, that excited you, didn't it?"

"Really, Banks," Chief Constable Riddle cut in from behind. "Don't you think this is getting a little out of hand?"

Clayton turned and looked at Riddle, a cruel smile on his thin lips. "Well, thank you, Jerry, for all your support. You're absolutely right. He's talking rubbish, of course. I'd never even met the girl."

"That doesn't matter," Banks went on, mentally kicking Riddle and trying to ignore his interruption. "Unlike Deborah, Ellen Gilchrist was a random victim. Wrong place, wrong time. You got lucky when Owen Pierce was arrested for the murder of Deborah Harrison, didn't you? You thought he would get convicted, sentenced and that would be an end to it. But when the trial was nearing its close, you started to worry that he might get off. The defense was good, the prosecution had only circumstantial evidence, and you'd heard rumors about evidence that would have convicted Pierce for certain had it been admissible. But you saw it all slipping away, and the focus perhaps shifting back towards you. So you went to Owen Pierce's house while the jury was deliberating, and you either found the door open from a previous break-in, or you broke in yourself and made it look like vandals. It doesn't really matter which. You took some hairs from Owen's pillow, and you stole an open film container which you guessed would have his fingerprints on it. You set out to deliberately frame Owen Pierce for the murder of Ellen Gilchrist, knowing we'd also put Deborah's murder down to him, too, and close the file on both of them. But, you know what? I think you also *enjoyed* it. Just the way you did with Deborah. And I think there would have been more if we hadn't caught you, wouldn't there? You've developed a taste for it."

"This is insane," Clayton said. "And you can't prove a thing."

"Oh, I think we can," Banks went on. "Look what we proved against Owen Pierce, and he didn't even do anything."

Clayton smiled. "Ah, but he got off, didn't he?"

Banks paused. "Yes. Yes, he did. But maybe you should talk to him about that. I'm sure he'd be very interested to meet you. Getting off isn't all it's cracked up to be in some cases. See, maybe you're right, Michael. Maybe we won't be able to convince a jury that a fine, upstanding citizen like yourself murdered two young girls. Perhaps even with the evidence of the journal and the diary and the hairs, if we find they match, we won't be able to prove it to them. But you know who *will* believe us, don't you, Michael? You know who knows quite well who 'Uncle Michael' is, who knows what Montclair is and that there are no locks on the bathroom doors there. You know exactly who *will* know who is the writer and who's the subject. Sir Geoffrey will know. And you'll have gained nothing. In some ways, I think I'd rather take my chances with a jury, or even go to jail, than incur the wrath of Sir Geoffrey over such a matter as the murder of his only daughter by the man he's trusted for more than twenty years, don't you?"

Clayton said nothing for a moment, then he croaked, "I want my solicitor. Now. Get my solicitor, right now. I'm not saying another word."

Bloody hell, thought Banks, here we go again. He called in the constable from outside the interview room. "Take him down to the custody suite, will you, Wigmore. And make sure you let him call his lawyer."

VI

Owen sat in the Nag's Head nursing his second pint and Scotch chaser, trying to pluck up the courage to go over the road and see Rebecca and Daniel. The problem was, he felt ashamed to face them. They had believed in his innocence, and he had let them down badly. He knew that if there were to be any sort of salvation or reclamation in this business at all, he would have to tell them the whole truth, including what he had done to Michelle. And he didn't know if he could do that right now. He could hardly even admit to himself that he had become exactly what everyone thought he was: a murderer.

He looked around at the uninspiring decor of the pub and wondered what the hell he was doing here again. It had seemed a nice irony when he saw the sign over the bridge— full circle—but now it didn't seem like such a good idea.

The Nag's Head was boisterous, with the landlord entertaining a group of cronies with dirty jokes around the bar and tables full of couples laughing and groups of underage kids who'd had a bit too much.

He didn't know what he was going to do after he finished his drinks: either go home and meet the police, or have another and go face Rebecca and Daniel. More drink wouldn't help with that, though, he realized. He would feel less like facing them if he were drunk. Best drink up and turn himself in, then, return to the custody suite, where he should feel quite at home by now.

"What did you say?"

Owen looked up at the sound of the voice. There was a lull in the conversation and laughter. The landlord was collecting empty glasses. He stood over Owen's table. "Sorry mate," he said. "I thought I heard you say something."

Owen shook his head. He realized he must have been muttering to himself. He turned away from the landlord's scrutiny. He could still feel the man looking at him, though, recognition struggling to come to the surface. He had a couple of days' growth, a few more pounds around the waist from lack of exercise and a prison pallor, but other than that he didn't look too different from the person who had sat alone in that same pub one foggy night last November.

Best finish his drinks and leave, he decided, tossing back the Scotch in one and washing it down with beer.

Then, all of a sudden, the landlord said, "Bloody hell, it *is* him! I don't bloody believe it. The nerve."

The men at the bar turned as one to look at Owen.

"It's him," the landlord repeated. "The one who was in here that night. The one who murdered those two young lasses."

Owen wiped his mouth with the back of his hand and stood up, edging towards the door.

"Nay, they let him off," someone said.

"Aye, but just because they hadn't got enough evidence," another said. "Don't you read t'papers?"

"It was a bloody cover-up."

"Bleeding shame, more like. Poor wee lasses."

"A travesty of justice."

By the time Owen actually got to the door, a journey that felt like a hundred miles, bar-stools were scraping against the stone floor and he was aware of a crowd surging towards him.

No time to sneak out surreptitiously now. He dashed through the door and ran across Kendal Road. Luckily, the traffic lights were in his favor. When he got to the other side of the road, he saw about five or six people standing outside the pub doors. For a moment, he thought they were going to give chase, but someone shouted something he didn't hear and they went back inside.

Owen still ran as if he were being chased. There was only one place he could go now. He dashed across North Market Street towards St. Mary's church. When he was through the gate, running down the tarmac path, he could see, even in the mist, that the kitchen light was on in the vicarage.

VII

Alone in his office at last, Banks went to close the blinds and looked out for a moment on the quiet cobbled market square and the welcoming lights of the Queen's Arms. Maybe he'd have a quick one there before going home. Still time. Finally, he closed the blinds, turned on the shaded table-lamp and lit a cigarette. Then he sifted through his tapes and decided on Britten's third string quartet.

For a long time he just sat there smoking, staring at the wall and letting Britten's meditative quartet wash over him. He thought about the Clayton interview, and especially about the new coldness in Chief Constable Riddle's manner towards his old lodge pal. Maybe Riddle wasn't so bad, after all; at least he had an open enough mind to change his opinions when the facts started to weigh heavily against them.

Then, when his cigarette was finished, Banks turned to Deborah's diary again, striving once more to understand what had happened between her and Clayton over the two months leading up to her death.

August 24

Disaster has struck! Mummy caught John and me in bed this afternoon. She was supposed to be at one of her charity meetings but she wasn't feeling well and came home early. It was a terrible scene with Mummy and John shouting at one another and I didn't like to see John at all behaving like that. I thought he was going to hit Mummy in the end but he broke a vase on the wall and a piece of pottery cut Mummy's face. Then when he'd gone Mummy said I absolutely must not see him again or she would tell Daddy. Then she cried and put her arms around me and I felt sorry for her. John said such terrible things, called her such horrible names and said he would do things to her I won't repeat even here in my private diary. I don't care if I never see him again. I hate him. He's gross. He even stole things from our house. He's just a common thief. A thief and a thickie. What could I ever have seen in him?

August 27
Michael came to the house today while Mummy and Daddy were out. He was absolutely livid about the other day with John. I didn't know Mummy had told him. He called me names and I thought at one point he was going to hit me. It was then I told him. I couldn't help it. I told him I'd read his journal about me and called him a dirty old man. He went so white I thought he was going to faint. Then he asked me what I was going to do. I said I didn't know. I'd just have to wait and see. Wait for what? he asked me. To see what happens, says I.

August 28
Michael really is rather handsome. And much more intelligent and sophisticated than John. Mary Taylor at school told me last term she had an affair with a married man, a friend of her father's, who was 38 years old! And she says he was wonderful and considerate at sex and bought her presents and all sorts of things. I think Uncle Michael might be even older than 38 but he's not fat and ugly or anything like most old people.

September 1
Michael came for dinner tonight. Mummy and Daddy were there, of course. I wore a tight black jumper and a short skirt. Out of the corner of my eye I could see him looking at my thighs and breasts when he thought I wasn't watching. It really is amazing how he can seem so normal and ordinary when we're all together, but when there's just him and me he's so passionate and can hardly control himself!

September 3
Michael came again today when everyone was out. He told me he felt such powerful desire for me he didn't

know if he could control himself. That was the word he used: desire. I don't think that anyone has ever desired me before. It feels rather exciting. Of course, he wanted to do it, and when I said no he got all upset and said if I let a no-good lout like John Spinks do it to me why wouldn't I let him? I must admit I don't know the answer to that. Except that he's Uncle Michael and I've known him all my life.

September 6

This is getting to be quite an adventure! Saw Michael again today and let him kiss me again. It made him happy for a while, then he said he wanted to kiss my breasts. I wouldn't let him do that but I let him touch them over my jumper. While he was doing it he took my hand and held it to the front of his trousers so I could feel he was really hard. I started to feel a bit scared because his grip was so strong and then I felt him go all wet and he gasped as if somebody had hit him just the way John used to do. Gross. I can't explain why I felt it then, but I started to panic a bit because I'd just been teasing really and this was UNCLE MICHAEL, and even if he isn't really my uncle I've still known him since I was a little girl. I just couldn't let him do it to me. It wouldn't be right. After he'd finished he went all quiet so I left.

September 8

School again. Sad, sad, sad. Saw Mucky Metcalfe in the corridor. Wonder if he knows I know he's been doing it with the vicar's wife?

There were no more entries until October, and Banks assumed that Deborah had been getting settled in at St. Mary's again in the interim. But even by late October, Michael Clayton still hadn't got the message.

October 24
Can't Uncle Michael understand that whatever it was
we had is over now? I've told him I don't love him, but
it doesn't do any good. He keeps coming to the house
when he knows I'm here alone. Now he says he just
wants to see me naked, that he won't even touch me if
I just take my clothes off in front of him and stand
there the way I did in the bath at Montclair. I suppose
it's flattering in a way to have a sophisticated older
man in love with you, but to be honest he doesn't seem
very sophisticated when he keeps wanting me to touch
that hard thing in his pants. I don't want to play any
more. I suppose he must still be living in hope, but
doesn't he understand that summer's over and I'm
back at school now?

Obviously he didn't, thought Banks. It hadn't been just a
summer romance for Michael Clayton; it had been a dark,
powerful obsession. And beneath all the veneer of sophisti-
cation and experience, Deborah had simply been a naïve
teenager misreading the depth of an older man's passion;
she was just a girl who thought she was a woman.

But even as Deborah grew worried by Clayton's persis-
tence, she always kept her secret, always lived in hope that
he would simply give up and stop pestering her. She clearly
knew what dreadful consequences would occur if she told
her parents, and she wanted to avoid that if she could. But
Clayton wouldn't give up and go away. He couldn't; he was
too far gone. Her final entry, dated the day before she died,
read,

November 5 (Bonfire Night)
Yesterday Uncle Michael grabbed me and held my
arm until it hurt and told me I had stolen his soul and
all sorts of other rubbish. I know it was cruel of me to
tease him, and to let him kiss me and stuff, but it was

just a game at first and he wouldn't let me stop it. I want him to stop it now because I'm getting frightened, the way he looks at me. You still wouldn't believe it if you saw him with other people around, but he really does change when he's only with me. It's like he has a split personality or something. I told him if he doesn't promise to leave me alone I'll tell Daddy when I get home from school tomorrow. I don't know if I will I don't really want to tell Daddy because I know what he gets like and what trouble it will cause. The house won't be worth living in. Anyway, we'll see what happens tomorrow.

Banks pushed the diary aside and lit another cigarette. The gaslights around the market square glowed through the gaps in the blinds. The quartet was reaching the end of its final movement now, the moving, introspective passacaglia, written when Britten was approaching death.

Why do we feel compelled to record our thoughts and feelings in diaries and on tape, Banks wondered, and our acts on video and in photographs? Perhaps, he thought, we need to read about ourselves or watch ourselves to know we are truly alive. Time after time, it leads to nothing but trouble, but still the politicians keep their diaries, ticking away like time bombs, and the sexual deviants keep their visual records. And thank the Lord they do. Without such evidence, many a case might not even get to court.

When the music finished, Banks sat in silence for a while, then stubbed out his cigarette. Just as he was about to get up and go for that pint before last orders, the telephone rang. He cursed and contemplated leaving it, but his policeman's sense of duty and his even deeper-rooted curiosity wouldn't let him.

"Banks here."

"Sergeant Rowe, sir. We've just had a report that Owen Pierce is at St. Mary's vicarage."

"Who called it in?"

"Rebecca Charters, sir. The vicar's wife. She says Pierce is ready to turn himself in for the murder of Michelle Chappel."

"But she's not dead."

"I suppose he doesn't know that."

"All right," said Banks. "I'll be right there."

He sighed, picked up his sports jacket and hurried out into the hazy darkness.

Acknowledgments

I would first of all like to thank several people for reading and commenting upon the manuscript through its several drafts: my agent, Dominick Abel; Cynthia Good, from Penguin Books Canada; Natalee Rosenstein, from Berkley; and my copy editor, Mary Adachi.

I would also like to acknowledge expert help from a variety of sources. Thanks, as ever, to Detective Sergeant Keith Wright, of Nottingham CID, who answered my frequently silly questions with his characteristic patience and humor. Thanks also to Pamela Newall, from the Centre for Forensic Sciences, for saving me from sounding like a complete idiot on DNA, to Paul Bennett for reading and commenting on the trial scenes, to John Halladay for further information on legal procedure and to Dr. Marta Townsend for the displacement.

In addition, I would like to offer special thanks to Elly Pacey and Nancy Galić for the Croatian insults and to Emily Langran for the Yorkshire schoolgirl slang. And, last but not least, I must thank John Irvine for keeping my computer going through thick and thin, and for the occasional wicked line.

As usual, any mistakes are entirely my own and are made in the interests of the story.

"The Alan Banks mystery-suspense novels are, simply put, the best series now on the market. Try one and tell me I'm wrong." —Stephen King

PETER ROBINSON

PLAYING WITH

0-06-019877-X • $23.95

On Sale: 1/20/04

wm WILLIAM MORROW
An Imprint of HarperCollins*Publishers*
www.harpercollins.com

CONTENTS

Chapter 1:

IRA Basics

1. Plan now and retire twice as rich

Studies show that people who become educated about their finances and play a role in planning and monitoring their IRAs wind up twice as rich as those who haven't a clue. Consider these three facts from a Dartmouth/Wharton study:

- **Wisdom pays**—Retirement planning is a strong predictor of retirement wealth. If you learn how money grows and how much you will need at retirement, you are much more likely to achieve your stated goals.

- **Money grows**—Those who plan are more likely to end up at retirement with twice the wealth of those who do not plan.

- **Start early**—Those who are financially literate when young are more likely to plan for retirement.

2. Avoid past years' mistakes

The Great Recession was painful for most IRA investors. But these valuable lessons were learned:

- **Get IRA advice.** If you are unsure what to do, consider hiring a financial advisor who understands IRA portfolio allocation, tax issues, diversification, distribution planning, hedging and emotional handholding.

- **Keep some cash.** Setting cash aside in your IRA will buffer your portfolio against downturns and let you invest when share prices are low.

- **Know your mix.** Proper allocation among stocks and bonds—and diversification among different stock and bond classes—is essential.

- **Stocks aren't certain.** Stocks are volatile, and stock-price growth comes after long periods of time. Even after 15 years, stock values can suddenly decline or remain flat for a period. Ease volatility by investing in a strategic mix of assets—such as stocks, bonds, annuities, cash, real estate and other investments.

- **Bonds have risks.** Many investors shooting for income continue to invest in individual bonds. But as we know now, any company—including "safe" ones—can go belly-up. That's why bond investments need to be highly diversified among many different types of fixed-income securities, through bond funds or individual bonds.

- **Market cycles end.** Both rising and declining markets have to be planned for and taken advantage of. The market has always gone in cycles. While a severe market downturn can cause financial anxiety, it will eventually end. But it can also be capitalized on with buying opportunities.

3. What are the IRA rules for 2019?

Contribution Levels

- **Up through age 49—**$6,000 for 2019 or your taxable compensation for the year, whichever is lower.
  (Visit **irahelp.com/2019** for all 2019 IRA and tax tables.)

- **Age 50 onward—**$7,000 for 2019 or your taxable compensation for the year, whichever is lower.
  (Visit **irahelp.com/2019** for all 2019 IRA and tax tables.)

Conversion Eligibility

- **Everyone qualifies** to convert a Traditional IRA or SEP IRA to a Roth IRA. After a two-year waiting period, SIMPLE IRAs can also be converted. Income restrictions on a conversion were repealed starting in 2010.

4. Do these myths sound familiar?

Many people who don't save enough in a 401(k) and IRA typically have five reasons why not. But those feel-good excuses are flawed. Here's why:

- **Myth: Taxes will be lower.** Many people believe that when they retire, their tax rates will be lower because they won't be earning as much income. But there's nothing stopping the government from raising them in future years. So withdrawals from a Traditional IRA years from now could actually face higher income taxes—even if you're not working.

- **Myth: You'll work longer.** When portfolios were down, many people shrugged and said they'll just have to work longer. Sounds good, but here's a stark fact: As you age, the odds are you physically won't be able to work as hard as you want—or as long as you once did.

- **Myth: Pensions will kick in.** As we know now, even companies that may once have been healthy sometimes end up filing for bankruptcy. Or restructure. Or face such hardships that they roll back benefits they once promised. This can include government and public pensions that were once thought to be secure.

- **Myth: Social Security starts at 62.** That's true—now. But there's nothing to say that the federal government won't raise the minimum age at which benefits start—or reduce benefits for those at specific income levels.

- **Myth: Inheritances will arrive.** Don't count on it. Many seniors are living longer today thanks to dietary changes and moderate exercise. Even when aging adults grow ill, medical care is so good that infirmities can be controlled and minimized for years. Lucky you—mom and dad will live forever!

5. Why bother saving in an IRA?

If you're contributing to a 401(k) at work, you may be wondering why you need an Individual Retirement Account (IRA). Or you may feel you can't afford to save the max in both. But opening and saving even a little in an IRA is important. Here's why:

- **Tax-free growth.** Assets in an IRA grow tax-free—meaning there are no taxes on capital gains when you sell assets within the account. Taxes are paid upon distribution.

- **Tax deduction.** You can always deduct your full Traditional IRA contribution if your modified adjusted gross income in 2019 is less than $103,000 (married filing jointly) or $64,000 (single) (visit **irahelp.com/2019** for all 2019 IRA and tax tables).

- **Investment freedom.** Unlike a 401(k), which typically offers a small menu of mutual funds, an IRA lets you invest in any securities you wish. In addition, you can use an IRA to diversify your total retirement portfolio by investing in assets not offered by your 401(k).

- **Long-range planning.** When you eventually leave your job, you will almost certainly wind up transferring the balance of your 401(k) into an IRA for greater investment choices, control and efficiency. You may as well open one now, even if you don't contribute the max each year.

6. What is a Traditional IRA?

The Individual Retirement Account (IRA) was created in 1974 with the enactment of the Employee Retirement Income Security Act (ERISA). The original version is commonly called a "Traditional IRA," which distinguishes it from other types of IRAs that have been introduced over the years. What you need to know about a Traditional IRA:

- **Contributions.** Each year you may contribute up to an amount set by the tax law—provided you earned at least that sum in salary or self-employment income (i.e. compensation). The max you can contribute is based on whether you are age 49 or younger—or age

50 or older. Contributions cannot be made once you reach the year you turn age 70 ½. (Visit **irahelp.com/2019** for current levels.)

- **Deadline.** Annual contributions can be made until April 15 of the following year.

- **Deduction.** If you are covered by a company plan, you can deduct your annual contribution if you meet the latest income levels (visit **irahelp.com/2019** for the current levels).

- **Gains.** Gains on assets in an IRA are not taxed until they are withdrawn, giving assets an enormous opportunity to compound and grow over time.

- **Withdrawals.** The Traditional IRA was created to encourage retirement savings. So withdrawals before age 59 ½ face both income tax and a stiff 10% penalty. You can withdraw penalty-free starting at age 59 ½—but withdrawals aren't mandatory. Starting at age 70 ½, you are required to take annual distributions based on the IRS' life-expectancy table.

- **Taxes.** Withdrawals face income taxes at your tax rate at the time.

- **Heirs.** The person or persons you want to receive your assets upon death should be named in your IRA beneficiary document. IRA assets shouldn't be passed through your will.

7. What is a Roth IRA?

The Roth IRA was named for William Roth, a U.S. senator from Delaware who sponsored the Taxpayer Relief Act of 1997. Here's what you need to know:

- **Qualifications.** Only taxpayers under specific income levels can open and contribute annually to a Roth IRA (visit **irahelp.com/2019** for the latest qualifying levels).

- **Contributions.** Each year you may contribute up to an amount set by the tax law, provided you earned at least that sum in salary or self-employment income. The max you can contribute is based on whether you are age 49 or younger—or age 50 or older (visit **irahelp.com/2019** for the latest levels). Annual contributions can be made at any age.

- **Deadline.** Annual contributions can be made up until April 15 of the following year.

- **Deduction.** There is no tax deduction for contributions to a Roth IRA.

- **Gains.** Gains on assets in a Roth IRA are generally not taxed, giving them an enormous opportunity to grow and compound over time.

- **Withdrawals.** Assets in a Roth IRA may be withdrawn after age 59 ½ tax-free if any Roth was opened more than five years earlier. That means every dollar growing in a Roth IRA can be yours to keep. In addition, there is no mandatory withdrawal age, meaning assets can continue to grow tax-free.

- **Penalty.** Gains withdrawn before age 59 ½ will face a 10% penalty plus taxation, as will certain pre-59 ½ distributions of converted funds.

- **Heirs.** The person or persons you want to receive your assets upon death should be named in your Roth IRA's beneficiary document. Roth IRA assets shouldn't be passed through your will.

- **Inheritance.** Upon death, a Roth IRA can pass estate-tax free to a spouse. Or it can pass to one or more non-spousal beneficiaries, though part of the assets may be needed to pay estate taxes. Non-spouse heirs must take distributions based on their life expectancies set by the IRS. But the required annual distributions are generally income-tax free. The catch is that a Roth IRA had to have been set up by the original Roth IRA owner more than five years before the distribution.

8. What is a SEP IRA?

A Simplified Employee Pension Individual Retirement Account (SEP IRA) is an IRA for the self-employed or small-business owner. The rules for a SEP IRA are the same as for a Traditional IRA (*see tip #6*)—with the following exceptions:

- **To qualify.** You must be a self-employed individual or small-business owner (with or without employees) whose venture generates income. You can open a SEP IRA even if you work for an employer and participate in another retirement plan—provided your side business generates income and complies with certain ownership guidelines.

- **Contributions.** You can contribute up to 20% of net earnings from self-employment—(25% of wages, if incorporated)—but not to exceed annual amounts set by the tax law (visit **irahelp. com/2019** for the latest levels). If your business has employees, all eligible employees must receive the same benefits under a SEP IRA plan. Unlike a Traditional IRA, you can continue to make contributions to your SEP IRA after age 70 ½, if you are still working for the company.

- **Taxes.** Contributions are deductible dollar for dollar. This means if you contribute $25,000 to your SEP IRA, you can deduct this amount from your income on tax returns. This feature makes SEP IRA contributions highly desirable from a retirement-planning and tax-savings standpoint.

9. Which IRA is right for you?

- **What's your income?** If your income level is under the eligibility threshold, open a Roth IRA.

- **Are you self-employed?** Open a SEP IRA and contribute up to 20% of your net income (25% if you're incorporated)—but not more than the annual amounts set by the tax law (visit **irahelp.com/2019** for the latest levels).

- **Do you have kids?** Open a Roth IRA for teens with salaried summer jobs. You can make the contributions on their behalf. So, if your child earned $2,000 over the summer, you can contribute up to that amount in his or her Roth IRA. They will thank you when they retire and can withdraw the accumulated assets tax-free.

10. Easy way to save $36,000

You can easily contribute at least $1,326 a year to an IRA. Here's how:

The average American winds up with $5.50 in spare change each week. Pool the coins along with $20 per week in stray singles, and you'll have $1,326 by year's end. Why bother? If you continue to contribute this sum annually for 15 years, and your IRA account earns a modest 6% annually on a compounded basis, you will wind up with nearly $36,000. That's hardly chump change.

11. What is a Roth IRA conversion?

The tax code lets you convert all or part of your Traditional IRA or SEP IRA to a Roth IRA. Prior to 2010, the tax code allowed such a conversion—but only if your annual income did not exceed $100,000. But starting in 2010, this income threshold was repealed. That means anyone can convert a Traditional IRA into a Roth IRA—regardless of annual income. What you need to know:

- **Benefit:** A Roth conversion grants you all the benefits of a Roth IRA—including tax-free withdrawals of earnings after five years of ownership and after reaching age 59 ½.

- **Drawback:** You must pay income tax on the portfolio's market value on the date of conversion.

12. Does a Roth IRA conversion pay?

In many cases, the answer is a resounding yes. If you can pay the income tax due on the portfolio's market value at the time of conversion, the move is a powerful one.

- **Here's why:** Historically, today's income-tax rates are relatively low. A conversion allows you to pay income tax at the current rate and get rid of Uncle Sam for life. So, for example, if a $500,000 portfolio in a Roth IRA grows to $1 million in 15 years, all of those dollars are yours. And you get to enjoy all of the benefits of a Roth IRA, including no mandatory withdrawals.

13. Roth IRA conversion questions

Converting your Traditional IRA to a Roth IRA is a terrific deal. Anyone can do this—regardless of annual income, but you will owe income tax on the conversion. Five big questions:

- **When doesn't it pay?** If you expect your income to decline in retirement and tax rates to be where they are now, a Roth conversion might not be ideal. That's because the tax hit on your withdrawals from a Traditional IRA in the future will likely be lower than what you would have to pay now to convert.

- **How is a conversion taxed?** If you convert part or all of a Traditional IRA to a Roth IRA, you will owe income tax on the assets' market value on the date of conversion. But if you have made nondeductible IRA contributions, you have to follow the IRS' pro-rata tax rule, which can be tricky. Consult a financial advisor or an accountant with specialized knowledge in this area.

- **How to cover the tax?** Ideally you want to use funds in taxable accounts to pay the tax. It doesn't make sense to tap an IRA or 401(k) to pay taxes and a 10% early-withdrawal penalty if you're under age 59 ½.

- **Can the tax be minimized?** Sure. Convert only part of the Traditional IRA.

- **What about a SEP IRA?** Yes, you can convert part or all of a SEP IRA. If you convert the entire SEP IRA, however, you can't continue making deductible contributions to your newly created Roth IRA. Instead, you'll have to set up a new SEP IRA account for future deductible contributions.

Getting tax-free income from a Roth IRA can be rewarding, but getting there from a Traditional IRA conversion can be daunting. You'll probably owe income tax on most or all of the retirement funds you convert.

What's more, a complete conversion will often push you into a higher tax bracket. For example, consider Andrew and Bonnie, who are married and file a joint tax return. During her career, Bonnie worked at a series of companies with 401(k) plans.

Whenever Bonnie would change jobs, she'd roll the 401(k) balance into her Traditional IRA. By the time the couple reached their 50s, eyeing retirement, there was $200,000 in Bonnie's IRA.

- **Their plan:** Convert Bonnie's Traditional IRA to a Roth IRA. However, all of the money in her IRA came from pre-tax 401(k) contributions. A complete rollover would add $200,000 to Bonnie and Andrew's taxable income for the year.

  Typically, their taxable income (after deductions) is around $120,000 a year. That puts them in the 24% tax bracket.

  Another $200,000 in taxable income from a Roth IRA conversion would push them all the way through the 22% and 24% brackets, well into the 32% bracket. They might owe about $60,000 in additional federal income tax.

- **Going partial:** Instead, Bonnie decides to convert only $25,000 of her IRA this year. That would increase the couple's taxable income to $145,000, still within the 22% tax bracket for 2019. The added tax would be $5,500 (22% of $25,000), which Andrew and Bonnie can manage. Bonnie plans to implement partial Roth IRA conversions year after year, staying within a tax bracket to hold down the tax bill. Eventually, her entire Traditional IRA will be moved to the Roth side, at a relatively low tax cost over a period of years.

- **Ed Slott's advice:** A series of partial conversions will make it easier to pay the tax from a taxable account. Then your entire Traditional IRA can become a Roth IRA without a haircut for withdrawals to pay the tax bill.

14. Yes, current tax rates are low

Federal income tax rates are at historic lows. Even if you're paying a top federal rate of 37%, your rate is relatively low and may rise to pay for the new wave of Congressional spending and deficits. (For a look at the 2019 tax rules, see Chapter 8.) Over time, the top tax rate has been as high as 94%. Remember, Congress can change the tax rates at any time for all taxpayers or just for those who earn more than a specific level.

Year	Top Federal Income Tax Rate
2018 - 2019	37%
2013 - 2017	39.6%
2003 - 2012	35%
2002	38.6%
2001	39.1%
1993 - 2000	39.6%
1991 - 1992	31%
1988 - 1990	28%
1987	38.5%
1982 - 1986	50%
1965 - 1981	70%
1964	77%
1954 - 1963	91%
1952 - 1953	92%
1946 - 1951	91%
1944 - 1945	94%

15. What's a recharacterization?

A recharacterization is a way to undo Traditional or Roth IRA contributions. In the past, this strategy could also be used to undo Roth IRA conversions. However, the Tax Cuts and Jobs Act (passed in December 2017), eliminated recharacterizations for Roth IRA conversions that took place after December 31, 2017. As a result, while you can still recharacterize a contribution, Roth IRA conversions are now irrevocable.

- **How it works:** Let's says you checked all the rules and determined you were eligible to open a Roth IRA. You went ahead and opened the account and began making contributions to the Roth IRA. However, in that same year you received a promotion that came with a significant raise. Because of the added income, you are no longer eligible to make Roth IRA contributions. Under the tax law, your contributions are now subject to a tax penalty. Basically, you just got penalized for doing great work. Not fair!

- **Solution:** You can recharacterize the Roth IRA contributions to a Traditional IRA. Whether the contributions are deductible in the IRA is going to depend on your income and whether you or your spouse are covered by a retirement plan at work. You would have to file Form 8606 with your income tax return to report any non-deductible contributions.

16. Who's your IRA beneficiary?

No matter what kind of IRA you own, request a copy of your signed beneficiary form for review. When you receive it, be sure that the people you want to inherit your IRA's assets are listed properly. Also provide your advisor and estate attorney with copies of the signed document.

- **Reason:** When you die, your IRA does not pass according to wishes in your will. Whatever IRA assets are left will pass to the person or persons named in your signed beneficiary document.

17. Inheriting an IRA: Spouse

Under the tax law, if you inherit a spouse's IRA, there are generally no estate or income taxes due—no matter how large your inheritance. But you have three choices regarding how to treat the IRA inheritance:

- **Option #1: You can roll** the inherited IRA assets into your existing IRA or one you set up in your own name.

- **Option #2: You can transfer** the inherited IRA assets into an Inherited IRA account. If your spouse was age 70 ½ or older, you must begin taking mandatory distributions by December 31 of the year following your spouse's death. If your spouse was younger than age 70 ½, you can delay distributions until your spouse would have turned age 70 ½.

- **Option #3: You can disclaim** all or part of the IRA inheritance within nine months of the IRA owner's death. You do not get to choose who is next in line to receive the disclaimed property. Instead, the assets will pass to the IRA's contingent beneficiary, as if you had died before the IRA's owner. Since the assets will be passing to a non-spouse, estate taxes may be owed based on the value of the IRA.

18. Inheriting an IRA: Non-spouse

If you inherit an IRA from a parent or someone who isn't your spouse, you have three choices:

- **Option #1: Take distributions.** Whether you inherit a Traditional IRA or a Roth IRA, you cannot roll the assets into your existing IRA as a non-spouse. Instead, you must set up an "Inherited IRA" and have the assets transferred directly in there. Rules…

  1. Begin taking minimum distributions from the Inherited IRA by December 31 of the year following the IRA owner's death.
  2. Minimum annual withdrawals are based on the IRS' Single Life Expectancy Table (visit **irahelp.com/2019** to view the IRS table).

- **Option #2: Take the total.** You can choose to take the full value of the inherited IRA as a lump-sum check. You will owe income tax on the sum if you inherited a non-spousal Traditional IRA. If you inherited a Roth IRA, you may owe income tax on earnings if the owner did not have any Roth IRA for at least five years.

- **Option #3: Disclaim it.** Your third option is to disclaim the inheritance within nine months of the IRA owner's death. Why would you do this? In most cases it's done to pass the inheritance to the next-in-line beneficiary who may need it more than you do. Either way, upon inheriting, you should immediately name heirs on the beneficiary form.

- **Ed Slott's advice:** Consult an IRA advisor on the appropriate choice. If you decide to take annual distributions or a lump sum from an inherited Traditional IRA, see if you can claim the IRD deduction ("income in respect of a decedent"). It's a deduction for inheritors of a Traditional IRA on which federal estate taxes were paid (see tip #69).

19. Did you inherit a Roth IRA?

- **If you're the spouse**—you can roll the inherited Roth IRA into your existing Roth IRA or a newly set-up Roth IRA in your own name. Then you can avoid taking distributions for life if you choose. You also can retitle the Roth IRA as your own. Either way, upon inheriting, you should immediately name heirs on the beneficiary form. When non-spouse heirs inherit from you, they will have to take required minimum distributions each year, although they can generally stretch them out over their lifetime—income-tax free.

- **If you're a non-spouse**—

  1. Begin taking minimum distributions from the inherited Roth IRA by December 31 of the year following the Roth IRA owner's death.

  2. Minimum annual withdrawals are based on the IRS' Single Life Expectancy Table (visit **irahelp.com/2019** to view the table). But the mandatory annual required distributions will generally be tax-free.

20. Beware of this costly IRA penalty

If you're a non-spouse who's inheriting a Roth IRA, you have to set up an "Inherited Roth IRA" to receive the assets.

- **Big trap:** Be sure to take the required minimum distribution (RMD) each year based on the IRS' life-expectancy table (visit **irahelp.com/2019** to view the table). If you don't take the distributions, you will owe a 50% penalty on each RMD you missed—even though the distribution remains tax-free.

21. What wealthy retirees do right

An IRA is likely to be one of your most valuable assets when you retire. While my wealthiest retired clients differ in net worth and retirement goals—all share similar behavior patterns regarding their IRAs and how they saved over time. Here are their saving secrets:

- **Get real.** Most wealthy clients who retire with sizable IRAs resisted becoming greedy over time. They set goals and maintained retirement portfolio allocations that matched their savings targets and risk tolerance levels over time. They also didn't second-guess their plan—even in 2008.

- **React smartly.** If your IRA remains properly allocated and highly diversified based on your age and goals, you have little to fear in terms of market swings. You also want to avoid the urge to invest in hot trends or go to 100% cash in a panic. Both moves often backfire.

- **Seek smart help.** Many of my clients who amassed sizable IRAs by retirement age did so with the help of a professional advisor who was educated in IRAs and tax strategies.

- **Watch carefully.** Studies show that if you plan correctly and track your spending and IRA statements, you are more likely to reach your goals. The reason is simple: If you take an interest in your money, you're more likely to care. And if you care, you're more likely to save more, spend less and invest strategically.

- **Withdraw wisely.** You want to leave assets in an IRA as long as possible—especially in retirement. Tax-deferred savings compound over time and have the best chance of greater growth. For income, you're always better off working part-time or withdrawing from taxable accounts first before tapping into your IRA.

- **Hedge risks.** We all fear unforeseen market mishaps. To guard against the impact of downturns, wealthy retirees take protective steps in their IRA portfolios and other accounts. For example, they set aside enough cash to cover emergencies, take out adequate insurance policies to protect against health and financial blows, and invest in a range of different, highly diversified investments to cushion against market setbacks.

- **Ed Slott's advice:** Most people can live comfortably on much less than they're spending now—if they find ways to spend wisely. Many wealthy retirees are happy with the little things in life and appreciate what they already own. Few overspend on cars, boats, homes or vacations. And when they do spend, they are extremely frugal.

Chapter 2:
Making Plans

22. Saving plenty isn't hopeless

No matter how much you need to save by the time you retire, never feel as though saving annually is hopeless. It's not, and even small amounts add up over time. The reason is the "compounded interest" you'll receive in tax-deferred retirement accounts like an IRA.

- **What's compound interest?** This is interest you earn not only on your initial contribution but also on accumulated amounts earned each year. Let's say you have $1,000 in an IRA investment and it earns 7% in the first year. You'll have $1,070. Now let's say that in the second year, your $1,070 earns 6%. You'll have $1,134. And so on, year after year. That's the power of compound interest.

- **Ed Slott's advice:** Set your annual IRA savings goal early in the year and find ways to reach that goal by setting aside money each week or month. Or consider having your IRA plan automatically withdraw the amount from your bank checking account each month. If the money is removed directly, you're less likely to miss it.

23. How much will you need to save?

This answer depends on how much you'll need each year for living expenses in retirement—or once you stop working full-time. How to estimate your savings goal:

- **Step 1.** Gather last month's bills, ATM slips and credit card receipts. Add them up—but leave out expenses that won't likely exist when you retire, such as college tuitions, mortgage payments, credit card debt, disability insurance premiums, etc.

- **Step 2.** Next, multiply your monthly sum by 12 for an annual total.

- **Step 3.** A dollar today will buy less in the future thanks to rising prices (inflation). So take your current annual total and see what it will be in the year you plan to retire. Use an online inflation calculator.

- **Step 4.** Subtract your estimated annual Social Security benefit and any estimated annual pension and annuity payouts. You can calculate your Social Security benefit at SSA.gov.

- **Step 5.** Now you know roughly how much income you'll need in your first year of retirement. But how many years of this income will be enough? While it's impossible to say with any certainty, you can use a life insurance company's life-expectancy table.

- **Step 6.** Multiply your annual retirement income by your years of life expectancy. The result is a rough estimate of how much you'll need to save by retirement. If it seems high, you'll have to cut back on your post-retirement living expenses. Of course, during retirement your savings will need to be invested properly so it keeps pace with inflation.

- **Step 7.** Clearly your goal is to save at least the amount you calculated. Even better is to save a sum that when invested conservatively at 5% will provide you with what you need each year, allowing you to leave your principal intact and pass as much as possible to heirs.

24. How much risk can you tolerate?

Once you know your estimated retirement age and savings goal, the next step is to evaluate how much risk you can tolerate.

- **What is risk?** Risk is a fancy word for fear. As we know from the economic turmoil of 2008, markets drop, sometimes considerably. When they do, investors grow fearful as their portfolios shrink in value. If your portfolio dropped in 2008 and you worried you might not have enough years left until retirement to make back what you lost, you likely were overexposed to stocks and took on too much risk.

- **Is safety risky?** Not investing at all is also risky—particularly if you have 15 years or longer until retirement. If you stick only with conservative investments paying a low rate of return, there's a high risk that your portfolio won't grow to the amount you need.

- **Striking a balance.** Risk is about the odds of being exposed to hardship and fear. Finding the right balance between safety and satisfaction requires a little rational thought. Start by looking at how many years you have left until retirement and what rate of return will satisfy your savings goal.

- **Ed Slott's advice:** The more years remaining until retirement, the more risk your portfolio can take on for a higher rate of return. As for your personal fear factor, that's important, too. Fear should play a cautionary role as you determine an ideal rate of return over time. Fear is only a problem if fear alone dictates your investment strategy.

25. What's your asset allocation?

After you figure out when you plan to retire, how much you'll need to save, and the level of risk you can tolerate, you need to determine the ideal asset allocation of your IRA portfolio. Ideally this exercise should be done with a financial advisor who fully understands how IRAs work and the tax benefits involved.

- **What is asset allocation?** Asset allocation is how you divide your savings among stocks, bonds, cash and other investments. Asset allocation is important for two reasons: By properly allocating savings, you maximize your portfolio's growth potential and minimize the negative impact of market declines.

- **How to allocate.** Your allocation levels will depend on when your savings will be needed and the realistic rate of return you can expect over that time period.

- **What's diversification?** Once you've decided what percentage of your portfolio should be devoted to stocks and bonds, the next step is to create a diversified mix of different types of stocks and bonds. This is done to further minimize portfolio jolts over time.

26. When to rebalance a portfolio

No matter how you allocate and diversify your IRA assets now, the mix you choose is likely to become lopsided after 12 months or even sooner. That's because markets are constantly in flux, changing the values of your investments.

- **Example:** If your allocation is supposed to be 50% stocks and 50% bonds, your investment values could change by year-end. How so? A $1,000 investment today in a stock fund may be worth $1,500 at the end of the year. And $1,000 invested in a bond fund may be worth $800. Therefore, your allocation will no longer be 50%-50%, and it will need to be brought back into line.

- **When to rebalance.** Each year, revisit your IRA portfolio to see if it's still allocated and diversified the way you originally planned. If the allocation is too far off, you will need to rebalance your IRA portfolio either alone or with the assistance of a financial advisor.

- **How to rebalance.** You can rebalance two ways: You can sell your position in stock or bond investments in your IRA that exceed your original allocation and invest the proceeds in positions that are below your target percentages. Or you can invest cash in either stock or bond positions to bring the allocation into line.

27. Risks of do-it-yourself planning

While the media has done a fine job over the past 15 years simplifying investing principals for average investors, some magazines and TV shows have oversimplified retirement planning. It's a highly complex process that requires in-depth knowledge and impartiality. Here's how do-it-yourself planners get into trouble:

- **Tip tipsy**—Without someone qualified to remind you of your investment plan, you're more likely to try to capitalize on someone else's hot tip.

- **Too positive**—People who think positively are often successful in life. But they also can get into hot water with their personal finances and investing. That's because positive thinkers tend to assume that markets and their investments will always rebound. As we witnessed in 2008, even the mightiest companies can go under, and markets may not rebound fast enough.

- **Hardly objective**—If you make your own financial and investment decisions without seeking professional advice, you're not going to be objective, no matter how hard you try.

- **Lax on laws**—Educated financial advisors keep up with the tax laws that affect retirement planning. If you make a move on your own without understanding or knowing these laws, you could pay more in taxes or lose out on opportunities.

- **Slow on strategies**—New ways to invest emerge all the time. Unless you're up on the different ways to capitalize on tax loopholes, trusts, insurance, annuities and other products, you may not achieve your retirement objectives.

28. Retirement dreams vs. reality

For years, age 65 was the magic number for retirement. Today and in the future, that age may no longer be quitting time. Plan for age 65 but don't assume that work stops then. The odds are greater that work will stop sooner—or later. Here's why:

- **Sudden retirement.** As we know, many people in their 50s recently found themselves out of work for the first time in their careers during the recession. What's more, many remained unemployed for a year or longer, forcing families to live on less or dip into their savings. When these people did find employment, the jobs typically paid less than what they had been earning. The lesson: Don't assume you'll be working until age 65 or at the salary you're earning now.

- **Much later retirement.** Work used to mean manual labor, so by age 65 most people were physically tired and in need of a much slower pace. Today, many people earn a living on their computers and love what they do. As a result, they intend to continue earning income well into their 70s—either because they want to or because they need to fund some aspect of their lifestyle or the needs of their children.

- **Ed Slott's advice:** When speculating about your retirement age, don't assume too much. The odds are that retirement will come sooner than you think and that your salary in your 60s and 70s will likely be considerably less than you made in your 40s or early 50s. This is why it's so important that you save as much as possible while you're young.

29. Why a financial advisor is essential

Retirement planning is more than just saving enough money for the years when you'll be working less. There are a wide range of complicated retirement issues that need to be considered, including taxes, estate planning and insurance. To retire comfortably, you need financial help. Here's what a financial advisor who's an expert in IRAs can do for you:

- **Less anxiety.** If you hire the right financial advisor, you'll be less likely to worry day after day about whether you've done enough or too little with your investments. Once you and your advisor create a financial plan, your advisor also will help you stick to it.

- **Reduced tracking.** If an advisor has carefully thought through what you need to do and you've implemented the plan, you're less likely to monitor the Dow Jones Industrial Average or S&P 500 day after day. Those are short-term concerns. Instead, you'll be thinking long-term.

- **Size management.** Your IRA is now (or will be soon) your most valuable asset. A qualified financial advisor is trained to manage portfolios as they grow in size and ensure that different asset categories in your portfolio are allocated properly to achieve your stated goals.

- **Coping with complexity.** IRAs have highly complex tax rules that when maximized can save you or your estate from paying much more than necessary in taxes.

- **Legacy management.** It is the job of your financial advisor, in tandem with an estate attorney and accountant, to smoothly transition IRA assets from one generation to the next, minimizing tax issues and maximizing protection.

- **Laws and loopholes.** No one wants to miss out on tax law changes. Only an educated financial advisor stays up on such changes.

30. How to find the right advisor

If you are serious about planning for retirement, you need a professional financial advisor. Believe it or not, I have found that less than 1% of financial advisors are competent IRA distribution specialists. This means that a vast majority of advisors are not up to speed on IRA distribution rules and are ill-equipped to help you plan using your IRA. Here's how to find the right professional advisor:

- **Stick with certification.** Anyone can call himself or herself a "financial advisor." You want an advisor who at least is subject to professional standards and maintains a level of financial education to meet those standards. These include CFP, CFA, ChFC and CPA. While certification does not guarantee competence, a professional designation does indicate at least a standard of education and accountability.

- **Consider specialties.** Two areas that have a big impact on retirement savings are taxes and insurance coverage. Your advisor should have designations such as CPA (accounting) or CLU (insurance), or have access to experts who do.

- **Focus on knowledge.** A financial advisor should know about the latest IRA rules. He or she also should know how to integrate your IRA into your broader retirement and estate planning. An advisor must show he or she is continually being educated in the specialized tax rules surrounding IRA accounts.

31. Questions to ask an advisor

How can you be sure a financial advisor is up to speed on IRA issues?

Ask the following questions:

ED SLOTT'S
ELITE
IRA
ADVISOR
GROUP℠

Find an advisor
at **irahelp.com**

1. **How** do you keep up to date on IRA rules?

2. **When** did you last attend an IRA training course? Ask to see the course manuals.

3. **Are** you up on the latest tax law changes?

4. **What** do you recommend I do with my lump-sum distribution from my company's retirement plan?

5. **Who** should be my IRA beneficiary?

6. **How** do you keep track of my IRA beneficiary forms?

7. **What** is my life expectancy and what is my required IRA distribution if I inherit an IRA? What about my beneficiary?

8. **What** will happen to my IRA after I die? How should an inherited IRA be titled and what's the minimum distribution that a beneficiary will have to take?

9. **How** will you integrate estate planning into your plans for my IRA?

10. **Who** will you turn to for help when you need clarification on IRA rules, estate planning and insurance? If the person says he or she knows it all and doesn't have to ask anyone—run.

Paying a fair price for advice

Among the questions to ask a prospective advisor, be sure to ask how he or she will be paid. You'll want to pay enough so you get good advice, but you don't want to overpay. Here are the major modes of compensation for financial advisors:

- **Traditional.** In the days when most financial advisors were known as brokers, they generally earned sales commissions. That's still true—many financial professionals depend on transaction fees to earn a living.

  Although commissions often get a bad rap, this model still makes sense for some investors, particularly for those who intend to hold their investments for the long-haul.

- **Percentage plays.** These days, many financial advisors rely upon fees rather than commissions. Among fee structures, the most common is charging a percentage of assets under management.

  Many advisors believe that this arrangement puts them "on the same side of the table" as their clients. They're motivated to increase your $500,000 portfolio to $600,000 because they will earn more. Similarly, they have a strong incentive to minimize any declines in your portfolio value, as that will decrease their fees as well.

  There certainly are good reasons why this arrangement has grown in popularity. Nevertheless, paying an asset management fee is not the best plan for everyone. If you seldom change your investments or you interact with your advisor infrequently, you should ask yourself if the fee you are paying is really worth it.

- **Alternate arrangements.** Other compensation structures include retainers, in which you pay a flat fee for advice during a specific time period, perhaps one year. Some advisors charge by the hour, just as accountants and attorneys commonly bill for their services. You may even find an advisor whose compensation includes some combination of the arrangements mentioned above.

- **Ed Slott's advice:** Don't be reluctant to ask an advisor about compensation. Get a written explanation and read it carefully to make sure you understand what you'll be paying.

Understand what you'll be getting, too. If you participate in a 401(k) plan, for instance, will that advisor help with those decisions, or will you simply continue what you've been doing? You can expect to pay your advisor in some manner, but you should be confident you'll receive a desirable amount of assistance in return.

32. Is your financial advisor honest?

Just because a financial advisor claims to be certified by a professional organization doesn't mean it's true. In the wake of all the recent financial scandals, it's now clear you have to do a little due diligence on the background of anyone you hire to handle your money.

- **Do it yourself**—Verify that your advisor has actually earned his or her credentials by calling the organizations that award certification. Also confirm with the organization that the advisor continues to satisfy ongoing educational requirements, that complaints have not been filed, and that the advisor has not been disciplined.

- **Hire a pro**—Consider hiring an online background-check firm or agency to verify your advisor's education degrees, any legal cases pending, liens and even dangerous levels of personal debt.

33. Does your advisor speak simply?

One of the most important qualifications of a financial advisor is the ability to explain complex matters simply. No matter whom you hire, eventually that person will be recommending investments for your IRA. If that person is unable to explain what the investment is and the rationale for you owning it, you have a big problem.

- **Ed Slott's advice:** Before you hire an advisor, ask him or her to explain a Roth IRA conversion, an annuity or how IRAs are distributed after death. If you cannot understand the explanation, or the advisor seems to grow impatient with your questions, there may be a communication problem and a big red flag.

34. How to manage an advisor

Even if you choose an honest, educated IRA advisor who understands the distribution and tax rules, and can explain them clearly, you still need to manage your advisor. You're the boss. The advisor works for you—just as though you were running a business. Here's how to keep your advisor on his or her toes:

- **Meetings**—For the first year, request that you and your advisor meet quarterly. Before these meetings, ask for an agenda of items to be covered.

- **Communication**—E-mails sent to your advisor should be answered promptly. Phone calls also should be returned promptly.

- **Statements**—If your advisor has invested your assets through several different firms, request a consolidated statement outlining your IRA portfolio.

- **Accountability**—Ask knowledgeable questions about your advisor's recommendations. Don't assume everything your advisor says is right or ideal. Questions about your assets are also likely to keep your advisor on his or her toes.

- **Pro-active**—Your advisor should not simply present you with advice and then wait for you to respond. Good advisors stay on clients to ensure that necessary steps are taken and decisions are made.

- **Education**—How is the advisor keeping up on the latest IRA tax rules? They are always changing.

35. How to hire the right CPA

Eventually you will need an accountant who is up on current tax laws, understands the best strategies to keep you from overpaying your taxes, prepares your tax returns on time, and has the skills or resources to assist you in the event of an audit.

- **Ed Slott's advice:** The best place to begin your search for a CPA is by asking friends and colleagues for recommendations. Just be sure you're not hiring more CPA than you need and that the person is suitable for someone with your net worth.

36. How to hire an estate attorney

Nearly 60% of Americans do not have estate plans—and most people who do, neglect to update them regularly. Without up-to-date estate plans in place, all of your hard work saving for retirement and hopes to preserve your wealth for heirs are at risk.

- **Ed Slott's advice:** Ask your financial advisor or friends and colleagues to recommend an estate attorney. Make sure the person understands IRA inheritance and distribution rules. The attorney also should understand the rules that govern distribution of assets to trust beneficiaries and heirs by trustees and estate plan administrators.

37. How to hire an insurance agent

Life insurance is an essential part of retirement planning. You may ask, "How can a life insurance policy benefit me if it won't pay out until I'm dead and gone?" While life insurance can be used to provide heirs with appropriate assets when you die, policies can also be used to guarantee heirs a specific sum so you can spend down what you've saved without worrying if there will be enough for them.

- **Ed Slott's advice:** When choosing a life insurance agent, look for someone who is independent or works with a top-rated, reputable life insurance company and can work with your financial advisor. In many cases, your financial advisor may already have an established relationship with an agent or can find one for you.

Chapter 3:
Minimizing Risks

38. Why knowledge leads to wealth

By now you may be asking yourself the following question: "If I've hired a financial advisor, a CPA and an estate attorney, why do I need to read the rest of this guide? Isn't it their job to know all this stuff?" The answer is yes—and no.

- **Ed Slott's advice:** Yes, your advisors should know all of the information in this guide. But as their employer, you need to be up on the best strategies for your needs and raise key issues with them. Smart retirement planning is an ongoing dialogue with advisors followed by action and fine-tuning along the way. The more you know, the better you'll be able to manage the process, protect your interests and prosper in retirement.

39. Big risks to your IRA savings

IRA planning is largely about maximizing the odds of reaching financial goals —and minimizing the risks that your wealth faces. These risks come in all shapes and sizes—including a recession, job loss, costly health crises, an unexpected death and even living longer than expected. Here's how these risks can be reduced:

- **Portfolio threats**—Market and economic risks to your IRA portfolio are offset through proper asset allocation, diversification and hedging.

- **Job threats**—The risk that IRA assets will be needed to pay bills following a layoff can be offset by setting aside enough emergency cash to cover your expenses until re-employment.

- **Health threats**—The risk that your IRA assets will be dramatically reduced to pay for health care is offset with health, disability and long-term care insurance.

- **Legacy threats**—The risk that your death will leave your family without sufficient income over time or that heirs won't inherit what you intended is offset with life insurance.

- **Tax threats**—The risk that your estate will owe more than necessary when you die in estate and income taxes is offset through strategic estate and tax planning.

40. Estate taxes made simple

When you die, the IRS considers all of the assets that are titled in your name or held jointly with your spouse to be part of your estate. The tax law generally allows you to pass all of your assets to your spouse tax-free. But if you die without a spouse, or you've left assets to children and other non-spouse heirs, these assets are tallied up and may face federal and state estate taxes. Such assets include the value of your retirement plans, your taxable accounts, real estate, and all other items of value owned by you.

- **Ed Slott's advice:** To preserve as much of the wealth you've built up as possible and to avoid overpaying your taxes, you and your financial advisor and estate attorney need to take steps to legally minimize the likelihood of taxation.

41. The case of the two Uncle Sams

When you die, your assets pass either to your spouse—or to children and other non-spouse heirs. Who gets what is spelled out in your will and in your retirement account beneficiary forms.

- **Problem:** Most estates will not pay federal estate tax, but some states have a state estate tax. The estate level at which state taxation begins is generally significantly lower. The federal government lets you subtract the amount of estate tax paid to a state from your federal estate-tax liability, up to a limit.

- **Ed Slott's advice:** Talk with your financial advisor and accountant about ways to minimize the impact of federal and state estate taxes. This is often done through gifting and life insurance, for example.

42. Avoid this death-benefit trap

When you take out a life insurance policy on your life, you typically name someone who will receive the cash death benefit when you die. This person is known as the policy's "beneficiary." If the beneficiary is your spouse, no estate taxes will generally be owed. But if the beneficiary is a child or other non-spouse heir, the death benefit will be counted as part of your estate and may be needed to pay estate taxes, reducing the cash payout.

- **Problem:** If you die and your spouse inherits your assets, no taxes are generally owed. But when your spouse dies, his or her much-larger estate will likely pass to your children, increasing the odds of an estate tax.

- **Ed Slott's advice:** While this is not a problem for most individuals in 2019 since the estate tax exemption is $11,400,000 per person (this amount sunsets after 2025) and is portable to a surviving spouse, ask your financial advisor and estate attorney about ways to minimize estate taxes when a surviving spouse dies.

43. What is term life insurance?

Term life insurance is the most basic type of policy. You pay a relatively low annual premium for coverage that remains in force for a specific number of years (the "term")—provided the premiums are paid. You can buy a "level term" policy in which the premium stays the same annually for the duration of the policy. Or you can buy annual renewable term, in which the premium starts out very low but inches up annually over the policy's term.

- **Ed Slott's advice:** A term policy typically is ideal for young couples who don't have a significant amount of income and want to maximize coverage and minimize annual premiums.

44. What is permanent life insurance?

The alternative to term life insurance is "permanent" insurance, which remains in force for the duration of your life, not a specific term—as long as the required annual premiums are paid. The premium for a permanent policy is higher than that for a term policy with the same death benefit for two reasons: The policy is in force for life, and part of your premium is deposited into a savings or "cash value" component. There are different kinds of permanent life insurance, so be sure to discuss them with your financial advisor or an insurance agent.

Retirement cash flow from life insurance

Most life insurance policies offer a prime tax benefit. When the insured individual dies, the beneficiary collects a death benefit and owes no income tax. That's true even if the decedent had paid, say, $500 in annual premiums and the beneficiary receives $250,000 or more from the insurer.

Some permanent life insurance policies have cash value. This generates two more tax benefits:

- **Tax-free buildup.** Cash value accumulation is not subject to income tax, inside the policy.
- **Tax-free lifetime cash flow.** The owner of a permanent life policy can withdraw money or take policy loans. This cash flow may be untaxed.

Generally, it takes years for such opportunities to become available. Permanent life policies often have upfront costs that depress the initial cash value. Eventually, sound policies can have substantial cash value, which the policyholder can tap.

Life insurance companies frequently provide "illustrations" to consumers considering permanent life insurance. These illustrations may show years of paying premiums followed by years of untaxed withdrawals or untaxed policy loans, or both. The illustrated cash flow to a living policy owner may be far greater than the premiums paid over time.

- **Ed Slott's advice:** You should buy life insurance because there is a genuine need for the death benefit, such as providing financial support to surviving loved ones. Once you decide to buy life insurance, and how much coverage you need, a permanent life policy might be a good choice if you are in it for the long term. After you have had a permanent life policy for a while and your cash value is substantial, you may decide to supplement your retirement income with periodic policy loans and withdrawals, tax-free. Just keep in mind that accessing your policy in that manner probably will reduce the death benefit.

  Warning! If you tap your policy for retirement cash flow, do so prudently. If you withdraw or borrow too heavily, your cash value may become insufficient and your policy might lapse. Not only would you lose your insurance coverage, you also could owe income tax on the investment earnings that had previously been sheltered inside the policy!

  Your insurance agent should be able to help you keep policy loans and withdrawals within acceptable levels.

45. How to protect your wealth

If the value of your estate is significant and will likely face estate taxes when you die ($11.4 million for individuals and $22.8 million for married couples in 2019), consider taking out a life insurance policy to cover the estate-tax tab. The death benefit of this policy will keep heirs from having to dip into the estate (their inheritance) to pay Uncle Sam.

46. Life insurance: Old and/or ill?

When it comes to buying life insurance, don't assume that someone who is old or ill won't qualify for a policy. If you want to cover sizable estate taxes with a life insurance policy, you almost always can secure coverage:

- **Little-known fact:** Some insurers have quotas to fill, and toward the end of each year will issue policies to even old and ill individuals by charging a high one-time premium.

47. Avoid this life insurance trap

To maximize the death benefit of a life insurance policy, don't own it in your name. If you own the policy in your name, the death benefit's value will be included as part of your estate and be subject to estate taxes, reducing the cash your non-spouse heirs will receive.

- **Ed Slott's advice:** Own the policy outside of your estate—perhaps by a trust. By having a trust own the policy, you're still insured and the death benefit will still be available to heirs. Upon your death, the policy's death benefit will pour into the trust—and not be included as part of your estate. Heirs will wind up receiving distributions from the trust based on the trust's terms.

48. Consider a life insurance trust

Many people who amass sizable estates by the time they retire wonder how they can pass as much of it as possible to heirs.

- **Tax traps:** You can't just hand the assets to heirs while you're alive. Uncle Sam can take an enormous bite in the form of a gift tax (visit **irahelp.com/2019** for the latest levels). On the other hand, if you wait until you die, the assets will be considered part of your estate and may face federal and state estate taxes.

- **Ed Slott's advice:** You can avoid any future estate tax traps by setting up a life insurance trust as the owner and beneficiary of a life insurance policy and naming heirs as the trust's beneficiaries. Then when you die, the sizable death benefit passes into the trust and is excluded from your estate. As a result, your heirs receive every dime you intended for them, not Uncle Sam.

49. Use your IRA to pay premiums

One way to pay a life insurance premium after age 59 ½ is to use your IRA. If you own a Traditional IRA, you'll owe income tax on the amount withdrawn. But the move still may pay since you'll be providing heirs with a tax-free inheritance in the form of the insurance policy's death benefit.

- **Ed Slott's advice:** If you believe that the top tax rates are likely to rise substantially in the years ahead, then it's far more attractive to pay the lower income tax now. Of course, this strategy makes sense only if the funds in an IRA or savings account aren't needed to pay your bills. Also ask your estate attorney and accountant about setting up a life insurance trust.

50. Provide for heirs and spend freely

Many people sacrifice for their kids. But most people go too far, tightening the screws on savings and enjoyment to ensure that heirs wind up with the largest possible inheritance, which is certainly noble. But what if you could leave heirs exactly what you want them to receive—and still enjoy your savings?

- **Ed Slott's advice:** Take a portion of your savings and buy a life insurance policy with a death benefit that covers what you want heirs to have. By doing this, heirs are covered and you're able to spend your savings as you wish. Just be sure to do this as early in life as possible, before health issues emerge and push premium costs up.

51. What's an annuity?

An annuity is purchased through an insurance company and guarantees the owner payments over a set number of years—or until death. An annuity can be purchased with a guaranteed death benefit—which means if you die, your beneficiaries will receive at least what you paid in premiums.

52. What are the annuity types?

There are two basic types of annuities—immediate and deferred:

- **Immediate annuity**—you invest a lump sum, typically at retirement. Regular payments from the annuity start immediately.
Deferred annuity—you invest and your contributions grow tax-deferred, like in a Traditional IRA. You can choose between a fixed or variable deferred annuity, depending on your tolerance for risk. Fixed means your contributions go into investments that earn a fixed rate of interest. Variable means your contributions grow based on market conditions, since they are typically invested in stock and bond annuity funds.

53. Why is an annuity attractive?

An annuity is designed to produce income for its owner in retirement. As a result, an annuity can function like a pension, making regular monthly payments. Such payments keep you from worrying that declining financial markets or the economy will hurt your investment income stream.

ED SLOTT'S
ELITE
IRA
ADVISOR
GROUP™
Find an advisor
at **irahelp.com**

- **Ed Slott's advice:** An annuity can be used as a hedge, providing you with a guaranteed income stream that your stock portfolio was supposed to generate but might not if the economy declines.

54. Why buy an annuity in an IRA?

Many advisors frown upon buying an annuity in an IRA, since annuity contributions already grow on a tax-deferred basis. But what if you don't have enough cash in a taxable account to buy an annuity that pays guaranteed income? That's when it may make sense to use IRA assets to buy an annuity within the IRA. Discuss your options with your financial advisor.

55. Aren't annuity fees high?

Admittedly, some annuities tend to have higher fees than other types of investments. But annuities can provide guaranteed income regardless of economic meltdowns and come with a death benefit, so they can't really be compared to most other investments.

- **Ed Slott's advice:** When comparing fees, weigh them against other annuities issued by insurance companies with similar attributes and ratings.

56. Essential estate-planning documents

Most Americans do not have a will or other estate documents. And if they do, the documents aren't likely up to date. What you need an estate attorney to draw up:

- **A will**—ensures that qualifying assets are distributed according to your wishes. It also names a guardian for minor children.

- **Durable power of attorney**—names a family member or friend to make financial decisions for you if you're incapacitated or unable to act.

- **Health-care proxy**—authorizes a family member or friend to make medical decisions if you are incapacitated. Make sure your doctor and hospital have an up-to-date copy.

- **Living will**—states your health-care and end-of-life wishes so the person making decisions knows what you want. Make sure your doctor and hospital also have this document.

- **Medical release**—Often called a HIPAA release (Health Insurance Portability and Accountability Act), this document lets a family member or friend access your medical records to monitor what is going on and make decisions.

Chapter 4

IRA Strategies

57. Affluent? You still can own a Roth IRA

You may be interested in contributing to a Roth IRA but think your income is too high. Are you out of luck? The answer is "no" and tax reform makes this clearer than ever by allowing a back-door Roth IRA conversion.

In 2019, if your modified adjusted gross income exceeds $203,000 (couples filing jointly) or $137,000 (single taxpayers), the tax code prohibits you from contributing to a Roth IRA (visit **irahelp.com/2019** for all 2019 IRA and tax tables). If your income exceeds these limits, take the following steps to own a Roth IRA:

> **Step 1: Open** a new 2019 Traditional IRA if you don't already have one before April 15, 2019, if you otherwise qualify (see Item 6).
>
> **Step 2: Make** the maximum 2019 contribution—$6,000 if you're age 49 or younger, $7,000 if you're age 50 or older.
>
> **Step 3: Convert** funds to a Roth IRA, which you've been allowed to do since the income limit restrictions were waived in 2010.
>
> **Step 4: Mind** the rules. You'll owe income tax on the conversion if you convert pre-tax funds, and the pro-rata rule will apply if you have after-tax funds in any of your IRAs. You won't be allowed to contribute to your new Roth IRA if your income exceeds the

annual IRS limits. Consult a financial advisor or accountant with specialized knowledge in this area.

Step 5: Exploit the loophole. Get around the income restriction by repeating this contribution-conversion strategy year after year.

- **In the past,** there have been concerns about the legality of back-door Roth IRA conversions. To some, this strategy seemed too good to be true and an attempt to exploit a loophole. These transactions have been consistently dogged by rumors that Congress or the IRS was ready to shut them down.

  Congress has put these fears to rest by confirming that the back-door Roth is an allowable strategy, with several references to the back-door Roth strategy included in Congress' Conference Committee report that accompanies the new law. IRS has also stated that this strategy is allowed.

58. Can Uncle Sam change his mind?

While you can convert a Traditional IRA to a Roth IRA regardless of your income, many people worry that the deficit-weary federal government will change its mind about the tax-free withdrawal status of Roth IRAs.

- **Ed Slott's advice:** Besides the political risks of officials advocating for such a change, Roth IRAs are funded with after-tax dollars. If taxes were to be imposed on Roth IRAs, no one would fund them, boxing the government out of tax revenue. Even if the Roth IRA's tax-free status were to change, existing accounts would likely be exempt from the new rules.

59. IRA conversion? Watch your 401(k)

If you're planning to convert a Traditional IRA to a Roth IRA, delay rolling over a 401(k) from a past employer into your Traditional IRA until the year following the conversion.

- **Reason:** For tax purposes, you want to keep your percentage of nondeductible contributions higher in the pro-rata formula the IRS uses to determine taxation on a conversion.

- **Ed Slott's advice:** You'll need to know which of your past IRA contributions were deductible and nondeductible. Consult your financial planner and accountant before making a move.

60. IRA conversion? Mind your annuity

If you hold a variable annuity in a Traditional IRA you plan to convert to a Roth IRA, have your financial advisor evaluate the annuity's value carefully. You can't use artificially deflated values for variable annuities.

- **Ed Slott's advice:** Get the actual fair-market value of the annuity from the issuing insurer.

61. Be sure of a Roth IRA conversion

The Tax Cuts and Jobs Act repealed the portion of the tax code that allowed for Roth recharacterizations. A recharacterization allowed a taxpayer to undo a Roth conversion as if it never happened. The benefits of a Roth IRA conversion remain unchanged — *you trade a tax bill now in exchange for tax-free Roth IRA distributions down the road.* That is still going to be a good deal for many people. Now that we are living in a world without recharacterization, you need to be very sure that it is the right strategy for you. With the "do-over" option no longer available, it is more important than ever, that you work with an educated financial advisor and carefully consider all the pros and cons before doing a Roth IRA conversion.

> *Note that Congress kept the ability for taxpayers to recharacterize contributions. An IRA contribution can be recharacterized to a Roth IRA contribution and vice-versa; a Roth IRA contribution can be recharacterized to a Traditional IRA. So be sure to consult with an educated financial advisor.*

62. No life insurance? Convert an IRA

Does a health problem make it impossible for you to qualify for life insurance? Or is a policy's annual premium prohibitively expensive? If you want non-spouse heirs such as children to inherit a sizable sum when you die, consider converting your Traditional IRA to a Roth IRA and naming those heirs as beneficiaries.

- **Reason:** During your life, there are no required distributions from your Roth IRA, and the Roth IRA will pass income-tax free to designated heirs provided five years have elapsed prior to inheritance.

- **Ed Slott's advice:** Be sure non-spouse heirs are named as beneficiaries on the newly converted Roth IRA.

63. Give a grandchild a cool $2.3 million

Most people who own a Traditional IRA assume they will spend down their account over the course of their lifetime. That's because the tax code requires owners of a Traditional IRA to take minimum distributions each year starting at age 70 ½. But here's a secret: The size of that distribution is based on IRS life-expectancy tables, which have you living much longer than standard actuarial tables. That's a good thing— meaning that assets will likely be left over in your Traditional IRA when you die if you take only the minimum required each year.

- **Ed Slott's advice:** Name one or more grandchildren the beneficiary of your Traditional IRA, and their inheritance could turn into millions of dollars. That's because a one-year-old's life expectancy is lengthy, and the amount that must be withdrawn annually from the Inherited IRA will be infinitesimal. So, a $100,000 IRA earning 6% annually will pay that child more than $2.3 million over 80 years.

64. How to set up a stretch IRA

The stretch IRA is simply a term used to describe the option that allows your individual beneficiaries to gain the maximum tax deferral period when they inherit your IRA by spreading their required minimum distributions over their lifetime.

This will make their inherited funds last the longest. The tax law allows this but only to designated beneficiaries. These are individual beneficiaries who are named on the beneficiary form.

There is some talk in Washington right now about limiting this option, but as of this writing, the stretch IRA benefit is alive and well, so this is a factor you should consider in your estate planning.

*As always, go to my website **irahelp.com** to find out the latest on this and any other major tax rule changes that could affect your retirement savings.*

Most people want the wealth they build up over a lifetime to last generations.

As noted in the previous tip, if your spouse won't need the assets that remain in your IRA when you die, name your children or grandchildren as the IRA's beneficiary. Then whatever remains in your IRA at death will pass to them. The Inherited IRA will likely grow larger over the life expectancy of those younger heirs. Here's some planning advice you can act on now so your beneficiaries will have more to stretch later:

- **Roll** assets from other retirement accounts into your Traditional IRA.

- **Plan** retirement spending carefully to preserve the assets in your Traditional IRA.

- **Tell** children about the IRA and your plans. Leave them a sealed letter outlining your wishes for them to stretch the Inherited IRA.

- **Or convert** all or part of your Traditional IRA into a Roth IRA—if you have the dollars in a taxable account to pay tax on the conversion. Why do this? A Roth IRA is more ideal than a Traditional IRA for stretching purposes. That's because there are no required minimum distributions for the original IRA owner. So your Roth IRA assets can continue to grow tax-free for an even longer period since you won't have to withdraw them when you turn age 70 ½.

65. Surviving spouse? Stretch your IRA

If your spouse inherits what's left in your IRA, he or she can set up a stretch IRA for children or grandchildren. What your spouse needs to do:

- **Roll** the inherited IRA into an IRA in their own name. Only a spouse can do this (non-spouses cannot).

- **Name** a child (or other heir) as the IRA's beneficiary. A surviving spouse does this by filling out the IRA's beneficiary form.

- **After** the surviving spouse dies, the assets will be counted as part of his or her estate, which may face estate taxes. The IRA passes to the heir, who must re-title the account as an inherited IRA. Otherwise the IRS could deem it distributed, which would result in income taxes.

66. When to decline an IRA inheritance

When one spouse dies, the surviving spouse is most often the beneficiary of the decedent's IRA. But the surviving spouse doesn't have to accept the inheritance. You have nine months to decline (disclaim) assets meant for you to inherit. Why would anyone decline to inherit an IRA? Here are the main reasons:

- **Assets aren't needed.** A surviving spouse with sufficient assets (or who receives life insurance proceeds) may not need the IRA assets and may want children or grandchildren to inherit them instead. By declining the inheritance, the IRA will pass to the next person named on the IRA's beneficiary form.

- **Estate-tax risk.** A surviving spouse inherits his or her spouse's assets tax-free. But when those assets pass to a spouse, they could result in a much larger estate when the surviving spouse dies, resulting in a stiff estate tax.

- **Ed Slott's advice:** One way to avoid passing along a future estate tax is to decline the IRA inheritance. When this happens, the assets will be counted as part of the decedent's estate and may face estate taxes. Then the heirs next in line as beneficiaries will receive the assets. Those inherited assets can grow large over time if heirs limit their withdrawals only to the required annual distributions. Disclaiming an inheritance is tricky. Before accepting assets, talk to your financial advisor and accountant.

67. Tricky IRA inheritance issues

Leaving assets to your spouse or a single heir is easy. But what if your life is more complicated? Here are three common inheritance scenarios that you should discuss with your advisor and estate attorney:

- **Multiple heirs**—IRA owners who want to pass IRA assets to multiple non-spouse heirs often wonder how to divide the wealth. First, complete the IRA beneficiary form so that all heirs are named. As for the share, dividing the inheritance equally by percentage is often easier and less likely to produce feuds than trying to divide assets fairly by dollars based on heirs' means.

- **New spouse**—People who divorce and remarry need to revisit who they want to inherit their IRA.

- **Single asset**—Naming IRA heirs is relatively simple. You complete the beneficiary form, and assets pass accordingly upon death. But if you are passing a home—an asset that can't neatly be divided—enormous friction can result if you leave heirs to figure out how to share the asset. Ask your estate attorney for strategies to ensure that the property passes equitably and that there are provisions in place for sharing or selling the property and protecting against possible taxes.

68. Steps if you inherit an IRA

The first step is to do nothing. You first want to hire a financial advisor who is educated in IRA strategies and distributions (*see tips #29-34*). Here are the issues you need to discuss with that advisor:

- **Accept or decline**—Just because you are the named beneficiary of an IRA doesn't mean you must accept it. In some cases, declining the inherited IRA may make more sense from a tax perspective.

- **Title properly**—If you accept the inherited IRA and you are not the spouse of the deceased, the IRA needs to be properly titled. It cannot be rolled into your existing IRA.

- **Distributions**—If you're not the spouse, you must take minimum distributions each year based on the IRS' life-expectancy table.

Minimum distributions from an IRA inherited by a non-spouse must begin by December 31 of the year following the IRA owner's death.

- **Beneficiary**—You will need to name a beneficiary for your Inherited IRA in case something happens to you. This is done by filling out the inherited IRA's beneficiary form.

- **Ed Slott's advice:** Avoid the temptation to withdraw the entire lump sum you inherit. For one, you'll face income tax on the full amount distributed to you. For another, the longer you leave assets in an account that can grow tax-free, the more you're likely to have over time.

69. Do you qualify for an IRD deduction?

In the past, the IRD deduction was one of the most overlooked tax breaks available to inheritors of an IRA, 401(k) or other property. But now with the increased estate tax exemptions, it will only be used by those who inherit from very large estates.

- **How it works:** If you inherit an IRA and take distributions, you'll owe income tax on the amount withdrawn. But if the person you inherited from had an estate that paid federal estate taxes, you are entitled to the IRD deduction, which can range as high as 40%.

- **Ed Slott's advice:** The IRD deduction can save you significant taxes and also is exempt from the alternative minimum tax (AMT). But figuring out your tax savings can be tricky, so consult your financial advisor or accountant.

70. Update your plan as life changes

You now have plenty of actionable, useful information to create a proactive plan to keep more of the money you have earned and make it last as long as you do. But, any plan has to leave room for changes and revisions as new events in your life unfold.

For example, events such as a birth, an illness, a death, an inheritance, a marriage, a divorce, a re-marriage, new grandchild, etc. You get the idea.

As situations change in your life, use the information in this guide to adapt and revise your plans, maybe changing a beneficiary or altering your estate plan. Tax law changes also need to be considered since they can have a major impact, especially when it comes to your tax-deferred retirement savings.

- **Ed Slott's advice:** Anticipate change, and when it comes, embrace it and ACT. It is essential to make educated and informed decisions, but they need to be reviewed and often revised to reflect changes in your life or new tax laws. Your plan should always be based on the most current information available.

Chapter 5:

In
Retirement

71. Can you afford to retire?

As you near retirement, you and your financial advisor need to calculate whether your savings will be able to meet your annual needs, which debt need to be paid off, and which accounts you'll turn to first for your post-retirement needs.

- **Ed Slott's advice:** With your financial advisor, make a list of income sources, including IRAs and other savings accounts, Social Security, pensions, etc. Determine how these assets need to be invested to match your risk tolerance and to be preserved for life expectancy. Also, find out how much to withdraw from which accounts.

72. Will your savings last a lifetime?

When you're young, your big goal is to save enough for retirement. When you retire, your big goal is to make sure you don't run out of what you've saved. Most people live longer than they assumed they would.

- **Ed Slott's advice:** Before you retire, consider whether you have enough to sustain your lifestyle during your retirement years. Then take steps to protect against devastating risks to those assets. Talk to your financial advisor about buying annuities to produce steady income for life. You can reduce the cost by buying annuities that don't start making payments until age 85, for example. Also discuss the savings realized if you move to a smaller home and take out long-term care insurance to minimize risks to savings.

73. Pre-retirement advisor questions

1. **How** much will I need to live on each year?

2. **What** sources will fund this amount?

3. **Which** assets should I turn to first if I'm at least age 59 ½?

4. **How** can I increase investment income?

5. **How** much emergency cash should I set aside?

6. **What** debts should I pay off before retirement?

7. **Should** I roll my 401(k) into my IRA?

8. **Should** I convert all or part of my Traditional IRA into a Roth IRA?

9. **How** can I make sure my life insurance policy is on schedule to pay off?

10. **Do** I need long-term care insurance?

74. Watch those nest-egg raids

Retirees who fear running out of assets in retirement frequently wonder how much they can safely withdraw from savings annually to fund their lifestyle.

- **Ed Slott's advice:** A withdrawal rate of 4% per year is good starting point when considering how to draw down your assets without running out of money is a good starting point. Withdrawal rates above 4% will increase the odds of running out of cash. Discuss this with your financial advisor so that all of your income assets are considered and factored into the withdrawal equation.

Playing by the "4% Rule"

The good news is that you probably won't run out of money in retirement, as long as the federal government can transfer electronic

Social Security payments into your bank account. The bad news? You may well run short of cash if you live beyond your life expectancy and deplete your portfolio.

To address this concern, financial advisors and academic researchers have come up with what's known as the 4% Rule. Here's the premise:

- **In the first year of your retirement** you should draw down no more than 4% of your portfolio.

- **In each succeeding year,** you can increase your portfolio withdrawal to keep up with inflation.

- **Judging by historic market returns,** this strategy will provide a high probability that your portfolio will last for 30 years or longer.

To put some numbers to this plan, assume that Fran retires with a $600,000 portfolio. In her first year without receiving a paycheck, she withdraws $24,000 (4% of $600,000) from her portfolio for spending money.

Assume that inflation is 3% that year. In Year Two of her retirement, Fran adds 3% ($720) to her annual drawdown, pulling out $24,720.

Suppose that inflation the next year goes up to 5%, so Fran would be scheduled to withdraw 5% more in Year Three, or $25,956. She could round up to a $26,000, to keep things simple.

And so on, year after year. Fran eventually will be withdrawing $30,000 or $40,000 or more in a given year with this plan, depending on how long she lives and the rate of inflation. Nevertheless, it's very likely her portfolio will last as long as she does.

- **Judgment calls.** Keep in mind that there is no penalty for bending the rules. You might, for example, skip the annual inflation increase after a steep drop in portfolio value. Alternatively, you might start with, say, a 5% withdrawal instead of 4% if you plan to eventually sell a valuable home and move into less expensive housing.

  In any case, you should realize that even a 4% withdrawal rate is greater than the current yields from stock dividends and high-quality bond interest. To draw down your portfolio in line with the 4% rule, you probably will have to sell some assets. Ask your wealth advisor to help you develop a plan for liquidating your portfolio assets.

- **Ed Slott's advice:** The main takeaway here is to make sure you have an idea about what size retirement fund you'll need to support your lifestyle. If you would like to withdraw $40,000 a year in your retirement, adjusted for inflation, you'd need a $1 million portfolio, using the 4% Rule. Increased saving may be the only way you can accumulate the desired amount by your retirement target date. Similarly, if you are already in retirement, the 4% rule can help you determine whether or not you may need to adjust your lifestyle in order to avoid running out of money.

75. When to take Social Security

Consider waiting until age 70 to receive Social Security checks. Your monthly payments will be higher than if you began at age 62 or 66, and over a long life the total payout will also be higher. But it is a complex decision, involving other assets, income taxes and estate plans, so it is best discussed with a financial advisor.

76. How to trim wasteful spending

Budgeting is hard for most people—particularly if you don't have a head for numbers or aren't highly organized. Spending is easy when you're younger and employed, because you have income coming in each month. But in retirement, watching where your dollars go is essential. The goal is to make your savings last.

- **Ed Slott's advice:** Make a list of your three types of monthly expenses —*fixed costs* such as utilities; *flexible expenses* such as food and gasoline; and *discretionary expenses* such as entertainment and travel. Get your monthly bills and jot down what you paid. Then add up the monthly total and multiply it by 12 for your estimated annual expenses. Don't forget to include insurance premiums, taxes and any other periodic expenses. Look for ways to reduce costs by saving money on flexible expenses and cutting back on discretionary expenses.

77. Keep savings safe and sound

We know that anything can happen to the economy—and at any time. The key, clearly, is not to be exposed to excessive risk when you need to preserve your retirement savings.

- **Ed Slott's advice:** Make sure your IRA and other savings accounts are properly allocated for your age and tolerance for risk. In retirement, your biggest risk is defined as running out of money.

78. When to take IRA withdrawals

If you're a retiree who's at least age 59 ½ and unsure whether to withdraw assets from your IRA, talk first with your financial advisor and accountant. Ideally, you want to take withdrawals from taxable accounts first before turning to an IRA. That's because the longer you leave assets in an IRA, the longer they can compound tax-free.

- **Ed Slott's advice:** When you withdraw assets from a Traditional IRA, calculate your tax hit immediately and set aside the cash. Too many people withdraw assets and spend it all. Then when tax time arrives, they don't have the money to pay Uncle Sam.

Avoid early withdrawal penalties

Your IRA is meant to provide retirement income, so there is generally a 10% early withdrawal penalty before you reach age 59 ½. That penalty is added to your regular income tax.

Suppose that Greg, age 52, pulls $10,000 from his IRA. If he is in a 22% tax bracket, he will owe $2,200 (22% of $10,000) in tax. He'll also owe a $1,000 penalty (10% of $10,000), so his effective tax rate on early withdrawals will be 32%.

- **Out of the penalty box.** Fortunately, there are several exceptions to the early withdrawal penalty. If Greg qualifies, he'll owe the $2,200 regular tax but not the $1,000 penalty.

Among several exceptions to the penalty, consider these:

- **Deductible medical expenses.** Suppose that Greg's adjusted gross income (AGI) is $60,000 this year and his unreimbursed medical expenses are $7,500. Greg will generally be entitled to deduct medical costs over 10% (this rate applies for 2019) of his AGI: $7,500-$6,000 = $1,500. Thus, $1,500 of Greg's $10,000 IRA withdrawal will escape the 10% penalty. This exception applies even if Greg does not itemize deductions on this year's tax return.

- **Health insurance.** Say Greg has lost his job this year and collected unemployment for at least 12 consecutive weeks. He paid a total of $4,800 for family coverage during the year. Greg can withdraw up to $4,800 from his IRA, penalty free.

- **College bills.** In another scenario, Greg pays $5,000 towards his son's college education this year as well as $2,000 so he can take a night school course towards his MBA. If so, he can take up to $7,000 from his IRA this year without owing the 10% penalty.

- **First home.** Greg also can take up to $10,000 from his IRA, penalty-free, to help pay for a first-time home purchase. The money might be used to help Greg's daughter buy her first home or for a home purchase by Greg himself, after going more than two years without owning a home. Note the last part of that sentence. "First-time homebuyer" doesn't have to mean first home, but the $10,000 number is a lifetime cap, not one you can utilize in totality for another home purchase five years down the road.

- **Disability.** If Greg becomes disabled and can't work, IRA distributions escape the 10% penalty.

- **Annuity.** Regardless of whether you are buying a first home or paying college bills or otherwise qualify for an exception, you can avoid the 10% early withdrawal penalty by taking a series of substantially equal periodic payments (SOSEPPs) from your IRA over your life expectancy.

- **Ed Slott's advice:** The SOSEPP rules are included in Section 72(t) of the tax code. By going to an Internet search engine, you can find many 72(t) calculators.

Suppose that Greg goes to an Internet 72(t) calculator and finds an approved method that permits him to withdraw $9,953 a year, penalty-free, from his $300,000 IRA. Greg takes that amount from his IRA and begins a SOSEPP.

A SOSEPP for this purpose must last five years or until age 59 ½, whichever comes later. Thus, Greg—now age 52—must take exactly $9,953 from his IRA each year until he reaches 59 ½. Any departure from this path will result in the 10% penalty being imposed on all of Greg's pre-59 ½ IRA withdrawals, plus interest. Work with your IRA custodian to set up your SOSEPP withdrawals.

79. Retiree tax breaks in 2019

Retirees get breaks on airlines and movie tickets. They also get breaks from the tax code:

- **Capital gains.** If you're in the lower tax brackets, long-term capital gains in 2019 are not taxed. However, don't get too comfortable with these numbers. While they're currently valid, they may change soon.

  As always, go to my website **irahelp.com** to find out the latest on this and any other major tax rule changes that could affect your retirement savings.

- **Real estate sales.** If you want to sell your home to relocate to a smaller one and you've owned your home for 20 or 30 years, your gain on the sale may exceed the tax exclusions of $500,000 for a couple or $250,000 for a single filer. To avoid capital gains taxes, you need to have big carry-forward losses from last year or sell portfolio losers to offset the gains on the home sale.

- **Reduce your estate.** If you have sizable assets that comfortably exceed what you'll need in retirement, consider making gifts to reduce your taxable estates (visit **irahelp.com/2019** for the latest maximum levels). You also can pay education expenses for grandchildren gift-tax free, provided your check is made out to the school. Or you can contribute to a 529 Education Savings Plan. Beginning in 2018, 529 accounts can be used to pay for K-12 education expenses.

80. Convert an IRA in retirement?

Much depends on your tax bracket in retirement and whether you have cash on hand to pay the income-tax bill. Starting in 2010, the IRS allowed all taxpayers to convert part or all of a Traditional IRA, a 401(k) or other company plan to a tax-free Roth IRA—regardless of household income! The catch? You have to pay income tax on the fair-market value of the account at the time of conversion. Which means you need the cash to do this.

- **Ed Slott's advice:** Many retirees live longer than expected, making a partial or full conversion extremely tax efficient. That's because the account is likely to grow over time and then pass to heirs tax-free—provided you have had a Roth IRA for five years. Also likely: Your current tax bracket may be higher in the future.

81. Convert an IRA for inheritance?

If you plan to pass your IRA to your children, converting part or all of your Traditional IRA to a Roth IRA likely makes sense. By converting, you will not have to take mandatory distributions starting at age 70 ½. Also, your children will not owe federal income tax on the Roth IRA they inherit provided you have had a Roth IRA for five years. If you're over age 59 ½, you can use the Traditional IRA assets to pay the tax without facing an early-withdrawal penalty. Better yet, pay the tax with other assets.

- **Ed Slott's advice:** If your goal is to pass any IRA to your children, be sure they are named on the IRA's beneficiary form.

82. Beware this IRA conversion trap

If you are age 70 ½ or older and you're already taking required minimum distributions (RMDs) from a Traditional IRA, you cannot dodge the annual RMD by converting the IRA to a Roth IRA. Rule: You must first take the required minimum distribution for the year and then convert the remaining Traditional IRA to a Roth IRA.

83. Know the IRA withdrawal rules

Starting at age 70 ½, you are required to begin taking distributions from a Traditional IRA. But how much do you have to take? That depends how you stack up on the IRS' life-expectancy tables. Each year's required minimum distribution is determined by dividing your IRA balance by the number of years the IRS expects you to be around.

- **Doing the math:** Check the IRS life-expectancy table at **irahelp.com/2019**. To calculate your 2019 RMD, find your age. Then divide the value of your IRA at the end of last year by the corresponding "distribution period." Or ask your accountant.

84. Watch out for retiree scams

Retirees are prime candidates for a wide range of financial scams and schemes. Beware of the following:

- **New advisors**—Always vet a new financial advisor, CPA or lawyer with care by running a background check on their credentials, education and any liens and legal actions pending.

- **Hot tips**—It's very easy to fall prey to advice from friends who claim to have done well with a particular investment. Resist the temptation to get in on the action. In most cases, such ventures may not be right for you and could wind up in disaster.

- **Phone pitches**—Don't be suckered by phone calls from people claiming to represent organizations and asking for personal information. The simple solution is to just hang up.

- **Door sales**—Steer clear of people who show up unannounced with low-cost offers to fix something on your house they've spotted from the street.

- **Social calls**—Beware of pitches from people who use the environment, animals, diseases or other heart-tuggers to hold your attention. Before donating to any charity, check on the charity's existence and make the donation directly through instructions on its website.

- **Pal of a pal**—Watch out for pitches by strangers who claim to be friends of your friends. This is one of the most effective ways to get victims to let down their guard.

- **Fishy e-mails**—Beware of e-mails from banks and financial institutions claiming there's a problem with your account. A real institution would not ask for personal information. To verify your account, never click on the link provided. Always go to your institution's website and access your account that way. Or call the number provided by the institution.

- **Going fast**—Avoid financial pitches that stress there's little time left, or there are only a few opportunities left for those who invest immediately.

- **New friends**—Sophisticated scammers befriend people and spend time developing trusting relationships before pitching a fraudulent deal.

- **Snail Mail**— IRS will always contact you by mail. Beware of e-mails or phone calls that say they are from IRS, especially if they make threats.

ED SLOTT'S
ELITE
IRA
ADVISOR
GROUP™
Find an advisor
at **irahelp.com**

85. Run a feud-free family meeting

Unless there's a reason why your children should not know about your finances, a family meeting with your financial advisor is a wise move—especially in retirement.

- **Ed Slott's advice:** Having your financial advisor present and officiating the meeting will keep the summit from sliding into personal issues or being used to settle old scores. By including your advisor, your children will receive a financial education, letting them become more confident managers of their finances and the advisors who are working for you.

86. Secrets of healthy family meetings

When you hold a family meeting with your financial advisor, draft questions and concerns in advance. Your children should know how to contact your life insurance representative, financial planners, accountants, and attorneys. In the meeting, note how the advisors respond to your children. This is a good indicator as to how helpful these advisors will be to your children in the future.

Chapter 6:
Social Security And Medicare

87. What Uncle Sam has to offer

Don't neglect Social Security and Medicare in your retirement planning. The former is a pension from the federal government. You've paid for it throughout your working years so you can collect in retirement. Married couples can generally get two Social Security checks each month.

Medicare is health insurance for seniors, subsidized by Uncle Sam himself. This program is not "Obamacare," as some people call the health insurance law now in effect. Again, you've paid into Medicare as long as you've been working, and a married couple usually gets coverage for both spouses.

- **Ed Slott's advice:** It's true that both Social Security and Medicare are currently expected to run short of money over the long run. However, tens of millions of American seniors are covered by these programs. Politicians in Washington will continue to tinker with their frameworks, but it's doubtful that benefits will be cut sharply. You can count on some form of Social Security and Medicare to be around when you retire.

Know Your Full Retirement Age (FRA)

When it comes to planning for many Social Security benefits, there's one factor that's more important than just about everything else: your full retirement age (FRA). Many of the benefits you may be eligible for are calculated based on how long before or after your FRA they are received. Plus, there are some more advanced Social Security claiming strategies that can only be used at your FRA or later.

Your FRA has nothing to do with when you actually retire, but rather, it is determined solely by when you were born. So whether you retire at 50 (lucky you!) or you work until 85 (good for you!), your full retirement age is unaffected. Depending upon the year of your birth, your full retirement age may be anywhere from 65 – 67 (although if your FRA is under 66 you should already be claiming any Social Security benefits you're entitled to).

Use this chart to determine your FRA:

Full Retirement Age (FRA)

Year of Birth*	Full Retirement Age
1937 or earlier	65
1938	65 and 2 months
1939	65 and 4 months
1940	65 and 6 months
1941	65 and 8 months
1942	65 and 10 months
1943 - 1954	66
1955	66 and 2 months
1956	66 and 4 months
1957	66 and 6 months
1958	66 and 8 months
1959	66 and 10 months
1960 and later	67

*If you were born on January 1 of any year, you should refer to the previous year. If you were born on the 1st of the month, your benefit—and your full retirement age—is figured as if your birthday was in the previous month.

88. Working and Social Security may not mix

You can start collecting Social Security retirement benefits as early as age 62, but there's a penalty for starting before your full retirement age. If you receive benefits during a year you are younger than your full retirement age for the entire year and you have more than $17,640 a year for 2019 of earned income, then you'll have $1 of Social Security benefits deducted for every $2 of earned income you have over the limit. If you receive benefits during the year you reach full retirement age and have more than $46,920 for 2019 of earned income, then you'll have $1 of Social Security benefits deducted for every $3 of earned income you have over the limit. This only applies to earned income up to the month before your full retirement age. Any deducted benefits will be credited to your account and added back to your Social Security checks AFTER you stop earning more than the limit or reach full retirement age.

- **Ed Slott's advice:** If you're still working before your normal retirement age, it usually doesn't pay to start Social Security. What's more, the younger you are when you start to take benefits the smaller your Social Security checks will be going forward. Married individuals who start before their normal retirement age may lose the chance to use some sophisticated tactics to maximize a couple's combined income from Social Security.

89. When sooner beats later

If you have stopped working, should you start Social Security at age 62, or soon thereafter? Maybe. It might make sense for one or both of these reasons.

- **You need the money.** With little or no earned income and a shortage of other resources, you might have to start Social Security for cash to pay your bills.

- **Your health isn't great.** By age 62, you might have developed a serious medical condition. Taking the money as soon as possible can make sense, especially if you are single.

If you don't have an immediate need for the money and you're healthy enough to anticipate a long retirement, waiting will increase the size of the Social Security checks you'll eventually receive. Long-term, you may come out ahead. Waiting may work especially well if you're married, and you have earned much more than your spouse over your career.

90. Social Security's 8% solution

If you don't start Social Security at age 62, you can start any time after that. The waiting game ends at age 70, though. There's no point in waiting longer because your Social Security benefits won't increase any more moving forward.

- **Why you should wait.** From age 62 to age 70, your monthly check goes up every month that you practice patience. When all the numbers are crunched, the annual increase is about 8% a year. That's 8% a year, guaranteed by the federal government, with no investment risk. Compare that with what you're getting now from your bank or your money market fund. It's a pretty good deal.

  What's more, that's 8% a year plus any cost-of-living boost. If inflation is, say, 3%, your total annual increase for waiting would be 11% that year.

  To give you an idea of the difference, suppose Al retired at his normal retirement age (66) in 2019. Assuming Al had paid the maximum in Social Security taxes over his career, his monthly Social Security benefit would have been $2,788, or $33,456 a year. But if you make the same assumption about Carol, who retired at age 70 in 2019, her monthly benefit would have been $3,680 a month, or $44,160 per year – and that's not even counting any cost-of-living adjustments!

91. Waiting = longevity insurance

Some people approach the start-versus-wait decision by looking at the break-even calculation. You might say, how long will I have to live for the amounts added to my monthly checks to catch up with the money I didn't receive while I waited? That's one way to make the decision.

Another way is to look at waiting as a means of buying "longevity insurance"—protection against running short of money in very old age. Today, many people are living into their late 80s, their 90s, and even hitting triple figures. That means 25+ years of retirement in many cases, and a real risk of emptying an investment portfolio. At that point, you'll really appreciate receiving a plumper Social Security check.

- **Ed Slott's advice:** The higher-earning spouse should generally wait to receive Social Security if that's practical. When one spouse dies, the survivor will continue to receive the larger of the two spouses' Social Security checks.

Coordinate with your spouse

If you are married, coordinating your own Social Security benefits with those of your spouse is an essential part of making sure you're maximizing the value of the Social Security benefits to which you're entitled. By coordinating your Social Security benefits with your spouse's benefits, you can help maximize income during both of your lifetimes, as well as for the survivor after one of you passes away. For a long time, the file-and suspend and restricted application strategies were two of the most common used by spouses to maximize Social Security benefits. Congress, however, passed a law in late 2015 eliminating these as potential strategies for many Boomers.

- **File and suspend –** Allows you to file for your Social Security benefits, but delay actually receiving those benefits. By doing so, your spouse may be able to claim a spousal benefit on your earnings history (which can only be done if you've filed). However, since you tell the Social Security Administration not to send you your own Social Security benefits, it allows them to continue to earn delayed credits.

  Warning! – You can only file and suspend once you've reached full retirement age or later. Additionally, this strategy is no longer viable for those requesting a suspension of their benefits as of April 2016. As a result of the law Congress passed in late 2015, after that time, your spouse will only be able to collect a spousal benefit if you are receiving your own benefit.

- **File a restricted application –** If your spouse has already filed for their own Social Security benefit or plans to do so, you can file what's known as a restricted application to tell the Social Security Administration to pay you only your spousal benefit. Your own benefit will be unaffected and can continue to earn delayed credits.

- **Warning! –** You can only file a restricted application once you've reached full retirement age or later. In addition, this strategy will no longer be viable for those individuals who turned 62 after January 1, 2016. As a result of the law Congress passed in late 2015, after that time if you file for your spousal benefit, you will also be deemed to be filing for your own benefit. Thus, you would no longer receive any delayed credits if your benefit is more than your spousal benefit.

92. IRAs can play a role in your Social Security decision

As you can see, waiting to start Social Security as late as possible, up to age 70, may pay off. But what if you need more cash flow while you're in your 60s? One approach is to tap your IRA then.

- **Conventional wisdom:** Many financial and tax advisors advocate delaying IRA distributions as long as possible. Required minimum distributions (RMDs) don't start until age 70 ½. The longer you continue tax-deferred buildup inside an IRA, the more wealth you can accumulate.

- **Ed Slott's unconventional advice:** Tapping your IRA during your 60s may be worthwhile if this tactic allows you to defer Social Security. Tax deferral inside an IRA is a real benefit, but this benefit is most valuable when you're in a high tax bracket and owe a substantial amount of income tax.

If you're in your 60s, in need of more cash flow, chances are that you have modest income and a small tax bill. Thus, IRA distributions won't be extremely taxing. Of course, once you're in your 60s, you're beyond the 10% early distribution penalty, which applies to those under age 59 ½.

93. A savvy sequence can slash your 70-something taxes

If you follow the traditional approach (start Social Security in your 60s, begin IRA withdrawals in your 70s), you probably will increase the income tax on your Social Security benefits. Reversing the procedure—drawing down your IRA so Social Security is delayed—can be a tax-saver

Why? A full explanation would involve delving into one of the most arcane provisions of the tax code, which is saying a lot. Here's the simple version:

- **When you collect Social Security,** some or most of your benefits may be taxed.

- **This tax is determined by a formula.** The formula counts almost all of your income, including IRA withdrawals, but only half of your Social Security benefits.

- **By delaying Social Security,** you'll get a larger check each month. The larger your monthly check of half-counted benefits, the less you'll have to tap your fully-counted IRA for spending money.

- **Doing the math,** accelerating fully countable IRA dollars while delaying half-countable Social Security dollars can mean a smaller tax bill once you start collecting your heftier Social Security checks.

94. Crowding out the tax collector

Under current law, IRA distributions are fully taxed. If you withdraw $10,000 from your IRA, you add $10,000 to your taxable income for the year.

On the other hand, no more than 85% of your Social Security benefits are taxed under current law. If you receive $10,000 from Social Security, no more than $8,500 will be added to your taxable income for the year. Many seniors include less than 85% of their benefits in taxable income because they have moderate income, and some report no taxable benefits at all.

- **Ed Slott's advice:** Any strategy that substitutes Social Security benefits for IRA withdrawals will be a tax-saver. If overall income tax rates rise in the future, as many people expect, this form of retirement income arbitrage will become even more tax-efficient.

95. Make a good idea even better with Roth accounts

As already mentioned, while $1 of IRA withdrawals counts as $1 for determining the taxation of your Social Security benefits, $1 of Social Security benefits only counts as 50 cents. So it pays to load up on Social Security income and reduce taxable IRA distributions.

What's more, withdrawals from Roth IRAs and Roth 401(k)s are best of all: qualified Roth distributions aren't taxable income and they don't count at all on the formula for taxing your Social Security checks.

Say Carl and Donna have $50,000 of Roth IRA distributions a year plus $40,000 from Social Security benefits and no other income. This couple, with no other income, would owe no tax on their Social Security benefits under the formula. Roth IRA distributions are tax-free for taxpayers who are at least age 59 ½ and have held the accounts at least five years.

- **Ed Slott's advice:** Contributing to a Roth 401(k) is one way to get money into tax-free territory while you work. Once you retire, and your tax bracket drops, you can take money from taxable investment accounts to pay the tax on converting Traditional IRA dollars to Roth IRA dollars.

96. Four for the money

Once you stop working, chances are you'll have four possible sources of income.

- **Taxable accounts.** This is money you have in banks, at brokers, or directly in mutual funds. These accounts have a variety of tax treatments. You may receive investment interest and dividends for spending money; you also can sell assets or take withdrawals to raise cash.

- **Tax-deferred accounts.** These include Traditional IRAs, SEP IRAs, and SIMPLE IRAs. You also may have money you kept in an employer plan such as a 401(k) or a pension. For these accounts, withdrawals typically are fully or mostly taxable.

- **Tax-free accounts.** Roth IRAs and Roth-type employer plans such as Roth 401(k)s offer tax-free withdrawals. Typically, distributions are completely tax-free after five years and after age 59 ½.

- **Social Security.** This is a federal life-long pension for workers and their spouses. Depending on the amount and type of your other income, Social Security benefits are tax-free or partially taxable.

- **Ed Slott's advice:** You'll have more spendable income in retirement if you plan to coordinate these sources of future income. The younger you are when you start to plan, the more cash flow you're likely to enjoy.

97. Ed Slott's retirement income plan

After you stop working, you'll need cash for living expenses. Here's a simplified suggested sequence. In realty, some combination of withdrawals across different types of accounts often produces the most tax-efficient results:

1. **Start with your taxable accounts.** In these low-yield times, investment interest and dividends alone probably won't pay your bills. You'll need to take withdrawals and sell assets. Fortunately, taxes on these transactions are likely to be scant.

2. **Move money from tax-deferred accounts such as Traditional IRAs and 401(k)s to your Roth IRA.** Again, these will be taxable transactions, but you probably won't owe much in tax if you're not working or you are in a lower tax bracket. Pay any tax from your taxable accounts.

3. **Draw down your tax-deferred accounts** once you've depleted your taxable accounts. Either use the money for spending or move dollars into your Roth IRA.

4. **Try to wait until age 70 to start Social Security benefits.** Among married couples, it sometimes makes sense for one spouse to start at full retirement age (66-67) while the other delays until 70. Dual-earner married couples who are 66 or older have the option to collect spousal payments worth half of the higher earner's benefit amount, and then later switch to payments based on their own, which would then be higher due to delayed claiming. However, people who turned 62 on January 2, 2016 or later are no longer able to claim a spousal benefit first and then later switch to a retirement benefit. Married retirees will now automatically receive the higher of the two benefit options and can no longer claim both types of payments at different times.

- **Bottom line:** The ideal endgame is to go into your 70s with maximum Social Security benefits and all of your savings in Roth accounts. Your Social Security benefits will be untaxed or lightly taxed, under current law, and Roth distributions won't be taxed. Roth IRAs have no RMDs so money you don't need can pass to your beneficiaries, for ongoing tax-free accumulation and distribution.

98. Learn the A-B-C-Ds of Medicare

Generally, Medicare is a great cost-saver. Workers and spouses typically qualify at age 65. Assuming you're not covered by an employer's health plan or by a former employer's retiree health benefits, you should sign up because Medicare offers cost-effective health insurance. There are two main components:

- **Part A.** This covers hospital bills after you pay a deductible of around $1,364 in 2019. For most seniors, there is no monthly charge for Part A.

- **Part B.** This covers doctors' visits and other medical expenses such as lab tests. The Standard Part B Premium is $135.50.

- **Ed Slott's advice:** Don't think that Medicare covers all medical costs: it doesn't. You'll still have various out-of-pocket expenses for your health care, and they can be meaningful. Many people buy supplemental "Medigap" policies from private insurers to limit their exposure to medical bills and "Part D" policies to help pay for prescription drugs.

Alternatively, you can join "Medicare Part C," also known as Medicare Advantage, and sign up for comprehensive health coverage through a private company. You won't need a Medigap policy then and you probably won't need a Part D plan, either. Out-of-pocket costs will be limited. The catch, though, is that you'll have to go to certain doctors and hospitals to get the cost savings.

The Medicare website, **medicare.gov,** has a find-a-plan feature to help you decide if you want a Medicare Advantage plan and, if so, which one.

99. Beware of Medicare Part B Premiums

As mentioned, most Medicare enrollees pay about $135.50 per month for Part B medical coverage. Seniors with higher incomes pay more. The amount depends on your modified adjusted gross income (MAGI). For this purpose, your MAGI is your regular adjusted gross income, plus any (supposedly) tax-exempt interest from municipal bonds or bond funds. Generally speaking, Medicare Part B premiums are based off of your tax return from two years prior. So, for instance, your 2019 Medicare Part B premiums will generally be based on your 2017 income.

In 2019, the standard Part B premium is $135.50 (or higher).

Here are the MAGI numbers for 2017 (for your 2019 premiums).

File individual tax return	File joint tax return	File married & Separate tax return	Monthly premium
$85,000 or less	$170,000 or less	$85,000 or less	$135.50
Above $85,000 up to $107,00	Above $170,000 up to $214,000	N/A	$189.60
Above $107,000 up to $133,500	Above $214,000 up to $267,000	N/A	$270.90
Above $133,500 up to $160,000	Above $267,000 up to $320,000	N/A	$352.20
up to $500,000	up to $750,000	up to $415,000	$433.40
Above $500,000	Above $750,000	Above $415,000	$460.50

Source: medicare.gov

Those Part B premium numbers are per Medicare enrollee. Thus, if a married couple includes two seniors on Medicare, with MAGI over $320,000, but less than $750,000, each spouse would owe $433.40 per month for Medicare Part B. That would be a total of $866.80 per month or almost $10,400 per year for health insurance.

100. Paring Part B premiums

Some planning can hold down your Medicare Part B premiums. The key is to realize that there is a two-year gap between actually receiving that high income and paying the super-premium for medical insurance. Consequently, since you may be eligible for Medicare at age 65, your reported income for every year starting at age 63 may determine your Part B premium. The earlier you start to plan, the better.

- **Ed Slott's advice:** A series of Roth IRA conversions can help you control your Part B premium. Any Roth IRA conversion after 2017 is irrevocable.

101. Appealing excessive Medicare premiums

As you can see, there's a time lag in imposing higher Part B premiums. What if you were working at age 63 or 64, earning a substantial amount, but retired by 65 or 66, with a much lower income? Can you ask for relief from the steep premium payments?

Yes, in some cases. If your income has gone down due to certain specific situations, you can ask for a lower premium. Those situations include:

1. You married, divorced, or became widowed.

2. You or your spouse stopped working or reduced your work hours.

3. You or your spouse lost income-producing property due to a disaster or other event beyond your control.

To support your claim, be ready to produce documentation, such as a death certificate or a letter from your former employer about your retirement.

102. Don't ignore the "health care IRA"

Before you reach Medicare age, you may be able to open a Health Savings Account (HSA). If so, an HSA can provide exceptional retirement planning opportunities, acting as an IRA for health care. HSAs can be extremely beneficial because they offer triple tax savings:

- **Tax-deductible contributions.**
- **Tax-free buildup** inside the HSA.
- **Tax-free distributions** for qualified health care expenses.

In order to have an HSA, you must have a qualified health insurance policy. Such policies have high deductibles, so you'll have low insurance premiums but ample out-of-pocket exposure before the insurance kicks in. With acceptable health insurance, you can contribute to an HSA—depending on your age and the coverage you have, deductible contributions could reach $8,000 for 2019.

If you wish, you can tap your HSA to pay medical costs right away. There are no time limits on withdrawals, though, so you can keep your HSA intact, growing untaxed, and use it for a tax-free source of cash to pay medical bills in retirement, including prescription drugs and qualified long-term care services.

- **Ed Slott's advice:** Some observers believe that HSA contributions should be Step Two in your retirement planning each year, right after making 401(k) contributions that your employer will match. The triple tax benefits of HSAs are cited to support such assertions. That strategy may or may not be best for you, depending on your personal circumstances, but it is true that you'll probably incur significant health care expenses after you reach age 65. Being able to pay those costs with pre-tax money would be a significant benefit.

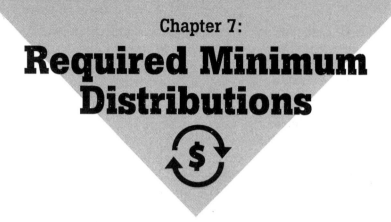

Chapter 7:
Required Minimum Distributions

103. Taking money from Traditional IRAs

When you have a Traditional IRA, there are two key milestones to keep in mind.

- **Age 59 ½.** Before then, you'll usually owe a 10% penalty on distributions, in addition to regular income tax. Some exceptions to this penalty apply, such as withdrawals for deductible medical expenses. Other retirement plans, such as 401(k)s, also incur this 10% surtax on early withdrawals, but the rules and the exceptions are not exactly the same as the IRA rules.

- **Age 70 ½.** Now you must take required minimum distributions (RMDs) from your Traditional IRA and, usually, from other retirement plans as well. However, if you are still working and own 5% or less of the company, you don't have to take RMDs from your current employer's retirement plan at that time, if the plan allows this. Additionally, if you own any qualifying longevity annuity contracts (QLACs) - a special type of retirement account annuity - you can delay RMDs until as late as the first day of the month after you turn 85. QLAC values are excluded for "regular" RMD calculations.

What's more, if you have put money into a Roth IRA, you never have to take RMDs from that account, at any age.

- **Ed Slott's advice:** If you need the money, you can withdraw more than your RMD amount—it's a required *minimum* distribution. You can also take distributions from your IRAs at any age, but try to wait until you are at least 59 ½ to avoid the 10% penalty. If you must tap your IRA even earlier, ask your tax pro if there's a penalty exception you can use.

104. Time your RMDs correctly

You're usually required to take RMDs once you reach age 70 ½, but that doesn't mean you must start exactly six months after your 70th birthday. Technically, the deadline is April 1 of the year after the year you reach that magic age. The tax code manages the feat of turning one day into over a year!

Suppose Betty was born on June 30, 1949, so she will be age 70 ½ on December 30, 2019. Betty must start RMDs from her IRA by April 1 of 2020, the following year.

Also suppose that Betty's neighbor Carol was born on July 1, 1949, so she won't be age 70 ½ until January 1, 2020. In this scenario, Carol doesn't have to start RMDs until April 1, 2021. Because of one day's (maybe only a few hours') difference in when they were born, Carol can wait a full year later to start taking RMDs.

Subsequent RMDs are due the following December 31, and every December 31 after that. Betty, in our example, must take her first RMD by April 1, 2020, and her second RMD by December 31, 2020, less than nine months later. From then on, she must take her RMD by every December 31, as long as there is money in her IRA.

Carol starts a year later than Betty, but Carol will be on a similar schedule for RMD deadlines.

- **Ed Slott's advice:** You may not want to wait until April 1 to take your first RMD. If you do, you'll have two RMDs in the year you begin, and that "doubling up" might push you into a higher tax bracket.

In the Betty example, she can take her first RMD in 2019, rather than wait until April 1, 2020. That will give her one taxable RMD per year and may allow her to stay in a lower tax bracket.

105. Calculate your RMD

The amount of your RMD generally depends on two things: your age and the amount in your IRA. Here's how you typically calculate it:

1. Look up the IRS Uniform Lifetime Table. You can find it at **irahelp.com/2019.**

2. Find your age as of December 31 of the year for which the RMD is due.

3. Find your life expectancy (in years).

4. Divide your life expectancy into your prior year-end account balance to find your RMD for the year.

In the example above, Betty reached age 70 ½ at the end of 2019 so she must take her first RMD by April 1, 2020. That's her RMD for 2019, the year in which she had her 70th birthday. Thus, her first RMD will be determined by age 70 on this IRS table.

On the Uniform Lifetime Table, at age 70 an IRA participant has a life expectancy of 27.4 years. If Betty had $100,000 in her IRA on December 31, 2018, she would divide $100,000 by 27.4 to get $3,650: that's the RMD Betty must take by April 1, 2020.

106. Be leery of illiquid assets

Many investors have turned away from stocks (volatile) and bonds (low-yielding) in recent years. They might look for alternatives to hold in their IRAs, and IRS regulations permit many types of IRA investments, from real estate to private businesses.

- **The catch:** Stocks and bonds and other traded securities are easy to value for the purpose of determining RMDs. You simply look at the traded prices on December 31 of each relevant year.

That's not always the case with illiquid assets, such as the medical office building bought inside your IRA. Nevertheless, the IRS requires the IRA custodian to put a value on all IRA assets and RMDs must be calculated based on that value, after age 70 ½. The cost of a valuation is paid by the IRA.

If the set value is too high, you'll withdraw too much from your IRA, pay too much in tax, and sacrifice untaxed wealth accumulation inside the account. However, if the set value is too low, you'll under-withdraw and take insufficient RMDs. This will expose you to a steep penalty, as explained below.

- **Ed Slott's advice:** If it's practical, consider eliminating hard-to-value assets from your IRA before age 70 ½, so RMD valuation won't be an issue. Otherwise, consult with a tax pro to work out a valuation plan that will pass muster with the IRS.

107. Take your RMD—*or else!*

The R in RMD stands for Required, and the cost of ignoring this requirement is steep. Any shortfall is subject to a 50% penalty!

Suppose Betty has an initial $3,650 RMD, as illustrated prior. If she takes only $3,000 from her IRA by the deadline, Betty will be $650 below the minimum so she'll owe a $325 penalty: 50% of $650. If Betty takes no RMD at all, the penalty will be 50% of the entire $3,650 RMD, or $1,825.

Moreover, those are the penalty amounts. Betty is still required to take her missed RMD, and report the taxable income from her IRA distribution in the year in which she takes the distribution.

108. Let your custodian do the counting?

As you can imagine, determining your RMD can involve a substantial amount of number crunching. Any mistake might generate a too-small RMD and a 50% fine for any insufficient distribution.

IRA custodians are required to send out letters to IRA owners early each year, calculating their RMD for the year or offering to do so. However, using the number provided by the IRA custodian could be a mistake. The custodian will generally only use the date of birth they have on file for you and the Uniform Lifetime Table to calculate your RMD. If your spouse is more than 10 years younger or if your date of birth is wrong, the calculation they do for you will be wrong. It never hurts to double check their math. After all, look where their math got them during the housing crisis!

- **Ed Slott's advice:** If you expect to use your RMD for spending money during the year, arrange with your custodian for monthly transfers from your IRA directly into your checking account. If that's not the case, waiting until year-end to take your annual RMD in a lump-sum will extend the time for potential tax-deferred buildup inside your IRA.

You should be aware that IRA custodians report to the IRS, too, so the tax collectors know who must withdraw from their IRAs. IRS may soon step up efforts to catch taxpayers who neglect this requirement to move money from one pocket to another.

ED SLOTT'S
ELITE
IRA
ADVISOR
GROUP
Find an advis
at **irahelp.co**

109. Mix and match IRA RMDs

Many people have more than one IRA. If so, you must calculate the RMD for each IRA to come up with your total RMD. Then you can take that RMD from any or all of your IRAs.

For example, suppose Art has one large IRA, another with $8,000 and yet another with $5,000. By adding up the RMDs from all three accounts, Art determines that he must take a total of $20,000 in RMDs this year.

Art decides to empty the two small IRAs, for a combined distribution of $13,000. Now, if he takes $7,000 from his large IRA, Art will have met his RMD for the year. Going forward, Art won't have to deal with paperwork from his two small IRAs; he will have only the large account, from which he will take all future RMDs.

If you have a SEP IRA or a SIMPLE IRA, you include that account among your IRAs when aggregating RMDs. However, you can't include inherited

IRAs in that calculation—they need separate RMDs (more about inherited IRAs below). And you can't combine IRAs with employer plans for aggregating RMDs.

- **Ed Slott's advice:** Unless you have a special reason to keep multiple IRAs, consider consolidating them when you reach the RMD stage, or drawing down any small accounts. This will make your life simpler in your 70s and later years.

110. Don't take your spouse's RMD

Among married couples, both spouses may have their own IRAs. Thus, when both spouses are older than 70 ½, they'll both have RMDs. Such couples should avoid a common error: taking all the RMDs from one spouse's IRA or IRAs.

Suppose that Grace has one IRA while her husband Joe has many IRAs, spread around several mutual fund companies. This year, Grace's RMD from her IRA is $18,000 while Joe's RMD total from all of his IRAs is $14,000.

Joe wants to take the $32,000 total RMD from his collection of IRAs, which will enable him to close out some IRAs and simplify his recordkeeping. After all, Joe reasons, the $32,000 of taxable IRA distributions will be reported on their joint tax return, so the couple will pay the proper amount of tax.

No harm, no foul….and no 50% penalty, Joe believes.

However, Joe is wrong. His reasoning will draw a yellow flag from the refs.

- **Ed Slott's advice:** The "I" in IRA stands for Individual. Each IRA owner should take RMDs from his or her own accounts. If not, the penalty will apply.

In the example above, Joe will have a $32,000 taxable distribution, drawing down his IRAs. Grace will have an $18,000 shortfall, and a 50% penalty ($9,000) for not taking her RMD. IRA beneficiaries also have RMDs, and aggregation rules to follow, as explained below.

111. IRA beneficiaries have RMDs, too

As explained previously, IRA beneficiaries have certain rules to follow. In simplest terms:

- **Any IRA beneficiary** can withdraw all of the money from the account, and pay any resulting income tax. (Roth IRA beneficiaries often won't owe income tax.)

- **A surviving spouse who is an IRA beneficiary** can roll the IRA to his or her name. From there, the RMD rules apply as they apply to any IRA owner, starting at age 70 ½.

- **All non-spouse IRA beneficiaries** not covered in the two points mentioned above are subject to RMD rules, even Roth IRA beneficiaries receiving tax-free distributions. Any RMD shortfall will trigger the 50% penalty.

- **Ed Slott's advice:** For maximum tax deferral through RMDs, IRA beneficiaries (other than surviving spouses rolling over the account to their own name) should retitle the account to an inherited IRA. Typically, IRA custodians will have a preference as to the form of an inherited IRA's title. RMDs for named or designated non-spouse beneficiaries should begin by December 31 of the year after the IRA owner's death.

112. IRA beneficiaries have their own RMD table

To take RMDs from an inherited IRA, you'll use yet another IRS table found at **irahelp.com/2019:** the Single Life Expectancy Table. Generally, beneficiaries look up their age in the year following the IRA owner's death. Young beneficiaries may enjoy tremendous wealth building over many decades of tax deferral.

Suppose, for example, that Nancy died in 2018 and left her $100,000 IRA to her grandson Phil. The first RMD is due by the end of 2019, the year of Phil's 20th birthday. On the IRS table, Phil has a life expectancy of 63 years at age 20. Thus, Phil takes an RMD of $1,587 ($100,000 divided by 63) in December 2019.

As you can see, Phil's RMD is 1.587% of the inherited IRA's value. As long as the IRA's investments earn more than 1.587%, the inherited IRA will continue to grow larger.

Going forward, Phil reduces his life expectancy by one year, every year. In 2020, in our example, Phil will have an RMD that's 1/62nd of the IRA value. In 2021, his RMD will be 1/61st of the IRA value. And so on. For years, the RMD will be a tiny fraction of the IRA amount so a successful investment plan, inside the IRA will enable the account to keep growing. If Phil only takes RMDs and the IRA money is invested well, he might withdraw hundreds of thousands of dollars from the $100,000 IRA he inherited.

113. Surviving spouses get extended life expectancy

Just to make things a little more complicated, the IRS has different rules for a surviving spouse who uses the same Single Life Expectancy Table to take RMDs from an inherited IRA—that is, for a surviving spouse who does not do a rollover to his or her own IRA.

Say a non-spouse begins RMDs from an inherited IRA at age 54 with a 30.5-year life expectancy. Each year, that beneficiary would reduce the life expectancy by one year: the RMD calculations would be 1/29.5, 1/28.5, 1/27.5, etc.

A surviving spouse, on the other hand, has no RMDs until the year their deceased spouse would have been age 70 ½. On top of that, spousal beneficiaries who do have to take RMDs (because their deceased spouse would have already reached age 70 ½) get to "recalculate" their life expectancy each year by looking up their life expectancy factor on the Single Life Expectancy Table. Since the factor often decreases by less than one, this allows for greater tax deferral in comparison to what non-spouse beneficiaries must withdraw.

For example, let's suppose a spousal beneficiary has to take their first RMD in the year they turn age 55. Their factor, obtained from the Single Life Expectancy Table, is 29.6. The following year, the spousal beneficiary would, once again, look at the Single Life Expectancy Table, this time finding a factor of 28.7. The difference between these two factors is 0.9. In comparison, a non-spouse beneficiary only looks at the table once – in the year after the IRA owner's death – and then subtracts one every year thereafter, resulting in a shorter life expectancy.

The longer life expectancy numbers used by surviving spouses produce smaller RMDs, smaller tax payments, and more potentially valuable tax deferral.

- **Ed Slott's advice:** Although most IRA beneficiaries who are surviving spouses will roll over the account to their own name, that's not always the case. A spouse beneficiary who will need to tap the IRA before age 59 ½ is often better off remaining as a beneficiary with an inherited IRA in order to avoid the 10% early withdrawal penalty.

Once the survivor reaches age 59 ½, beyond that 10% penalty, he or she can roll over the IRA to his or her own name. Then they can defer RMDs until their age 70 ½. There is no time limit on the ability of a surviving spouse to execute such an IRA rollover.

114. RMDs for multiple beneficiaries

Calculating the RMD when Mary leaves her IRA to her son John is relatively straightforward. John (or his tax pro, or the IRA custodian) can go to the IRS life expectancy table for beneficiaries and do the math.

But what if Mary leaves her IRA to her son John and her daughter Sue? In such cases, the shorter life expectancy is used. If John is older than Sue, John's life expectancy will dictate RMDs from the IRA Mary left to her children. If John and Sue had a kid sister, Ashley, who was also a co-beneficiary, John's shortest life expectancy would still determine RMDs for that inherited IRA.

- **Ed Slott's advice:** In some situations, this rule is inconvenient and may become extremely costly for some heirs. Therefore, multiple IRA beneficiaries should mark their calendars to meet two key deadlines: September 30 of the year after the IRA owner dies and December 31 of the year after the IRA owner dies.

115. Determine the designated beneficiaries

By September 30 of the year after death, the "designated beneficiaries" will be determined. In some situations, acting before then can be helpful. For example:

- **When a charity or nonprofit organization** is among the IRA beneficiaries. Suppose Al's IRA had been left to the children, Craig and Diane, but it also included Al's alma mater as a beneficiary of 10%. A charity or nonprofit has no life expectancy—effectively the shortest among the beneficiaries—so the IRA would have to be fully distributed in a relatively short time period. In that situation, Craig and Diane would lose some potentially valuable tax deferral inside the IRA.

In this example, Craig and Diane can have the IRA custodian distribute 10% of the IRA account to the university, as payment in full. As long as the university is paid before September 30 of the year after the IRA owner's death, this will remove the college as a beneficiary, leaving only Craig and Diane as designated beneficiaries. Then the children can stretch RMDs over Craig's life expectancy.

116. Beneficiaries can go separate ways

If September 30 of the year after an IRA owner's death is the deadline for designating beneficiaries, what occurs three months later, on December 31? That's the deadline for separating an inherited IRA into multiple inherited IRAs, one for each beneficiary.

For example, imagine an IRA was left to the surviving spouse Barbara (50%), son Craig (25%), and daughter Diane (25%). Barbara rolled over her 50% share before the September 30 deadline, leaving Craig and Diane as co-beneficiaries of the IRA that remained. Assuming the IRA contained $400,000 at the owner's death, Craig and Diane would have an IRA worth $200,000.

Then, Craig and Diane would have until December 31 of that year to separate the account into two $100,000 inherited IRAs. They would both have until that date to take the first RMD from their own inherited IRAs.

- **Ed Slott's advice:** By separating IRAs, each beneficiary gains more control over his or her own account. They can choose their own investments and decide whether to take only the RMDs each year or withdraw larger amounts. What's more, now each IRA beneficiary will be able to use his or her own life expectancy for calculating RMDs.

If Craig is 50 when he starts to take RMDs, he'll take those RMDs over a 34.2-year life expectancy. However, if Diane is 40 at that time, she can use a 43.6-year life expectancy to take RMDs from her inherited IRA. The longer life expectancy may allow Diane to take smaller RMDs, enjoy more tax deferral, and thus build more wealth within her inherited IRA.

117. Trusts have their pros and cons

Some IRA owners name a trust as beneficiary. That is, when they die, their IRA will pass to a trust instead of to one or more individuals.

Example: When Edna Franklin fills out the beneficiary form for her IRA account, she enters "Franklin Family Trust" as her beneficiary. The trust document lists Edna's three children as the trust beneficiaries. A trustee is named who will manage the money inside the IRA after Edna dies and handle subsequent distributions.

- **Advantages:** Leaving your IRA (or any other asset) to a trust can be a good idea if you have an heir who is inexperienced in managing large amounts of money, is likely to squander the inheritance, or has other financial concerns. Suppose Edna's son Gregg bets (and loses heavily) on ball games, while her daughter

Heather is a doctor, exposed to malpractice judgments. With a trust beneficiary, the IRA funds will be safer than if they had been left outright to Edna's children.

- **Drawbacks:** Any trust involves time and money to create and administer. A trust that is named as the beneficiary of an IRA may be able to take RMDs over an extended time period, extending tax deferral, but that will be the case only if the trust meets several criteria set out by the tax code.

Assuming the trust qualifies as a "look-through" trust, RMDs will be based on the life expectancy of the oldest trust beneficiary. Generally, the trust beneficiaries will not be able to split the inherited IRA and take RMDs over their individual life expectancies. Therefore, the younger trust beneficiaries will lose some potential tax deferral.

- **Ed Slott's advice:** Don't name a trust as your IRA beneficiary because you think it offers tax benefits. It doesn't. However, if you have concerns as to how your loved ones will handle the IRA they'll inherit, a trust can provide protection. Be sure to work with an attorney who is knowledgeable about the IRA rules for trust beneficiaries.

118. Still more rules on aggregating RMDs

Some RMDs from inherited IRAs may be aggregated, but that's not always true. In order for you to aggregate these RMDs, you must have inherited IRAs from the same IRA owner.

Scenario 1: Suppose Ron inherited two IRAs from his mother. Each year, Ron will calculate the RMD from each of these inherited IRAs. He can add up the RMDs and take the total withdrawal from either IRA, or both.

Scenario 2: Now suppose it's five years later and Ron inherits an IRA from his uncle. In this case, Ron can still aggregate the RMDs from his mother's IRAs, but he must do a separate calculation, based on his life expectancy at the time, in order to take RMDs from his uncle's IRA. Whatever the RMD turns out to be, Ron must take the distribution for his uncle's IRA from that inherited account.

Scenario 3: Taking the example one step further, suppose Ron reaches age 70 ½, so he must take RMDs from his own IRA. Again, those RMDs must come from his own IRA; if he has more than one IRA, Ron can aggregate the RMDs and take the total from any or all of his own IRAs. However, he can't take RMDs for his own IRA from the inherited IRAs, and he can't take RMDs for the inherited IRAs from his own IRA.

Common to all scenarios: If Ron doesn't take all the RMDs from the correct accounts, he'll owe a 50% penalty on all the RMDs that were left in place when they should have been withdrawn.

119. Requesting RMD forgiveness

The previous items have focused on taking the right RMD amount from the right place and thus avoiding a 50% penalty. However, there might be circumstances in which you under-withdraw or just forget the RMD altogether. If that should happen, and you're facing a stiff fine, you can ask the IRS to waive the penalty. In order to succeed, you must demonstrate that the shortfall was due to a reasonable error and that you have taken the right actions to make up for your lapse.

You use IRS Form 5329, *Additional Taxes on Qualified Plans (Including IRAs) and Other Tax-Favored Accounts* to report the missed distribution and to calculate the penalty. To request a waiver, you must fill out the form and attach a letter of explanation.

- **Ed Slott's advice:** When you submit Form 5329 with a statement requesting a waiver of the penalty, don't include payment for the 50% penalty. IRS no longer requires that payment be sent in with the form.

120. Making up missed RMDs

Before you file Form 5329 to request a waiver of the 50% penalty, you should actually take all the required distributions you've missed, as soon as you make the discovery of an RMD shortfall. Do the calculations, or have your tax professional do them, and move all the RMD amounts from your IRA to your taxable bank or investment account.

Suppose you missed a $10,000 RMD for 2017 and a $12,000 RMD for 2018. You should withdraw a total of $22,000 from any or all of your Traditional IRAs in 2019, thus incurring $22,000 of taxable income for 2019. Of course, you should be sure to also take your 2019 RMD by year-end.

- **Ed Slott's advice:** Assume that an IRS examiner will scrutinize your request for a penalty waiver. Therefore, you should do everything you can to help the IRS agent understand what you have done to correct your error.

  One possible approach is to ask your IRA custodian for separate checks that match each missed RMD. In the above example, you could ask your custodian for a $10,000 IRA distribution and a $12,000 distribution from your IRA with no taxes withheld. Make photocopies and then deposit the two checks into a taxable account.

121. File all necessary forms

If you owe penalties for multiple years, you must file a Form 5329 for each year in order to get a full waiver. These can be forms you file alone or ones that you file with an income tax return.

Previously, we gave the example of missed RMDs in 2017 and 2018. In such a situation, you should file two Forms 5329, one for each of those years. You can file a solo Form 5329 for 2017. If you have not yet filed your 2018 income tax return, you would attach Form 5329 for that year (or both years) to the tax return. Either way, attach a photocopy of the relevant distribution check to the Form 5329, showing that you have received that year's belated RMD from the IRA custodian.

- **Ed Slott's advice:** You shouldn't file an amended tax return as part of your request for a penalty waiver. Once you've missed an RMD for, say, 2017, you can't withdraw IRA money in 2019 and have it count for 2017. Instead, you'll take a makeup RMD in 2019, report that withdrawal on your 2019 tax return, and pay tax on that amount of income.

122. Conquering Form 5329

Requesting a waiver on Form 5329 doesn't require an advanced degree in computer science, but it's not child's play, either. Making a common mistake can be costly.

The danger lies in Part VIII of the form, labeled "Additional Tax on Excess Accumulation in Qualified Retirement Plans (Including IRAs)." Here's how to sidestep the trap:

- **On line 52,** enter the amount of the RMD that you were required to take.

- **On line 53,** enter the total of IRA distributions that you actually took during that calendar year.

- **On line 54,** enter "zero," and write "RC" (for reasonable cause) in the margin. Do not enter the amount of the RMD you missed.

- **On line 55,** enter "zero" again.

- **Ed Slott's advice:** The instructions for line 54 of Form 5329 can be confusing, but you should be sure not to put any number on that line. If you put any amount there, you won't get the waiver you're requesting. Instead, the IRS will impose the 50% penalty tax and request payment in full.

123. State your case for a penalty waiver

When you file Form 5329, requesting a waiver of the 50% penalty for a missed RMD, be sure to attach a waiver request. Emphasize that you have taken an IRA distribution equal to the missed RMD, as evidenced by the attached copy of the distribution check from your IRA custodian.

Your statement also should include an explanation for missing the RMD. Unfortunately, the IRS has not issued any notices or rulings that would indicate what's considered to be a good reason for getting a penalty waiver.

- **Ed Slott's advice:** Just saying "I forgot" is not likely to get the penalty dismissed. You'll need to show a reasonable cause. Here are some explanations that the IRS might accept:

  1. Illness or death in the family.

  2. Failure on the part of your IRA custodian, which didn't inform you of your RMD.

  3. Failure on the part of the Post Office, so notices about RMDs never reached you.

  4. Problems with a reputable tax preparer.

  5. Exceptional stress, which might involve a divorce, a lost job, a home foreclosure, the closing of a family business, etc.

In any event, your statement should apologize for the inadvertent oversight, point out that the missed RMDs have been taken, and promise to make every attempt to make all future RMDs on time.

124. Charitable thoughts about RMDs

RMDs generate unwelcome taxes, but a missed RMD generates a steep penalty, and there is no sure way to have that penalty waived. What's more, taking an RMD inflates your adjusted gross income (AGI), and a higher AGI can have expensive consequences throughout your tax return. Just to name a couple of examples, a higher AGI can cost you medical deductions and prevent you from deducting losses from investment property.

- **Now for the good news:** Fortunately, there is a way to satisfy your RMD requirement without getting snared by all these tax traps. You can utilize a tax break called a qualified charitable distribution (QCD). Here's how it works:

ED SLOTT'S
ELITE
IRA
ADVISOR
GROUP™
Find an advisor
at **irahelp.com**

Suppose Ellen is 75 years old, with an RMD from her Traditional IRA of $20,000 this year. Ellen, who is charitably inclined, chooses to transfer $20,000 from her IRA to her favorite charity this year.

That $20,000 can be a QCD, satisfying her RMD and absolving her from the 50% penalty. It's true that Ellen won't get the usual tax deduction for this charitable donation, but it's also true that Ellen won't have to include that $20,000 distribution in her AGI, and that exclusion can have multiple tax-saving benefits.

QCDs are especially valuable to seniors who (a) have an IRA and (b) take the standard deduction on their tax return, so they don't deduct charitable contributions. Such IRA owners get no tax benefit from their donations so they might as well make them from their IRA and avoid the taxable income from their RMDs.

125. Breaking down the QCD tax break

Now that the QCD is a permanent part of the tax code, it's even more important to know how to make one properly. Here's what you need to know:

- You have to be at least age 70 ½ as of the date of the transfer to use the tax break.

- IRA beneficiaries as well as IRA owners over age 70 ½ can make QCDs, which will count as RMDs.

- The annual limit is $100,000 of QCDs per donor, so a couple in that age range can donate up to $200,000 ($100,000 each) from their respective IRAs.

- Your IRA custodian must make a payment to the charity or charities you designate, not to you. Public charities and nonprofit organizations (colleges and museums, for instance) generally are acceptable recipients.

- Donations to a donor-advised fund, a private foundation, or a supporting organization won't be acceptable as a QCD.

- The charitable recipient must receive your name and address, so it can send you the required acknowledgment. This letter should state that it received the money and did not provide you with any benefit in return.

Chapter 8:
2019
Tax Update

Tax Reform Is Here!

Here's What It Means for You:

On December 22, 2017, the **Tax Cuts and Jobs Act** was signed into law. This far-reaching piece of legislation overhauled the tax code. What does it all mean for you and your retirement plan? Here are some highlights.

Big Changes!

Tax reform kept seven tax brackets and lowered the top rate to 37% for individuals. The alternative minimum tax (AMT) has been scaled way back. The standard deduction is now $12,200 in 2019 for singles and $24,400 for those who are married, filing jointly, and the child credit has been expanded. Personal exemptions are suspended.

Many popular deductions have been eliminated or scaled back. The state and local tax deduction is limited to $10,000, and the mortgage interest deduction will be limited to the first $750,000 in mortgage interest debt for new home purchases.

These changes, like most of the changes tax reform brings for individuals, are scheduled to sunset after 2025. Tax reform also brought sweeping reform to corporate taxation. Changes on the corporate side, unlike the individual side, are permanent.

Your Retirement Plan

When it comes to your retirement plan, the big news may be what was NOT changed by tax reform.

Your ability to make pretax salary deferrals to your 401(k) is unchanged.

Proposals to require after-tax contributions, instead of pre-tax (i.e., the so called "Rothification" concept), never made it into the final legislation. Despite rumors of its demise, *the stretch IRA also remains on the table* as a planning strategy for you to leave your retirement funds to your heirs.

Roth IRA conversions may make more sense than ever.

Tax brackets have been lowered and the AMT has been limited to a very few taxpayers. This may be the time to have a conversation about conversion with your advisor. These changes are currently scheduled to sunset in a few years, so there is a window of opportunity here. Now may be the time to act. No one knows for sure what the future will bring, but higher tax rates are a strong possibility. Converting now locks in today's low rates and avoids the worries of future tax uncertainty.

Tax reform's changes to the "kiddie tax" may be yet another reason to convert to a Roth IRA.

The new law taxes children's unearned income at tax bracket rates imposed on trusts and estates, not the rate paid by parents or the child's own rate. The new rates can be much higher. Required minimum distributions (RMDs) from an inherited IRA are ordinary unearned income taxable at top rates. So, distributions to children from inherited Traditional IRAs can get hit with very high rates very quickly, even if parents pay lower rates. Converting to a Roth IRA eliminates this worry because RMDs from inherited Roth IRAs are generally tax free.

Recharacterization of Roth IRA conversions is not available for conversions done in 2018 or later.

Conversions are now irrevocable. A Roth conversion may still be the right strategy for you, but you must be sure. You will want to be certain that there is enough money available outside of your IRA to pay the taxes. Because there is no "do-over," advice from a knowledgeable advisor is more important than ever. Doing smaller, or partial, conversions to hedge your bets may be a strategy worth undertaking. Also, waiting until closer to the end of the year when you have a better understanding of your tax situation may be a wise move.

Recharacterization of contributions survives.

This is good news for those who change their mind about the type of IRA to which they want to contribute. For example, if you discover your Traditional IRA contribution is not deductible, you can still recharacterize that contribution to a Roth IRA if you are eligible to make a Roth contribution for the year.

Consider a back-door Roth IRA if your income is too high for you to make Roth IRA contributions.

If you had concerns about this tactic in the past, you can rest easy. The committee reports that were released along with the new law explicitly mentioned the tactic on four separate occasions. However, you must have taxable compensation and be under age 70 ½ for the year to be eligible. Also, the pro-rata formula will apply.

Qualified charitable distributions (QCDs) are more valuable than ever.

The QCD has always been a great tool for those who have an IRA and are charitably-minded. With tax reform expanding the standard deduction and doing away with many popular deductions, it is expected that fewer taxpayers than ever will itemize their deductions. This means that even though the charitable deduction remains, fewer taxpayers will use it. A QCD is a way you can still get a tax break for your charitable contribution while also using the new expanded standard deduction. If you are over 70 ½, you can transfer up to $100,000 tax-free directly from your IRA to the qualifying charity of your choice. These funds will not be included in your income for the year, and you can even use a QCD to satisfy your RMD.

Tax reform does away with the itemized deduction for advisory fees for your IRA.

Consider paying these fees directly from your Traditional IRA instead of out of pocket. Although it reduces the amount growing tax-deferred, you get a break by using pretax dollars. Because Roth IRAs are an after-tax account, this strategy won't work there.

Tax reform also does away with your ability to claim a loss on your IRA.

This was only available if you cashed out all your IRAs of the same type and the total distribution was less than your basis, so it was uncommon. However, now it is eliminated.

You will have more time to roll over a plan loan offset if you leave your job or the plan is terminated.

Old rules only gave you sixty days to roll over the unpaid loan balance. Tax reform will extend this rollover deadline until your tax return due date (including extensions) for the year during which the loan offset occurred. This can help if you are between jobs and need more time to come up with the cash.

Bipartisan Budget Act of 2018 Impacts Retirement Plans

On February 9, 2018, President Trump signed the Bipartisan Budget Act of 2018 (BBA) into law. While the new law is best known for keeping the government open, it also includes some provisions that impact retirement plans.

California Wildfire Disaster Relief

In 2017, Congress passed legislation with a package of tax relief for victims of Hurricanes Harvey, Irma, and Maria. Left out in the cold were the victims of the 2017 California wildfires. The BBA remedies this omission by including tax relief provisions for these taxpayers, mirroring those put in place last year for the hurricane victims.

- **Qualified Wildfire Distributions:** An individual who had their principle residence in the California wildfire disaster area and who sustained an economic loss due to the wildfires is eligible to take a distribution from a qualified retirement plan or IRA without being subject to the 10% early distribution penalty. The distribution must be made from October 8, 2017 to December 31, 2018 and cannot exceed $100,000. The income can be included ratably over a three-year period on the individual's tax return, and a taxpayer has three years to recontribute those funds back to a plan or IRA.

- **Repayment of Home Loan Distributions:** The BBA also grants relief to individuals who took hardship distributions for a home purchase (or construction) or an IRA distribution that qualified as a first-time homebuyer purchase. Under the new law, if the loan or construction was cancelled due to the California wildfire disaster, the individual can recontribute those funds back to a retirement plan or IRA. To qualify, the distribution must have been received after March 31, 2017 and before January 15, 2018. In addition, the funds must be recontributed between October 8, 2017 and June 30, 2018.

- **Increase in Plan Loan Limit:** Employer plan loan limits were increased, and the repayment period was extended, for qualified individuals with a principle residence in the California wildfire disaster area. Generally, plan loans are limited to the lesser of $50,000 or one-half of the vested account balance. For these individuals, the plan loan limit is increased from $50,000 to $100,000, and the "one-half rule" is removed. To qualify, the loans must be issued between February 9, 2018 and December 31, 2018. Moreover, if these individuals had outstanding plan loans at the time of the disaster, the repayment period can be extended.

Hardship Distribution Rule Changes

The BBA made some direct changes to the hardship distribution rules. These changes are effective for plan years beginning after December 31, 2018.

- **Elimination of the Six-Month Prohibition on Contributions:** Under current law, once a participant receives a hardship distribution, he or she is prohibited from making contributions to the plan for six months. The BBA directs the IRS to remove this six-month prohibition.

- **Expansion of Eligible Hardship Distribution Funds:** The BBA also expands the types of retirement funds that are eligible for a hardship distribution. Currently, the employee can only receive a hardship distribution of his or her elective salary deferral contributions. Under the BBA, hardship distributions will include any qualified non-elective contributions, qualified matching contributions and the earnings on salary contributions.

- **No Longer the Last Resort:** The BBA also eliminates the rule that required participants to take plan loans before accessing hardship distributions.

The BBA also broadly directs the IRS to make any changes necessary to ease the hardship distribution rules. This could be the first step towards correcting the problem with casualty loss hardship distributions that arose when Congress changed the deduction rules for casualty losses in the Tax Cuts and Jobs Act. This change has no effect on the qualifications to deduct casualty losses (which only applies to federal disaster areas). It only applies to accessing funds as hardship distributions due to a casualty loss.

However, until IRS issues further guidance, plans that have adopted the safe harbor hardship distribution rules will have to limit access to hardship distributions related to casualty losses. Of course, keep in mind that any guidance the IRS provides could be retroactive.

Rollover of Wrongful Levy

If the IRS wrongfully levies a retirement plan or IRA and returns those funds (plus interest) to the taxpayer, the BBA allows the taxpayer to roll over the amount received to a retirement plan or IRA. The rollover must be completed by the individual's tax filing due date for the year in which the funds are returned. This deadline does not include any extensions. The new law applies to levied funds returned to a taxpayer in tax years beginning after December 31, 2017. The rollover does not count for purposes of the one-rollover-per-year rule.

Your Estate Plan

The estate, gift and generation skipping tax exemptions are increased to $22,800,000 (married couple) or $11,400,000 per person for 2019.

The top rate stays at 40%, and the step-up in basis stays intact. But these changes are only through the end of 2025, and then the exemptions go back to the $5 million per person indexed for inflation. With such high exemptions available, few estates will be hit with the estate tax. However, those that are subject to the tax will be hit hard. If that is you, talk to your advisor about strategies such as maximizing gifts over the next few years. When planning, don't overlook the state estate tax, which can have much lower exemptions than the newly increased federal ones.

Education Savings

529 plans have been expanded. Previously, these accounts could only be used for higher education expenses. Now, 529 accounts can distribute up to $10,000 annually per student to pay for public, private, or religious primary or secondary school costs.

Contribution limits have been increased for ABLE accounts.

If you have family members with disabilities, tax reform brings some good news in the form of increased contribution limits. Also, the designated beneficiary of the ABLE account can claim the Saver's Credit for contributions made to their account. The Saver's Credit was previously only available for retirement plan contributions.

Distributions from 529 plans can now be rolled over to an ABLE account, if that ABLE account is owned by the designated beneficiary of that 529 account or a family member.

Rollovers count towards the annual contribution limit.

Other Provisions of Interest

- The Affordable Care Act's individual mandate, which penalizes people who do not have health care, will go away in 2019.

- In the past, taxpayers could claim a deduction for major losses arising from fire, storm, or similar casualties, with some limitations. Tax reform will restrict this. Personal casualty losses will be deductible only if the losses are due to a federally declared disaster. If you are not in a federally declared disaster area, casualty losses will no longer be deductible.

- The corporate tax rate was cut from 35% to 21% starting in 2018. The AMT for corporations has been eliminated. Tax reform also creates a 20% business income deduction with some limits for pass-through businesses such as partnerships and shareholders of S-corporations, LLCs and partnerships. Unlike the majority of the tax cuts for individuals under tax reform, these changes for businesses are permanent. Now may be a good time to investigate changing your business structure to maximize your benefits under the new rules.

- For 2019, taxpayers may deduct only the amount of the total unreimbursed allowable medical care expenses that exceeds 10% of the adjusted gross income.

Good Advice Is Essential

Do you have questions about your own situation? These big changes mean that now more than ever, good advice is essential. A qualified financial advisor can help guide you through all the new rules and ensure that you are best positioned to take advantage of the breaks and avoid the pitfalls.

Overview of the 2019 Tax Rates

Taxable Income Brackets for 2019 Ordinary Income Tax Rates

Marginal Tax Rate	Married Filing Joint	Single
10%	$0 - $19,400	$0 - $9,700
12%	$19,401 - $78,950	$9,701 - $39,475
22%	$78,951 - $168,400	$39,476 - $84,200
24%	$168,401 - $321,450	$84,201 - $160,725
32%	$321,451 - $408,200	$160,726 - $204,100
35%	$408,201 - $612,350	$204,101 - $510,300
37%*	$612,351 or more	$510,301 or more

* The top rate is effectively 40.8% for those subject to the 3.8% Medicare surtax on net investment income

Capital Gains and Qualified Dividends

The top tax rate for long-term capital gains and dividends remains at 20%

2019 Capital Gains Tax Brackets:

Married filing jointly	
$0 - $78,750	0%
$78,751 - $488,850	15%*
$488,851 or more	20%**

Single	
$0 - $39,375	0%
$39,376 - $434,550	15%*
$434,551 or more	20%**

*Some of those in the 15% capital gains bracket will pay 18.8% if they are subject to the 3.8% net investment income tax

**In nearly all cases the 20% capital gains rate will be 23.8%, after adding the 3.8% net investment income tax, which applies at lower income amounts.

Trust tax rates reach the 20% capital gains tax rate after $12,950 of taxable income.

Kiddie Tax Changes

The so called *"kiddie tax"* is now at trust tax rates.

2019 Trust Tax Rates

10%	$0 - $2,600
24%	$2,601 - $9,300
35%	$9,301 - $12,750
37%	Over $12,750

The kiddie tax applies to the unearned income of children under age 18 (under age 24 for full-time students). Under prior law this income was taxed at the rate paid by the child's parents. But starting in 2018, this income is taxed at trust tax rates. This could result in the child's unearned income being taxed at rates higher or lower than the rate paid by the parents.

Estate Tax

The exemptions for estate, gift and generation skipping tax in 2019 are now up to $11,400,000.

The top rate is 40%

2019 Estate & Gift Exemption Amounts	
Estate Tax	$11,400,000
Generation Skipping Tax	$11,400,000
Gift Tax	$11,400,000
Annual Gift Tax Exclusion	$15,000

Estate Tax Portability

The portability feature for the estate and gift tax exemptions is now permanent, providing married couples with a total exemption of up to $22,800,000.

The estate tax return, Form 706, must be filed to get portability of a deceased spouse's remaining exemption.

There is no portability of the generation skipping transfer (GST) tax exemption.

ABOUT ED SLOTT

Ed Slott was named *"The Best" source for IRA advice by the Wall Street Journal.*

He is a nationally recognized professional speaker and has starred in several nationally aired public television specials including the most recent, — *Retire Safe & Secure! with Ed Slott (2019).*

Slott created *The IRA Leadership Program*™ and *Ed Slott's Elite IRA Advisor Group^{SM}*, which were developed specifically to help financial professionals earn recognition as leaders in the IRA marketplace.

Mr. Slott is an accomplished author of many financial and retirement-focused books, including most recently *Ed Slott's Retirement Decisions Guide: 2019 Edition* (IRAHelp, 2019) and *Fund Your Future: A Tax-Smart Savings Plan in Your 20s and 30s* (IRAHelp, 2018). Slott also publishes *Ed Slott's IRA Advisor*, a monthly IRA newsletter. He is a personal finance columnist for numerous financial publications.

As a thought leader in the retirement industry, Slott is often quoted in *The New York Times, The Wall Street Journal, Forbes, Money, Kiplinger's, USA Today, Investment News* and a host of additional national magazines and financial publications. He has appeared on numerous national television and radio programs. Mr. Slott is also a consultant to financial information websites.

He is a past Chairman of the New York State Society of CPAs Estate Planning Committee and editor of the IRA planning section of the *CPA Journal*. Mr. Slott is the recipient of the prestigious *"Excellence in Estate Planning"* and *"Outstanding Service"* awards presented by The Foundation for Accounting Education. He is a former Board member of The Estate Planning Council of New York City and an Accredited Estate Planner (AEP) distinguished.

For more information:

Website: irahelp.com

Email: info@irahelp.com

Twitter: @theslottreport

Facebook: AmericasIRAExperts

LinkedIn: Ed Slott and Company

YouTube: EdSlottandCompanyIRA